W9-CIX-910

PENGUIN BOOKS

SHARPE'S SWORD

Bernard Cornwell was born in London in 1944, raised in South Essex, and educated at London University. He worked for several years as a producer and writer for BBC television, taking charge of its current affairs department in Northern Ireland, and in 1978 he became editor of Thames Television's *Thames at Six* program. His interest in the Napoleonic Wars, pursued since his schooldays, was ignited by C. S. Forester's Hornblower novels, and in his spare time he began his research for the Richard Sharpe novels. Mr. Cornwell is now a full-time writer.

SHARPE'S SWORD

RICHARD SHARPE AND THE
SALAMANCA CAMPAIGN,
JUNE AND JULY 1812

Bernard Cornwell

PENGUIN BOOKS

For Peggy Blackburn, with love

PENGUIN BOOKS
Viking Penguin Inc., 40 West 23rd Street,
New York, New York 10010, U.S.A.
Penguin Books Ltd, Harmondsworth,
Middlesex, England
Penguin Books Australia Ltd, Ringwood,
Victoria, Australia
Penguin Books Canada Limited, 2801 John Street,
Markham, Ontario, Canada L3R 1B4
Penguin Books (N.Z.) Ltd, 182–190 Wairau Road,
Auckland 10, New Zealand

First published in the United States of America by
The Viking Press 1983
Published in Penguin Books 1987

LIBRARY OF CONGRESS CATALOGING IN PUBLICATION DATA
Cornwell, Bernard.
Sharpe's sword.
1. Salamanca, Battle of, 1812—Fiction.
2. Peninsular War, 1807–1814—Fiction.
3. Great Britain—History, Military—19th century—
Fiction.   I. Title.
PR6053.O75S55   1987   823'.914   86-30426
ISBN 0 14 01.0264 7

Printed in the United States of America by
Offset Paperback Mfrs., Inc., Dallas, Pennsylvania
Set in Baskerville

'A knight errant – to cut a long story short – is beaten up one day and made Emperor the next.'

Don Quixote
by Miguel Cervantes (1547–1615)
Translated by J. M. Cohen

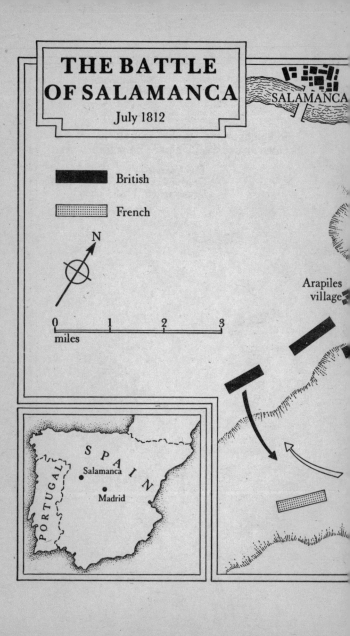

THE BATTLE OF SALAMANCA

July 1812

British

French

N

0   1   2   3
miles

SALAMANCA

Arapiles village

SPAIN

PORTUGAL

Salamanca

Madrid

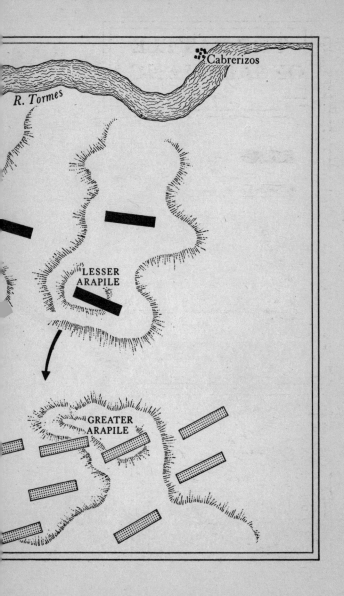

Cabrerizos

R. Tormes

LESSER
ARAPILE

GREATER
ARAPILE

PART ONE

Sunday, June 14th
to
Tuesday, June 23rd
1812

PROLOGUE

The tall man on horseback was a killer.

He was strong, healthy, and ruthless. Some men thought he was young to be a full Colonel in Napoleon's Imperial Guard, but no-one took advantage of his youth. A single glimpse of his curiously pale eyes, pale-lashed eyes, eyes that gave his strong, handsome face a chill of death, was enough to make men offer respect to Colonel Leroux.

Leroux was the Emperor's man. He went where Napoleon sent him and he performed his master's tasks with skill and pitiless efficiency. Now he was in Spain, sent there by the Emperor himself, and Colonel Leroux had just made a mistake. He knew it, he cursed himself for it, but he was also planning how to escape his self-imposed predicament.

He was trapped.

He had ridden with a cavalry escort to a miserable village huddled at the edge of the great plains of Leon and there had found his man, a priest. He had tortured the priest, stripping the skin inch by inch from the living body, and in the end, of course, the priest talked. They all talked to Colonel Leroux in the end. Yet this time he had taken too long. At the moment of victory, at that very moment when the priest could take the pain no longer and screamed out the name which Leroux had come so far to learn, the German cavalry erupted into the village. Men of the King's German Legion who fought for Britain in this war savaged the French Dragoons, their sabres rising and falling, their hoofbeats drumming a rhythm behind the screams of pain, and Colonel Leroux had run.

He had grabbed one companion, a Captain of the cavalry escort, and together they had ridden desperately north, cutting their way through one group of Germans, and now, an hour later, they had stopped at the edge of a wood that grew about a sudden, quick stream that tumbled towards the River Tormes.

The Dragoon Captain looked behind. 'We've lost them.'

'We haven't.' Leroux's horse was streaked with white sweat, its flanks heaved, and the Colonel felt the terrible heat of the sun smashing through his gorgeous uniform; red jacket looped with gold, green overalls reinforced with leather with the silver buttons running down each leg. His black fur colback, thick enough to stop a sword blow to the head, hung from his pommel. The light breeze could not stir his sweat-plastered blond hair. He suddenly smiled at his companion. 'What's your name?'

The Captain was relieved by the smile. He was frightened of Leroux and this sudden, unexpected friendliness was a welcome change. 'Delmas, sir. Paul Delmas.'

Leroux's smile was full of charm. 'Well, Paul Delmas, we've done great things so far! Let's see if we can lose them for good, eh?'

Delmas, flattered by the familiarity, smiled back. 'Yes, sir.' He looked behind again, and again he could see nothing except for the bleached grassland silent under the heat. Nothing seemed to move except the wind-ripple of grass, and a solitary hawk, wings motionless, that easelessly rode the cloudless sky.

Colonel Leroux was not deceived by the emptiness. He had spotted the dead ground as they rode and he knew the Germans, good professionals, were out in the plain, spreading the cordon that would drive the fugitives towards the river. He knew too that the British were marching eastwards, that some of their men would be following the river, and he guessed that he and his companion were being driven into an ambush. So be it. He was trapped, outnumbered, but not beaten.

He could not be beaten. He had never been beaten, and now, above all other times, he had to regain the safety of the French army. He had come so near to success, and when he completed the job then he would hurt the British as they had rarely been hurt in this war. He felt the surge of pleasure at the thought. By God, he would hurt them! He had been sent to Spain to discover the identity of El Mirador, and he had succeeded this afternoon, and now all that remained was to take El Mirador back to some torture chamber and squeeze from the British spy the names of all the correspondents in Spain, Italy, and France who sent their messages to El Mirador in Salamanca. El Mirador collected information from throughout Napoleon's empire, and though the French had long known the code-name, they had never discovered his identity. Leroux had, and so he had to escape this trap, he had to take his captive back to France, and there he would destroy the net of British spies who all worked for El Mirador. But first he must escape this trap.

He let his horse walk into the cool greenness of the wood. 'Come on, Delmas! We're not finished yet!'

He found what he wanted just a few yards into the wood. A fallen beech tree, its trunk rotten, lay in front of a tangle of brambles and wind-driven leaves from last year's autumn. Leroux dismounted. 'Time to work, Delmas!' His voice was optimistic and cheerful.

Delmas did not understand what they were doing, was frightened to ask, but he followed Leroux's example and stripped off his jacket. He helped the Colonel clear a space behind the log, a hiding place, and Delmas wondered how long they would have to crouch in thorny discomfort until the Germans gave up the hunt. He smiled diffidently at Leroux. 'Where do we hide the horses?'

'In a minute.' Leroux dismissed the question.

The Colonel seemed to be measuring the hiding place. He drew his sword and poked at the brambles. Delmas watched the sword. It was a weapon of exquisite craftsmanship, a straight-bladed, heavy cavalry sword made by Kligenthal as were most of the French cavalry blades, but this sword had been made specially for Leroux by the finest craftsman at Kligenthal. It was longer than most swords, heavier too, for Leroux was a tall, strong man. The blade was beautiful, a sheen of steel in the dappled green light of the wood, and the hilt and guard were made of the same steel. The handle was bound by silver wire, the sword's sole concession to decoration, but despite its plainness, the weapon proclaimed itself as a beautiful, exquisitely balanced killing blade. To hold that sword, Delmas thought, must be to know what King Arthur felt when he slid Excalibur, smooth as grey silk, from the churchyard stone.

Leroux straightened up, seemingly content. 'Anything behind us, Delmas?'

The Dragoon Captain turned. Nothing disturbed the peace of the beeches and oaks. 'No, sir.'

'Keep watching. They're not far behind.'

Leroux guessed he had ten minutes which was more than enough. He smiled at Delmas's back, measured the distance, and lunged.

He wanted this kill to be quick, painless, and with a minimum of blood. He did not want Delmas to cry out and startle anyone who might be further into the trees. The blade, as sharp as the day it had left its maker, pierced the base of Delmas's head. Leroux's strength, an enormous strength, drove it through bone, through the spinal cord, and into the brain. There was a soft sigh and Delmas crumpled forward.

Silence.

Leroux guessed he would be captured, and he knew too that the British would not let Colonel Leroux be exchanged for a British Colonel captured by the French. Leroux was a wanted man and he had seen to that himself. He worked by fear, he spread horror about his name, and all his victims, once dead, were inscribed with his name. He would leave a patch of skin untouched and on the patch he would incise two words. *Leroux fecit.* Just as if he were a sculptor boasting a fine piece of work, he would leave his mark. 'Leroux made this.' If Leroux was captured he could expect no mercy. Yet the British would not give a fig for Captain Paul Delmas.

He changed uniforms with the corpse, working with his usual speed and efficiency, and when he was done he pushed his uniform, together with Delmas's corpse, into the hiding place. He covered them swiftly with leaves and brambles, leaving the body to be eaten by beasts. He drove Delmas's horse away, not caring where it went, and then he mounted his own horse, placed Delmas's tall, brass helmet on his head, and turned north towards the river where he expected to be captured. He whistled as he walked the horse, making no attempt to hide his presence, and at his side hung the perfect sword, and in his head was the secret that could blind the British. Leroux could not be beaten.

Colonel Leroux was captured twenty minutes later. British Greenjackets, Riflemen, rose suddenly from cover inside the wood and surrounded him. For a moment Leroux thought he had made a terrible mistake. The British, he knew, were officered by gentlemen, men who took honour seriously, but the officer who captured him seemed as hard and ruthless as himself. The officer was tall, tanned, with dark hair hanging unruly beside a scarred face. He ignored Leroux's attempt to be pleasant, ordering the Frenchman to be searched, and Leroux had a moment of alarm when a huge Sergeant, even bigger than the officer, found the folded piece of paper between saddle and saddlecloth. Leroux pretended to speak no English, but a Rifleman was brought who spoke bad French, and the officer questioned the Frenchman about the paper. It was a list of names, all Spanish, and beside each name was a sum of money.

'Horse-dealers.' Leroux shrugged. 'We buy horses. We're cavalry.'

The tall Rifle Officer heard the translation and looked at the paper. It could be true. He shrugged and pushed the paper into his pack. He took Leroux's sword from the big sergeant and the Frenchman could see the sudden lust in the Rifle Officer's eyes. Curiously for an infantryman, the Rifleman also wore a heavy cavalry sword, but where Leroux's was expensive and beautiful, the Rifle Officer's sword was cheap and crude. The British officer held the sword and felt the perfect balance. He wanted it. 'Ask what his name is.'

The question was asked and answered. 'Paul Delmas, sir. Captain in the Fifth Dragoons.'

Leroux saw the dark eyes rest on him. The scar on the Rifleman's face gave him a mocking look. Leroux could recognise the man's competence and hardness, he recognised too the temptation that the Rifleman had to kill him at this moment and take the sword for himself. Leroux looked about the clearing. The other Riflemen seemed just as pitiless, just as tough. Leroux spoke again.

'He wants to give his parole, sir.' The Rifleman translated.

The Rifle Officer said nothing for a moment. He walked slowly about the prisoner, the beautiful sword still in his hand, and when he spoke he did so slowly and clearly. 'So what's Captain Delmas doing on his own? French officers don't travel alone, they're too frightened of the Partisans.' He had come in front of Leroux again, and the Frenchman's pale eyes watched the scarred officer. 'And you're too bloody cocky, Delmas. You should be more scared. You're up to no bloody good.' He was behind Leroux now. 'I think I'll bloody kill you.'

Leroux did not react. He did not blink, did not move, but just waited until the Rifle Officer was in front of him again.

The tall Rifle Officer stared at the pale eyes as if they

would give him a clue to the riddle of the officer's sudden appearance. 'Bring him along, Sergeant. But watch the bastard.'

'Yes, sir!' Sergeant Patrick Harper pushed the Frenchman towards the path and followed Captain Richard Sharpe out of the wood.

Leroux relaxed. The moment of capture was always the moment of greatest danger, but the tall Rifleman was taking him to safety, and with him went the secret Napoleon wanted. El Mirador.

CHAPTER 1

'God damn it, Sharpe! Hurry, man!'

'Yes, sir.' Sharpe made no attempt to hurry. He painstakingly read the piece of paper, knowing that his slowness irritated Lieutenant Colonel Windham. The Colonel slapped a booted leg with his riding crop.

'We haven't got all day, Sharpe! There's a war to win.'

'Yes, sir.' Sharpe repeated the words in a patient, stubborn tone. He would not hurry. This was his revenge on Windham for allowing Captain Delmas to have parole. He tipped the paper so that the firelight illuminated the black ink.

'I, the undersigned, Paul Delmas, Captain in the Fifth Regiment of Dragoons, taken prisoner by the English Forces on 14th June, 1812, undertake upon my Honour not to seek to Escape nor to Remove myself from Captivity without Permission, and not pass any Knowledge to the French Forces or their Allies, until I have been Exchanged, Rank for Rank, or Otherwise Released from this Bond. Signed, Paul Delmas. Witnessed by me, Joseph Forrest, Major in His Britannic Majesty's South Essex Regiment.'

Colonel Windham rapped with his crop again, the noise loud in the predawn chill. 'Dammit, Sharpe!'

'Seems to be in order, Sir.'

'Order! Blood and hounds, Sharpe! Who are you to say what's in order! Good God! I say it's in order! I do! Remember me, Sharpe? Your commanding officer?'

19

Sharpe grinned. 'Yes, sir.' He handed the parole up to Windham who took it with elaborate courtesy.

'Thank you, Mr. Sharpe. We have your gracious permission to get bloody moving?'

'Carry on, sir.' Sharpe grinned again. He had come to like Windham in the six months that the Colonel had commanded the South Essex, a regard that was also held by the Colonel for his wayward and brilliant Captain of the Light Company. Now, though, Windham still seethed with impatience.

'His sword, Sharpe! For God's sake, man! Hurry!'

'Yes, sir.' Sharpe turned to one of the houses in the village where the South Essex had bivouacked. The dawn was a grey line in the east. 'Sergeant!'

'Sir!'

'The bloody frog's sword!'

'Sharpe!' Colonel Windham's protest sounded resigned.

Patrick Harper turned and bellowed into one of the houses. 'Mr. McDonald, sir! The French gentleman's sword, sir, if you'd get a move on, sir!'

McDonald, Sharpe's new Ensign, just sixteen years old and desperately eager to please his famous Captain, hurried from the house with the beautiful, scabbarded blade. He tripped in his haste, was held by Harper, and then he came to Sharpe and gave him the sword.

God, but he wanted it! He had handled the weapon during the night, feeling its balance, knowing the power of the plain, shining steel, and Sharpe had felt the lust to own this sword. This was a thing of lethal beauty, made by a master, worthy of a great fighter.

'Monsieur?' Delmas's voice was mild, polite.

Beyond Delmas Sharpe could see Lossow, the Captain of the German Cavalry and Sharpe's friend, who had driven Delmas into the prepared trap. Lossow had held the sword too, and shaken his head in mute wonder at the weapon. Now he watched as Sharpe handed the weapon to the

Frenchman, a symbol that he had given his parole and could be trusted with his personal weapon.

Windham gave an exaggerated sigh. 'Now, perhaps, we can start?'

The Light Company marched first behind Lossow's cavalry screen, striking up onto the plains before the day's heat rose in the sky to blind them with sweat and choke them with warm, gritty dust. Sharpe went on foot, unlike most officers, because he had always gone on foot. He had entered the army as a private, wearing the red jacket of the line Regiments and marching with a heavy musket on his shoulder. Later, much later, he had made the impossible jump from Sergeant to officer, joining the elite Rifles with their distinctive green jacket, but Sharpe still marched on foot. He was an infantryman and he marched as his men marched, and he carried a rifle as they carried their rifles or muskets. The South Essex were a redcoat Battalion, but Sharpe, Sergeant Harper, and the nucleus of the Light Company were all Riflemen, accidentally attached to the Battalion, and they proudly retained their dark green jackets.

Light flooded grey on the plain, the sun hinting with a pale red strip in the east of the heat to come, and Sharpe could see the dark shapes of the cavalry outlined on the dawn. The British were marching east, invading French-held Spain, aiming at the great city of Salamanca. Most of the army was far to the south, marching on a dozen roads, while the South Essex with Lossow's men and a handful of Engineers had been sent north to destroy a small French fort that guarded a ford across the Tormes. The job had been done, the fort abandoned by the enemy, and now the South Essex marched to rejoin Wellington's troops. It would take two days before they were back with the army and Sharpe knew they would be days of relentless heat as they crossed the dry plain.

Captain Lossow dropped behind his cavalry to be beside Sharpe. He nodded down at the Rifleman. 'I don't trust your Frenchman, Richard.'

'Nor do I.'

Lossow was not discouraged by Sharpe's curt tone. He was used to Sharpe's morning surliness. 'It's strange, I think, for a Dragoon to have a straight sword. He should have a sabre, yes?'

'True.' Sharpe made an effort to sound more sociable. 'We should have killed the bastard in the wood.'

'That's true. It's the only thing to do with Frenchmen. Kill them.' Lossow laughed. Like most of the Germans in Britain's army, he came from a homeland that had been overrun by Napoleon's troops. 'I wonder what happened to the second man.'

'You lost him.'

Lossow grinned at the insult. 'Never. He hid himself. I hope the Partisans get him.' The German drew a finger across his throat to hint at the way the Spanish Guerilleros treated their French captives. Then he smiled down at Sharpe. 'You wanted his sword, *ja?*'

Sharpe shrugged, then spoke the truth. '*Ja.*'

'You'll get it, my friend! You'll get it!' Lossow laughed and trotted ahead, back to his men. He truly did believe that Sharpe would get the sword, though whether the sword would make Sharpe happy was another matter. Lossow knew Sharpe. He knew the restless spirit that drove the Rifleman through this war, a spirit that drove Sharpe from achievement to achievement. Once Sharpe had wanted to capture a French standard, an Eagle, something never done before by a Briton, and he had done it at Talavera. Later he had defied the Partisans, the French, even his own side, in taking the gold across Spain, and in doing it he had met and wanted Teresa. He had won her too, marrying her just two months ago, after he had been the first man across the death-filled breach at Badajoz. Sharpe, Lossow suspected, often got what he wanted, but the achievements never seemed to satisfy. His friend, the German decided, was like a man who, searching for a crock of gold, found ten and rejected them all because the pots were the wrong shape. He laughed at the thought.

They marched two days, bivouacking early and marching before dawn and, on the morning of the third day, the dawn revealed a smear of fine dust in the sky, a great plume that showed where Wellington's main force covered the roads leading towards Salamanca. Captain Paul Delmas, conspicuous in his strange rust-red pantaloons and with the tall, brass helmet on his head, spurred past Sharpe to stare at the dust cloud as if he hoped to see beneath it the masses of infantry, cavalry and artillery that marched to challenge the greater forces of France. Colonel Windham followed the Frenchman, but reined in beside Sharpe. 'A damn fine horseman, Sharpe!'

'Yes, sir.'

Windham pushed back his bicorne hat and scratched at his greying scalp. 'He seems a decent enough fellow, Sharpe.'

'You talked to him, sir?'

'Good God, no! I don't speak Froggy. Snap! Come here! Snap!' Windham was shouting at one of his foxhounds, perpetual companions to the Colonel. Most of the pack had been left in Portugal, in summer quarters, but half a dozen outrageously spoiled dogs came with the Colonel. 'No, Leroy chatted to him.' Windham managed to convey that the American Major was bound to speak French, being a foreigner himself. Americans were strange, anyone was strange to Windham who did not have true English blood. 'He hunts, you know.'

'Major Leroy, sir?'

'No, Sharpe. Delmas. Mind you, they hunt bloody queer in France. Packs of bloody poodles. I suppose they're trying to copy us and just can't get it right.'

'Probably, sir.'

Windham glanced at Sharpe to see if his leg was being pulled, but the Rifleman's face was neutral. The Colonel courteously touched his hat. 'Won't keep you, Sharpe.' He turned to the Light Company. 'Well done, you scoundrels! Hard marching, eh? Soon over!'

It was over at mid-day when the Battalion reached the hills directly across the river from Salamanca. A messenger had come from the army, ordering the South Essex to that spot while the rest of the army marched further east to the fords that would take them to the north bank. The French had left a garrison in the city that overlooked the long Roman bridge and the job of the South Essex was to make sure that none of the garrison tried to escape across the river. It promised to be an easy, restful afternoon. The garrison planned to stay; the guard on the bridge was nothing more than a formal gesture.

Sharpe had been to Salamanca four years before with Sir John Moore's ill fated army. He had seen the city then in winter, under a cold sleet and an uncertain future, but he had never forgotten it. He stood now on the hill crest two hundred yards from the southern end of the Roman bridge and stared at the city over the water. The rest of the Battalion were behind him, out of sight of the French guns in the forts, and only the Light Company and Windham were with him. The Colonel had come to see the city.

It was a place of honey-coloured stone, a riot of belfries and towers, churches and palaces, all dwarfed by the two Cathedrals on the highest hill. The New Cathedral, three centuries old with its two domed towers, was huge and serene in the sunlight. This city was not a place of trade, like London, nor a granite-faced fortress, like Badajoz, but a place of learning, of prayer, of grace, of beauty that had little purpose but to please. It was a city of gold above a river of silver, and Sharpe was happy to be back.

The city had been spoiled, though. The French had razed the south western corner of Salamanca and left just three buildings. The three had been changed into fortresses, given ditches and walls, loopholes and embrasures, and the old houses and churches, colleges and monasteries had been

24

ruthlessly pulled down to give the three forts a wide field of fire. Two of them overlooked the bridge, denying its use to the British, the third was closer to the city centre. All three, Sharpe knew, would have to be taken before the British left the city and pursued the French army that had withdrawn to the north.

He looked down from the forts to the river. It flowed slowly under the bridge between green trees. Marsh harriers, their wing tips flicked up, glided between green islands. Sharpe looked again at the magnificence of the golden-stoned Cathedral and looked forward to entering the city. He did not know when that would be. Once the far end of the bridge was secured by the Sixth Division, the South Essex would march two miles east to the nearest ford and then go north to join the rest of the army. Few men of Wellington's forces would see Salamanca until Marmont's army was defeated, but it was enough for Sharpe, at this moment, to stare at the intricate, serene beauty across the river and to hope that soon, very soon, he would have a chance to explore the streets once more.

Colonel Windham's mouth twitched into a half smile. 'Extraordinary!'

'Extraordinary, sir?'

Windham gestured with his riding crop at the Cathedral, then at the river. 'Cathedral, Sharpe. River. Just like Gloucester.'

'I thought Gloucester was flat, sir.'

Windham sniffed at the comment. 'River and cathedral. Much the same, really.'

'It's a beautiful city, sir.'

'Gloucester? Of course it is! It's English. Clean streets. Not like that damned place.' Windham probably never ventured out of the main street of any English town to explore the rubbish clogged alleyways and rookeries. The Colonel was a countryman, with the virtues of the country, and a deep suspicion of all things foreign. He was no fool, though Sharpe suspected that Lieutenant Colonel Windham sometimes liked to play the fool to avoid that most hurtful of all English insults; being too clever by half. Windham now twisted in his saddle and looked back at the resting Battalion. 'Here comes that Frenchman.'

Delmas saluted Windham. Major Leroy had come with him and translated for the Colonel's benefit. 'Captain Delmas asks when he can be sent on to Headquarters, sir.'

'In a damned hurry, ain't he?' Windham's tanned leathery face scowled, then he shrugged. 'Suppose he wants to get exchanged before the damn frogs run all the way to Paris.'

Delmas was leaning far down from his saddle to let one of the Colonel's dogs lick his fingers. Leroy spoke with him while Windham fidgeted. The Major turned back to the Colonel. 'He'd be grateful for an early exchange, sir. He says his mother is ill and he's keen to get news of her.'

Sharpe made a sympathetic noise and Windham barked at Sharpe to be quiet. The Colonel watched the Frenchman fussing his dogs with approval. 'I don't mind, Leroy. Damned if I know who's going to escort him to Headquarters. Do you fancy a hack?'

The Major shook his head. 'No, sir.'

Windham screwed himself around again and peered at the Battalion. 'I suppose we can ask Butler. He's usually willing.' He caught sight of Ensign McDonald, much closer. 'Does your young man ride, Sharpe?'

'Yes, sir. No horse, though.'

'You have bloody strange ideas, Sharpe.' Windham half disapproved of Sharpe's belief that an infantry officer should walk like his men. It made sense for some officers to be mounted. They could see further in battle, and be seen by their men, but a Light Company fought on foot in the skirmish line and a man on horseback was a plain target. Sharpe's officers wore their boots out. McDonald had heard the exchange between Sharpe and Windham and he came close and looked eager. Major Leroy swung himself off his own horse.

'You can take mine. Ride her easy!' Leroy opened his pouch and took out a folded piece of paper. 'Here's Captain Delmas's parole. You give that to the Officer of the Day at Headquarters, understand?'

'Yes, sir.' McDonald was excited.

Leroy gave the Ensign a leg up onto the horse. 'You know where Headquarters is?'

'No, sir.'

'Nor does anyone.' Windham grumbled. He pointed south. 'Go that way till you find the army, then go east till you find Headquarters. I want you back here by dusk and if Wellington asks you to dinner, say you're spoken for.'

'Yes, sir.' McDonald grinned delightedly. 'Do you think he might, sir?'

'Get away with you!' Windham acknowledged Delmas's salute. The Frenchman turned once more to look at Salamanca, staring intently as though looking to see if any British troops had yet made their journey back from the fords and were entering the city streets. Then the pale eyes turned to Sharpe. Delmas smiled. 'Au revoir, M'sieur.'

Sharpe smiled back. 'I hope your mother's pox gets better.'

Windham bristled. 'Damned unnecessary, Sharpe! Fellow was perfectly pleasant! French, of course, but pleasant.'

Delmas trotted obediently behind the sixteen year old Ensign and Sharpe watched them go before turning back to the gorgeous city across the river. Salamanca. It would be the first bloodless victory of Wellington's summer campaign, and then Sharpe remembered it would not be quite bloodless. The makeshift fortresses left in the city would have to be reduced so that Wellington could pour his supplies and reinforcements across the long Roman bridge. The city of gold would have to be fought for so that the bridge, built so

27

long ago by the Romans, could help a new army in a modern war.

Sharpe wondered that a bridge so old still stood. The parapets of the roadway were crenellated, like a castle wall, and almost in the centre of the bridge was a handsome small fortress arched above the road. The French had not garrisoned the tiny fort, leaving it in the possession of a statue of a bull. Colonel Windham also stared at the bridge and shook his head. 'Bloody awful, eh Sharpe?'

'Awful, sir?'

'More damned arches than bones in a rabbit! An English bridge would be just two arches, ain't I right? Not all that waste of damned good stone! Still, I suppose the Spanish thought they were bloody clever just to get it across, what?'

Leroy, his face still terribly scarred from Badajoz, answered in his laconic voice. 'The Romans built it, sir.'

'The Romans!' Windham grinned happily. 'Every damned bridge in this country was built by the Romans. If they hadn't been here the Spanish would probably never cross a river!' He laughed at the idea. 'Good, that! I must write it home to Jessica.' He let his reins drop onto his horse's neck. 'Waste of time this. No damn frogs are going to try and cross the bridge. Still, I suppose the lads could do with a rest.' He yawned, then looked at Sharpe. 'Your Company can keep an eye on things, Sharpe.'

Sharpe did not answer. The Colonel frowned. 'Sharpe?'

But Sharpe was turning away from the Colonel, unslinging his rifle. 'Light Company!'

By God! And wasn't instinct always right? Sharpe was pulling back the flint of his rifle, moving ahead of Windham's horse while to his right, down in the small valley which approached the southern end of the bridge was Delmas.

Sharpe had seen the movement in the corner of his eye and then, in a moment of shock, recognised the baggy pantaloons, the brass helmet, and only a rifle could stop the Frenchman now. Only a rifle had the range to kill the fugitive whom Sharpe's instincts had said not to trust. Damn the parole!

'Good God!' Colonel Windham saw Delmas. 'Good God! His parole! God damn him!'

God might well damn Delmas, but only a Rifleman could stop him reaching the bridge and the safety of the French forts on the far side. Delmas, low on his horse's neck, was a hundred yards from the Riflemen, with the same distance to go to the bridge entrance. Sharpe aimed for the big horse, leading the galloping beast with his foresight, tightening his finger on the trigger and then his view was blocked by Colonel Windham's horse.

'View halloo!' Windham, his sabre drawn, was spurring after the Frenchman, his dogs giving tongue either side.

Sharpe jerked his rifle up, cursing Windham for blocking the shot, and stared, hopelessly, as the Frenchman, his honour broken with his parole, raced for the bridge and safety.

CHAPTER 2

Windham's horse blocked all the Riflemens' shots for a few crucial seconds, but then the Colonel dropped into the concavity of the hillside and Sharpe re-aimed, fired, and was moving down the hill before he could see where his bullet had gone. The powder stung his face from the pan, he smelt the acrid smoke as he ran through it, and then he heard a fusillade of shots from his handful of Riflemen.

Sharpe had missed, but one of his men, Hagman probably, struck Delmas's horse. The Frenchman was pitched forward, the horse down on its knees, while dust spumed up to hide the dying horse and falling man.

'Skirmish order!' Sharpe yelled, not wanting his men to be bunched into an easy target for the French artillery in the fortresses across the river. He was running fast now, pumping his arms left and right to tell his men to spread out, while ahead Lieutenant Colonel Windham raced up towards the fallen Delmas.

The Frenchman scrambled to his feet, glanced once behind, and began running. The hounds bayed, stretched out, while Windham, sabre reaching forward, thundered behind.

The first French cannon fired from the fortress closest to the river. The sound of the gun was flat over the water, a boom that echoed bleakly above the beauty of river and bridge, and then the shot struck short of Windham, bounced, and came on up the hill. The French gun barrels would be cold, making the first shots drop short, but even a bouncing shot was dangerous.

'Spread out!' Sharpe shouted. 'Spread out!'

More guns fired, their reports mingling like thunder, and the wind of one bouncing shot almost wrenched Windham from his horse. The beast swerved and only the Colonel's superb horsemanship saved him. The spurs went back, the sword was held out again, and Sharpe watched as the running Frenchman stopped and turned to face his pursuer.

Another gun from the fortress, a different note to this firing, and the hillside seemed to leap with small explosions of soil where the canister bullets, sprayed from the bursting tin can at the gun's muzzle, pecked at the soil. 'Spread out! Spread out!' Sharpe was running recklessly, leaping rough ground, and he threw away his fired rifle, knowing one of his men would retrieve it, and clumsily drew his huge, straight sword.

Windham was angry. Honour had been trampled by the breaking of Delmas's parole, and the Colonel was in no mood to offer the Frenchman mercy. Windham heard the canister strike the ground, heard an agonised yelp as one of his hounds was hit, and then he forgot everything because Delmas was close, facing him, and the British Colonel stretched out with his curved sabre so that its point would spear savagely into the fugitive's chest.

It seemed to Windham that Delmas struck with his sword too soon. He saw the blade coming, was just bracing his arm for the shock of his own blade meeting the enemy, and then Delmas's beautiful sword, as it had been intended to do, slammed viciously into the mouth of Windham's horse.

The animal screamed, swerved, reared up, and Windham fought for control. He let his sabre hang by its wrist-strap as he sawed at the reins, as he saw blood spray from his injured horse's mouth, and as he struggled he never saw the Frenchman move behind, swing, and never knew what killed him.

Sharpe saw. He shouted helplessly, uselessly, and he saw the great sword slam blade-edge into the Colonel's back.

Windham seemed to arch away from the stroke. Even in

death his knees gripped the horse, even as his head dropped, as his arms went limp and the sabre dangled uselessly. The horse screamed again, tried to shake the dead man from the saddle. It fled away from the man who had hurt it, still bucking and hurting, and then, almost mercifully, a barrel-load of canister threw man and horse into a bloodied mess on the turf.

The hounds sniffed at the dead man and dying horse. Its hooves drummed the dry earth for an instant, the hounds whimpered, and then the horse's head was down. Blood drained quickly into the parched soil.

Delmas was limping. The fall must have hurt him, but still he hurried, gritting his teeth against the pain, but now Sharpe was gaining. There were houses at the bridge's southern end, a small outpost of the university city across the river, and Sharpe saw the Frenchman disappear behind a wall. Delmas was almost onto the bridge.

Another canister load of musket balls flayed into the turf, filling the summer air with their whip-crack of death, and then Sharpe saw Patrick Harper, the giant Sergeant, racing up on his right with his seven-barrelled gun held in his hand. Sharpe and Harper were nearing the houses, nearing the safety afforded by their walls from the French guns in the fortresses, but Sharpe had a sudden premonition of danger. 'Go wide, Patrick! Wide!'

They swerved right, still running, and as they cleared the corner of the house to get their first glimpse of the roadway running straight across the wide river, Sharpe saw too the kneeling Frenchman pointing a brace of pistols at the place where he expected his pursuers to appear. 'Down!'

Sharpe sprawled into Harper, sending them both in a bruising fall to the earth, and at that moment the pistols cracked and the two balls sounded sibilant and wicked over their heads.

'Jesus!' Harper was heaving himself upright. Delmas had already turned and was limping onto the bridge, hurrying

32

towards the northern bank beneath the three fortresses.

The two Riflemen ran forward. They were safe for a moment, hidden from the gunners by the houses, but Sharpe knew that as soon as they emerged onto the bridge the canisters would begin to rattle the ancient stones. He led Harper left, into what little protection the crenellated, low parapet might give, but the very instant that they stepped onto the bridge was the moment they both instinctively dropped to the roadway, heads covered, appalled by the sudden storm of canister that tangled the air above the bridge.

'God save Ireland.' Harper muttered.

'God kill that bastard. Come on!'

They crawled, keeping below the parapet, and their pace was pitifully slow so that Sharpe could see Delmas opening the gap between them. In his path the Frenchman seemed to leave a maelstrom of striking shot, screaming stone shards chipped from the road, the noise of metal on stone, yet the Frenchman was untouched, kept safe by the gunner's accuracy, and Sharpe could sense that Delmas was escaping.

'Down, sir!' Harper unceremoniously pushed Sharpe with a huge hand, and Sharpe knew that the horrid seven-barrelled gun was being aimed over his head. He clapped his hands to his ears, abandoning the sword for a second, and waited for the explosion above his head.

It was a horrid weapon, a gift from Sharpe to his Sergeant, and a gun that only a huge man could handle. It had been made for the Royal Navy, intended as a weapon to be fired from the topworks down onto the packed decks of enemy ships, but the vicious recoil of the seven half-inch barrels had thrown the sailors clear out of the rigging, sending them falling with fractured shoulders onto their own decks. Patrick Harper, the huge Irishman, was one of the few men who had the brute strength to use one, and now he aimed the stubby, bunched barrels at the pantalooned figure that was limping beneath the arch of the small fortress.

He pulled the trigger and the gun belched smoke, bullets, and burning wadding that fell onto Sharpe's neck. It was a deadly gun at close range, but at fifty yards, the distance of Delmas's lead, it would be a lucky bullet that hit. A single word over Sharpe's head told him the Irishman had missed.

'Come on!'

A half dozen Riflemen had crawled onto the bridge after Sharpe and Harper, the rest stayed in the lee of the buildings and frantically loaded their weapons in hope of a clear shot. Sharpe pushed on, cursing the canister that screamed above the roadway. One ball, freakishly ricocheting from the far parapet, struck his boot heel, and Sharpe swore. 'We'll have to bloody run, Patrick.'

'Sweet Jesus!' The Donegal accent could not hide his feelings about running through the storm of shot. Harper touched the crucifix he wore about his neck. Since he had met Isabella, the Spanish girl he had saved from the rape at Badajoz, he had become more religious. The two might live in mortal sin, but Isabella made sure her huge man paid some respect to their church. 'Say the word, sir.'

Sharpe waited for another grinding barrelful of canister to crash onto the roadway. 'Now!'

They sprinted, Sharpe's sword heavy in his pumping arm, and the air seemed filled with the sound of death and the fear rose in him, fear at this ghastly way of dying, hit by canister and unable to strike back. He skidded into the safety of the small archway beneath the fortress and fell against the wall. 'God!'

They had survived, God only knew how, but he would not try it again. The air had seemed thick with shot. 'We'll have to bloody crawl, Patrick.'

'Anything you say, sir.'

Daniel Hagman, the oldest man in Sharpe's Company, and the best sharpshooter in the Battalion, methodically loaded his rifle. He had been a poacher in his native

Cheshire, caught one dark night, and he had left wife and family to join the army rather than face the awful justice meted out by the Assizes. He did not use a cartridge with its rough powder, instead he measured his charge from the fine powder kept in his Rifleman's horn, and then he selected a bullet and rammed it down the barrel. He had wrapped the bullet in a greased leather patch, a patch that would grip the rifling when the gun was fired and give a spin to the bullet which made the weapon so much more accurate than the smooth-bore musket. He primed the gun, aimed, and in his mind was the memory of Rifleman Plunkett who, four years before, had sent a bullet a full and astonishing eight hundred yards to kill a French General. Plunkett was a legend in his regiment, the 95th, because the Baker Rifle was not reckoned to be truly accurate much over two hundred yards, and now Hagman had a clear sight of his target just a hundred yards away.

He smiled. At this range he could pick his spot, and he chose the lower spine, letting the foresight settle a little above it, letting half his breath out, holding it, and then he squeezed the trigger.

He could not miss at that range. The rifle slammed into his shoulder, smoke jetting from pan and muzzle, the burning powder stinging his cheek.

The canister screamed onto the bridge, four cannon-loads fired at once, and Hagman never knew what happened to his bullet. It never reached Delmas. Somewhere in the metal over the bridge the bullet was lost, a freak chance, but Delmas still lived, still limped on towards the safety of the far bank.

Yet there was still a chance. The fortresses were built on top of the hill above the river and once the bridge was close to the northern bank the guns could not see the roadway. In a few more yards, Sharpe knew, he would be able to stand up and run in safety, and Delmas knew it too. The Frenchman forced himself on, ignoring the pain, refusing to be beaten, and he managed to force his hurting body into a slow run that took him even further ahead.

Then it seemed that everything would be lost. There were shouts ahead and Sharpe looked up to see blue uniforms running down the hill towards the bridge. Voltigeurs! French Light infantry, their red epaulettes distinctive in the sunlight, and Sharpe swore for he knew that these troops had been sent out of the fortresses to see Delmas to safety. A dozen Frenchmen were coming down the hill, while others waited at its crest.

Sharpe crawled, pushing himself on, Harper's breathing hoarse behind him. It truly did seem hopeless now. The Voltigeurs would reach Delmas long before Sharpe or Harper could, but he would not give up. A shard of stone, chipped by a canister strike, clanged on the metal scabbard of his sword while another skinned across his knuckles and drew bright blood.

The Voltigeurs were at the bridge's end, lining it, fumbling their muskets into the firing position, and Delmas was just feet away. A rifle bullet cracked past Sharpe, he saw a French Voltigeur duck away from the passing of the bullet, and then another Frenchman pitched forward. Forward! Sharpe looked up. There was musket smoke from the houses of the city which bordered the wasteland the French had cleared about the fortresses. 'Look!' He pointed up. 'The Sixth must have got here!'

It was not the Sixth Division. The muskets were being fired by the citizens of Salamanca, venting their anger on the French who had occupied the city for so long. The Voltigeurs were caught between the two fires; the Riflemen firing across the long bridge and the Spaniards aiming from behind.

'Come on!' They had reached the safe part of the bridge, that part which could not be reached by the guns, but at the same moment Delmas had stumbled into the arms of his rescuers who were already retreating, taking the fugitive up towards the forts.

Sharpe and Harper ran, not caring about the odds, and the French Voltigeur officer calmly turned six of his men around, lined them, and brought their muskets up into the aim.

Sharpe and Harper split automatically, Harper going to the right of the bridge, Sharpe to the left, so that the enemy would have to choose between two smaller targets. Sharpe was shouting now, an incoherent shout of rage that would frighten the enemy, and he could hear Harper bellowing to his right.

Another rifle bullet cracked past them, hitting a Frenchman in the knee and his shout of sudden pain made the others nervous. Two of their number were wounded, both men crawling back towards the hill. Behind them Spanish muskets fired, before them the Riflemen were firing down the long length of the bridge between the two huge men who were screaming defiance at them. The four remaining Voltigeurs pulled their triggers, wanting only to retreat to the safety of the fortresses.

Sharpe sensed the wind of the musket balls, knew he was not hit, and he had the huge sword ready for its first strike. The enemy skirmishers were going backwards, retreating after Delmas, but the officer tried to hold them. He shouted at them, pulled at one of them, and when he saw it was hopeless he turned himself with his long, slim sword waiting for Sharpe.

It was the French officer's bravery that made the four men turn. Their muskets were not loaded, but they still had bayonets which they twisted onto their muskets, but they were too late to save their Lieutenant.

Sharpe could see the fear in the man's eyes; wished that he would turn and run, but the man insisted on staying. He moved to block Sharpe, bringing his sword up to lunge, but the huge cavalry sword beat it aside in a numbing, ringing blow, and then Sharpe, not wanting to kill the man, shoulder charged and sent the officer flying backwards onto the roadway of the bridge's entrance.

The four Voltigeurs were coming back, bayonets out-stretched. Sharpe turned towards them, teeth bared, sword ready, but suddenly he could not move. The French Lieuten-ant had grabbed his ankle, was holding on for dear life, and the Voltigeurs, seeing it, suddenly hurried to take advantage of Sharpe's loss of balance.

It was a fatal mistake. Patrick Harper, the Irishman, counted himself a friend of Sharpe, despite the disparity in rank. Harper was hugely strong, but, as with so many strong men, he had a touching gentleness and even placidity. Harper was mostly content to let the world go by, watching it with wry humour, but never so in battle. He had been raised on the songs and stories of the great Irish warriors. To Patrick Harper, Cuchulain was not an imaginary hero from a remote past, but a real man, an Irishman, a warrior to emulate. Cuchulain died at twenty-seven, Harper's present age, and he had fought as Harper fought, with a wild battle song intoxicating him. Harper knew that mad joy too, he had it now as he charged the four men and shouted at them in his own, old language.

He was swinging the heavy seven-barrelled gun like a club. The first stroke beat down a musket and bayonet, beat down onto a Frenchman's head, and the second stroke threw two men down. Harper was kicking now, stamping them down, using the gun as a mace into which he put all his giant strength. The fourth man lunged with his bayonet and Harper, taking one hand from his club, contemptuously pulled the musket towards him and brought his knee up into the stumbling enemy's face. All four were down.

The French officer, lying on the ground, watched aghast. His hand nervelessly let go of Sharpe's ankle, saving himself from the downward stab of the huge sword. More Riflemen were coming now, safe on that part of the bridge that could not be reached by the enemy gunners.

Harper wanted more. He was climbing the hillslope,

negotiating the rubble of the houses which the French had blown up to give their forts a wide barrier of waste ground. He went past the two wounded men who, like their comrades below, would be prisoners, and Sharpe followed the Sergeant. 'Go right! Patrick! Go right!'

Sharpe could not understand it. Delmas, safe with the other Voltigeurs, was not going towards the fortresses. Instead he was limping right towards the city, towards the balconied houses from which the Spaniards fired. A Voltigeur officer was arguing with him, but Sharpe saw the big Dragoon officer order the man silent. Two other Voltigeurs were detailed to help Leroux, to almost carry the limping man up the slope and Sharpe did not understand why Delmas would go towards the scattered musket fire of the civilians. It was insane! Delmas was within yards of the safety of the forts, but instead he was aiming to plunge into a hostile city into which, at any moment, the Sixth Division of Wellington's army would march. Delmas was even risking the Spanish musket fire, the closer to which he limped the more dangerous it became.

Then it was no danger. Sharpe, climbing up behind the Dragoon, saw a tall, grey-haired priest appear on one of the balconies of the houses and, though Sharpe could not make out the words, he could hear the priest bellowing in a huge voice. The man's arms flapped up and down, unmistakeably telling the civilians to stop firing. Damn the priest! He was letting Delmas get into the tangle of alleys, and the civilians were obeying the grey-haired man. Sharpe swore and redoubled his efforts to catch the group of Frenchmen. Damn the bloody priest!

Then Sharpe had to forget Delmas and the priest. The other Voltigeurs, seeing the speed with which Sharpe and Harper were climbing the hillside, had been sent down to deal with them. The first bullets struck dust from the rubble and Sharpe had to roll into cover because the musket fire was too heavy. He heard Harper swear, looked for him, and saw the Irishman rubbing his thigh where he had bruised it in his own swift fall behind a block of stone. The Sergeant grinned. 'Didn't someone say this would be an easy afternoon?'

Sharpe looked behind him. He guessed he was halfway up the slope, a hundred feet above the river, and he could see three of his Riflemen shepherding the prisoners into a huddle. Four more climbed towards them and one of them, Parry Jenkins, was shouting incoherently and pointing beyond Sharpe. At the same instant Harper yelled. 'In front, sir!'

The Voltigeurs, annoyed perhaps at the impudence of the Riflemen's charge, were determined to take the two men isolated on the slope. They had fired their volley and now a dozen of them came down with bayonets to either take prisoners or finish Sharpe and Harper off.

Frustration filled Sharpe with anger. He blamed himself for letting Delmas escape. He should have insisted to Colonel Windham that the man could not be trusted, and now Windham was dead. Sharpe had to presume that poor young McDonald was dead too, killed at sixteen by a bastard who had broken his parole and who was now escaping up the hill. Sharpe came up out of his hiding place with a huge anger, with the great, heavy, ill-balanced sword in his hand, and as he went to meet the Frenchmen it seemed to him, as it so often did in battle, that time slowed down. He could clearly see the face of the first man, could see the gapped, yellowed teeth beneath the straggly moustache, and he could see the man's throat and he knew where his blade would go and he swung, the steel hissing, and the sharpened tip slashed the enemy's throat and Sharpe was already bringing it back in an upswing that crashed a second man's musket aside, bit into the man's forearm so that he dropped the weapon and was helpless as the downswing slammed through shako and skull.

Harper watched for an instant, grinning, because he was used to the fearsome spectacle of Richard Sharpe going fierce into battle and then he joined in. He left the seven-barrelled gun behind and used a length of fire-blackened timber with which he flailed the red-epauletted enemy until, their courage broken, they were scrambling back up the hill. Harper looked at his Captain whose reddened blade had defeated four men in less than half a minute. He bent down to retrieve the big gun. 'Have you ever thought about joining the army, Mr. Sharpe?'

Sharpe was not listening. He was staring at the houses where the priest had stopped the civilians from firing, and now Sharpe was smiling because the priest might be able to order civilians, but he could not order British soldiers about. The Sixth Division had arrived! He could see the red uniforms at the hilltop, he could hear the crackle of muskets, and Sharpe drove himself up the slope so he could find out where Delmas was. Harper followed.

They dropped at the crest. To their right the houses were dotted with red uniforms, to their left were the three forts to which the Voltigeurs were retreating and Delmas was with them! He had been headed off by the Sixth Division and had been forced towards the fortresses. That was a victory of a kind, Sharpe supposed, because now the treacherous Frenchman was trapped in the forts. He looked behind and saw the river bank thick with British troops who marched west along the road beside the Tormes to finish off the cordon about the three strongholds. Delmas was trapped!

The French cannons fired again, canister blasting over the wasteland to rattle on the houses, smashing windows and flimsy shutters, aimed at driving the newly arrived British troops into cover.

Sharpe watched Delmas. He watched as the man was helped into the ditch in front of the nearest, smallest fort. Watched as the brass helmet appeared again and the Frenchman was pulled into one of the cannon embrasures. Sharpe watched his enemy go into the fort. The bastard was trapped! The sword was in Salamanca and it might yet belong to Sharpe.

Sharpe looked at Harper. 'That's it. Bastard got away.'

'Not next time, sir.' Harper twisted around and stared over the river. A knot of officers were in the shelter of the houses on the far bank, another group of men, unmolested by the French gunners, were carrying Windham's body up the hill. Harper could see the foxhounds following the sad cortege. As he watched, so the gunners fired again at the bridge. They would let the British take away their dead, but they would still not yield passage of the river. Harper nodded at the bridge. 'Don't think we can go back, sir.'

'No.'

'Not a bad wee city to be stuck in, sir.'

'What?' Sharpe had only been half listening. He had been thinking of Delmas. The Frenchman had murdered Windham, and probably murdered McDonald too. A man who killed while still on parole was a murderer.

'I said it's not a bad wee city . . .'

'I heard you, Patrick.' Sharpe looked at the Sergeant, remembering the fight. 'Thank you.'

'For what? Do you think we should join the lads?'

'Yes.'

They scrambled down the hill to join the few Riflemen who, like themselves, were marooned on the northern bank of the river. One of them had retrieved Sharpe's rifle and carried it all the way across the bridge. He gave it back to his Captain. 'What do we do now, sir?'

'Now?' Sharpe listened. Faintly he could hear a rhythmic booming, a sound overlaid with a slight, tinny melody. 'Hear that?'

They listened. Parry Jenkins grinned. 'It's a band!'

Sharpe slung his rifle. 'I think we should join in.' He guessed that the Sixth Division was making their formal entry into the city; bands playing and colours flying, and he pointed down the river bank to the east. 'That way, lads, then up into the city.' The route would take them far from the French cannons pointing across the wasted south-western

42

corner of the city. 'And listen, lads!' They looked at him. 'Just stay together, you understand? We're not supposed to be here and the bloody Provosts would just love a chance to put a real soldier in chains.' They grinned at him. 'Come on!'

He was wiping the blood from his big sword as he led them along the river bank and then up into a steep alleyway which pointed towards the two Cathedrals on the hilltop. They were behind the houses from which the Spanish civilians had fired at Delmas, where the priest had checked their fire, and Sharpe thought he recognised the tall, grey-haired figure that climbed ahead of him.

He quickened his pace, leaving his Riflemen behind, and the noise of his boots on the cobbled street made the priest turn. He was a tall, elderly man whose face seemed filled with amusement and charity. He smiled at Sharpe and glanced at the sword. 'You look as if you want to kill me, my son.'

Sharpe had not known exactly why he had pursued the priest, except to vent his anger at the man's interference with the afternoon's fight. The priest's perfect English took him by surprise, and the man's cool tone annoyed him. 'I kill the King's enemies.'

The priest smiled at Sharpe's dramatic tone. 'You're angry with me, my son. Is it because I stopped the civilians shooting? Yes?' He did not wait for an answer, but went on placatingly. 'Do you know what the French will do to them if they get a chance? Do you? Have you seen civilians put against a wall and shot like sick dogs?'

Sharpe's anger spilt into his voice. 'For Christ's sake! We're here now, not the bloody French!'

'I doubt if it's for His sake, my son.' The priest irritated Sharpe by continuing to smile. 'And for how long are you here? If you don't defeat the main French armies then you'll be running back to Portugal and we can expect those Frenchmen to be in our streets again.'

Sharpe frowned. 'Are you English?'

'Praise the Lord, no!' For the first time the priest sounded shocked by something Sharpe had said. 'I'm Irish, my son. My name is Father Patrick Curtis, though the Salamantines call me Don Patricio Cortes.' Curtis stopped as Harper shepherded the curious Riflemen past the two men. Harper took them on up the street. Curtis smiled again at Sharpe. 'Salamanca is my city now, and these people are my people. I understand their hatred of the French, but I must protect them if the French ever rule here again. That man you were chasing. Do you know what he would do to them?'

'Delmas? What?'

Curtis frowned. He had a strong face, deeply lined, dominated by enormous, busy grey eyebrows. 'Delmas? No! Leroux!'

It was Sharpe's turn to be puzzled. 'I was chasing a man in a brass helmet. A man with a limp.'

'That's right! Leroux.' He saw Sharpe's surprise. 'He's a full Colonel in Napoleon's Imperial Guard. Philippe Leroux. He's ruthless, my son, especially against civilians.'

The priest's calm, informative voice had not mollified Sharpe, who kept his voice hostile. 'You know a lot about him.'

Curtis laughed. 'Of course! I'm Irish! We're always interested in other people's business. In my case, of course, it's also God's business to know about people. Even people like Colonel Leroux.'

'And it was my business to kill him.'

'As the centurion said on Golgotha.'

'What?'

'Nothing, my son. A comment in poor taste. Well, Captain?' Curtis made the rank a question, and Sharpe nodded. The priest smiled. 'It's my pleasant duty to welcome you to Salamanca, even if you are English. Consider yourself duly welcomed.

'You don't like the English?' Sharpe was determined not to like the elderly priest.

'Why should I?' Curtis still smiled. 'Does the worm like the plough?'

'I suppose you'd prefer the French?' Sharpe was still convinced that Curtis had stopped the firing to spare the man who had called himself Delmas.

Curtis sighed. 'Dear, oh dear! This conversation, if you'll forgive me, Captain, is getting tiresome. I'll bid you good-day, my son. I expect we'll meet again soon. Salamanca's a small enough town.' He turned and walked ahead of Sharpe, leaving the Rifle Officer annoyed. Sharpe knew he had been bested by the priest, that Curtis's calmness had easily deflected his anger. Well, damn the priest, and damn Colonel Philippe Leroux. Sharpe walked on, hurrying past Curtis without acknowledging him, and his head was busy with his need for revenge. Leroux. The man who had murdered Windham, had murdered McDonald, had broken his parole, had escaped Sharpe, and who possessed a sword fit for a great fighter. Colonel Leroux; a worthy enemy for this summer of war and heat.

CHAPTER 3

Sharpe overtook his men and led them along beside the two Cathedrals and into streets that were crowded with people ready to celebrate the city's release from the French. Blankets had been hung from the poorer balconies, flags from the richer, while women leaned over window ledges and balustrades. 'Vive Ingles!'

Harper bellowed back at them. 'Viva Irlandes!' Wine was pressed on them, flowers tossed to them, and the cheerful holiday crowd jostled the Riflemen as they moved towards the music and the city centre. Harper grinned at Sharpe. 'The Lieutenant ought to be here!'

Sharpe's Lieutenant, Harold Price, would have been inordinately jealous. The girls were beautiful, smiling, and Price would have been torn by indecision like a terrier not knowing which rat to take first. A woman, monstrously fat, jumped up and down to plant a kiss on Harper's cheek and the Irishman swept her up in his arms, kissed her happily, and put her down. The crowd cheered, loving it, and a small child was handed to the Sergeant who took her, skinny legs flailing, and put her on his shoulders. She drummed on his shako top, beating with the band sound, and beamed at her friends. Today was holiday in Salamanca. The French were gone, either north with Marmont or else into their three cordoned fortresses, and Salamanca was free.

The street opened into a courtyard, gorgeously decorated with carvings, and Sharpe remembered the place from his last visit. Salamanca was a town like Oxford or Cambridge, a

46

University town, and the courtyard was part of the University. The stones of the buildings had been carved as delicately as silver filigree, the workmanship of the masons breathtakingly skilled, and he saw his men staring in wonder at the riotous stone. There was nothing like this to be seen in England, perhaps anywhere in the world, yet Sharpe knew that the best of Salamanca was still to come.

Bells pealed from a dozen belfries, a cacophony of joy that clashed with the army band. Swallows in their hundreds were wheeling and swooping over the rooftops, the harbingers of evening, and he pushed on, nodding and smiling at the people, and he noticed in the next street how the doors still bore the chalk marks left by the French billeting officers. Tonight the Sixth Division would be in these houses, and welcomed more readily because the British paid for their rooms and for their food. The French had gone. And Sharpe smiled because Leroux was trapped in the forts, and then he wondered how it would be possible to arrange it so that he could be present when the Sixth Division assaulted the forts.

The street ended in a wide space and Sharpe saw the tips of bright bayonets bobbing rhythmically over the heads of the crowd towards an archway. Harper put the small girl down, releasing her to run and join the crowd lining the parade route, and the Light Company men followed Sharpe towards the archway. Like all the Riflemen in Sharpe's Company, Harper had been here before, back in the winter of '08, and he remembered the Plaza Mayor that lay beyond this archway. It was in the Plaza Mayor that the Sixth Division gathered for the formal parade to mark the British entry into Salamanca.

Sharpe stopped just sort of the archway and looked at Harper. 'I'm going to find Major Hogan. Keep the lads together, and meet me here at ten o'clock.'

'Yes, sir.'

Sharpe looked at the men with Harper, rogues all of them. They were typical of the drunks, thieves, murderers and runaways who had somehow become the best infantry in the world. He grinned at them. 'You can drink.' They gave ironic cheers and Sharpe held up a hand. 'But no fights. We're not supposed to be here and the bloody Provosts would love to beat the hell out of you. So stay out of trouble, and keep your mates out of trouble, understand? Stick together. You can drink, but I'm not carrying anyone home tonight, so stay on your feet.' Sharpe had reduced the army's regulations to three simple rules. His men were expected to fight, as he did, with determination. They were not to steal, except from the enemy or unless they were starving. And they were never to get drunk without his permission. They grinned at him and held up wine that had been given them. They would have sore heads in the morning.

He left them and pushed his way through the crowds that lined the archway. He knew just what to expect, but still it took his breath away as he stood for a moment and just stared at what he thought was the most beautiful place he had seen in his life; Salamanca's Plaza Mayor, the Great Plaza. It had been finished just thirty years before and had taken seventy years to build, but the time had been well spent. The square was formed of continuous houses, each of three storeys above the arched colonnade and every room facing the Plaza opened onto a wrought iron balcony. The severity of the buildings' design was softened by decorated scrollwork, carved coats of arms, and a spire studded balustrade that edged the sky. The houses met at the north side of the Plaza in a splendid Palacio, higher than the houses and more ornate, and on the eastern side, full in the rays of the descending sun, was the Royal Pavilion. The stone of the whole Plaza was golden in the late afternoon, traced with a thousand, thousand shadows cast by balconies, shutters, carvings and spires. Swallows laced the air of the huge space. The Plaza was of royal dimensions. It spoke of grandeur, pride and magnificence, yet it was a public place and belonged to the citizens of Salamanca. The meanest person could walk and linger in its glory and imagine himself in the residence of a King.

Thousands of people were now crammed into the Plaza's immensity. They lined the triple balconies and waved scarves and flags, cheered, and tossed blossoms into the paved square. Crowds were thick in the shadowed arcade beneath the colonnade's eighty-eight arches, and their cheering threatened to drown the band that played beneath the Palacio to whose music the Sixth Division made their solemn and formal entry.

This was a moment to savour, a moment of glory, the moment when the British took hold of this city. The Plaza Mayor had sensed this moment, was making a celebration of it, yet in the very centre of the noise and colour sat a quiet man who looked, on his tall horse, to be almost drab. He wore no uniform. A plain blue coat, grey trousers, and unadorned bicorne hat sufficed Wellington. Before the General marched his troops, the men who had followed him from Portugal through the savage horrors of Ciudad Rodrigo and Badajoz.

The first Battalion of the 11th Regiment, their jacket facings as deep a green as the valleys of North Devon from whence they came, were followed by the Shropshires, red facings on red jackets, their officers' coats laced in gold. The swords swept up to salute the plain, hook-nosed man who stood quiet in the riot of noise. The 61st were there, a long way from Gloucestershire, and the sight of them made Sharpe remember Windham's scornful comparison of the two Cathedral cities. The Colonel would have loved this. He would have tapped his riding crop in time with the music, have criticised the faded jackets of the Queen's Royals, blue on red, second infantry of the line behind the Royal Scots, but he would not have been in earnest. The Cornishmen of the 32nd marched in, the 36th of Hereford, and all of them marched with colours uncased, colours that stirred in the small wind and showed off the musket and cannon scars of

49

the smoke-tinged flags. The colours were surrounded by Sergeants' halberds, the wide blades burnished to a brilliant silver.

Hooves sounded by the archway where Sharpe had entered and Lossow, his uniform miraculously brushed, led the first troop of King's German Legion Light Dragoons into the Plaza. Their sabres were drawn, slashing light, and the officers wore fur edged pelisses casually draped over the gold-laced blue jackets. The Plaza seemed crammed with troops, yet still more came. The brown jackets of the Portuguese Cacadores, Light troops, whose green shako plumes nodded to the music's tempo. There were Greenjackets too, not Riflemen of the 95th, Sharpe's old Regiment, but men of the 60th, the Royal American Rifles. He watched them enter the square and he felt a small burst of pride at the sight of their faded, patched uniforms and the battered look of their Baker Rifles. The Rifles were the first onto any battlefield, and the last to leave it. They were the best. Sharpe was proud of his green jacket.

This was just one division, the Sixth, while beyond the city and shielding it from the French field army were the other Divisions of Wellington's force. The First, the Third, the Fourth, the Fifth, the Seventh, and the Light Divisions, forty-two thousand men of the infantry marched this summer. Sharpe smiled to himself. He remembered Rolica, just four years before, when the British infantry had numbered just thirteen and a half thousand men. No one had expected them to win. They had been sent to Portugal with a junior General, and now that General saluted his troops as they marched into Salamanca. At Rolica, Wellington had fought with eighteen guns, this summer's battle would hear more than sixty British cannon. Two hundred cavalry had paraded at Rolica, now there were more than four thousand. The war was growing, spreading across the Peninsula, up into Europe, and there were rumours that the Americans were beating the drum against England while Napoleon, the ringmaster of it all, was looking north to the empty Russian maps.

Sharpe did not watch the whole parade. In one of the eight streets that led to the Plaza he found a wineshop and bought a skin of red wine that he decanted, carefully, into his round, wooden canteen. A gipsy woman watched him, her black eyes unreadable, one hand holding a baby high on her breast, the other plunged deep into her apron where she clutched the few coins she had begged during the day. Sharpe left a few mouthfuls in the skin and tossed it to her. She caught it and jetted the wine into the baby's mouth. A stall beneath the Plaza archway was selling food and Sharpe took some tripe, cooked in a spiced sauce, and as he drank his wine, ate the food, he thought how lucky he was to be alive on this day, in this place, and he wished he could share this moment with Teresa. Then he thought of Windham's body, blood smeared on the dry ground, and he hoped that the Frenchmen shut up in the forts were hearing the band and anticipating the siege. Leroux would die.

The parade finished, the soldiers were marched away or dismissed, yet the band played on, serenading the nightly ceremony in which the people of Salamanca played out a stately flirtation. The townspeople walked in the Plaza each evening. The men walked clockwise at the outer edge of the square, while the girls, giggling and arm in arm, walked counter-clockwise in an inner ring. British soldiers now joined the outer promenaders, eyeing the girls, calling out to them, while the Spanish men, jealous, watched coldly.

Sharpe did not join the circle. Instead he walked in the deep shadow of the arcade, past the shops that sold fine leathers, jewels, books, and silks. He walked slowly, licking the garlic from his fingers, and he was a strange figure in the holiday crowd. He had pushed his shako back, letting his black hair fall over the top of the long scar that ran, beside his left eye, to his cheek. It gave him a sardonic, mocking look when his face was at rest. Only laughter or a smile softened the rigour of the scar. His uniform was as tattered as any Rifleman's. The scabbard of his long sword was battered. He looked what he was, a fighting soldier.

He was looking for Michael Hogan, the Irish Major who served on Wellington's staff. Sharpe and Hogan had been friends for most of this war and the Irishman, Sharpe knew, would make good company on this night of celebration. Sharpe had another reason, too. Hogan was in charge of Wellington's intelligence gathering, sifting through the reports which came from spies and Exploring Officers, and Sharpe hoped that the small, middle-aged Major could answer some questions about Colonel Philippe Leroux.

Sharpe stayed beneath the colonnade, heading towards the group of mounted officers who crowded about the General. The Rifleman stopped when he was close enough to hear their loud laughter and confident voices.

He could not see Hogan. He leaned against a pillar and watched the mounted men, gorgeous in their full dress uniforms, and he was unwilling to join the favour seeking group who crowded round the General. If Wellington picked his nose, Sharpe knew, there would be plenty of officers willing to suck his fingers clean if it brought them one more golden thread for their uniforms.

He tilted the canteen, shut his eyes, and let the raw wine scour his mouth. 'Captain! Captain!'

He opened his eyes, but could not see who had shouted, and he presumed that it was not for him and then he saw the priest, Curtis, pushing his way out of the group of horsemen around Wellington. The damned Irishman was everywhere. Sharpe did not move except to cork his canteen.

Curtis walked towards him and stopped. 'We meet again.'

'As you said we would.'

'You can always believe a man of God.' The elderly priest smiled. 'I was hoping you might be here.'

'Me?'

Curtis gestured towards the mounted officers. 'There's

someone who would be relieved, very relieved, to hear from you that Leroux is safely shut up in the fortresses. Would you be so kind as to confirm it?' He gestured again, inviting Sharpe to walk with him, but the tall Rifleman did not move.

'Don't they believe you?'

The elderly priest smiled. 'I'm a priest, Captain, a Professor of Astronomy and Natural History, and Rector of the Irish College here. Those aren't suitable qualifications, I'm afraid, for these warlike matters. You, on the other hand, will be believed on this subject. Would you mind?'

'You're what?' Sharpe had thought the man just an interfering priest.

Curtis smiled gently. 'I'm eminent, dreadfully eminent, and I'm asking you to do me a kindness.'

Sharpe did not move, still unwilling to walk into the circle of elegant officers. 'Who needs reassurance?'

'An acquaintance. I don't think you'll regret the experience. Are you married?'

Sharpe nodded, not understanding. 'Yes.'

'By Mother Church, I hope?'

'As it happens, yes.'

'You surprise me, and please me.' Sharpe was not sure whether Curtis was teasing him. The priest's bushy eyebrows went up. 'It does help, you see.'

'Help?'

'Temptations of the flesh, Captain. I am sometimes very grateful to God that he has allowed me to grow old and immune to them. Please come.'

Sharpe followed him, curious, and Curtis stopped suddenly. 'I don't have the pleasure of your name, Captain.'

'Sharpe. Richard Sharpe.'

Curtis smiled. 'Really? Sharpe? Well, well!' He did not give Sharpe any time to react to his apparent recognition. 'Come on then, Sharpe! And don't go all jellified!'

With that mysterious injunction Curtis found a way through the horses and Sharpe followed him. There must have been two dozen officers, at least, but they were not, as Sharpe had first thought, crowded around Wellington. They were looking at an open carriage, pointing away from Sharpe, and it was to the side of the carriage that Curtis led him.

Someone, Sharpe thought, was indecently rich. Four white horses stood patiently in the carriage traces, a pow-dered-wigged driver sat on the bench, a footman, in the same livery, on a platform behind. The horses' traces were of silver chain. The carriage itself was polished to a sheen that would have satisfied the most meticulous Sergeant Major. The lines of the carriage, which Sharpe supposed was a new-fangled barouche, were picked out in silver paint on dark blue. A coat of arms decorated the door, a shield so often quartered that the small devices contained in its many compartments were indistinguishable except at very close inspection. The occupant, though, would have stunned at full rifle range.

She was fair haired, unusual in Spain, and fair skinned, and she wore a dress of dazzling whiteness so that she seemed to be the brightest, most luminous object in the whole of Salamanca's golden square. She was leaning back on the cushions, one white arm negligently laid on the carriage side, and her eyes seemed languid and amused, bored even, as though she were used to such daily and lavish adulation. She held a small parasol against the evening sun, a parasol of white lace that threw a filmy shadow on her face, but the shadow did nothing to hide the rich, full mouth, the big, intelligent eyes, or the slim, long neck that seemed, after the tanned, brown skin of the army and its followers, to be made of a substance that was of heavenly origin. Sharpe had seen many beautiful women. Teresa was beautiful, Jane Gibbons, whose brother had tried to kill him at Talavera, was beauti-ful, but this woman was in another realm. Curtis rapped the carriage door. Sharpe was hardly aware of any other person, not even of Wellington himself, and he watched the eyes come to him as she listened to Curtis' introduction. 'Captain

54

Richard Sharpe, I have the honour to name you La Marquesa de Casares el Grande y Melida Sadaba.'

She looked at him. He half expected her to offer him a white-gloved hand, but she just smiled. 'People never remember it.'

'La Marquesa de Casares el Grande y Melida Sadaba.' Sharpe marvelled that he had got the words out without stammering. He understood exactly what Curtis meant by jellification. She raised an eyebrow in mock surprise. Curtis was telling her, in Spanish, about Leroux. Sharpe heard the name mentioned, and saw her glance at him. Each glance was stupefying. Her beauty was like a physical force. Other women, Sharpe guessed, would hate her. Men would follow her like lap dogs. She had been born beautiful and every artifice that money could buy was enhancing that beauty. She was glorious, tantalising, and, he supposed, untouchable to anyone less than a full-blooded lord and, as he always did when he saw something that he wanted, but could not hope to have, he began to dislike it. Curtis stopped and she looked at Sharpe. Her voice sounded bored. 'Leroux is in the forts?'

He wondered where she had learned English. 'Yes, Ma'am.'

'You're certain?'

'Yes, Ma'am.'

She nodded, dismissing him, and it seemed to Sharpe that his reassurances had not been wanted, nor welcomed. Then she turned back to him and raised her voice. 'You do seem so much more soldierlike, Captain, than these pretty men on their horses.'

He was not supposed to reply. The remark had been made, he suspected, purely to annoy her gallant admirers. She did not even bother to see what effect it had on them, but merely drew a silver-tipped pencil from a small bag and began writing on a piece of paper. One man rose to the bait, a foppish cavalry officer whose English drawl spoke of aristocratic birth.

'Any brute can be brave, Ma'am, but a curry-comb always improves it.'

There was a moment's silence. La Marquesa looked up at Sharpe and smiled. 'Sir Robin Callard thinks you're an uncombed brute.'

'Rather that than a lap dog, Ma'am.'

She had succeeded. She looked at Callard and raised an eyebrow. He was forced to be brave. He stared at Sharpe, his face furious. 'You're insolent, Sharpe.'

'Yes he is.' The voice was crisp. Wellington leaned forward. 'He always has been.' The General knew what La Marquesa was doing, and he would stop it. He hated duelling among his officers. 'It's his strength. And weakness.' He touched his hat. 'Good day, Captain Sharpe.'

'Sir.' He backed away from the carriage, ignored by La Marquesa who was folding her piece of paper. He had been dismissed, contemptuously even, and he knew that a tattered Captain with an old sword had no place among these scented, elegant people. Sharpe felt the resentment rise sour and thick within him. Wellington needed Sharpe when there was a breach to be taken at Badajoz, but not now! Not among his Lordship's own kind. They thought Sharpe was a mere brute who needed a curry-comb, yet he was a brute who kicked, clawed and scratched to preserve their privileged, lavish world. Well damn them. Damn them to a stinking hell. Tonight he would drink with his men, not one of whom would dream of owning as much money as the worth of a single silver trace chain from La Marquesa's coach. Yet they were his men. Damn the bitch and the men who sniffed about her. Sharpe would prove he did not care a damn for them.

'Sharpe?'

He turned. A handsome cavalry officer, hair as gold as La Marquesa's, uniform as elegant as Sir Robin Callard's, stood smiling at him. The man's left arm was in a sling that covered the blue and silver of his jacket, and for a second Sharpe thought this man must be Callard's second come to offer a duel. Yet the cavalry officer's smile was open and friendly, his voice warm. 'I'm honoured to meet you, Sharpe! Jack Spears, Captain.' He grinned broadly. 'I'm glad you twisted Robin's nose. He's a pompous little bastard. Here.' He held a folded piece of paper to Sharpe.

Sharpe took it reluctantly, not wanting anything to do with the glittering circle about the blue and silver barouche. He unfolded the pencil written note. 'I am giving a small reception this evening at 10 o'clock. Lord Spears will direct you.' It was signed, simply, 'H'.

Sharpe looked at the startlingly handsome cavalryman. 'H?'

Spears laughed. 'Helena, La Marquesa de tiddly-tum and tummly-tid, and the object of an army's combined lust. Shall I tell her you'll come?' His voice was relaxed and friendly.

'You're Lord Spears?'

'Yes!' Spears unleashed all his charm on Sharpe. 'By the Grace of God and the timely bloody death of my elder brother. But you can call me Jack, everyone else does.'

Sharpe looked again at the note. Her handwriting was childishly round, like his own. 'I have other business tonight.'

'Other business!' Spears' cry of mock amazement made some of the promenading Salamantines look curiously at the young, handsome cavalry officer. 'Other business! My dear Sharpe! What other business could possibly be more important than attempting to breach the fair Helena?'

Sharpe was embarrassed. He knew Lord Spears was being friendly, but Sharpe's encounter with the Marquesa had made him feel shabby and inadequate. 'I have to see Major Hogan. Do you know him?'

'Know him?' Spears grinned. 'He's my lord and master. Of course I know Michael, but you won't see him tonight, not unless you go south a couple of hundred miles.'

'You work for him?'

'He's kind enough to call it work.' Spears grinned. 'I'm

one of his Exploring Officers.'

Sharpe looked at the young Lord with a new respect. The Exploring Officers rode far behind enemy lines, wearing full uniform so they could not be accused of spying, and relying on their swift, corn-fed horses to ride them out of trouble. They sent back a stream of information about enemy movements, entrusting their messages and maps to Spanish messengers. It was a lonely, brave life. Spears laughed. 'I've impressed the great Sharpe, how wonderful! Was it important to see Michael?'

Sharpe shrugged. In truth he had used Hogan's name as an excuse for avoiding La Marquesa's invitation. 'I wanted to ask him about Colonel Leroux.'

'That prize little bastard.' For the first time there was something other than gaiety in Spears' voice. 'You should have killed him.' Spears had evidently overheard the priest's brief conversation with La Marquesa.

'You know him?'

Spears touched the sling. 'Who do you think did this? He nearly caught me one dark night last week. I tumbled out of a window to escape him.' He smiled again. 'Not very gallant, but I didn't fancy the noble line of Spears coming to an end in a Spanish fleapit.' He clapped Sharpe's shoulder with his free hand. 'Michael will want to talk to you about Leroux, but in the meantime, my dear Sharpe, you are coming to the Palacio Casares tonight to drink La Marquesa's champagne.'

Sharpe shook his head. 'No, my lord.'

'My lord! My lord! Call me Jack! Now tell me you're coming!'

Sharpe screwed the paper into a ball. He was thinking of Teresa and feeling noble that he was rejecting the invitation. 'I'm not coming, my lord.'

Lord Spears watched Sharpe walk away, cutting across the circling walkers in the Plaza Mayor, and the cavalryman smiled to himself. 'Ten to one you do, my friend, ten to one you do.'

CHAPTER 4

Sharpe had wanted to go to La Marquesa's; the temptation was on him all night, but he stayed away. He told himself that he did so because he did not care to go, but the truth was, and he knew it, that he was frightened of the mockery of La Marquesa's witty, elegant friends. He would be out of place.

He drank instead, listening to the stories of his men and chasing away the one Provost who tried to challenge their presence in the city. He watched them betting on cockfights, watched them losing their money because the prize birds had been fed rum-soaked raisins, and he pretended that he would rather be with them than with anyone else. They were pleased, he knew, and he felt ashamed because it was a pretence. He watched yet another dead cockerel being taken from the blood-soaked ring, and he thought of the luminous woman with the gold hair and white skin.

Nothing kept the small group of Riflemen in Salamanca and so, the next morning, they marched early to the San Christobal Ridge where the main army waited for the French. They marched with sore heads and sour throats, leaving the city behind and going to the place they belonged.

They all expected a battle. The French had been man-oeuvred out of Salamanca, but Marmont had left the garrisons behind in the three fortresses, and it was obvious to even the least soldier that once the French Marshal had been reinforced from the north then he would come back to rescue his men trapped in the city. The British waited for him, hoping he would attack the great ridge that barred the road to the city, the ridge behind which Sharpe reunited his men with the South Essex.

McDonald was dead, buried already, killed by a thrust of Leroux's sword between his ribs. Major Forrest, in temporary command after the death of Windham, shook his head sorrowfully. 'I'm truly sorry about the boy, Richard.'

'I know, sir.' Sharpe had hardly had time to know the Ensign. 'You'll want me to write to his parents?'

'Would you? I've written to Windham's wife.' Forrest was shaving from a canvas bucket. 'A letter seems so inadequate. Oh dear.' Forrest was a kind man, even a meek man, and he was ill-suited to the trade of warfare. He smiled at Sharpe. 'I'm glad you're back, Richard.'

'Thank you, sir.' Sharpe grinned. 'Look at that.'

Isabella, small and plump, was brushing at Harper's jacket even as she welcomed him tearfully. The whole Battalion was bivouacked on the grassland, their wives and children in attendance, and as far as Sharpe could see, east and west, other Battalions waited behind the ridge. He walked up to the crest and stared north at the great plain that was bright with poppies and cornflowers. It was over those flowers, over the sun-bleached grass, that the enemy would come. They would come to crush the one army that Britain had in Spain, one army against five French, and Sharpe stared at the heat-blurred horizon and watched for the tell-tale spark of light reflected from sword or helmet that would say the enemy was coming to do battle.

They did not come that day, nor the next, and as the hours passed so Sharpe began to forget the events of Salamanca. Colonel Leroux lost his importance, even the golden haired Marquesa became a remote dream. Sharpe did his job as Company Commander and he filled his time with the day to day rhythm of soldiering. The books had to be kept up to date, there were punishments to mete out, rewards to be given, quarrels to ease, and always the business of keeping bored men up to their highest standard. He forgot Leroux, he forgot La Marquesa, and on the third day on the San Christobal Ridge he had good reason to forget.

It was a perfect day, the kind of summer's day that a child might remember for ever, a day when the sun shone from a burnished sky and spilt light on the poppies and cornflowers that were spread so lavishly in the ripening wheat. A small breeze stole the venom of the sun and rippled the crops, and onto that perfect stage, that setting of gold, red and blue, came the army of the enemy.

It seemed almost a miracle. An army marched on dozens of roads, its flanks far from each other, and in a summer's campaign it was usual for a man never to see more than a half dozen other Regiments. Yet suddenly, at the order of a general, the scattered units were drawn together, brought into one great array ready for battle and Sharpe, high on the wind-cooled ridge, watched Marmont perform the miracle.

The cavalry came first, their breastplates and sword blades reflecting the sun in savage flashes at the watching British. Their horses left trampled paths in the flower-strewn wheat.

The infantry were behind, snakes of blue-jacketed men who seemed to fill the plain, spreading east and west, and among them were the guns. The French artillery, Napoleon's own trade, who made their batteries in full view of the ridge and lifted the burning barrels from the travelling position to the fighting position. Major Forrest, watching with his officers, grinned. 'There's enough of them.'

'There usually are, sir,' Sharpe said.

Hussars, Dragoons, Lancers, Cuiraisseurs, Chasseurs, Guardsmen, Grenadiers, Voltigeurs, Tirailleurs, Infantry, Artillery, Bandsmen, Engineers, Ambulance men, Drivers, Staff, all of them pulled by the beat of the drum to this place where they became an army. Fifty thousand men brought to this patch of land half the size of a country parish, a patch of land that might become well-manured with their blood. The

Spanish farmers said the crops grew twice as well the year after a battle.

The French could not see the British. They saw a few officers on the hilltop, saw the flash of light from an occasional telescope aimed at them, but Marmont had to guess where Wellington's troops were hidden behind the ridge. He would have to guess where to make his attack, knowing all the while that his fine troops might climb the ridge's scarp only to be suddenly faced with the red-jacketed infantry that could fire their Brown Bess muskets faster than any army in the world. Marmont would have to guess where to attack, and Generals do not like guessing.

He did not guess that first day, nor the next, and it seemed as if the two armies had come together only to be paralysed. Each night men from British Light Companies would go down the hill towards the French to act as picquets against a night attack, but Marmont did not risk his army in the darkness. Sharpe went one night. The noise of the French army was like the noise of a city, its lights were a sprawl of fires scattered as lavishly as the poppies and cornflowers. It was cold at night, the upland not holding the day's heat, and Sharpe shivered, Leroux and La Marquesa forgotten, waiting for the battle to erupt on the long ridge.

On Monday, after early breakfasts, the road from Salamanca was crowded with people coming to stare at the two armies. Some walked, some rode, some came in carriages, and most made themselves comfortable on a hill beside the village of San Christobal and were irked that the armies were not fighting. Perhaps because the spectators had arrived, there seemed a greater sense of urgency in the British lines, and Sharpe watched as his men once more prepared for battle. Flints were reseated in the leather patch that was gripped in the screw-tightened jaws of the rifle cocks, hot water was swilled into barrels that were already cleaned, and Sharpe sensed the fear that all men have before battle.

Some feared the cavalry and in their minds they rehearsed the thunder of a thousand hooves, the dust rolling like a sea fog from the charge and shot through with the bright blades that could slice a man's life away or, worse, hook out his eyes and leave him in darkness for life. Others feared musket fire, the lottery of an unaimed bullet coming in the relentless volleys that would fire the dry grass with burning wads and roast the wounded where they fell. All feared the artillery, coughing its death in fan-like swathes. It was best not to think about that.

A hundred thousand men, before and behind the ridge, feared on that perfect day of heat, poppies and cornflowers. The smoke from the French cooking fires of the night drifted in a haze to westward while the gunners prepared their instruments of slaughter. Surely today they would fight. Some men in both armies hoped for the battle, seeking in combat the death that would release them from the pains of diseased bodies. The spectators wanted to see a fight. Why else had they come the long six hot miles from Salamanca?

Sharpe expected battle. He had gone to a Regiment of Dragoons and tipped the armourer to put a new edge on the long sword. Now, at midday, he slept. His shako was tipped over his face and he dreamed that he was lying flat, a horseman riding about him, and the sound of the hooves was distinct in his dreams. He could not rise, even though he knew the cavalryman was trying to kill him, and in his dream he struggled and then felt the lance tip at his waist and he jerked himself sideways, twisting desperately, and suddenly he was awake and a man was laughing above him. 'Richard!'

'Christ!' The horse had not been a dream. It stood a yard away, its rider dismounted and laughing at him. Sharpe sat up, shaking the sleep from his eyes. 'God, you frightened me!' Major Hogan had woken him by tapping his belt with a booted foot.

Sharpe stood up, drank tepid water from his canteen, and only then grinned at his friend. 'How are you, sir?'

'As well as the good Lord permits. Yourself?'

'Bored with this waiting. Why doesn't the bastard attack?' Sharpe looked at his Company, most of whom dozed in the sun as did the men of the South Essex's other nine companies. A few officers strolled in front of the somnolent lines. The whole British army seemed asleep, except for a few sentries on the skyline.

Major Hogan, his grey moustache stained yellow by the snuff to which he was addicted, looked Sharpe up and down. 'You're looking well. I hope you are because I might need you.'

'Need me?' Sharpe was putting on his black shako, picking up rifle and sword. 'What for?'

'Come for a walk.' Hogan took Sharpe's elbow for a second and steered him away from the Light Company up the long slope that led to the ridge-crest. 'You have news of Colonel Leroux for me?'

'Leroux?' For a brief moment Sharpe was lost. The events of Salamanca seemed so long ago, even far away, and his mind at this moment was concerned with the battle that would be fought for the San Christobal Ridge. He was thinking of skirmishers, of Riflemen, not about the tall, pale-eyed French Colonel who was in the city's fortresses. Hogan frowned.

'You met him?'

'Yes.' Sharpe laughed ruefully. 'I met the bastard.' He told Hogan about the capture of the Dragoon officer, of the parole, of the man's escape, and finally how he had chased him up the hill. Hogan listened intently.

'You're certain?'

'That he's in the forts? Yes.'

'Truly?' Hogan had stopped, was staring hard at Sharpe. 'You're really certain?'

'I saw him climb in. He's there.'

Hogan said nothing as they finished the climb to the ridge top. They stood there, where the ground dropped steeply away to the great plain where the French were gathered. Sharpe could see an ammunition tumbril coming forward to the closest battery and he had to fight back the thought that his own death might be on that cart.

Hogan sighed. 'God damn it, but I wish you'd killed him.'

'So do I.'

Hogan stared, Sharpe suspected without seeing, at the French army. The Major was thoughtful, worried even, and Sharpe waited as he took from his pocket a scrap of paper. Hogan thrust it at Sharpe. 'I've carried that for two months.'

The paper meant nothing to Sharpe. It had groups of numbers written like words in a short paragraph. Hogan smiled wryly. 'It's a French code, Richard, a very special code indeed.' He took the paper back from Sharpe. 'We have a fellow who can read these codes, a Captain Scovell, and damned clever he is too.' Sharpe wondered what the story was behind the scrap of paper. A French messenger ambushed by Partisans? Or one of the Spaniards who tried to smuggle messages through hostile territory, the paper hidden in a boot-heel or hollow stick, a man captured and killed so that this piece of paper could reach Hogan? The French, Sharpe knew, would send four or five identical messages because they knew that most would be intercepted and delivered to the British.

Hogan stared at the numbers. 'It's one thing to decode these messages, Richard, it's another to understand them. This one's the Emperor's own code! How about that?' He smiled in understandable triumph at Scovell's victory. 'It was sent from the man himself to Marshal Marmont and I'll tell you what it says.' He read from the numbers as if they were words. '"I send you Colonel Leroux, my own man, who works for me. You are to afford him whatever he requests." That's all, Richard! I can read it, but I can't understand it. I know that a Colonel Leroux is here to do a special job, a job for the Emperor himself, but what's the job? Then I hear more things. Some Spaniards have been tortured, skinned alive, and the bastard signed them with his name. Why?' Hogan folded the paper. 'There was something else. Leroux got Colquhoun Grant.'

That shocked Sharpe. 'Killed him?'

'No, captured him. We're not exactly trumpeting that failure about.'

Sharpe could understand Hogan's misery. Colquhoun Grant was the best of the British Exploring Officers, a colleague of Lord Spears who rode brazenly on the flanks of the French forces. Grant was a severe loss to Hogan, and a triumph for the French.

Sharpe said nothing. To his right he could see, half a mile away, the General and his staff bunched on the skyline. An aide-de-camp had just left the small group and was spurring back down the ridge towards the British forces. Sharpe wondered if something was about to happen.

The French were making a move, yet not a particularly forceful one. Directly ahead of Sharpe and Hogan, at the foot of the ridge scarp, was a small knoll that disturbed the smoothness of the plain where the French were gathered. Two enemy Battalions had come slowly forward and now lined the knoll's crest. They were no threat to the ridge and, having taken the tiny summit, they seemed content to stay there. Two field guns had come with them.

Hogan ignored them. 'I have to stop Leroux, Richard. That's my job. He's taking my best people and he's killing them if they're Spanish and capturing them if they're British, and he's too bloody clever by half.' Sharpe was surprised by the gloom in his friend's voice. Hogan was not usually downcast by setbacks, but Sharpe could tell that Colonel Philippe Leroux had the Irish Major desperately worried. Hogan looked up at Sharpe again. 'You searched him?'

'Yes.'

'Tell me again what you found. Tell me everything.'

Sharpe shrugged. He took off his shako to let the small breeze cool his forehead. He spoke of that day in the wood, of

66

the prisoner's seeming arrogance. He mentioned the sword, he spoke of his suspicion that Leroux pretended not to understand English. Hogan smiled at that. 'You were right. He speaks English like a bloody native. Go on.'

'There isn't any more. I've told you everything!' Sharpe looked behind the ridge to see where the aide-de-camp had ridden, and an urgency suddenly came over him. 'Look! We're moving! Christ!' He crammed his shako back on.

The South Essex, together with another Battalion, had been stirred into activity. They had stood up, dressed their ranks, and now they were climbing the hill in companies. They were going to attack! Sharpe looked north, at the small knoll, and he knew that Wellington was meeting the French move with a move of his own. The French would be pushed off the small hill, and the South Essex was to be one of the two Battalions that did the pushing. 'I must go!'

'Richard!' Hogan held his elbow. 'For God's sake. Nothing else? No papers? No books? Nothing hidden in his helmet, I mean, God, he must have had something!'

Sharpe was impatient. He wanted to be with his men. The Light Company would be first into the attack and Sharpe would lead them. Already he was forgetting Leroux and thinking only of the enemy skirmishers he would face in a few minutes. He snapped his fingers. 'No, yes. Yes. There was one thing. Jesus! A piece of paper, he said it was horse dealers or something. It was just a list!'

'You have it?'

'It's in my pack. Down there.' He pointed to the place the South Essex had left. The Battalion was halfway up the slope now, the Light Company already stretching ahead. 'I must go, sir!'

'Can I look for the paper?'

'Yes!' Sharpe was running now, released by Hogan, and his scabbard and rifle thumped as he hurried towards his men. The leather casings were being stripped from the colours so that the flags, unfurled, spread in the small breeze, their tassels bright yellow against the Union Flag. He felt the surge of emotion because the Colours were a soldier's pride. They were going to fight!

'Are they going to fight?' La Marquesa de Casares el Grande y Melida Sadaba had come to San Christobal hoping for a battle. Lord Spears was with her, his horse close to the elegant barouche, while La Marquesa herself was chaperoned by a dowdy, middle-aged woman who was wilting of the heat in a thick serge dress. La Marquesa wore white and had her filmy parasol raised against the sun.

Lord Spears tugged at his sling to make it comfortable. 'No, my dear. It's just a redeployment.'

'I do believe you're wrong, Jack.'

'Ten guineas says I'm not.'

'You owe me twice that already.' La Marquesa had taken out a small, silver telescope that she trained on the two British Battalions. They were marching towards the crest. 'Still, I'll take you, Jack. Ten guineas.' She put the telescope in her lap and picked up a folding ivory fan with which she cooled her face. 'Everyone ought to see a battle, Jack. It's part of a woman's education.'

'Quite right, my dear. Front row for the slaughter. Lord Spears' Academy for Young Ladies, battles arranged, mutilations our speciality.'

The fan cracked shut. 'What a bore you are, Jack, and just a tiny bit amusing. Oh look! Some of them are running! Do I cheer?'

Lord Spears was realising that he had just lost another ten guineas that he did not have, but he showed no regret. 'Why not? Hip, hip . . .'

'Hooray!' said La Marquesa.

Sharpe blew his whistle that sent his men scattering into the loose skirmish chain. The other nine companies would fight in their ranks, held by discipline, but his men fought in pairs, picking their ground and being the first to meet the enemy. He was on the crest now, the grass long beneath his boots, and his skirmish line was going down towards the enemy. Once again he forgot Leroux, forgot Hogan's concern, for now he was doing the job for which the army paid him. He was a skirmisher, a fighter of battles between the armies, and the love of combat was rising in him, that curious emotion that diluted fear and drove him to impose his will on the enemy. He was excited, eager, and he led his men at a swift pace down the hillside to where the enemy skirmishers, the Voltigeurs, were coming out to meet him. This was his world now, this small saddle of land between the escarpment and the knoll, a tiny piece of grassland that was warm in the sun and pretty with flowers. There he would meet his enemy and there he would win. 'Spread out! Keep moving!' Sharpe was going to war.

CHAPTER 5

Wellington did not want to attack. He saw little sense in sending his army down into the plain, but he was frustrated by the French reluctance to attack him. He had sent two Battalions against the two enemy Battalions on the knoll in the hope that he could provoke Marmont into a response. Wellington wanted to entice the French up onto the ridge, to force their infantry to climb the steep slope and face the guns and muskets that would suddenly appear to blast the tired enemy in chaos and horror back the way they had come.

Such thoughts were far from Richard Sharpe. His job was altogether more simple, merely to take on an enemy Light Company and defeat them. The British, unlike the French, attacked in line. The French had a taste for attacking in columns, great blocks of men driven like battering rams at the enemy line, columns propelled by the serried drummers in their midst, marching beneath the proud eagle standards that had conquered Europe, but that was not the way of Wellington's army. The two red-coated Battalions made one line, two ranks deep, and it marched forward, its ranks wavering because of the uneven ground, marching towards the French defensive line, three ranks deep, broken only where the field guns waited to fire.

Sharpe's Company was ahead of the British line.

His job was simple enough. His men had to weaken the enemy line before the British attack crashed home. They would do it by sniping at the officers, at the gunners, worrying the morale of the Frenchmen, and to stop them doing it, the French had sent out their own skirmishers. Sharpe could see them clearly, blue-jacketed men with white crossbelts and red shoulders, men who ran forward in pairs and waited for the Light Company. Sweat trickled down Sharpe's spine.

His Light Company was outnumbered by enemy skirmishers, but he had an advantage denied the French. Most of Sharpe's men, like the enemy, carried muskets that, though quick to load and fire, were inaccurate except at point blank range. Yet Sharpe also had his green-jacketed Riflemen, the killers at long range, whose slow-loading Baker Rifles would dominate this fight. The grass-stalks were thick, pulling at his boots, brushing against the metal scabbard heavy at his side. He looked to his right and saw Patrick Harper walking as easily as if he was strolling in the hills of his beloved Donegal. The Sergeant, far from looking at the French, was staring over their heads at a hawk. Harper was fascinated by birds.

The French gunners, judging their range, put fire to the priming tubes and the two field guns hammered back on their trails, pulsed smoke in a filthy cloud and crashed their shot at the opposing hillside. The gunners had deliberately aimed short for a cannon-ball could do more damage if it bounced waist high amongst the enemy. They called that bounce a 'graze' and Sharpe watched it, spewing grass, dirt and stones on its passage. The ball grazed among his men and slammed up the hill to graze again before it struck a file of the South Essex behind.

'Close up! Close up!' Sharpe could hear the Sergeants shouting.

The noise would start now. Shots, shouts, screams. Sharpe ignored it. He heard the guns, but he watched only his enemy. A Voltigeur officer, a sabre at his side, was spreading his men out and pointing towards Sharpe. Sharpe grinned. 'Dan?'

'Sir?' Hagman sounded cheerful.

'You see that bastard?'

'I'll get him, sir!' The French officer was as good as dead already. It was always the same. Look for the leaders, officers or men, and kill them first. After that the enemy would waver.

Richard Sharpe was good at this. He had been doing it for nineteen years, his whole adult life, more, indeed, than half his life, and he wondered if he would ever be good for anything else. Could he make things with his hands? Could he earn a living by growing things, or was he just this? A killer on a battlefield, legitimised by war for which, he knew, he had a talent. He was judging the distance between the skirmishers, picking his moment, but part of his mind worried about the coming of peace. Could he soldier in peacetime? Was he to lead his men against hunger-rioters in England or against Harper's countrymen in their ravaged island? Yet there was no sign of this war ending. It had lasted his lifetime, Britain against France, and he wondered if it would last the lifetime of his little daughter, Antonia, of whom he saw so little. Twenty seconds to go.

The guns were at their rhythm now, the roundshot slamming at the attackers and in a few seconds they would change to canister to spray the hillside with death. Harper's job was to stop that.

Ten seconds Sharpe guessed, and he saw a Frenchman kneel and bring his musket into his shoulder. The musket was aimed at Sharpe, but the range was too great to cause worry. For a second Sharpe thought of poor Ensign McDonald who had so wanted to distinguish himself in the skirmish line. Damn Leroux.

Five seconds, and Sharpe could see his opposing Captain looking nervously left and right. The smoke from the cannons was thickening, the noise hammering at Sharpe's eardrums. 'Now!'

He had lost count of the number of times he had done this. 'Go! Go! Go!'

This was rehearsed. The Light Company broke into a run, the last thing the enemy expected, and they went left and right, confusing their enemy's aim, and they closed the range to put pressure on the enemy's nerve. The Riflemen stopped first, wicked guns at their shoulders, and Sharpe heard the first crack which spun the enemy officer backwards, hands up, blood spraying suddenly, and then Sharpe was on his knee, his own rifle at his shoulder, and he saw the puff of smoke where the man had been who was aiming for him and he knew the musket ball had gone wide. Sharpe aimed up the hill. He looked for the enemy Colonel, saw him on his horse, aimed slowly, squeezed, and grinned as he glimpsed the Frenchman fall back from the saddle. That would be Sharpe's last shot in this battle. Now he would fight his men as a weapon.

More rifles cracked, firing into the smudge of smoke about the nearest gun. If the gunners could be killed, that was good, but at the least the bullets whistling about their weapon would slow their fire and spare the South Essex some of the ghastly canister.

'Sergeant Huckfield! Watch left!'

'Sir!'

The men fought in pairs. One man fired while the other loaded, and both sought targets for each other. Sharpe could see four enemy down, two of them crawling backwards, and he saw that unwounded men were hurrying to help the wounded. That was good. When the uninjured went to help their comrades it meant they were looking for an excuse to leave the battle.

Sharpe's muskets were firing fast now and his men were going forward, paces at a time, and the enemy were going backwards. The field gun opposite the South Essex had slowed down and Sharpe smiled because he had nothing to do. His men were fighting as he expected them to fight, using their intelligence, pushing the enemy back, and Sharpe looked behind to see where the main Battalion was.

The South Essex were fifty yards behind, coming steadily forward, and on their muskets were bayonets, bright in the sun, and behind them, on the ridge slope, were the bodies broken by the cannon.

'Rifles! Go for the main line! Kill the officers!'

Make widows on this field! Kill the officers, crumble the enemy morale, and Sharpe saw Hagman aim, fire, and the other Riflemen followed. Lieutenant Price was directing the musket fire, keeping the enemy skirmishers pinned back and releasing the Rifles to fire above their heads. Sharpe felt a surge of pride in his men. They were good, so good, and they were showing the spectators just how a Light Company should fight. He laughed aloud.

They were at the foot of the slope now, the enemy Light troops driven back towards their own line, and in a few seconds the South Essex would catch up with their Light Company. They had a hundred yards to go into the attack.

Sharpe pulled his whistle from its holster, waited a few seconds, then blasted out the signal to form company. He heard the Sergeants repeat the signal, watched his men come running towards him for now their skirmishing task was done. Now they would form up on the left of the attacking line and go in like the other Companies. The men sprinted towards him, tugging out bayonets, and he clapped them on the shoulders, said they had done well. Then the Company was formed, marching, and they were climbing the knoll over the blood of their enemies.

The field gun had stopped firing. The smoke was drifting clear.

Sharpe walked in front of his men. The great sword scraped on the scabbard throat as it came clear.

The French line levelled their muskets.

Boots swished through the grass. It was hot. The powder smoke stung men's nostrils.

'For what we're about to receive,' a voice said.

'Quiet in the ranks! Close up!'

'Keep your dressing, Mellors! What the hell do you think you're doing? Get in line, you useless bastard!'

Boots in the grass, the French line seeming to take a quarter turn to the right as the muskets go back into the shoulders. The muzzles, even at eighty yards, look huge.

'Get your bayonet up, Smith! You're not ploughing the bloody field!'

Sharpe listened to the Sergeants.

'Steady, lads, steady!'

The French officers had their swords raised. The cannon smoke had cleared now and Sharpe could see that the field gun had gone. It had been taken back, away from the infantry.

'Take it like men, lads!'

Seventy yards and the French swords swept down and Sharpe knew they had fired too soon. The smoke rippled from the hundreds of muskets, the sound was like the falling of giant stakes, and the air was thick with the thrumming of the balls.

The attacking line was jerked by the balls. Some men fell backwards, some stumbled, most kept stolidly on. Sharpe knew the enemy would be frantically reloading, fumbling with cartridges and ramrods, and he instinctively quickened his pace so that the South Essex might close the gap before the enemy had recharged their weapons. The other officers hurried too, and the attacking line began to lose its cohesion. The Sergeants yelled. 'It's not a sodding steeplechase! Watch your dressing!'

Fifty yards, forty, and Major Leroy, whose voice was twice as loud as Forrest's, bellowed at the South Essex to halt.

Sharpe could see some enemy muskets being rammed. The Frenchmen were looking nervously at their enemy so close.

Leroy filled his lungs.

'Level your muskets!'

The Light Company alone was not loaded. The other

companies levelled their muskets and beneath each muzzle the seventeen inch bayonet pointed towards the French.

'Fire!'

'And charge! Come on!'

The crash of that volley, the smoke, and then the redcoats were released from the Sergeants' discipline and they were free to take the blades up the hill to savage the enemy who had been shattered by the close volley.

'Kill the bastards. Go on! Get in with them!' And the cheer carried them up the slope, screaming mad, wanting only to get at the men who had threatened them during the long approach march, and Sharpe ran ahead of his men with his long sword ready.

'Halt! Form up! Hurry!'

The enemy had gone. They had fled the bayonets as Sharpe had guessed they would. The enemy Battalions were running full tilt back towards the main army, and the redcoats were left holding the small knoll which bore the dead and wounded of their enemy. The looting had begun already, practised hands stripping the casualties of clothes and money. Sharpe sheathed his unblooded sword. It had been well done, but now he wondered what was next. Twelve hundred British troops held the small hill, the only British troops on a plain that was peopled with more than fifty thousand Frenchmen. That was not his concern. He settled down to wait.

'They've run away!' La Marquesa sounded disappointed.

Lord Spears grinned. 'That was only a ten guinea battle, my dear. For two hundred you get the whole spectacle; slaughter, dismemberment, pillage, and even a little rape.'

'Is that where you come in, Jack?'

Spears laughed. 'I've waited so long for that invitation, Helena.'

'You'll have to wait a little longer, dear.' She smiled at him. 'Was that Richard Sharpe?'

'It was. A genuine hero, and all for ten guineas.'

'Which I doubt I'll ever see. Is he truly a hero?' Her huge eyes were fixed on Spears.

'Good Lord, yes! Absolutely genuine. The poor fool must have a death wish. He took an Eagle, he was first into Badajoz, and there's a rumour he blew up Almeida.'

'How delicious.' She opened her fan. 'You're a little jealous of him, aren't you?'

He laughed, because the accusation was not true. 'I wish to have a long, long life, Helena, and die in the bed of someone very young and breathtakingly beautiful.'

She smiled. Her teeth were unusually white. 'I rather want to meet a real hero, Jack. Persuade him to come to the Palacio.'

Spears twisted in his saddle, grimacing suddenly because the arm in its sling hurt. 'You feel like slumming, Helena?'

She smiled. 'If I do, Jack, I'll come to you for guidance. Just bring him to me.'

He grinned and saluted. 'Yes, Ma'am.'

The French would not be goaded into battle. They made no attempt to throw the British off the knoll. Marmont could not see beyond the great ridge and he feared, sensibly, to attack Wellington in a position of the Englishman's choosing.

Smoke drifted from the knoll, dissipating into shimmering heat over the grass. Men lay on the ground and drank brackish warm water from their canteens. A few desultory fires burned from the musket fire, but no-one moved to stamp them out. Some men slept.

'Is that it?' Lieutenant Price frowned towards the French.

'You want more, Harry?' Sharpe grinned at his Lieutenant.

'I sort of expected more.' Price laughed and turned round to look at the ridge. A staff officer was riding his horse recklessly down the slope. 'Here comes a fancy boy.'

'We're probably being pulled back.'

Harper gave a massive yawn. 'Perhaps they're offering us free entrance to the staff brothel tonight.'

'Isabella would kill you, Harps!' Price laughed at the thought. 'You should be unattached, like me.'

'It's the pox, sir. I couldn't live with it.'

'And I can't live without it. Hello!' Price frowned because the staff officer, instead of riding towards the Colours where the Battalion's commanding officer would be found, was aiming straight for the Light Company. 'We've got a visitor, sir.'

Sharpe walked to meet the staff officer who called out when he was still thirty yards away. 'Captain Sharpe?'

'Yes!'

'You're wanted at Headquarters. Now! Do you have a horse?'

'No.'

The young man frowned at the reply and Sharpe knew he was considering yielding up his own horse to expedite the General's orders. The consideration did not last long in the face of the steep uphill climb. The staff officer smiled. 'You'll have to walk! Quick as you can, please.'

Sharpe smiled at him. 'Bastard. Harry?'

'Sir?'

'Take over! Tell the Major I've been called to see the General!'

'Aye aye, sir! Give him my best wishes!'

Sharpe walked away from the Company, between the small fires, and up the hillside that was littered with the torn cartridge papers of his skirmishers. Leroux. It had to be Leroux who was pulling Sharpe back towards the city. Leroux, his enemy, and the man who possessed the sword Sharpe wanted. He smiled. He would have it yet.

CHAPTER 6

Wellington was angry, the officers about him nervous of his irritability. They watched Sharpe walk up to the General and salute.

Wellington scowled from the saddle. 'By God, you took your time, Mr. Sharpe.'

'I came as fast as I could, my lord.'

'Dammit! Don't you have a horse?'

'I'm an infantryman, sir.' It was an insolent reply, one that made the aristocratic aides-de-camp that Wellington liked look sharply at the dishevelled, hot Rifleman with the scarred face and battered weapons. Sharpe was not worried. He knew his man. He had saved the General's life in India and ever since there had been a strange bond between them. The bond was not of friendship, never that, but a bond of need. Sharpe needed a patron, however remote, and Wellington sometimes had reluctant need of a ruthless and efficient soldier. Each man had a respect for the other. The General looked sourly at Sharpe. 'So they didn't fight?'

'No, sir.'

'God damn his French soul.' He was talking of Marshal Marmont. 'They march all this bloody way just to pose for us? God damn them! So you met Leroux?' He asked the question in exactly the same tone in which he had damned the French.

'Yes, my lord.'

'You'd recognise him again?'

'Yes, my lord.'

'Good.' Wellington sounded far from pleased. 'He's not to escape from us, d'you understand? You're to capture him. Understand?'

Sharpe understood. He would be going back to Salamanca and his job, suddenly, was to trap the pale-eyed French Colonel who even had Wellington worried. 'I understand, sir.'

'Thank God somebody does.' The General snapped. 'I'm putting you under Major Hogan's command. He seems to have the knack of making you toe the line, God knows how. Good day, Mr. Sharpe.'

'My lord?' Sharpe raised his voice for the General was already wheeling away.

'What is it?'

'I have a whole Company that would recognise him, sir.'

'You do, do you?' Wellington's bad mood had driven him into clumsy sarcasm. 'You want me to strip the South Essex of a Light Company just to make your life easier?'

'There are three forts, my lord, a long perimeter, and one man can't have eyes everywhere.'

'Why not? They expect it of me.' Wellington laughed, breaking his bad mood with an extraordinary suddenness. 'All right, Sharpe, you can have them. But don't you lose him. Understand? You will not lose him.' The blue eyes conveyed the message.

'I won't lose him, sir.'

Wellington half smiled. 'He's all yours, Hogan. Gentlemen!'

The staff officers trotted obediently after the General, leaving Hogan alone with Sharpe.

The Irishman laughed quietly. 'You have a deep respect for senior officers, Richard, it's what makes you into such a great soldier.'

'I'd have been here sooner if that bastard had lent me his horse.'

'He probably paid two hundred guineas for it. He reckons

it's worth more than you are. On the other hand that nag cost ten pounds, and you can borrow it.' Hogan was pointing towards his servant who was leading a spare horse towards them. Hogan had anticipated Sharpe arriving on foot and he waited as the Rifleman climbed clumsily into the saddle. 'I'm sorry about the panic, Richard.'

'Is there a panic?'

'God, yes. Your piece of paper started it.'

Sharpe hated riding. He liked to be in control of his destiny, but horses seemed not to share that wish. He gingerly urged it forward, hoping it would keep pace with Hogan's walking animal and, somehow, he managed to stay abreast. 'The list?'

'Didn't it look familiar?'

'Familiar?' Sharpe frowned. He could only remember a list of Spanish names with sums of money beside them. 'No.'

Hogan glanced behind to make sure his servant was out of earshot. 'It was in my handwriting, Richard.'

'Yours? Good God!' Sharpe's hands fumbled with the rein while his right boot had come out of the stirrup. He never understood how other people made riding look easy. 'How in hell's name did Leroux get a list in your handwriting?'

'Now there's a question to cheer up a dull morning. How in hell's name did he? Horse dealers!' He said the last words scornfully, as if Sharpe had been at fault.

The Rifleman had managed to get his foot back into the stirrup. 'So what was it?'

'We have informants, yes? Hundreds of them. Almost every priest, doctor, mayor, shoemaker, blacksmith and anyone else you care to mention sends us snippets of news about the French. Marmont can't break wind without ten messages telling us. Some of them, Richard, are very good messages indeed, and some of them cost us money.' Hogan paused as they passed a battery of artillery. He returned a Lieutenant's salute, then looked back at Sharpe. 'Most of them do it out of patriotism, but a few need money to keep their loyalty intact. That list, Richard, was my list of payments for the month of April.' Hogan looked and sounded sour. 'It means, Richard, that someone in our headquarters is working for the French, for Leroux. God knows who! We've got cooks, washerwomen, grooms, clerks, servants, sentries, anyone! God! I thought I'd just misplaced that list, but no.'

'So?'

'So? So Leroux has worked his way through that list. He's killed most of them in ways that are pretty horrid, and that's bad enough, but the really bad news is yet to come. One man on that list, a priest, just happened to know something that I'd rather he hadn't known. And now, I think, Leroux knows it.'

Sharpe said nothing. His horse was ambling happily enough, going westward on the track that led behind the ridge. He would let Hogan tell his unhappy tale at his own pace.

The Irish Major wiped sweat from his face. 'Leroux, Richard, is damned close to hurting us really badly. We can afford to lose a few priests and mayors, but that's not what Leroux wants. We can afford to lose Colquhoun Grant, but that isn't what Leroux came here to do either. There's one person, Richard, we can't afford to lose. That's the person Leroux came to get.'

Sharpe frowned. 'Wellington?'

'Him too, maybe, but no. Not Wellington.' Hogan slapped irritably at a fly. 'This is the bit I shouldn't tell you, Richard, but I'll tell you a little of it, just enough so you know how important it is for you to stop that bastard getting out of the forts.' He paused again, collecting his thoughts. 'I told you we have informants throughout Spain. They're useful, God knows they're useful, but we have informants of much more value than that. We have men and women in Italy, in Germany, in France, in Paris itself! People who hate Bonaparte and want to help us, and they do. A regiment of Lancers leaves Milan and we know it within two weeks, and we know where they're going and how good their horses are, and even the name of their Colonel's mistress. If Bonaparte bawls out a General, we know about it, if he asks for a map of Patagonia we hear about it. Sometimes I think we know more about Bonaparte's empire than he does, and all, Richard, because of one person who just happens to live in Salamanca. And that person, Richard, is the person Leroux has come to find. And once he's found them, he'll torture them, he'll find out all the names of the correspondents throughout Europe, and suddenly we'll be blind.'

Sharpe knew better than to ask who the person was. He waited.

Hogan smiled wryly. 'You want to know who it is? Well, I won't tell you. I know, Wellington knows, and a few Spaniards know because they're responsible for passing the messages to Salamanca.'

'The priest knew?'

'Aye. The priest on my list knew, and now, God rest his soul, he's dead. Most of the messengers don't know the real name, they just know the codename. El Mirador.'

'El Mirador.' Sharpe repeated the words.

'Right. El Mirador, the best damned spy in Britain's service, and our job is to stop Leroux finding El Mirador. And the easiest way to do that, Richard, is for you to stop Leroux. He'll try and escape, I know that, and I can guess when he'll do it.'

'When?'

'During our attack on the forts. He can't do it at any other time. We've got those forts surrounded, but in the turmoil of a fight, Richard, he'll have his plans ready. Stop him!'

'That's all? Stop him? Capture him?'

'That's all, but don't underestimate him. Capture him and give him to me and I promise you Colonel Leroux will not see daylight again till this war's over. We'll lock him up so tight he'll wish he hadn't been born.'

Sharpe thought about it. It would not be so difficult. The

Sixth Division had sealed off the forts, and even in an attack the cordon of men would still ring the wasteland. All that would be left was for Sharpe, or one of his Company, to recognise Leroux among the prisoners. He grinned at Hogan, wanting to cheer him up. 'Consider it done.'

'If you're doing it, Richard, I will.' It was a nice compliment.

They had ridden close to the hill on which the spectators had gathered and Sharpe looked to his right to see a grinning figure coming towards them on a fiery, well-ridden horse. Even one-handed Lord Spears was a finer horseman than Sharpe could hope to be. His Lordship was in high spirits.

'Michael Hogan! By the Good Lord! You're looking dull as a parson, sir! Where are your Irish spirits? Your carefree, devil-may-care attitude to life's daily toil?'

Hogan looked with some fondness at the cavalryman. 'Jack! How's the arm?'

'Totally mended, sir. As good as the day it was born. I'm keeping it in a sling so you won't send me back to work. Richard Sharpe! I watched your Company at work. They were hungry!'

'They're good.'

'And you're both invited to a pique-nique. Now.' He grinned at them.

'A what?' Hogan frowned.

'A pique-nique. It's a French word, but I suppose we'll all be using it soon. For you peasants who don't speak French it means a simple, light repast taken in the open air. We've got chicken, ham, spiced sausages, some delicious cake, and best of all some wine. We, of course, are myself and La Marquesa de Casares el Grande y Melida Sadaba. You're both specifically invited.'

Hogan smiled. It seemed that Sharpe accepting the responsibility for Leroux had lifted a weight from his shoulders. 'La Marquesa! It's time I rubbed shoulders with the aristocracy!'

'What about me?' Spears looked aggrieved. 'Am I not noble enough for you? Good Lord! When my ancestors ate the forbidden fruit in Eden they insisted on having it served on a silver platter. You're coming?' This last he addressed to Sharpe.

Sharpe shrugged. Hogan was insisting on going, so Sharpe was forced to follow, and though part of him yearned to see La Marquesa again, another, greater part of him was scared of the encounter. He hated being tempted by things he could not have, and he could feel his mood becoming surly as he climbed the hill behind Hogan and Spears.

La Marquesa watched them come. She raised a languid hand in greeting. 'Captain Sharpe! You've at last accepted one of my invitations!'

'I'm with Major Hogan, Ma'am.' The instant he said it, he regretted it. He had been trying to say that he had not come willingly, that he was not her slave, but his words made it sound as though he had need to be forced into her company. She smiled.

'I owe Major Hogan my thanks.' She turned her lavish beauty onto the Irishman. 'We've met, Major.'

'Indeed we have, Ma'am. At Ciudad Rodrigo, I remember.'

'So do I, you were most charming.'

'The Irish usually are, Ma'am.'

'Such a pity the English haven't learned from their neighbours.' She looked at Sharpe who sat, miserable, on his uncomfortable horse. She smiled again at Hogan. 'You're well?'

'Indeed, Ma'am, and thank you, Ma'am. Yourself? Your husband?'

'My husband, ah!' She fanned her face. 'Poor Luis is in South America, suppressing one of our Colonial rebellions. It seems so silly. You're here to liberate our country while Luis is busy doing the opposite somewhere else.' She laughed, then looked again at Sharpe. 'My husband, Captain Sharpe, is a soldier, like you.'

85

'Indeed, Ma'am?'

'Well not quite like you. He's much older, much fatter, and he dresses much better. He's also a General, so perhaps he's not quite like you.' She patted the leather seat of the barouche between herself and her perspiring chaperone. 'I have some wine, Captain, won't you join me?'

'I'm quite comfortable, Ma'am.'

'You don't look it, but if you insist.' She smiled. She was, as he remembered, dazzlingly beautiful. She was a dream, something of exquisite fineness, someone of whom Sharpe was resentful for he found her beauty overwhelming. She still smiled at him. 'Jack tells me you're a true hero, Captain Sharpe.'

'Not at all, Ma'am.' He was wondering if he should go and fetch his Company, and make his excuses to Major Forrest who would be hugely unhappy at losing his Light troops.

Lord Spears guffawed with laughter. 'Not a hero! Listen to him! I love it!'

Sharpe frowned, embarrassed, and looked to Hogan for help. The Irishman grinned at him. 'You took an Eagle, Richard.'

'With Harper, sir.'

'Oh God! The modest hero!' Lord Spears was enjoying himself. He imitated Sharpe's reluctant voice. 'It was all an accident. Eagle just dropped off its staff, straight into my hands. I was picking wild flowers at the time. Then I lost my way at Badajoz. Thought I was going to church parade and just happened to climb this breach. Very awkward.' Spears laughed. 'God damn it, Richard! You even saved the Peer's life!'

'Arthur's life?' La Marquesa asked. She looked with interest at Sharpe. 'When? How?'

'The Battle of Assaye, Ma'am.'

'Battle of Assaye! What's that? Where was it?'

'India, Ma'am.'

'So what happened?'

'His horse was piked, Ma'am. I happened to be there.'

'Oh, God help us!' Spears' smile was friendly. 'He only fought off thousands of bloody heathens and says he happened to be there.'

Sharpe's embarrassment was acute. He looked at Hogan. 'Should I fetch my Company, sir?'

'No, Richard, you should not. It can wait. I'm thirsty, you're thirsty, and her Ladyship is kindly offering wine.' He bowed to La Marquesa. 'With your permission, Ma'am?' He held his hand out for the bottle that the chaperone held.

'No, Major! Jack will do it. He has the manners of a servant, don't you Jack?'

'I'm a slave to you, Helena.' Spears took the bottle happily, while Hogan brought Sharpe a glass. Sharpe's horse had moved some feet away from the carriage in search of greener grass and Sharpe was glad to be out of La Marquesa's earshot. He drank the wine quickly, finding himself to be parched, and discovered Hogan at his elbow. The Irishman smiled sympathetically.

'She's got you in full retreat, Richard. What's the matter?'

'It's not my place, sir, is it? That's my place.' He nodded down the hill to where the South Essex relaxed on their knoll. The French were not moving.

'She's just a woman, trying to be friendly.'

'Yes.' Sharpe thought of his wife, the dark haired beauty who would despise this aristocratic luxury. He glanced at La Marquesa. 'Why does she speak such good English?'

'Helena?' Even Hogan, Sharpe noted, seemed to know her well enough to use her Christian name. 'She's half English. Spanish father, English mother, and raised in France.' Hogan drank his own wine. 'Her parents were killed in the Terror, very nasty, and Helena managed to escape to an Uncle in Spain, in Saragossa. Then she married the Marques de Casares el Grande y Melida Sadaba, and became as rich as the hills. Houses all over Spain, a couple of castles, and a very good friend to us, Richard.'

'What are you talking about?' Her voice carried to them and Hogan turned his horse.

'Business, Ma'am, just business.'

'This is a pique-nique, not an Officers' Mess. Come here!' She made Spears give Sharpe more wine that he drank just as fast as the first glass. The crystal goblet was ridiculously small.

'You're thirsty, Captain?'

'No, Ma'am.'

'I have plenty of bottles. Some chicken?'

'No, Ma'am.'

She sighed. 'You're so hard to please, Captain. Ah! There's Arthur!'

Wellington was, indeed, returning westward along the track behind the ridge.

Spears twisted in his saddle to look at the General. 'Ten to one he comes up here to see you, Helena?'

'I'd be surprised if he didn't.'

'Sharpe!' Spears grinned at him. 'Two guineas he won't come?'

'I don't gamble.'

'I do! Christ! Half the bloody estate's gone.'

'Half of it?' La Marquesa laughed. 'All of it, Jack. All of it, and a lot more. What will you leave your heir?'

'I'm not married, Helena, thus none of my bastards can be described as an heir.' He blew her a kiss. 'If only your dear husband would die I would be on my knees to you. I think we'd make a handsome couple.'

'And how long would my fortune last?'

'Your beauty is your fortune, Helena, and that is safe for ever.'

'How pretty, Jack, and how untrue.'

'The words were said by Captain Sharpe, my dear, I just repeated them.'

The huge blue eyes looked at Sharpe. 'How pretty, Captain Sharpe.'

He was blushing because of Spears' lie and he hid it by wrenching the reins harshly about and staring at the quiescent French. Lord Spears followed him and spoke softly. 'You fancy her, don't you?'

'She's a beautiful woman.'

'My dear Sharpe.' Spears leaned over and led the Rifleman's horse forward a few paces. 'If you want her, try her.' He laughed. 'Don't worry about me. She won't look at me. She's very discreet, our Helena, and she's not going to endure Jack Spears boasting round the city that he tucked his feet in her bed. You should mount an attack, Sharpe!'

Sharpe was angry. 'You mean lovers from the servant's hall keep quiet, because they're so grateful?'

'Your words, friend, not mine.'

'True.'

'And if you must know, you may be right.' Spears was still friendly, but his words were low and forceful. 'Some people think the meat in the servant's hall is better than the thin stuff served in the banquet hall.'

Sharpe looked at the handsome face. 'La Marquesa?'

'She gets what she wants, you get what I want.' He grinned. 'I'm doing you a favour.'

'I'm married.'

'God help me! Do you say your prayers every night?' Spears laughed aloud, then turned for hoofbeats presaged Wellington's arrival at the head of his staff. The General reined in, doffed his bicorne hat, then cast a cold glance at Spears and Sharpe.

'You're well escorted, Helena!'

'Dear Arthur!' She offered him her hand. 'You have disappointed me!'

'I? How?'

'I came for a battle!'

'So did we all. If you have any complaints you must address them to Marmont. The fellow absolutely refuses to attack!'

She pouted at him. 'But I so hoped to see a battle!'

'You will, you will.' He patted his horse's neck. 'I'll lay you odds that the French will sneak away tonight. I gave them their chance and they turned it down, so tomorrow I'll take those forts.'

'The forts! I can watch from the Palacio!'

'Then pray Marmont sneaks away tonight, Helena, for if he does I'll lay on a full assault for you. All the battle you could wish!'

She clapped her hands. 'Then I will give a reception tomorrow night. To celebrate your victory. You'll come?'

'To celebrate my victory?' Wellington seemed positively skittish in her presence. 'Of course I'll come!'

She waved a hand round all the horsemen gathered about the elegant barouche. 'You must all come! Even you, Captain Sharpe! You must come!'

Wellington's eyes met Sharpe. The General gave a thin smile. 'Captain Sharpe will be busy tomorrow night.'

'Then he will come when his business is finished. We shall dance till dawn, Captain.'

Sharpe felt, though he did not know if it was meant, a subtle mockery in the eyes that watched him. Tomorrow. Tomorrow he would face Leroux, tomorrow he would fight that sword, and Sharpe felt the desire to fight. He would beat Leroux, this Colonel who had put a chill of fear into the British, he would face him, fight him, and he would drag him captive from the wasteland. Tomorrow he would fight, and these foppish aristocrats would watch from La Marquesa's Palacio and suddenly Sharpe knew what reward he wanted for facing Colonel Philippe Leroux. Not just the sword. He would have that anyway as the spoils of war, but something else. He would have the woman. He smiled at her for the first time, and nodded. 'Tomorrow.'

CHAPTER 7

Tired cavalry scouts came back to the city in the early Tuesday hours. Marmont's army had gone north in the night. The French had abandoned the garrison of the forts in the city, they would bide their time now and hope that at some point in the summer they would catch Wellington flat-footed and fight a battle more on their own terms.

The fortresses served no purpose now for Wellington. They had failed to bring Marmont to battle for their rescue, and they stopped his supply trains using the long Roman bridge, so the fortresses would be destroyed. La Marquesa would get her battle, and Sharpe would have to seek Leroux among the prisoners.

If there were prisoners. It had seemed a light thing for the General to promise La Marquesa an assault of the three buildings, but Sharpe could see that the defenders would not easily give in. He had stared long and hard at the buildings, marooned in their waste ground, and the more he looked, the less he liked.

The waste ground was split by a deep gorge that ran southwards towards the river. On the right of the gorge was the largest of the French forts, the San Vincente, while to the left were the forts of La Merced and San Cayetano. An attack on any one of the three forts would be savaged by gunfire from the others.

The three buildings had been convents until the French evicted the nuns and turned this corner of the city into a stronghold. For nearly a week now the convents had been under fire from British guns, yet the artillery had done remarkably little damage. The French had prepared the buildings well.

Out of the levelled houses that had surrounded the convents they had made a crude glacis that bounced the roundshot up and over the defensive works. They had buttressed walls behind the deep ditch which surrounded each convent and over their gun emplacements and troop shelters they had made huge, thick roofs. Each roof was like a massive box filled with earth, designed to soak up the British howitzer shells that fell with fluttering smoke from the sky. The French garrisons were surrounded, trapped, but it would be hard for the British to break in.

Sharpe paraded his Company, not entirely by chance, outside the Palacio Casares. The huge gates stood open, revealing the central courtyard in the middle of which a fountain splashed into a raised pool. The courtyard was paved, filled with flowers in ornate tubs, and Sharpe stared through the shadows of the archway at the great door above the formal steps. The house seemed deserted. Thickly woven straw mats had been lowered over the windows, blotting the sun, and the water in the fountain was the only sign of movement in the great, rich house.

Above the gateway, on the tall, blank, outer wall, the coat of arms that decorated the barouche door was carved in pale gold stone. Above that, high above, Sharpe could see plants growing at the wall's top, evidence perhaps of a balcony or even roof garden and it was there, he knew, that La Marquesa would get her view, above the rooftops, of the wasteland and the forts. Not that she would see much. The attack would be made at last light. Sharpe would have preferred a night attack, but Wellington distrusted them, remembering the closeness of disaster to success that the night had brought in Seringapatam so long ago.

He turned away from the house, to his Company, and he knew that he had become obsessed with this woman. It seemed to him to be ridiculous, to be an ambition of impossible proportions, but now he was snagged on it. His job was to kill Leroux, to protect the unknown figure of El Mirador, yet his mind stayed with La Marquesa.

'Sir?' Harper came to formal attention. 'Company ready for inspection, sir!'

'Lieutenant Price!'

'Sir?'

'Weapons, please.' Sharpe trusted his men. None would go into battle with unserviceable weapons. Price could look at them, tug at screwed flints, feel bayonet edges, but he would find nothing. Sharpe could hear the assault troops being paraded. They were all Light troops, the best of their Battalions, and they were assembling way back from the wasteland, hoping that the sudden eruption of the attack would take the French by surprise. The siege guns still fired. Four eighteen pounders had been dragged across the fords and brought to the city and the huge, iron guns hammered at the forts.

'Listen to me.' He spoke quietly. 'We're not here for heroics. It's not our job to capture the forts, understand?' They nodded. Some grinned. 'The other Light companies do that. Our job is to find one man, the man we captured. So we stay behind the attack. If we can we move to one side, out of the firing line. I don't want casualties. Keep your heads down. It's skirmish order all the way. If we capture the forts, then our job is to search the prisoners. Normal squads. I don't want anyone going off on their own. There's no bloody reward so don't go in for heroics. And remember. This bastard killed young McDonald and he killed Colonel Windham. He's dangerous. If you find him, or if you think you've found him, tie the sod up. And I'm paying ten guineas for his sword.'

'What if it's worth more, sir?' It was Batten's voice; the whining, grumbling, never satisfied Batten. Harper started towards him, but Sharpe held up a hand.

'It is worth more, Batten, probably twenty times more, but if you sell it to anyone else but me I'll have you digging latrines for the rest of the bloody war. Clear?'

The others grinned. A private soldier could hardly expect to sell a valuable sword on the open market. He would be accused of stealing it, and the penalty for theft could be hanging. Some Sergeants would pay more, but not much more, and make their profit in Lisbon. Ten guineas was a big sum, more than a year's wages after deductions and the Company knew it was a fair offer. Sharpe raised his voice again. 'No bayonets. Load, but flints down. We don't want them knowing we're coming. One musket banging off and they'll be giving us canister for supper.' He nodded at Harper. 'Right turn, you know where we're going.'

Harper kept his voice low. 'Right turn!'

'Captain Sharpe!' It was Major Hogan, hurrying towards the main battery where the eighteen pounders sounded.

'Sir!' Sharpe snapped to attention, saluted. In front of the Company they were formal, correct.

'Good luck!' Hogan grinned at the men. They knew him well, the Riflemen had spent weeks with him before they were forcibly joined to the South Essex, the redcoats remembered him from Badajoz or nights when he had come to seek Sharpe's companionship. The Irish Major looked at Sharpe, turned his back to the men, and made a resigned gesture. 'Good luck to you.'

'Not good?'

'No.' Hogan sniffed. 'Some idiot messed up the ammunition supply. We've got about fifteen rounds for each gun! What the hell use is that?'

Sharpe knew he meant the big eighteen pounders. 'What about the howitzers?'

Hogan had taken out his snuff box and Sharpe waited while the Major inhaled his usual huge pinch. He sneezed. 'God and his Angels!' He sneezed again. 'Bloody howitzers! They're not denting the bloody place! A hundred and sixty rounds for six guns. It's no way to run a war!'

'You're not hopeful.'

'Hopeful?' Hogan waited as an eighteen pounder fired one of its precious, dwindling ammunition stock. 'No. But we've persuaded the Peer to attack just the centre fort. We're firing at that.'

'The San Cayetano?'

Hogan nodded. 'If we can grab that, then we can build our own batteries there and hammer the others.' He shrugged. 'Surprise is everything, Richard. If they don't expect us . . .' He shrugged again.

'Leroux may not be in the San Cayetano.'

'He probably isn't. He's probably in the big one. But you never know. They may all surrender if the middle one falls.'

Sharpe reflected that it could be a long night. If the other forts did decide that resistance was futile then the surrender negotiations could take hours. There were, he guessed, a thousand men in the three garrisons and they would be difficult to search in the darkness. He glanced ruefully at the Palacio Casares behind him. There was a chance, a good chance, that he would never manage to arrive on time. Hogan caught the glance. 'You invited?'

'To the celebration? Yes.'

'So's the whole damned town. I just hope there's something to celebrate.'

Sharpe grinned. 'We'll surprise them.' He looked round to see his Company being marched into an alleyway and he gestured at their backs. 'I must go.'

Three hundred and fifty men, the Light Companies of two brigades of the Sixth Division, were crammed into a street that ran behind the houses facing the wasteland. It was the closest cover to the centre fort, the San Cayetano, but no one, apart from a handful of officers, was allowed to look at the ground they had to cover. Surprise was everything. There were twenty ladders, each surrounded by its carrying party, and they would be the first to rush the two hundred yards towards the fort's ditch. They would jump into the excavation and then put the ladders against the palisade.

Sharpe could hear the crack of rifles, startling the swallows who flew in the dusk. Riflemen had surrounded the forts for the six days since the army had entered Salamanca, living uncomfortably in shallow pits of the waste ground, sniping at the French embrasures. The evening sounded normal. The French could not have detected anything unusual in the rhythm of the siege. The big guns fired intermittently, the rifles cracked, and as the light faded so did the sound of the firing. It would seem, Sharpe hoped, a peaceful night in the three forts built on the hill above the slow-sliding river Tormes.

A big Sergeant with a scarred face tugged at a rung of one of the ladders. It bent, fractured, and the Sergeant spat moodily against a wall. 'Bloody green wood!'

Harper was loading his seven-barrelled gun, carefully measuring powder from his Rifleman's horn. He grinned up at Sharpe. 'Met that Irish priest while you were chatting with the Major, sir. Wished us luck.'

'Curtis? How the hell does he know? I thought this was secret.'

Harper shrugged, then tapped the butt of the huge gun on the ground. 'Probably saw this lot march in, sir.' He jerked his head at the Light Companies. 'Don't exactly look as if they've come for a Regimental dance.'

Sharpe sat and waited, head back against the wall, the loaded rifle between his knees. It seemed strange, on this perfect summer's evening, the light fading into translucent grey, to think of the vast, secret war that shadowed the war of guns and swords. How had the priest known this attack was to take place tonight? Were there French spies in Salamanca who also knew? Who might have already warned the fortresses? Sharpe supposed there might be. It was possible that the French were ready, eagerly awaiting the first attack that they would shred with canister.

96

Sharpe had only seen one French spy. He had been a small Spaniard, jolly and generous, who had purported to be a lemonade seller outside Fuentes d'Onoro. He proved to be a Corporal in one of the Spanish Regiments that fought for the French and Sharpe had watched the man hung. He had died with dignity, a smile on his lips, and Sharpe wondered what bravery it took to be such a man. El Mirador, Sharpe supposed, had that bravery. He had lived in Salamanca, under French occupation, and still he had sent his stream of intelligence towards the British forces in Portugal. Tonight Sharpe was fighting for that brave man, for El Mirador, and he looked up at the fading light and knew that the attack must come soon.

'Sharpe?' A senior officer was looking at him. Sharpe struggled to his feet and saluted.

'Sir?'

'Brigadier General Bowes. I'm in command tonight, but I gather you have your own orders?' Sharpe nodded. Bowes looked curiously at the strange figure, dressed half as an officer and half as a Rifleman. The Brigadier seemed satisfied. 'Glad you're with us, Sharpe.'

'Thank you, sir. I hope we can be useful.'

Bowes gestured abruptly towards the hidden fort. 'There's a crude trench for the first seventy yards. That'll cover us. After that it's up to God.' He looked with frank admiration at the wreath on Sharpe's sleeve. 'You've done this sort of thing before.'

'Badajoz, sir.'

'This won't be as bad.' Bowes moved on. The attackers were standing up, straightening their jackets, obsessively checking the last few details before the fight. Some touched their private talismans, some crossed themselves, and most wore the look of forced cheerfulness that hid the fear.

Bowes clapped his hands. He was a short man, built strongly and he climbed on a mounting block set beside one of the houses. 'Remember, lads! Quiet! Quiet! Quiet!' This

97

was the Sixth Division's first battle in Spain and the men listened eagerly, wanting to impress the rest of the army. 'Ladders first. After me!'

Sharpe cautioned his own men to wait. Harper would lead the first squad, then Lieutenant Price, while Sergeant McGovern and Sergeant Huckfield had the others. He grinned at them. Huckfield was new to the Company, since Badajoz, promoted from one of the other companies. Sharpe remembered when, as a private, Huckfield had tried to lead the mutiny before Talavera. Huckfield owed his life to Sharpe, but the bargain had been good. He was a conscientious, solid man, good with figures and the Company books, and the memory of that distant day, three years before, when Huckfield had nearly led the Battalion into mutiny was faded and unreal.

The street emptied, the attackers filing into the wasteland, and Sharpe still waited. He did not want his Company mixed with the others. He almost held his breath, listening for the first shot, but the night was silent. 'All right, lads. Keep yourselves quiet.'

He went first, through the passage between the houses, and the ground dropped into a steep pit that had been made when the sappers threw up one of the flanking batteries. The nine-pounders were silent behind their fascines.

He could see the other companies ahead, crammed into the shallow trench. It had not been made for the attack, instead it was the remnants of a small street and it gave cover because the destroyed houses either side were banks of rubble. He dared not raise his head to look at the San Cayetano. There was a hope that the French were dozing, not expecting trouble, but he had no reason to suppose that their sentries would be any the less watchful because the night was quiet.

A ladder, far ahead, banged on rubble and there was the sound of loose stones falling. He froze, his senses acute for an enemy reaction, but still the night was quiet. There was a soft background noise, unceasing, and he realised it was the wash of water against the piles of the bridge arches. An owl sounded, south of the river. The light was pearl grey, the west soaked in crimson, the air warm after the day's heat. The people of Salamanca, he knew, would be walking the stately circles in the great Plaza, sipping wine and brandy, and it would be a night of rich beauty in the city. Wellington was waiting, fearing surprise was lost, and Sharpe suddenly thought of La Marquesa, up on her roof or balcony, staring at the darkening shadows of the wasteland. A bell struck the half-hour past nine.

He heard a scraping and clicking ahead and knew that the attackers were fixing bayonets ready to run from the cover and rush the jumbled waste ground towards the San Cayetano. Lieutenant Price caught Sharpe's eye and gestured at one of his men's bayonets. Sharpe shook his head. He did not want the blades to betray the position of his company, far back, and they had no business, anyway, in attacking the fort.

'Go!' Bowes' voice broke the silence, there was a scramble of feet and the sunken road ahead of Sharpe heaved with bodies that clambered over and through the rubble. This was the moment of danger, the first appearance, for if the French were ready, expecting them, the guns would fire now and decimate the attack.

They fired.

They were small guns in the forts, some were old and captured four pounders, but even a small gun, loaded with canister, can destroy an attack. Sharpe knew the figures well enough. A four pound canister was a tin can, packed with balls, sixty or eighty to a can, and when it was fired the tin burst apart at the gun's muzzle and the balls spread, like duckshot, in a widening cone. Three hundred yards from the muzzle the cone would be ninety feet across, good odds for a single man in the line of fire, but not if several guns' cones intersected. The San Cayetano, ahead of the attack, had only four guns, but the San Vincente, across the gorge, the biggest fort, could bring twenty to bear on the flank of the British attack.

They all fired. One first, followed in a handful of seconds by the rest, and the noise of the guns was different, deeper than usual, somehow more solid and Sharpe looked aghast at Harper. 'They're double shotted!'

Harper nodded, shrugged. Two canisters to a gun, say seventy balls in each, and twenty four guns firing. Sharpe listened to the metal hell that was criss-crossing the rubble and tried to work out the figures. Three thousand musket balls, at least, had greeted the attack, ten to each man, and in the silence after the volley he could hear the screams of wounded and then the rattle of muskets from the French embrasures. He could see nothing. He looked at the Company. 'Stay there!'

He climbed the rubble side of the street, rolled over its crest and found cover behind a timber baulk. Bowes was alive, sword drawn, and ahead of the attack. 'On! On!'

Ladder parties, miraculously alive, came off the ground where they had dived for shelter and began struggling over the jumbled stones. Each ladder was thirty feet, cumbersome on the shadowed ground, but the men were moving and, behind them, more figures advanced towards the dark bulk of the San Cayetano.

The attackers cheered, still confident despite the first, shattering discharge, and it was a miracle to Sharpe that so many had lived through the screaming cones. He slid his rifle forward, leafed up the sight, and then the second shots sounded from the French.

This volley was more ragged than the first. The gunners were loading as fast as they could, single canister only, and the faster crews would fire first. The balls bellowed from the embrasures, clattered on the stones, whirled the dead and wounded in limp disarray, and Sharpe cursed the French. They had known! They had known! There had been no surprise! They had double shotted the guns, had the matches ready for the fuses, and the attack stood no chance. The canisters burst and spread their death over the attackers, gun after gun, the shots coming singly or in small groups, and the lead balls hammered like hard rain on the stones, timber and bodies in the wasteland.

The two forts were ringed with smoke. The third, off to Sharpe's left, was silent as if its guns, insultingly, were not needed. He could hear the French now, cheering their work as the gunners heaved at their weapons, loaded and fired, loaded and fired, and their flames sprang across the ditch, split the smoke, and licked behind the shredding canister.

'Rifles!'

There was not much they could do, but anything was better than being a spectator of this slaughter. He shouted again. 'Rifles!'

His Riflemen poured over the lip of the rubble. He had trained a half dozen of the redcoats to use the Bakers, weapons left by men killed in the last three years, and they came, too. Harper dropped beside him, eyebrows raised, and Sharpe gestured at the nearest fort. 'Go for the embrasures!'

They might kill a gunner or two, not much, but something. He heard the first shots, fired himself when the smoke showed a target, but the attack was done. The British did not know it. The men still went forward, shoulders hunched as if pushing into a storm, and they left their dead and wounded on the ground. Screams pierced the harsh sound of guns and Sharpe prayed with each new discharge of canister that a ball might end the screaming. Bowes was still up, still going ahead, taking his sword against the artillerymen and, behind and to each side, the survivors refused to give up. They were scattered now, less susceptible to the rain of lead, but too few to hope for victory. A ladder party actually made the ditch. Sharpe saw them jump in, heard the muskets fire from the palisade, and then he saw the Brigadier, limned against the spreading pall of smoke, and Bowes was hit. He seemed to dance on the spot, feet skittering to keep him upright and his sword fell as his hands clutched at his stomach. His head went back in a silent scream, more shots threw him forward and still he tried to stand, and then it was as if a whole barrel load of canister slammed the quivering figure, threw it flat, and the wasteland was suddenly empty of running men.

The attackers had gone to ground, defeated, and the French jeered at them, shouted insults, and the cannon fire died away.

There were no more men to throw into the attack, except Sharpe's Company and he was not going to sacrifice them to the gunners. At Badajoz the army had gone on attacking, again and again into worse fire than this, in a smaller space, until it had seemed to Sharpe that all the canister in all the world could not go on killing the stream of men that had poured at the breaches. This attack had started with three hundred and fifty men, and there were no more. It was done.

The cannon smoke turned the dusk into false night and the French threw a lighted carcass, packed straw soaked with oil and bound in canvas, over their parapet. Shouts came from the wasteland. 'Back! Back!'

Some men risked the fire, stood up, and ran. The French stayed silent. More men plucked up courage and the survivors, bit by bit, began their retreat. Still the French held their fire, happy that the British had given up, and men stopped to pick up their wounded. Sharpe looked at his Riflemen. 'Back you go, lads.'

They were silent, depressed. They were used to victory, not defeat, but Sharpe knew they had been betrayed. He looked at Harper. 'They knew we were coming.'

'Like as not.' The huge Irishman was easing the flint of his rifle, unfired, into the safe position. 'They had the guns double-loaded. They knew.'

'I'd like to get the bastard who told them.'

Harper did not reply. He gestured ahead of them and Sharpe saw a man, staggering in the rubble, coming towards them. He had the red facings of the 53rd, the Shropshires, and his face was the colour of his uniform. Sharpe stood up, slung his rifle, and called to the man. 'Here! Over here!'

The man seemed not to hear. He was walking, almost drunkenly, weaving on the stones, and Sharpe and Harper ran towards him. The man was moaning. Blood poured from his skull. 'I can't see!'

'You'll be all right!' Sharpe could not see the man's face through the blood. His hands, musket discarded, were clutched at his stomach. He seemed to hear Sharpe, the blood-soaked head quested towards the sound, and then he fell into Sharpe's arms. The hands came away and blood pumped onto Sharpe's jacket and overalls. 'It's all right, lad, it's all right!'

They laid him down and the man began to choke. Harper twisted his torso over, cleared the man's throat with his finger, and shook his head at Sharpe. The Shropshire man vomited blood, moaned, and muttered again that he could not see. Sharpe undid his canteen, poured water on his eyes, and the blood, soaked there from a canister wound on his forehead, cleared slowly away. 'You'll be all right!'

The eyes opened, then shut immediately as a pain spasm shook him and blood seemed to well from his midriff. Harper tore at the man's uniform. 'God save Ireland!' It was a miracle he was still alive.

'Here!' Sharpe undid his officer's sash, handed it across, and Harper pushed it beneath the body, caught the end, and tied it as a crude bandage round the horrid wound. He looked at Sharpe. 'Head or legs?'

'Legs.'

He took the man's ankles, they lifted him, and struggled with the burden back towards the houses. Other men were limping on the stones. The French were silent.

They put the man down in the street, full now once again with men, and Sharpe bellowed for bandsmen. The soldier was fighting for his life, the air scraping in his throat, and it seemed impossible that he could survive the wounds. Sharpe shouted again. 'Bandsmen!'

An officer, his uniform unstained by dust or blood, his red facings and gold lace new and pristine, looked past Sharpe. 'Dale. No musket.' He was dictating to a bespectacled clerk.

'What?' Sharpe turned and looked at the Lieutenant. Harper raised his eyes to heaven, then looked at Sergeant McGovern. The two Sergeants grinned. They knew Sharpe and knew his anger.

'Equipment check.' The Lieutenant looked at Sharpe's rifle, then at the great sword, then at the Rifleman's shoulder. 'If you'll excuse me, sir.'

'No.' Sharpe jerked his head towards the wounded man. 'Are you planning to charge him?'

The Lieutenant looked round for escape or support, then sighed. 'He has lost his musket, sir.'

'It was broken by French shot.' Sharpe's voice was quiet.

'I'm sure you'll put that in writing, sir.'

'No. You will. You were out there, weren't you?'

The Lieutenant swallowed nervously. 'No, sir.'

'Why not?'

'Sir! I was ordered to stay here, sir!'

'And no one ordered you to make life a bloody misery for the men who went out, did they? How many battles have you been in, Lieutenant?'

The Lieutenant's eyes looked round the circle of grim, interested faces. He shrugged. 'Sir?'

Sharpe reached over to the clerk-Corporal and took the notebook out of his hand. 'You write "destroyed by enemy" against everything, understand? Everything. Including the boots they lost last week.'

'Yes, sir.' The Lieutenant took the notebook from Sharpe and gave it to the clerk. 'You heard the man, Bates. "Destroyed by enemy".' The Lieutenant backed away.

Sharpe watched him go. His anger had not vented itself and he wanted to strike out at something, at someone, because the men had died through treachery. The French had been ready, warned of the attack, and good men had been thrown away, and he bellowed again. 'Bandsmen!'

Two musicians, doing their battlefield job of tending the wounded, came and crouched by the injured Dale. They lifted him clumsily onto a stretcher. Sharpe stopped one of them as they were about to go. 'Where's the Hospital?'

'Irish College, sir.'

'Look after him.'

The man shrugged. 'Yes, sir.'

Poor bloody Dale, Sharpe thought, to be betrayed in his first battle. If he survived he would be invalided out of the army. His broken body, good for nothing, would be sent to Lisbon and there he would have to rot on the quays until the bureaucrats made sure he had accounted for all his equipment. Anything missing would be charged to the balance of his miserable wages and only when the account was balanced would he be put onto a foul transport and shipped to an English quayside. There he was left, the army's obligation discharged, though if he was lucky he might be given a travel document that promised to reimburse any parish overseer who fed him while he travelled to his home. Usually the overseers ignored the paper and kicked the invalid out of their jurisdiction with an order to go and beg somewhere else. Dale might be better off dead than face all that.

Lieutenant Price, wary of Sharpe's anger, saluted. 'Dismiss, sir?'

'Dismiss and get drunk, Lieutenant.'

Price grinned with relief. 'Yes, sir. Morning parade?'

'Late one. Nine o'clock.'

Harper could still hear the suppressed rage in Sharpe, but he was one man who did not fear the Captain's anger. He nodded at Sharpe's uniform. 'Not planning on any formal dinner tonight, sir?'

The uniform was soaked with Dale's blood, dark against the green, and Sharpe cursed. He brushed at it uselessly. He had planned on going to the Palacio Casares and then he thought how La Marquesa had wanted a battle, and had been given one, and now she could see how a real soldier looked instead of the dripping confections of gold and silver who called themselves fighting men. Harper's uniform was bloody, too, but Harper had Isabella waiting for him and suddenly Sharpe was tired of being alone and he wanted the golden haired woman and his anger was such that he would use it to take him into her palace and see what happened. He looked at the Irish Sergeant. 'I'll see you in the morning.'

'Yes, sir.'

Harper watched Sharpe walk away and let out a deep breath. 'Someone's in for trouble.'

Lieutenant Price glanced at the huge Sergeant. 'Should we go with him?'

'No, sir. I think he fancies a fight. That Lieutenant didn't give him one so he's going to look for another one.' Harper grinned. 'He'll be back in a couple of hours, sir. Just let him cool off.' Harper raised his canteen to Price and shrugged. 'Here's to a happy night, sir. A happy, bloody night.'

CHAPTER 8

Sharpe's resolution to go to La Marquesa waned as he neared the Palacio Casares. Yet he had said to Harper that he would not be back until morning and he could not face slinking back early with his tail between his legs and so he walked on. Yet with every step he worried more about the state of his uniform.

The streets were still filled with men from the Light Companies who waited for dismissal while the final rosters were taken. The wounded, on stretchers and carts, were being carried to the surgeons' knives and many of the dead were still on the wasteland. The unwounded living stood with bitter, angry expression and the citizens of Salamanca hurried by in the shadows, averting their eyes, hoping the soldiers would not vent their anger on helpless civilians.

The arch gates of the Palacio Casares were wide open, flickering with lights cast by resin torches and Sharpe, like the fearful citizens, kept to the shadows on the far side of the street. He leaned against the wall and pulled his blood-soaked jacket straight. He did up the top buttons and tried to force the high collar, that had long lost its stiffness, into a decent shape round his neck. He wanted to see her.

Candles showed in the hallway. Their light was splintered by the fountain in the courtyard centre. The raised pool was surrounded by the silhouettes of British uniforms, officers' uniforms, and while most seemed to be taking the air, or smoking a cigar in the night's coolness, others were puking helplessly on the flagstones. The defeat, it seemed, had not affected the celebration. The courtyard was surrounded by light, the once masked windows ablaze with candles, and music came gently across the street. It was not the spirited thump of martial music, nor the full-bellied sound of soldiers' taverns, but the thin, precious tinkle of rich peoples' music. Music as expensive as a crystal chandelier, and Sharpe knew that if he walked over the street, through the tall arch, and over to the hallway he would feel as foreign and strange as if he had been plunged into the court of the King of Tartary. The house was lit like a festival, the rich were at play, and the dead who lay shredded by the canister just a quarter mile away might never have existed.

'Richard! By the moving bowels of the living saints! Is that you?' Lord Spears was in the gateway. In one hand was a cigar that beckoned to him. 'Richard Sharpe! Come here, you dog!'

Sharpe smiled, despite his mood, and crossed the street. 'My lord.'

'Will you stop "my lording" me? You sound like a damned shop-keeper! My friends call me Jack, my enemies what they like. Are you coming in? You're invited. Not that it makes any difference, every damned mother's son in town is here.'

Sharpe gestured at his uniform. 'I'm hardly in a fit state.'

'Christ! What's a fit state? I'm drunk as an Archbishop, wits gone to the four winds.' Spears was, Sharpe could see, slightly unsteady. The cavalryman linked his free arm, the cigar clenched between his teeth, into Sharpe's and steered the Rifleman into the courtyard. 'Let's have a look at you.' He stopped Sharpe in the light, turned him, and looked him up and down. 'You should change your tailor, Richard, the man's robbing you blind!' He grinned. 'Bit of blood, that's all. Come here!' He tossed the cigar into the pool and scooped water with his good hand, throwing it on Sharpe's uniform and rubbing it down. 'How was it out there?'

'Bloody.'

'So I see!' He was on one knee, slapping at Sharpe's overalls. 'It cost me a heavy purse.'

'How?'

Spears looked up and grinned. 'I had a hundred on you getting into the fort before midnight. Lost it.'

'Dollars?'

Spears stood up and inspected his handiwork. 'Spanish dollars, Richard? I'm a gentleman. Guineas, you fool.'

'You haven't got a hundred guineas.'

Lord Spears shrugged. 'Fellow has to keep up a decent appearance. If they knew I was as broke as a virgin whore they'd cut me dead.'

'Are you?'

Spears nodded. 'I am, I am. And I don't even have her remedy for making good the loss.' He cocked his head to one side, still inspecting Sharpe. 'Not bad, Richard, not bad. The weapons add a touch of roughness to the ensemble, but I think we can improve you.' He looked round the courtyard and saw Sir Robin Callard, blind drunk, collapsed against a flower tub. Spears grinned. 'Robin bloody Callard, 'pon my soul. He never could take his drink.' He led the way towards the collapsed staff officer. 'I was at school with this poxy little swine. He used to wet his bed.' Spears bent down and tugged at Callard. 'Robin? Sweet Robin?'

Callard gagged, threw himself forward, and Spears pushed his head down between his knees. Once he had him bent double he plucked the fur-trimmed cavalry pelisse from the shoulders, then tugged at the cravat. It was pinned. Callard's head jerked and lolled, he made a drunken protest, but Spears banged the head down again, tugged harder, and the cravat came free. Spears came back to Sharpe. 'Here. Wear these.'

'What about him?'

'He can roger the moon, for all I care. You wear 'em, Richard, and throw them away tomorrow. If the little bastard wakes up and wants them back we'll shove him head-

109

first into the cess-pit. He'll think he's back home.'

Sharpe tucked the cravat into his collar, then draped the pelisse, dark red trimmed with black fur, so that the sleeve hung loose by his left side. Spears grinned at the effect, laughed as Sharpe slung the rifle over the decorative garment. 'You look ravishing. Shall we go and find something to ravish?'

The hall was crowded with officers and people of the town and Spears pushed through them, shouting at friends, waving indiscriminately. He looked back at Sharpe. 'Eaten?'

'No.'

'There's a trough in there! I should get your face in it!'

Sharpe found himself in a vast room, lit by a thousand candles, and on the walls were great, dark oil paintings that showed men in solemn armour. A table ran the length of the room, beside one wall, and it was covered with a white cloth spread with heaped dishes. Half the foods he did not even recognise; small birds, brown from the ovens, dripping with clear, sticky sauce, and next to them a plate of strange fruits, fantastically decorated with palm leaves, and glistening with ice that sweating servants replenished as they dashed up and down the table's length. Sharpe took a goose-breast, bit it, and discovered he was ravenous. He took one more to eat while he watched the strange throng.

Half were officers. There were British, German, Spanish and Portuguese, and the colours of their uniforms spanned the whole of a painter's tray. The rest were civilians, richly and sombrely dressed, and the men, Sharpe guessed, outnumbered the women five to one. They outnumbered the pretty women a hundred to one. A group of British Dragoon officers had invented their own game at the far end of the room, lobbing bread rolls like howitzer shells high over the crowd so they fell indiscriminately amongst a sober group of Spaniards who were pretending that the bread cannonade was merely a figment of their imaginations. Spears whooped at them as they fired, correcting their aim, calling the fall of shot and then, delighted with the game, tossed a whole roasted chicken to one of the group. They chanted the fire orders. 'Sponge out! Load! Prime! Stand back! Fire!' The chicken sailed into the air, turning and dripping, then splatted down and scored a glancing blow on the high mantilla and carefully constructed hair of a Spanish matron. She rocked forward slightly, oblivious, apparently, of the Dragoons' cheers, and her companions looked silently at the ruined, gaping, wire-threaded interior of her piled hair. It seemed to leak a little dust from its remains. One of the men stooped down and tore off a chicken wing and began to munch at it.

Spears waved at Sharpe. 'God, Richard, isn't this fun?'

Sharpe pushed through the crowd. 'Is the General here?'

'What do you think?' Spears gestured at the cavalry officers. 'They wouldn't dare if he was here. No, the word is he isn't coming. Lickin' his wounds, so to speak.' He was shouting over the crowd's noise.

Sharpe was introduced to the cavalry officers, a whirl of names, bonhomie, unmemorable faces, and then Spears pushed him through the doorway, back to the hall, and up a huge staircase that separated in two great curves either side of a statue. The statue, which was of a decorous maiden holding a pitcher of water, had been crowned with a British shako.

Sharpe had thought that the room with the food must be the main room of the Palacio, but he was shown, at the stair's top, through a door and into a hall that took his breath away. It was the size of a cavalry drill hall, lined with huge paintings, topped by a ceiling of intricate plaster, and lit by great chandeliers, each a universe of candles, and the crystal winked and dazzled, glittered and shook, above the uniforms of the officers, silver and gold, lace and chain, and above the dresses and jewels of the women. 'Jesus!' The word was torn from him involuntarily.

'He sent His apologies.' Spears grinned at him. 'Do you like it?'

'It's incredible!'

'She married one of the richest devils in Spain, and the dullest.' Spears suddenly bowed to a middle-aged civilian. 'My lord!'

The civilian nodded gravely to Spears. 'My lord.' He was English, plump, with an angry face. He looked at Sharpe, quizzing him up and down with a raised monocle. Sharpe's uniform was still wet with water and blood. 'Who are you?'

Spears stepped in front of Sharpe. 'It's Callard, my lord. You remember him?'

His lordship waved Spears aside. 'We have appearances to keep up, Callard, and you are a disgrace. Retire and change.'

Sharpe smiled. 'I'll rip your windpipe out of your fat throat if you don't take your fat arse out of that door in two seconds.' The smile had disguised a terrible anger that hammered at the man. For one second the plump man looked as if he would protest, and then he fled, rump going from side to side, leaving Sharpe angry and Lord Spears almost helpless with laughter.

'God, you're precious, Sharpe. You know who that was?'

'I couldn't give a damn.'

'So I see. Lord Benfleet. One of our politicians, come to put some spine into the Dagoes. His nickname, you'll be pleased to know, is Lord Bumfleet. Come on.' He took Sharpe's elbow and steered him to the top of the steps. 'Who do we know here? Who else can you upset?'

An orchestra was playing on a raised dais that was set into a great arch topped by a gilded scallop. The musicians, wigged heads bowed, seemed to be scraping obsequiously for the circling mass on the floor. Among the people standing at the edges of the floor Sharpe saw the dark habits of sleek churchmen, their faces flushed with drink and good food. One face was not flushed. Sharpe saw the bushy eyebrows, and then the hand raised in recognition across the width of the room. Spears saw the gesture. 'You know him?'

'Curtis. He's a professor at the University here.'

'He's a bloody traitor.'

'He's what?' Sharpe was startled by the sudden severity in Spears' voice. 'Traitor?'

'Bloody Irishman. God knows, Richard, some of the Irish are all right, but some of them turn my stomach. That one does.'

'Why?'

'He fought against us, did you know that? When the Spanish were on the side of the French he was a chaplain on a naval ship. He volunteered as soon as he knew they would fight the English. He even boasts about it!'

'How do you know?'

'Because the Peer had a lot of so called eminent citizens to dinner one night, his Irish bloody eminence among them, and they sat and griped about the quality of the food. He should be bloody shot.'

Sharpe looked over the dancers to where Curtis was listening to a Spanish officer speak. The Irishman did seem to crop up at the most unexpected places. He had stopped the citizens firing at Leroux and only this evening he had said to Harper that he had known of the coming attack. An Irishman who had no love for the English. Sharpe pushed the thought away. He was seeing spies everywhere, when all that mattered was the utter defeat of Leroux.

Sharpe was not comfortable in this room. This was not his world. The musicians, who had taken a brief pause, started again and the men bowed to ladies, led them to the floor, and Lord Spears grinned at him. 'D'you dance?'

'No.'

'I somehow thought you'd say that. It's very simple, Richard. You keep your feet moving, pretend you know what you're doing, and pull their little waists firmly into your loins. One trip round the floor and you'll know if you're in luck. You should try it!' He dived into the crowd and Sharpe turned away, took a glass from a passing servant, and found a corner where he could stand and drink the wine.

He was out of place here. It was not just the clothes. Any man, he supposed, could get a tailor to dress him like a lord, but it was not just a question of money. How did a man learn which of a dozen knives and forks to pick up first? Or how to dance? Or how to make light conversation with a Marquesa, joke with a Bishop, or how, even, to give orders to a butler? They said it was in the blood of a man's birth, ordained by God, yet upstarts like Napoleon Bonaparte had come from low birth to the glittering pinnacle of the richest country on earth. He had asked Major Leroy once, the loyalist American, if there was no social distinction in the fledgling United States, but the Major had laughed, spat out a shred of cheroot, and intoned solemnly to Sharpe. '"We hold these truths to be self-evident, that all men are created equal." You know what that is?'

'No.'

'The rebels' Declaration of Independence.' Leroy had spat another tobacco shred from his tongue. 'Half the bastards who signed it had slaves, the other half would run a mile rather than shake the hand of a slaughterman. No. I give them fifty years and they'll all want titles. Barons of Boston and Dukes of New York. It'll happen.'

And Sharpe, standing in the shards of a myriad refracted candle flames, guessed Leroy was right. If you took every person in this room and abandoned them, Robinson Crusoe style, on an empty island, then inside a year there would be a duke, five barons, and the rest would be serfs. Even the French had brought back the aristocracy! They had murdered it first, as they murdered La Marquesa's parents, and now Bonaparte was making his Marshals into Princes of this and Dukes of that and his poor, honest brother had been made into King of Spain!

Sharpe looked at the sweating faces over tight collars, the thick thighs laced tight in military uniforms, the ridiculous costumes of the women. Take away the money, he supposed, and they would look like anyone else, softer perhaps, flabbier, but the money, and the birth, gave them something that he lacked. An assurance? An ease of moving through the rich waters of society? Then should he bother? He could walk away from the army, when the war was done, and Teresa would have a home for him in Casatejada among the wide fields that were her family's property. He need never say 'my lord' again, or 'sir', or feel belittled by an elegant fool, and he felt an anger inside him at the unfairness of life and, at the same time, a determination that one day he would have them respecting him. God rot them all!

'Richard! Are you going?'

Spears whirled off the dance floor, climbed the two steps to where Sharpe was standing, and brought with him a small, dark-haired girl with brightly rouged cheeks. 'Say hello to Maria.'

Sharpe half bowed to her. 'Senorita.'

'We are formal.' Spears grinned at him. 'You're not going, are you?'

'I was.'

'You can't, my dear fellow! Positively can't. You'll have to see La Marquesa, at least. Press her exquisite fingers to your lips, murmur "charmed", and compliment her on her frock.'

'Tell her from me she looked wonderful.' He had not seen her, though he had looked, in either room.

Spears slumped back in mock resignation. 'Are you a dull dog, Richard? Don't tell me that the hero of Talavera, the Conqueror of Badajoz, is creeping back to his lonely cot to say a few prayers for lame dogs and orphans! Enjoy yourself!' He gestured at the girl. 'Do you want her? She's probably as clean as they come. Really! You can have her! There are plenty more down there.' Maria, who obviously spoke not a word of English, looked devotedly up into Spears' handsome face.

Sharpe wondered why Spears was so friendly. Perhaps his Lordship needed a strong arm to protect him from his gambling creditors or maybe, as he had accused La Marquesa, Spears liked the company of his social inferiors. Whatever, it did not matter. 'I'm going. It's been a long day.'

Spears shrugged. 'If you must, Richard. If you must. I did try.'

'Thank you, my lord.'

Sharpe took one last look at the ballroom, at the circling, brilliant people beneath the great chandeliers, and he knew he had been foolish in coming to this place. La Marquesa was not to be his reward. He had been presumptuous in even coming. He nodded to Spears, turned, and walked onto the upper landing. He stopped behind the shako-hatted statue and stared up at the great, painted ceiling, and he could not imagine owning one hundredth of one hundredth part of all this wealth. He would go back and tell Harper of it.

'Senor?' A servant had appeared beside him. The man was aloof, liveried, and with a supercilious look in his eye.

'Yes?'

'This way, senor.' The man plucked Sharpe's sleeve towards a tapestry against the wall.

Sharpe shook the hand off, growled, and he saw alarm come into the servant's eyes.

'Senor! *Por favor!* This way!'

It suddenly occurred to Sharpe that the man only had these two words of English, words he had been coached in, and only one person gave orders in this house. La Marquesa. He followed the man towards the hanging tapestry. The servant glanced around the landing, making sure that no-one was watching, and then he swiftly drew back one heavy corner of the great cloth. Behind it was a low, open doorway. 'Senor?'

There was urgency in the man's voice. Sharpe ducked under the lintel and the footman, staying on the landing, let the tapestry fall back into place. Sharpe was alone, quite alone, in a musty and total darkness.

CHAPTER 9

He stood quite still, the air cooler on one side of his face, the sound of revelry muffled by the thick tapestry. He put out his left hand slowly, found the open door, and swung it shut. The hinges were well greased. It moved soundlessly until the latch clicked into place and then Sharpe leaned against it and let his eyes adjust slowly to the darkness.

He was on a small, square landing between two staircases. To his right the steps went downwards into utter darkness, to his left they climbed and at their head he could see a pale square that might have been the night sky except that it was curiously mottled and had no stars. He went to his left, climbing slowly, and his boots grated on the stone steps until he came out onto a wide balcony.

He saw now why there were no stars visible. The open side and roof of the balcony were enclosed by a small-latticed screen, dense with climbing plants, and the effect was to make the balcony comfortably cool. The plant stems had been trained so there were wide gaps between them and he crossed to the nearest gap and rested his shako peak on the lattice so he could see out. The lattice moved. He started back, then realised that the screen was a series of hinged doors, any of which could be opened so that the sun could flood onto the flagstones. The city was spread beneath him, grey moonlight on tiles and stone, the glow of fires reddening some of the buildings.

The balcony was deserted. Rush mats lay at its centre, making a path between troughs planted with small shrubs and stone benches supported by carved, crouching lions. He walked slowly along the balcony's length and his eye caught strange, intermittent flashes of light from his right. They seemed to come from the balcony floor where it met the wall of the Palacio and he stopped, crouched, and saw that the lights came from a series of tiny windows that looked into the ballroom below. They were like spyholes. Beyond the palm-sized panes of glass were tunnels that must go through stone and plaster and each revealed a small patch of the great ball-room. Sharpe saw Lord Spears circle through his spyhole, his pelisse round Maria's shoulders and his one good arm some-where beneath the pelisse. Sharpe stood up and walked on.

The balcony turned to the right and Sharpe stopped at the corner. The rush mats on the new stretch were overlaid with rugs and there were doors, shut and shuttered, that led into the Palacio's interior. At the far end, hard against a blank wall, Sharpe could see a table that was set with food and wine. The crystal and china winked with the reflected light of a single candle, shielded by glass, that stood in a niche of the wall. Only two chairs stood by the table, both empty, and Sharpe felt the stirring of his instinct, of danger, and he wondered why he had been invited to what looked like a very small party indeed. It made no sense, despite Spears' ex-planation, for La Marquesa de Casares el Grande y Melida Sadaba to invite Captain Sharpe to this private, expensive, and luxurious balcony.

Halfway down the balcony a huge brass telescope was mounted on a heavy iron tripod. Sharpe walked to it and pushed open a lattice door next to the instrument and saw, as he had guessed, that it pointed toward the night's battlefield. The wasteland was pale in the moonlight, the fortresses dark, and Sharpe could see the ravine clearly that ran between the San Vincente and the smaller forts. There was the glow of fire tingeing the roofline of the San Vincente's courtyard and he knew the French were celebrating their victory around the flames, but fearing, too, the next assault. There were other fires, small torches that were hand-held in the wasteland where men searched for the wounded and dead. The French ignored them. Sharpe suddenly shivered. For no reason he remembered the burning of the dead after the assault on Badajoz just a few weeks before. There had been too many bodies to bury so they had been stacked in layers, timber between the stripped corpses, and the fires had burned darkly and he remembered how the corpses on the top layer had sat up in the heat, almost as if they were alive and begging for rescue, and then the corpses below had also begun to bend in the great fire and, as if to blot out the vision, he pulled shut the lattice door with a loud click.

'What are you thinking?' Her voice was husky. He turned and La Marquesa was standing by the table, by a door that had opened silently, and a woman servant was in the doorway offering a shawl. La Marquesa shook her head and the servant disappeared, shutting the door as noiselessly as it had opened. La Marquesa was light in the darkness. Her golden hair seemed glowing to Sharpe, spun with gossamer fine radiance, and her dress was a brilliant white. It left her shoulders and arms bare and he could see the shadows of her collarbones and he wanted to put his hands on that fine, pale skin because she was, in a Palacio of priceless and beautiful objects, the most perfect of them all. He felt clumsy.

'I was told to compliment you on your frock.'

'My dress? I suppose that was Jack Spears?'

'Yes, Ma'am.'

'He never saw me.' She leaned over the table and Sharpe saw her light a small cigar from the candle. He was amazed. He was used to the women of the army smoking their short clay pipes, but he had never seen a woman with a cigar before. She blew a plume of smoke that drifted up to the lattice. 'I saw you, though, both of you. You were glowering at the ballroom, hating it all, and he was wondering where he could find an empty bedroom to take that silly girl. Do you smoke?'

'Sometimes. Not now, thank you.' Sharpe gestured at the spyholes. 'Did you see through those?'

She shook her head. 'The palace is full of spyholes, Captain. Riddled with secret passages.' She walked towards him, her feet quite silent on the rugs. Her voice seemed different to Sharpe, this was not the same woman who had been excited and enthusiastic at San Christobal. Tonight she spoke crisply, with a confident authority, and all traces of wide-eyed naivete had gone. She sat on a cushioned bench. 'My husband's great-great-grandfather built the Palacio and he was a suspicious man. He married a younger wife, like me, and he feared she would be unfaithful so he built the passages and the peepholes. He would follow her round the building, she in light and he in darkness, and everything she did, he watched.' She told the story as if it was a much-told tale, of interest to the listener, but holding boredom for herself. She shrugged, blew smoke upwards, and looked at him. 'That's the story.'

'Did he see anything he shouldn't have?'

She smiled. 'It's said she discovered about the passages and that she hired two masons. One day she waited until her husband was in a long tunnel that bends round the library. It has only one entrance.' Her eyes were huge in the dimness. Sharpe watched her, entranced by the line of her throat, the shadows on her skin above the low white dress, by the wide mouth. She chopped down with the cigar. 'She gave a signal and the masons nailed the entrance shut and then they laid stones over it. After that she made the servants pleasure her, one by one, two by two, and all the time they could hear the husband screaming and scrabbling beyond the wall. She told them it was rats and told them to keep going.' She shrugged. 'It's just a nonsense, of course, not true. The pride of this house would not allow it, but the people of Salamanca tell the story and certainly the passages exist.'

'It's a harsh story.'

'Yes. It goes on that she died, strangled by the ghost of her husband, and that will be the fate of any mistress of this house who is unfaithful to her husband.' She glanced up at

Sharpe as she said the last words and there was a curious hostility in her expression, a challenge perhaps.

'You say the story isn't true?'

She gave a crooked, secret smile. 'How very indelicate of you, Captain Sharpe.' She drew on the cigar, hardening the red point of the tobacco. 'What did Lord Spears tell you about me?'

He was startled by the directness of her question, by the inference that she was commanding him to answer. He shook his head. 'Nothing.'

'How very unlike Jack.' She drew on the cigar again. 'Did he tell you that I asked him to make you come here?'

'No.'

'I did. Aren't you curious why?'

He leaned against the frame of the lattice. 'I'm curious, yes.'

'Thank God for that! I was beginning to think there wasn't a human feeling in your body.' Her voice was harsh. Sharpe wondered what game she was playing. He watched as she tossed the cigar onto the flagstones of the balcony and, as it landed, it showered sparks like a musket pan fired at night. 'Why do you think, Captain?'

'I don't know why I'm here, Ma'am.'

'Oh!' Her voice was mocking now. 'You find me on my own, ignoring all my guests, not to mention the proprieties, and there's a table set with wine, and you think nothing?'

Sharpe did not like being toyed with. 'I'm only a humble soldier, Ma'am, unused to the ways of my betters.'

She laughed, and her face suddenly softened. 'You said that with such delicious arrogance. Do I make you uncomfortable?'

'If it pleases you to, yes.'

She nodded. 'It pleases me. So tell me what Jack Spears whispered to you?' The inflection of command was back in her voice, as if she talked to her postilion.

Sharpe was tired of her games. He let his own voice be as harsh as hers. 'That you had low tastes, Ma'am.'

She went very still and tense. She was leaning forward on the bench, her hands gripping its edge, and Sharpe wondered if she was about to shout for her servants and have him thrown out. Then she leaned back, relaxed, and waved a hand at the elegant balcony. 'I thought I had rather high tastes. Poor Jack thinks everyone is like him.' Her voice had changed again, this time she had spoken with a soft sadness. She stood up and walked to the lattice, pushing open one of the doors. 'That business tonight was a shambles.'

The previous subject seemed to have been forgotten, as if it had never existed. Sharpe turned to look at her. 'Yes.'

'Why did the Peer order the attack? It seemed hopeless.'

Sharpe was tempted to say that she had wanted a battle, almost pleaded with Wellington for one, but this new, crisp woman was not someone he wanted to annoy, not at this moment. 'He's always impetuous at sieges. He likes to get them done.'

'Which means many deaths?' Her fingers were beating a swift tattoo on the frame of the lattice.

'Yes.'

'What happens now?' She was staring at the forts and Sharpe was staring at her profile. She was the loveliest thing he had ever seen.

'We'll have to dig trenches. We'll have to do everything properly.'

'Where?'

He shrugged. 'Probably in the ravine.'

'Show me.'

He went to her side, smelling her, feeling her closeness to him and he wondered if she could detect his trembling. He could see a silver comb holding up her piled hair and then he looked away and pointed at the gorge. 'Along the right hand side, Ma'am, close to the San Vincente.'

She turned her face to his, just inches away, and her eyes were violet in the moonlight that threw shadows beneath the high cheekbones. 'How long will that take?'

'It could be done in two days.'

She kept her face turned up and her eyes stayed on his eyes. He was aware of her body, of the bare shoulders, of dark shadows that promised softness.

She turned abruptly away and crossed to the table. 'You haven't eaten.'

'A little, Ma'am.'

'Come and sit. Pour me some wine.' There were partridges roasted whole, quails stuffed with meat and peppers, and small slices of fruit, that she said were quinces, that had been dipped in syrup and sugar. Sharpe took off his shako, propped his rifle against the wall, and sat. He did not touch the food. He poured her wine, moved the bottle to his own glass, and she stared at him, half smiling, and spoke in a detached, curious voice. 'Why didn't you kiss me just then?'

The bottle clinked dangerously against his glass. He set it down. 'I didn't want to offend you.'

She raised an eyebrow. 'A kiss is offensive?'

'If it's not wanted.'

'So a woman must always show that she wants to be kissed?'

Sharpe was feeling desperately uncomfortable, out of his place in a world he did not understand. He tried to shrug the topic away. 'I don't know.'

'You do. You think that a woman must always invite a man, yes? And that then leaves you guiltless.' Sharpe said nothing, and she laughed. 'I forgot. You're just a humble soldier and you don't understand the ways of your betters.'

Sharpe looked at the beauty across the table and he tried to tell himself that this was just another woman, and he a man, and that there was nothing more to it than that. He could behave as if she was any woman he had ever known, but he could not convince himself. This was a Marquesa related to Emperors, and he was Richard Sharpe, related to no one apart from his daughter. The difference was like a screen between them and he could not shift it. Others might, but not he. He shrugged inwardly. 'That's right, Ma'am. I don't understand.'

She picked another cigar from the box on the table and leaned over the candle in the niche to light it. She sat down and stared at the cigar glow as if she had never seen it before. Her voice was soft again. 'I'm sorry, Captain Sharpe. I don't mean to offend.' She looked up at him. 'How many people do understand? How many, do you think, live like this? One in a hundred thousand? I don't know.' She looked at the thick rugs, at the crystal on the table. 'You think I'm fortunate, don't you.' She smiled to herself. 'I am. Yet I speak five languages, Captain, and all I am expected to do with them is order the daily meals. I look in a mirror and I know just what you see. I open my doors and all those pretty staff-officers flood in and they flatter me, charm me, amuse me, and they all want something of me.' She smiled at him, and he smiled back. She shrugged. 'I know what they want. Then there's my servants. They want me to be lax, to be undemanding. They want to steal my food, my money. My Confessor wants me to live like a nun, to give to his charities, and my husband wants me to sail to South America. Everyone wants something. And now I want something.'

'What?'

She pulled on the cigar, looking at him through the smoke. 'I want you to tell me if there's going to be a battle.'

Sharpe laughed. He sipped the wine. He had been brought up to this balcony to tell her something that any officer, British or Spanish, German or Portuguese, could tell her? He looked at her and her face was serious, waiting, so he nodded. 'Yes. There has to be. We haven't come this far to do nothing, and I can't see Marmont giving up the west of Spain.'

She spoke with deliberation. 'So why didn't Wellington attack yesterday?'

He had almost forgotten that it was only yesterday that they had sat on the hilltop and watched the two armies. 'He wanted Marmont to attack him.'

'I know that. But he didn't, and the Peer outnumbered

him, so why didn't he attack?'

Sharpe reached forward and cut at a partridge. The skin was crisp and honeyed. He gestured with the slice of meat towards the lights of the spyholes. 'There are a dozen generals down there, three dozen staff officers, and you ask me? Why?'

'Because it pleases me!' Her voice was suddenly harsh. She paused to draw on the cigar. 'Why do you think? If I ask one of them they'll smile politely, become charming, and tell me, in so many words, not to worry my head about soldiering. So I'm asking you. Why didn't he attack?'

Sharpe leaned back, took a deep breath, and launched into his thoughts. 'Yesterday the French had their back to a plain. Marmont could have retreated endlessly, in good order, and the battle would have stopped by nightfall. There'd have been, oh . . .' he shrugged, 'say, five hundred dead on each side? If our cavalry was better there might have been more, but it would decide nothing. The armies would still have to fight again. Wellington doesn't want a series of small indecisive skirmishes. He wants to trap Marmont, he wants him in a place where there's no escape, or where he's wrong footed, and then he can crush him. Destroy him.'

She watched the sudden passion in Sharpe, the cruelty of his face as he imagined the battle.

'Go on.'

'There isn't any more. We take the forts and then we go after Marmont.'

'Do you like the French, Captain Sharpe?'

It struck him as a curious question, the wrong question. She meant, surely, did he dislike the French? He made a gesture of indecision. 'No.' He smiled. 'I don't dislike them. I don't have reason to dislike them.'

'Yet you fight them?'

'I'm a soldier.' It was not that simple. He was a soldier because there was nothing else for him to be. He had discovered all those years ago that he could do the job and do it well, and now he could not imagine another life.

Her eyes were curious, huge and curious. 'What do you fight for?'

He shook his head, not knowing what to tell her. If he said 'England' it would sound pompous, and Sharpe had a suspicion that if he had been born French then he would have fought for France with as much skill and ferocity as he served England. The Colours? Perhaps, because they were a soldier's pride, and pride is valuable to a soldier, but he supposed the real answer was that he fought for himself to stop himself sliding back into the nothingness where he began. He met her eyes. 'My friends.' It was as good an answer as he could think of.

'Friends?'

'They're more important on a battlefield.'

She nodded, then stood up and walked down the balcony trailing smoke behind her. 'What do you say to the charge that Wellington can't fight an attacking battle? Only a defensive battle?'

'Assaye.'

She turned. 'Where he crossed a river in the face of the enemy?'

'Yesterday you knew nothing about Assaye.'

'Yesterday I was in public.' The cigar glowed again.

'He can attack.' Sharpe was impressed by her intelligence, by her knowledge, but he was also mystified. There was something catlike about La Marquesa. She was quiet in her movements, beautiful, but she had claws, he knew, and now he knew she had the intelligence to use them skilfully. 'Believe me, Ma'am, he can attack.'

She nodded. 'I believe you. Thank you, Captain Sharpe, that's all I wanted to know.'

'All?'

She turned to the lattice and opened a window in it. 'I want to know if the French are coming back to Salamanca. I want to know if Wellington will fight to stop that happening.

You've told me he will. You weren't boasting, you weren't trying to impress me, you gave me what I wanted; a professional opinion. Thank you.'

Sharpe stood up, not sure if the visit was done and he was being dismissed. He walked towards her. 'Why did you want to know?'

'Does it matter?' She still stared at the fortresses.

'I'm curious.' He stopped behind her. 'Why?'

She looked back at the table. 'You forgot your musket.'

'Rifle. Why?'

She turned round to face him and gave him another of her hostile stares. 'How many men have you killed?'

'I don't know.'

'Truly?'

'Truly. I've been a soldier for nineteen years.'

'Do you get frightened?'

He smiled. 'Of course. All the time. It gets worse, not better.'

'Why's that?'

'I don't know. I sometimes think because the older you get, the more you have to live for.'

She laughed at that. 'Any woman will tell you otherwise.'

'No, not any woman. Some, maybe. Some men, too.' He gestured at the faraway sound of the party. 'Cavalry officers don't like getting old.'

'You're suddenly very wise for a humble soldier.' She was mocking him. She put the cigar to her mouth and smoke drifted between them.

She had still not answered his question and he still did not understand why he had been brought to this balcony where the leaves stirred in the night breeze. 'You could have asked a thousand people in this town the questions you've asked me, and got the same answers. Why me?'

'I told you.' She pointed with the cigar to his rifle. 'Now why don't you pick up the rifle and go?'

Sharpe said nothing. He did not move. Somewhere in the

town there were raised voices, drunken soldiers fighting in all probability, and a dog howled at the moon from another street, and he saw her eyes look at his cheek. 'What are those black stains?'

Sharpe was becoming used to her sudden questions that had no relevance to the previous conversation. She seemed to like to tease him, bring him almost to the point of anger, and then deflect him with some irrelevance. He brushed his right cheek. 'Powder stains, Ma'am. The gunpowder explodes in the rifle pan and throws them up.'

'Did you kill someone tonight?'

'No, not tonight.'

They were standing just two feet apart and Sharpe knew that either could have moved away. Yet they stayed still, challenging each other and he knew that she was challenging him to touch her and he was tempted suddenly, to break the rules. He was tempted to walk away, as Marmont had simply walked away from Wellington's army, but he could not do it. The full mouth, the eyes, the cheekbones, the curve of her neck, the shadows above the white lace-frilled dress had caught him. She frowned at him. 'What does it feel like? To kill a man?'

'Sometimes good, sometimes nothing, sometimes bad.'

'When is it bad?'

He shrugged. 'When it's unnecessary.' He shook his head, remembering the bad dreams. 'There was a man at Badajoz, a French artillery officer.'

She had expected more. She tipped her face to one side. 'Go on.'

'The fight was over. We'd won. I think he wanted to surrender.'

'And you killed him?'

'Yes.'

'How?'

He gestured at the big sword. 'With this.' It had not been that simple. He had hacked at the man, gouged him, disembowelled the corpse in his great rage until Harper had stopped him.

She half turned away from him and stared at the scarcely touched food on the table. 'Do you enjoy killing? I think you do.'

He could feel his heart beating in his chest as if it had expanded. It was thumping hollowly, sounding in his ear-drums, and he knew it as a compound of fear and excitement. He looked at her face, profiled against the broken moonlight, and the beauty was overpowering, unfair that one person could be so lovely and his hand, almost of its own volition, came slowly up, slowly, until his finger was under her chin and he turned the face towards him.

She gave him a calm, wide-eyed expression, then stepped away from him so his arm was left suspended in mid-air. He felt foolish. Her face was unfriendly. 'Do you enjoy killing?'

He had been made to touch her, so she could back away and make him feel foolish. She had brought him here for her small victory, and he knew defeat. He turned away from her, walked to his rifle, slung it on his shoulder, and started back down the balcony without a word. He did not look at her. He walked past her, smelling the tobacco smoke from her cigar.

'Colonel Leroux enjoys killing, Captain.'

For a second he almost kept on walking, but the name of his enemy stopped him. He turned.

'What do you know of Leroux?'

She shrugged. 'I live in Salamanca. The French were in this house. Your job is to kill him, yes?'

Her voice was challenging again, impressing him with her knowledge, and again he had the feeling that he was involved in a game of which she only knew the rules. He thought of Leroux in the forts, of the cordon of men about the waste-land, of his own Company in their billets. He had a simple job and he was making it complicated.

'Good night, Ma'am. Thank you for the meal.'

'Captain?'

He kept walking. He went round the corner, past the lights of the spyholes, and he felt a freedom come on him. He would be true to Teresa, who loved him, and he quickened his pace towards the secret staircase.

'Captain!' She was running now, her bare feet slapping the rush mats. 'Captain!' Her hand pulled at his elbow. 'Why are you going?'

She had teased him earlier, mocked him for not kissing her, withdrawn when he had touched her. Now she held his arm, was pleading with him, her eyes searching his face for some reassurance. He hated her games.

'God damn you to hell, Ma'am.' He put his left arm about her back, half lifted her, and kissed her on the mouth. He crushed her, kissing her to hurt, and when he saw her eyes close, he dropped her. 'For God's sake! Do I enjoy killing? What am I? A bloody trophy for your rotten wall? I'm going to get drunk, Ma'am, in some flea-bitten hovel in this bloody town and I might take a whore with me. She won't ask me bloody questions. Good night!'

'No!' She held him again.

'What do you want? To save me money?' He was harsh, feeling his hurt. She was more beautiful than he could have imagined a woman to be.

'No.' She shook her head. 'I want you, Captain, to save me from Colonel Leroux.' She said it almost bitterly and then, as if ashamed of the kiss, she turned and walked away from him.

'You what?'

She went on walking, back to the corner and onto the lighted side of the balcony. Once again she had surprised him, but this time he felt there was no game. He followed.

She was standing by the telescope, staring through the lattice, and Sharpe propped his rifle against the wall and went close behind her. 'Tell me why?'

'I'm frightened of him.' She stared away from him.

'Why?'

'He'll kill me.'

There was a silence and it seemed to Sharpe to be like a great abyss over which he was suspended on a single, fine blade-edge. One false move and the moment would be lost, finished, and it was as if he and she were alone high above the dark night and he saw the shadow between her shoulder blades, a dark shadow running down into the intricate lace of her dress, and it seemed to him that there was nothing on this dark earth so mysterious, so frightening, or as fragile as a beautiful woman. 'He'll kill you?'

'Yes.'

He put his right hand up, slowly, and put his long finger against her shoulder blade, a touch so gentle that it could have been a strand of her golden hair. He slid the finger down her warm, dry skin and she did not move.

'Why will he kill you?'

His fingertip explored the ridges of her spine. Still she did not move and he let his other fingers down, then pushed them slowly up towards her neck. She was very still.

'You've stopped calling me "Ma'am".'

'Why will he kill you, Ma'am?'

His fingers were on the nape of her neck where they could feel the wisps of hair that had escaped from the silver combs. He moved his hand right, very slowly, letting his fingers trace and stroke the curve of her long neck. She began to turn and his hand, as if frightened of breaking something very fragile, leaped an inch from her skin. She stopped, waited till she was touched again, and turned to face him.

'Do your friends call you Dick?'

He smiled. 'Not for many years.' His arm was tense from the effort of holding it still, hovering on her skin, and he waited for her to speak again, knowing that she had suddenly asked an irrelevant question because she was thinking. She seemed oblivious of his hand, but he knew she was not, and his heart still thumped inside him, and the moment was still there. Her eyes flicked between his.

'I'm frightened of Leroux.' She said it flatly.

He let the palm of his hand drop onto the curve of her neck. Still she seemed to take no notice. His fingers curled onto her back. 'Why?'

She gestured at the balcony. 'You know what this is?'

He shrugged. 'A balcony.'

For a few seconds she said nothing. His hand was feather-light on her neck and he could see the shadows move on her skin as she breathed. He could hear the beat of his heart. She licked her lips. 'A balcony, but a special kind of balcony. You can see a long way from here, and it's built so you can do that.' Her eyes, trusting and serious, were on his. She was speaking simply, as if to a child, so that he would understand her. It was, Sharpe thought, with his hand still on her neck, yet another face of this remarkable woman who changed like lake water, but something in her tone told him that now she was not playing. If there was a true Marquesa, this was she. 'You can see the roads over the river, and that's why it was built. My husband's great-great-grandfather didn't want to spy only indoors. He liked to watch his wife when she rode out of the palace, so he built this balcony like a watch-tower. They're not unusual in Spain, and they have this lattice for a special reason. No one can see in, Mr. Sharpe, but we can see out. It's a special kind of balcony. In Spanish a balcony is "balcon", but this isn't a "balcon". Do you know what it is?'

Sharpe's hand was utterly still. He did not know the answer, but he could guess. The word almost stumbled as he spoke it, but he said it aloud. 'Mirador?'

She nodded. 'El Mirador. The watch-place.' She looked at his face. She could see a pulse throbbing in his cheek beside the sword scar. His eyes were dark. She raised an eyebrow as if in question. 'You know, don't you?'

He hardly dared speak, he hardly dared breathe. He moved his hand, sliding it gently onto her back so that his fingertips touched the skin of her spine. The wind stirred the leaves above them.

She frowned slightly. 'Do you know?'

'Yes, I know.'

She closed her eyes, seemed to sigh, and he pulled with his hand and she came, so easily, into his chest. Her hair was below his chin, her face cradled in his rough uniform, and her voice was small and pleading.

'No one must know, Richard, no one. Don't tell anyone that you know, not even the General! No one must know. Promise me?'

'I promise.' He held her close, the wonder of it in his head.

'I'm frightened.'

'Is that why you wanted me here?'

'Yes. But I didn't know if I could trust you.'

'You can trust me.'

She tipped her head up to his and he could see that her eyes were gleaming. 'I'm frightened of him, Richard. He does terrible things to people. I didn't know! I never knew it would be like this.'

'I know.' He leaned down and her face did not move. He kissed her and suddenly her arms were round him and she clung to him fiercely and kissed him fiercely as if she wanted to suck the strength from him into her own self. Sharpe held her, his arms round the slim body, and he thought of what his enemy would do to this perfect, lovely, golden woman, and he despised himself for distrusting her because he knew, now, that she was braver than he, that she had led her lonely life in the great Palacio, surrounded by enemies, and in danger, always, of a terrible death. El Mirador!

His hand pressed on her back and, through the lace, hanging in fringes, he felt the hooks of her dress, and he slipped his hand between the hooks, felt her skin, and then pressed the bottom hook between finger and thumb, the finger and thumb that were more used to the pressure of flint on mainspring, and the hook slid out of the loop, and he moved his hand up to the second, pressed again, it opened, and she dropped her face onto his chest, still clinging to him. He could not believe this was happening, that he, Richard

133

Sharpe, was on this mirador, this night, with this woman, and he moved his hand to the last hook, pressed it back through the loop and he could feel the metal scraping as it moved, and she seemed to stiffen in his arms. He froze.

She looked up at him and her eyes searched his face as though she needed some reassurance that this man could truly keep her from Leroux's long Kligenthal. She gave a small smile. 'Call me Helena.'

'Helena?' The hook snapped free, he moved his hand, and he sensed the wings of the dress fall away and he put his hand back, stroked, and it was pressed into the rich curve at the small of her back. Her skin was like silk.

Her smile went, all the harshness came back. 'Let go of me!' It was snapped like an order, her voice loud. 'Let go of me!'

He had been a fool! She had wanted protection, not this, and now he had offended her by imagining what was not to be, and he let go of her, bringing his hand back, and she stepped away from him. Her face changed again. She laughed at him, laughed at his confusion, and she had ordered him away so that she could stand free and let the dress, light as thistledown, rustle to the floor. She was naked beneath the dress and she stepped back to him over its folds. 'I'm sorry, Richard.'

He put his arms round her, her skin was pressed against his uniform, his sword belt, his ammunition pouch, and she clung to him and he stared at the dark bulk of the San Vincente and he swore that the enemy would never reach her, never, not while there was breath in his body or while his arm could lift the heavy sword whose hilt was cold on her flank. She hooked a leg round his, lifted herself up, and kissed him again and he forgot everything. The Company, the forts, Teresa; all were scoured away, whirled far off by this moment, by this promise, by this woman who fought her own lonely war against his enemies.

She lowered herself to the floor, took his hand, and her face was grave and innocent. 'Come.'

He followed, obedient, in the dark Salamantine night.

PART TWO

Wednesday, June 24th
to
Wednesday, July 8th
1812

CHAPTER 10

Sharpe found himself resenting the progress of the trench that was being dug in the ravine. He knew that once the excavation reached the midpoint between the San Vincente and San Cayetano forts then the second assault was imminent. The second assault could hardly fail. The ammunition supply to the heavy guns had been restored, cart after cart came across the San Marta ford and screeched into the city and each cart was loaded with the huge roundshot. The guns fired incessantly, grinding at the defences, and to make it worse for the French the gunners heated the shot to a red heat so that the balls lodged in the old timbers of the convents and started fires that the French tried desperately to control.

For four nights Sharpe watched the bombardment, each night from the mirador, and the red-hot shot seared in the darkness and crashed into the crumbling forts. The fires blazed, were damped down, then blazed again and only the small hours of the morning brought a respite for the defenders. Some nights it seemed to Sharpe as if no one could live through the battering of the forts. The shot streaked over the wasteland while, high overhead, the fuses of the howitzer shells spun and smoked then plunged down to explode in flowering dark flame and thunder. The crackle of the flames rivalled the cracks of the Riflemen, creeping nearer, and each morning showed more damage; more embrasures opened wide, their guns unseated, smashed, useless. Wellington was in a hurry. He wanted the forts taken so that he could march north in pursuit of Marmont.

When the forts fell Sharpe knew he would go north. The Light Company would rejoin the regiment and he would leave Salamanca, leave La Marquesa, leave El Mirador, and each moment, marked by the slow extension of the attacker's trench, was precious to him. He left the Palacio each morning, going out by the secret staircase that led into an alleyway beside the stables, and he went back each afternoon when the only disturbance of Salamanca's siesta was the sound of the gunners crumbling at the forts.

The Light Company were puzzled, Patrick Harper most of all, but Sharpe said nothing and they could only speculate where their Captain disappeared each day and night. On the first morning he came back to them he had bathed, his uniform had been cleaned, mended and pressed, but he offered no explanation. Each morning he exercised the Company, marching them into the countryside and going through the evolutions of skirmishing. He drove them hard, not wanting them to become soft because of their stay in this soft city. Each afternoon he released them to their freedom while he went, secretly and cautiously, to the small door in the stable alley. Behind the door the stairs led to the private, top floor where only La Marquesa's most trusted servants were allowed and where, almost to Sharpe's disbelief, he found himself deep in a passionate affair.

He had lost his fear of her. She was no longer La Marquesa, now she was El Mirador, and though she was still a flawless woman she was also a person to whom he listened avidly. She spoke of her life, talking bitterly of the death of her parents. 'They were not even French, but they took them. They killed them. The scum.' Her hatred of the revolution was total. Sharpe had worked out her age from the tales she told him. She had been ten when the mob came to take her parents, so now she was twenty eight, and in the years between she had studied the forces of a world that had

138

taken her parents' lives. She spoke to him of politics, of ambitions, and she showed him letters from Germany that spoke of Napoleon gathering a vast army that she said was destined for Russia. She had news too from across the Atlantic, news that spoke of an imminent American invasion of Canada, and Sharpe, sitting in the mirador, had the sense of watching a whole world drawn into a maelstrom of flame and shot like that which hammered, unceasing, below.

Above all Helena spoke of Leroux, of his famed savagery, and of the fear she had that he would escape. Sharpe smiled. 'He can't escape.'

'Why not?'

He had gestured at the wasteland. 'It's ringed, totally. No one can get through, not even a rat!'

That was his one certainty, that the Light troops which surrounded the beleaguered forts were too vigilant, too thick on the ground, for Leroux to slip past. Leroux, as Hogan had said, would try to escape in the chaos of the successful assault. Sharpe's problem would be to make sense of that chaos and to recognise the tall Frenchman.

Helena had shrugged. 'He'll disguise himself.'

'I know. But he can't hide his height, and he has a weakness.'

'A weakness?' She had been surprised.

'The sword.' Sharpe smiled, knowing he was right. 'He won't lose that sword, it's part of him. If I see a tall man with that sword then I won't care if he's dressed as a British General of Division. That's him.'

'You sound very sure.'

'I am.' He sipped at the cool, white wine and thought of the joy of owning that sword. The Kligenthal would be his, within a week, but with it would come the loss of this woman.

The loss would be secret, as it had to be, yet there were times when he wanted to shout his present joy from the rooftops, and times when it was hard to disguise. He walked towards the Company billets one dawn, crossing the great Plaza, and there was a shout from one of the upper balconies. 'Sharpe! You rogue! Stay there!'

Lord Spears waved at him, turned into the building and reappeared a moment later in one of the doorways of the arcade. He walked, yawning, into the dawn light and then stopped. 'By God, Richard! You look almost human! What have you done to yourself?'

'Just cleaned the uniform.'

'Just cleaned the uniform!' Lord Spears mimicked him, then prowled round the Rifleman, peering at him. 'You've been putting your boots under someone's bed, haven't you? Sweet Christ, Richard, you think I can't spot a sin at a thousand paces? Who is she?'

'No one.' Sharpe grinned in embarrassment.

'And you're damned cheerful for the early morning. Who is it?'

'I told you, no one. You're up early.'

'Up early? I haven't been to bloody bed. I've been at the bloody cards again. I've just lost the Irish lands to some boring man.'

'Truly?'

Spears laughed. 'Truly. It's not bloody funny, I know, but Christ!' He shrugged. 'Mother's going to be upset. Sorry, Mother.'

'Have you got anything left?'

'The dower house. Few acres in Hertfordshire. A horse. Sabre. The family name.' He laughed again, then linked his good arm into Sharpe's and led him across the Plaza. His voice was serious, pleading. 'Who have you been with? Someone. You weren't home last night and that frighteningly enormous Sergeant of yours didn't know where you were. Where were you?'

'Just out.'

'You think we Spears are foolish? That we don't know? That we can't be sympathetic to a fellow sinner?' He stopped, pulled his arm free, and clicked his fingers. 'Helena! You bastard! You've been with Helena!'

'Don't be so ridiculous!'

'Ridiculous? Nonsense. She never appeared at that party of hers, she was said to be ill, and she hasn't been seen since. Nor have you. Good God! You lucky bastard! Admit it!'

'It is not true.' Even to Sharpe it sounded lame.

'It is true.' Spears was grinning with delight. 'All right, if it ain't true, who were you with?'

'I've told you, no one.'

Spears took a deep breath and bellowed at the shuttered windows of the Plaza. 'Good morning Salamanca! I have an announcement to make!' He grinned at Sharpe. 'I'll tell them, Richard, unless you admit the truth to me.' He took another deep breath.

Sharpe interrupted him. 'Dolores.'

'Dolores?' Spears' grin grew wider.

'She's a cobbler's daughter. She likes Riflemen.'

Spears laughed. 'You don't say! Dolores, the cobbler's daughter? Are you going to introduce me?'

'She's shy.'

'Oh! Shy. How the hell did you meet her, then?'

'I helped her in the street.'

'Of course!' Spears pretended total belief. 'You were on your way to feed the stray dogs or help the orphans, right? And you just helped her. Dropped her cobbles, had she?'

'Don't mock. She's only got one leg. Some bastard sawed off the bottom two inches of her peg.'

'A one-legged cobbler's daughter? Saves her father a decent bit of money, no doubt. You're a liar, Richard Sharpe.'

'I swear it.'

Spears took a huge breath and bellowed again. 'Richard Sharpe has rogered Dolores! The cobbler's hopping daughter!' He roared with laughter at his own joke and bowed to some astonished labourers who were dismantling the barri-

141

cades that had been used for the previous day's bullfight. He linked his arm with Sharpe again and dropped his voice. 'How is La Marquesa?'

'How would I know? I haven't seen her since we were at San Christobal.'

'Richard! Richard! You're too clever for me. I wish you'd admit it, even if it isn't true, it would be a perfectly delicious scandal.'

'I can't see that stopping you spreading it.'

'True, but no one believes me!' Spears sighed, then suddenly became serious. 'Let me ask you one more question.'

'Go on.'

'Have you heard of "El Mirador"?'

'El Mirador?' In his surprise, Sharpe checked.

Spears stopped as well. 'You have, haven't you?'

'Only as a name.' Sharpe wished he had not betrayed his surprise.

'A name? What connection?'

Sharpe paused to think of an answer. It crossed his mind that this could be some kind of a test, arranged by La Marquesa, to see if he was really trustworthy. It brought home to him, as if he had forgotten, the total secrecy that had to surround her. He shrugged. 'No connection. Is he one of the Guerilla leaders?'

'Like El Empecinado?' Spears shook his head. 'No, he's not a Partisan, he's a spy here in Salamanca.'

'Ours or theirs?'

'Ours.' Spears bit his lip, then turned fiercely on Sharpe. 'Think! Try to remember! Where did you hear it?'

Sharpe was taken aback by the sudden passion, then had an inspiration. 'You remember Major Kearsey? I think he mentioned it, but I can't remember why. It was two years ago.'

Spears swore. Kearsey had been, like Lord Spears, an Exploring Officer, but he was dead, swept off the ramparts of Almeida when Sharpe blew up the magazine.

142

'How do you know about him?' Sharpe asked.

Spears shrugged. 'You hear rumours as an Exploring Officer.'

'Why is it so important now?'

'It's not, but I'd like to know.' He jerked the arm in its sling. 'When this is healed I'll be back to work and I'll need friends everywhere.'

Sharpe began walking again. 'Hardly in Salamanca. The French have gone.'

Spears matched Sharpe's stride. 'Only for the moment, Richard. We have to defeat Marmont first, otherwise we'll be scuttling back to Portugal with our tails between our legs.' He looked at Sharpe. 'If you hear anything, will you tell me?'

'About El Mirador?'

'Yes.'

'Why don't you ask Hogan?'

Spears yawned. 'Maybe I will, maybe I will.'

At midday Sharpe went to the main battery and watched the gunners heating the solid shot in their portable furnaces. The assault, he knew, had to be close, even the next day, and it would mark the end of his visits to the Palacio Casares. He wished the gunners were not so industrious. He watched them slaving at the bellows fixed to one end of the forge while other men shovelled the coal from the bunker at the far end. In the centre was the cast iron furnace, roaring in the noon heat, the flames escaping at the bottom of the casing, and he marvelled that men could work with that heat, under the sun. It took fifteen minutes to heat each eighteen pounder shot until the red glow had gone deep into the iron and the ball could be dragged from the crucible with long tongs and rolled carefully onto the metal cradle, carried by two men, that took the shot to the gun. The barrel was loaded with powder, then with a thick wad of soaking cloth that stopped the heated shot from igniting the charge. It was rammed home swiftly, the men eager to preserve the red-heat, and then the gun bellowed and the shot left the smallest, finest trace of smoke in its flat trajectory into the demolished French defences. Hardly an enemy gun replied now. The next assault, Sharpe knew, would meet small resistance. He wondered if Leroux was already dead, the body laid out with the others killed in the siege, and that thus these gunners would already have done Sharpe's work.

He found La Marquesa writing at a small desk in her dressing room. She smiled at him. 'How is it progressing?'

'Tomorrow.'

'For certain?'

'No.' He could hardly hide the regret in his voice, but he sensed that she shared it, and he wondered at that. 'The Peer will make the decision tomorrow, but he won't need to wait. It'll be tomorrow.'

She laid the pen down, stood up, and kissed him swiftly on the cheek. 'So tomorrow you'll take him?'

'Unless he's dead already.'

She walked onto the mirador and pushed open one of the lattice doors. The San Vincente showed two fires, pale in the strong sun, and the San Cayetano smoked where a fire had been extinguished by the defenders. She turned back to him. 'What will you do with him?'

'If he doesn't resist, then he's a prisoner.'

'Will you parole him?'

'No, not again. He'll be shackled. He broke parole. He won't be exchanged, he won't be treated well, he'll just be sent to England, to a prison, and he'll be held there until the war ends.' He shrugged. 'Who knows? Maybe he can be tried for murder because he killed men when he was on parole.'

'So tomorrow I'm safe?'

'Until they send another one to find you.'

She nodded. He was used to her now, to her gestures, to her sudden dazzling smiles, and he had forgotten the coquettish, teasing woman he had met at San Christobal. That was the public face, she told him, while he saw the private and he wondered if he would see her again, in the future, and he would see the public face surrounded by fawning officers and he would feel a terrible, keen jealousy. She smiled at him. 'What happens to you when it's done?'

'We'll join the army.'

'Tomorrow?'

'No. Sunday perhaps.' The day after tomorrow. 'We'll march north and bring Marmont to battle.'

'And then?'

'Who knows? Madrid perhaps.'

She smiled again. 'We have a house in Madrid.'

'A house?'

'It's very small. No more than sixty rooms.' She laughed at him. 'You'll be very welcome though, alas, it has no secret entrance.' It was unreal, Sharpe knew. They never talked of her husband, or of Teresa. They were secret lovers, Sharpe and a lady, and they would have to stay secret. They had been given these few days, these nights, but fate was going to take them apart; he to a battle, she to the secret war of letters and codes. They had this night, tomorrow's battle, and then, if they were lucky, just one more night, the last night, and then they were in fate's hands. She turned to look once more at the fortresses. 'Will you fight tomorrow?'

'Yes.'

'I can watch you.' She gestured at the telescope on its heavy tripod. 'I will watch you.'

'I'll try not to be tempted into anything rash because of that.'

She smiled. 'Don't be rash. I want you tomorrow.'

'I can bring you Leroux in chains.'

She laughed, a touch of sadness in the sound. 'Don't do that. Remember he may not know who El Mirador is, yet. He might guess, and then he might escape.'

'He won't escape.'

'No.' She reached out for his hand and led him into the shade of the Palacio. He lowered a wooden-slatted blind against the sunlight and turned to see her on the black-curtained bed. She looked beautiful, pale against the darkness, as fragile as alabaster. She smiled. 'You can take your boots off, Captain Sharpe. Siesta time.'

'Yes, Ma'am.'

Later that afternoon he held her as she slept and she seemed to jump each time the big guns sounded. He kissed her forehead, pushing back the golden hair from her skin, and she opened her eyes sleepily, pushed her body closer to his, and murmured to him. She was only half awake. 'I'll miss you, Richard, I'll miss you.'

He soothed her, as he would a child, and knew that he would miss her too, but fate was inexorable. Outside, beyond the blind, beyond the lattice, the guns hastened their fate, and they clung to each other as if the press of their bodies might be imprinted on their memories for ever.

CHAPTER 11

'Where the hell have you been?' Hogan was truculent, sweating in the heat.

'Here, sir.'

'I looked for you last night. Damn it, Richard! You could at least let people know where you are! Suppose it was important!'

'Was it, sir?'

'As it happens, no.' Hogan conceded it grudgingly. 'Patrick Harper said he'd heard you were with some cobbler's daughter. Doris or something, and that she didn't have any legs.'

'Yes, sir.'

Hogan opened his snuff box. 'Damn it, Richard, your marriage is your affair, but you're damned lucky to have Teresa.' He sniffed violently, to cover his feelings. Sharpe waited for the sneeze, it came, and Hogan shook his head. 'God's Blood! I won't say anything.'

'Nothing to say, sir.'

'I hope not, Richard, I hope not.' Hogan paused, listening to the sizzling sound as a red hot shot was rammed onto the soaked wadding. The gun fired, bellowing noise at the houses, drifting the bitter smoke back where the two officers talked. 'Have you heard from Teresa, Richard?'

'Not for a month, sir.'

'She's chasing Caffarelli's men. Ramon wrote me.' Ramon was her brother. 'Your child's fine and bonny, in Casatejada.'

'That's good, sir.' Sharpe was not certain whether Hogan was trying to make him feel guilty. Perhaps he should feel guilty, yet he did not. He and La Marquesa were so temporary, their loving doomed to be of such a short time, that somehow it did not affect his long term plans. And he could not feel guilty about protecting El Mirador. It was his job.

Hogan glanced at Sharpe's Company, paraded in the street, and grunted that they looked good. Sharpe agreed. 'The rest has suited them, sir.'

'You know what to do?'

'Yes, sir.'

Hogan wiped his forehead. The noonday sun was searing the city. He repeated his orders despite Sharpe's answer. 'Go behind the assault, Richard. And no one's to leave, understand? No one, unless you've seen their face, and when you've found the bastard, bring him to me. If I'm not here, I'll be at Headquarters.'

'Yes, sir.'

The Company filed into the new trench that led, in safety, down the gorge towards the Tormes. Overhead the shot still rumbled, still crashed into the fortresses, and the attacking troops were cheerful and confident. This time they could not fail. The San Cayetano had been so battered that one wall was virtually gone and that was the first fort which was to be attacked. It would be a daylight attack, hard on the echoes of the siege guns, and the troops were happy because the French guns were mostly silent. A Rifle Lieutenant was to lead the Forlorn Hope, but neither he nor his men wore the strained and hopeless look of other Forlorn Hopes. A Forlorn Hope expected to die. Their job was to draw the enemy's fire, to empty the defending guns before the main attack erupted into the breach. The volunteers grinned at Sharpe. They recognised him and envied the laurel wreath badge on his arm. 'Won't be like Badajoz, sir.'

'No, you'll be fine.'

Sharpe could see at the far end of the ravine the silver

waters of the Tormes sliding quietly towards the far off sea. His men had fished the waters in their long, restful afternoons and they would miss the trout. Sharpe saw Harper staring at the water. 'Sergeant?'

'Sir?'

'What's this I hear about Doris? Something you said to Major Hogan?'

'Doris, sir?' Harper looked innocent, then gauged that Sharpe was not upset. 'You mean Dolores, sir. I might have said something.'

'How did you hear about it?'

Harper pulled back the flint of his seven-barrelled gun. 'Me, sir? I think Lord Spears was looking for you one day. He might have mentioned it.' He grinned at Sharpe conspiratorially. 'Legless, I hear, sir.'

'You hear wrong. It's not true.'

'No, sir. Course not, sir.' Harper whistled tunelessly and stared up at the cloudless sky.

There was a stirring in the trench, groans as men got to their feet and fixed long bayonets onto muskets, and Sharpe realised that the cannonade had stopped. This was the moment of attack, yet it had none of the tension of the previous attack, when these same Battalions had been shredded by the French guns. Today it would be easy, instinct told them that, easy because the vicious heated shot from the great guns had turned the fortresses into hell for their garrisons. The Rifle Lieutenant drew his sabre, waved at his Forlorn Hope, and climbed the side of the trench. At the summit, with no fire coming from the enemy, he halted. He gestured his men down. 'Stop! Stop!'

'What the devil?' A Lieutenant Colonel pushed his way down the trench. His neck was constricted by a tight, leather stock, and his face was red and glistening in the heat. 'Go on, man!'

'They're surrendering, sir! A white flag!'

'Good God!' The Colonel clambered up the trench side

and stared at the San Cayetano, then at the San Vincente. 'Good God!'

The British troops in the trench jeered at the French and shouted insults. 'Fight, you buggers! Are you afraid?'

The Colonel bellowed at them. 'Quiet! Quiet!'

Only the San Cayetano showed a white flag, the other forts were silent, no defenders apparent in their casements. Sharpe wondered if this were a trick, some convoluted plot by Leroux to gain his freedom, but he could not understand it if it was. Whether they were defeated by bayonets, or simply surrendered, the French garrisons would still be at the mercy of their captors and Sharpe would still be able to search their ranks for the tall, cold-eyed man with the long Kligenthal sword. The Company settled down in the trench. Rumours worked their way up and down the excavation, that the French merely wanted to send out their wounded, then that the enemy wanted time to negotiate their surrender. Some of the men slept, snoring gently, and the quiet of the afternoon, without the gunfire, seemed remarkably peaceful to Sharpe. He looked to his left and could see, over the roofs, the dark lattice of the mirador. There was a square black hole that showed where La Marquesa would be watching through her telescope. He wanted this afternoon done, the prisoners paraded, and Leroux safely chained at Headquarters. Then he could go back to the small doorway, climb the stone stairway, and have the last Salamantine night in the Palacio Casares.

A French-speaking officer took a speaking trumpet onto the trench parapet and shouted at the San Cayetano. Rough translations were passed in the trench. The French wanted to get orders from the fortress commander in the San Vincente, but Wellington was denying them the chance. The British would attack in five minutes and the garrison had a choice. Fight or surrender. As if to reinforce the message the eighteen pounders fired a last volley and Sharpe heard flames roar and crackle behind him as the San Vincente caught fire again. The San Cayetano officer shouted at the British, the French-speaking British officer shouted back, and then another messenger came down the trench and shouted up at the man with the speaking trumpet. The order was plainly heard in the trench. The enemy had wasted enough time in argument. They were to remove the white flag because the assault was now coming. The command was passed on in French, the Lieutenant Colonel drew his sword, turned to the packed trench, and shouted for them to go.

They cheered. Their bayonets were fixed, they wanted revenge, and the men hurled themselves up the side of the ravine, ignoring the Forlorn Hope that was now just part of the main attack, and Sharpe went with them. No guns fired from the French embrasures. The San Vincente, when Sharpe turned to look at it, was blazing fiercely. The gunners in the biggest French fort were fighting the flames, not serving the guns, and the assault was untroubled by canister. The white flag had gone from the San Cayetano, withdrawn into the shattered defences, and in its place was a rank of French infantrymen. The enemy were filthy, smeared by smoke and dust, and they levelled their muskets at the attack. They glanced at each other, not certain if they had surrendered or not, but the sight of the attackers, swarming in loose order over the rubble, decided them. They fired.

It was a small volley, hardly effective, and it only served to wound a handful of men and goad the others on. There was a ragged cheer, the first redcoats were in the ditch that was half filled with fallen masonry, and then they climbed the crude breach towards the fort.

The French had no fight in them. The infantrymen threw down their muskets before the attackers reached them. They were ignored, shoved aside, and the troops poured into the convent's interior. The building still smoked, showing where the fires had been, and now it filled with cheering British, intent on loot, and Sharpe stopped at the glacis lip and looked behind him. Sergeant McGovern's squad were there, where they should be, and Sharpe cupped his hands. 'Stop anyone leaving! Understand!'

'Yes, sir!'

Sharpe grinned at Harper. 'Let's go hunting.' He drew his sword, wondering if this would be the last time he ever used this sword, and jumped into the ditch. The climb onto the defences was easy, thanks to the collapse of the convent wall into the ditch, and Sharpe ran up the stones, hoping against hope that Leroux would be in this first building. He could be in any of the three. The French had not been able to leave the forts, thanks to the ring of Light Companies, but there had been no way of stopping them moving between the buildings in the dark of night.

'God save Ireland!' Harper paused at the top. The San Cayetano resembled a charnel house whose corpses had been crushed and burned. The unwounded prisoners were gathering in the central courtyard, but they left on the ramparts, on firesteps, beside guns, a grisly remnant of the garrison. The eagerness of the attackers for revenge was checked by the horror. The redcoats were kneeling by the wounded, giving them water, and every soldier could imagine what life had been like, these last few burning hours, under the close bombardment of the guns. One man was close to the breach, on a stretcher where Sharpe presumed he had been laid so he could be taken swiftly to the hospital, and the screaming, horrid figure seemed to sum up the garrison's suffering. He was an artillery officer and the plain, blue uniform reminded Sharpe of the man he had killed at Badajoz. This man would not live long. His face was half masked in blood, a shapeless mass where one eye had been, and his belly appeared to have been torn open by a splinter of wood or shattering iron that had left his guts, blue-sheened between thick blood, open to the sky and flies. He heaved, he screamed, he shouted for help, and even the men who were used to suffering and sudden death found the agony unbearable and gave the horrid wound a wide berth. Between screams the man panted, moaned, and cried. Two French infantrymen, unwounded, squatted fearfully beside the officer. One held his hand. The other tried to contain the terrible blue-red wound that had smeared the uniform with blood where it had not been scorched with fire. Sharpe looked at the artillery officer. 'Be quicker to shoot him.'

'And a dozen others, sir.' Harper nodded at other men, some almost as badly wounded, some burned beyond a human face any more, and Sharpe climbed back to the breach top and shouted at McGovern. 'The wounded will come out! Let them up!'

Carts were already waiting at the trench head, beside the main battery, to take the French to the hospital. Sharpe checked them out, one by one, and then looked at the prisoners in the courtyard. Leroux was not there. Somehow Sharpe was not surprised. He expected Leroux to be in the main fort, the San Vincente, and he hurried as he began to search the San Cayetano for he knew that the assault on the other forts must begin soon. He raced up stairs inside the convent, throwing doors open onto empty rooms, coughing when he had to dash down a smoke filled corridor to explore rooms threatened by flame, but the fort was deserted. The French were prisoners, downstairs, and the only men in the upper rooms were British soldiers rifling the possessions of their erstwhile enemies. Even those men Sharpe looked at carefully for it was not beyond a possibility that Leroux would have disguised himself in British uniform, but Leroux was not there.

A shout came from below and Sharpe ran to the last room he had not searched. It was empty as the others, except for a telescope, mounted like La Marquesa's on a tripod, that a small Welsh soldier was struggling to lift. 'Leave it!'

The man looked offended. 'Sorry, sir.'

Sharpe could see the tripod marks on the wooden floor and he carefully aligned the telescope again on the old marks. He guessed that perhaps it had been used for receiving telegraph messages, when the French army had been close to the city, but he could not be sure. He peered through the glass, saw open sky, and tilted the tube downwards. The glass pointed through a tiny window. Anyone using it from the tripod marks could see scarce a thing through that tiny space. A patch of sky and then, the glass steadied, and Sharpe saw the dark square, and saw the circle of light that he knew was the brass-bound lens of La Marquesa's glass. He grinned. Someone had tried to watch La Marquesa on her mirador and he could not blame them, for it must have been hell to be pinned in this tiny fort and an officer had set up the glass, far enough back so that it would not reflect any betraying light, and he must have prayed and hoped for a glimpse of that perfect beauty to relieve the perfect hell that sliced apart a man's intestines. He stayed for a moment, hoping he would see her, but there was no sign of her. He remembered the shout from below and gestured at the glass. 'You can have it, soldier.'

He ran down the stairs, joining Harper who had searched the rooms again, and the shout proved to be the discovery of the French magazine. The building smouldered and, beneath their feet, the powder barrels waited that could blow them into fine scraps. A British officer had organised a chain of men and the barrels were heaved up, passed through the court-yard, to be piled in the ditch. Sharpe pushed past the chain, ignoring their protests, but Leroux was not in the cellar.

The other two forts had still not surrendered, yet the British walked quite openly and unconcerned in the space outside the San Cayetano. No French guns fired, no canister riddled the air. Sergeant Huckfield had brought his squad to join McGovern's, and the two Sergeants saluted as Sharpe came out of the breach. McGovern shook his head dourly. 'No sign of him, sir?'

'No.' Sharpe sheathed his sword. Lieutenant Price was waiting in the trench, ready to go to the San Vincente, and Sharpe thought of the long afternoon ahead. He wanted to get back to La Marquesa, he wanted this chore done, and he began to resent the long search in the heat. He looked at Huckfield. 'Take your men to La Merced. Wait for me there.' He did not expect Leroux to be in the smallest fort, but it had to be covered. He switched to McGovern. 'Let four of your men stay here, just in case he's hiding. The rest to the big one.'

'Sir. I'd be happier with six.'

'Six it is.' He thought what might happen if Leroux had found a hiding place in the smoking ruins. 'And you stay, too, Mac.'

'Sir.' McGovern nodded gravely.

God, but it was hot. Sharpe took off his shako and wiped his face. His jacket was undone, swinging free. He clambered down the ravine side, staring up at the San Vincente, and as he watched he saw the Portuguese troops begin their climb towards the big, blazing fortress. Let the bastards surrender quickly, he thought, and he hurried, the sweat soaking the new, fine linen shirt that La Marquesa had given him. He would have to bathe in the Palacio, he thought, and he remembered the unbelievable luxury of the huge tub, filled by a relay of servants, and the strange sensation of being immersed in hot water. He smiled at the memory and Patrick Harper wondered what his Captain was thinking.

The Portuguese were not resisted. The small figures jumped into the ditch, clambered through the cannon emplacements, and no muskets fired. The French had had enough. Sharpe looked at his squads. 'Come on!'

The air was stifling. Close to the big fort, it was even hotter, fuelled by the fires that blazed unchecked in the building. Some Frenchmen, ignored by the Portuguese, were already leaping from the defences and Price led his squad to cut off their flight. Sharpe hurried up the crude glacis, the heat burning at him, and then he led Harper's squad into the big defences to find the same picture they had seen before. The wounded needed attention, the living surrendered, the dead stank in the collapsed stones and timber. The Portuguese were already pulling the powder barrels from the cellars, rolling the kegs to safety, while others herded prisoners and looted French packs. There was no sign of Leroux. Three huge Frenchmen were pulled out of the ranks and Sharpe stared at them, trying to fit their faces to his mental image, but none was Leroux. One had a hare lip, and he could not imagine the Imperial Guard Colonel faking that disfigurement, one was too old, and the third seemed some kind of simpleton who grinned with feeble good-will at the Rifle Officer. It was not Leroux. Sharpe looked at the burning buildings, then at Harper. 'We'll have to search.'

They searched. They looked in every room that could be entered and tried to look even in those where no human could stay alive. Once Sharpe teetered on the brink of a broken floor, staring hopelessly into a roaring fire that swept upwards, white hot, and he heard the fall of great timbers and knew that no man could live in that. He put a hand on his ammunition pouch and the leather was almost too hot to touch and he went back, suddenly fearing that the rifle ammunition would explode, and he felt the first stirrings of doubt, of frustration. He was soaked with sweat, begrimed, and still the sun burned down on the furnace building, the prisoners milled outside and Sharpe cursed Leroux.

Price panted in the heat. 'I haven't seen him, sir.'

Sharpe pointed at a separate group. 'Who are they?'

'Wounded, sir.'

He looked at the wounded. He even made one man take off a dirty bandage from his head, and wished he had not. The man was terribly burned and he was not Leroux. Sharpe looked at the scene on the glacis. 'How many prisoners?'

'Four hundred here, sir. At least.'

'Search them again!' They marched up the ranks, stopping at each man, and the French prisoners looked at them dully. Some were tall, and those were pushed out of the ranks into a separate group, but it was hopeless. Some had no teeth, others were the wrong age, some were similar but not Leroux.

'Patrick!'

'Sir?'

'Find that officer who spoke French. Ask him to see me.'

The officer came and gladly helped. He asked prisoners if they knew of the tall Colonel Leroux or else of Captain Delmas, and most shrugged, but one or two volunteered help and said they remembered a Captain Delmas who had fought so well at Austerlitz, and one remembered a Leroux who had been in the town guard at Pau, and the sun smashed down, bounced off the broken stones, and the sweat trickled into Sharpe's eyes, stinging them, and it was as if Leroux had vanished from the face of the earth.

'Sir?' Harper pointed across the ravine. 'The little one's surrendered.'

They crossed the ravine again and, now that the third fort had surrendered, the wounded who had been taken from the San Cayetano and the San Vincente were allowed up the trench. Sharpe wondered how many had died as they waited in the burning sun. The artillery officer whose guts had been laid open by a flying splinter still lived, his face with the bloody mess where there had been an eye rocked back and forth, and Sharpe saw Harper touch his crucifix as the Sergeant watched the stretcher being carried towards the waiting carts. There but for the grace of God, thought Sharpe, and then they climbed up the ravine and headed towards La Merced.

Leroux was not there. Leroux was in none of the forts and Sharpe and Harper walked the wide, burning wasteland again to the San Vincente and once again they searched the prisoners on the glacis. Leroux was not there. Pray as Sharpe might, he could not make one face fit the French Colonel. He looked at the French-speaking officer in frustration. 'Someone must know!'

The Lieutenant Colonel was impatient. He wanted the prisoners moved, to release his men from guarding them in the afternoon heat, but Sharpe stubbornly went down the ranks again. He wiped the sweat from his eyes, searched the faces, but he knew it was no good. He nodded reluctantly to the Colonel. 'I'm through, sir.'

He was not through. He searched the burning convent again, went down into the coolness of the huge cellar that had been the magazine, but there were no signs of the fugitive. It was Harper who finally admitted what Sharpe did not want to admit. 'He's not here, sir.'

'No.' But he would not give up. If Leroux had escaped, and for the life of him he could not see how, then La Marquesa was in danger. It might take the Frenchman days, or weeks, or just hours before he made his move and Sharpe thought of her body in that man's hands and he hacked with his sword at an open cupboard as if it might conceal a false compartment. He let the rage subside. 'Search the dead.' It was quite possible that Leroux was among the dead, but Sharpe suspected the tall, clever Colonel would not have exposed himself to the artillery fire. Yet Sharpe must search the corpses.

The dead stank. Some had been dead for two days, unburied in the heat, and Sharpe raked the bodies off the pile and, the nearer the bottom he reached, the more he knew that Leroux was not here. He went out again, onto the glacis, and stared at the other two forts. La Merced was empty, its garrison marching away into captivity, and only McGovern with his small picquet stood guard on the San Cayetano. Sharpe looked at Harper's squad. They were tired, worn out, and he gestured at them to sit down. He took off his jacket and gave it to Lieutenant Price. 'I'm going for one more look at the San Cayetano.'

'Yes, sir.' Price was coated with sweat-streaked dust.

Harper came with Sharpe, but no one else, and for the fourth time they climbed the ravine and the two tall Riflemen walked slowly towards the first fort to fall. Sergeant McGovern had seen nothing. His men had searched the building again, but he swore it was empty, and Sharpe nodded. 'Go back to Lieutenant Price, Mac. Send a man to bring Sergeant Huckfield back.'

La Merced had received very little of the bombardment and there were no corpses in the smallest fort, so the only hope left was the dead in the San Cayetano. Sharpe and Harper went slowly into the ghastly courtyard and looked at the grisly pile. There was nothing for it but to search.

The corpses lolled unnaturally after they had been raked down from the stack. Sharpe looked at each face, and each was a stranger, and then he went up to one of the less damaged parapets and stared with Harper across the river. The clean, green hills were pale in the sunlight. He looked at his hands, stained with the dirt and blood of death, and swore long and foully.

Harper offered his canteen and said nothing. He knew what Sharpe was thinking; that the Light Company had pulled an easy duty, a detachment that had given them days by the river and nights in wine shops, and in return they had failed in the one thing they had been asked to do.

Huckfield's men filed beneath the parapet and the Sergeant looked up at Sharpe and offered help. Sharpe shook his head. 'There's nothing here! Go on. We'll join you in a minute.'

'What now, sir?' Harper sat on the parapet.

'I don't know.' He glanced at the small fort, La Merced, and wondered if he should search it again, but he knew it was empty. He could wait for the fires to burn down in the San Vincente and then rake through the ashes looking for a body. By God! He would do it! And he would pull the damned convents down, stone by bloody stone, until he had found the Frenchman. His new shirt was stained and stinking, glued to his chest with sweat. He thought of La Marquesa, of the coolness of her rooms, of the bath that waited for him and the chilled wine on the mirador. He shook his head. 'He can't have escaped. He can't!'

'He did before.' Harper offered cold comfort.

Sharpe thought of La Marquesa's silk smooth skin ripped from her body, inch by inch, and the thought of Leroux torturing her made him shut his eyes.

Harper swilled his mouth with water and spat it into the ditch. 'We can search again, sir.'

'No, Patrick. It's no damned good.' He stood up and walked wearily down the steps into the courtyard. He hated to admit failure, but he did not think another search would reveal anything. He stopped, waiting for Harper, and stared at a French corpse that had been disembowelled. The man was naked, his wound had laid him open so that his spine was visible through his stomach, but Sharpe was not seeing anything. He was just staring, his thoughts hammering at him. Harper saw the stare and looked himself at the corpse.

'Funny, that.'

'What?' Sharpe was startled from his reverie.

Harper nodded at the corpse. 'That other poor bugger was gutted, just like that. Except the other one lived.'

'Yes.' Sharpe shrugged. 'Funny things, wounds. Remember Major Collett? Not a mark on him. Other poor bastards live with half their stuffing taken out.' He was making conversation, trying to hide his disappointment. He moved away, but Harper still stared at the corpse. 'You coming? Patrick?'

Harper crouched and batted at the flies with a hand. 'Sir?' His voice was worried. 'Would you say this one had his full kit, sir? I know he's a bloody mess, so he is, but . . .'

'Oh God in heaven! Christ!' Sharpe knew that the corpse's guts could have been lost in an explosion, they could have been tossed to the stray dogs that scavenged the wasteland at night, or they could have been scooped out to make the perfect disguise. 'Oh Christ!'

They began running.

CHAPTER 12

They ran, forcing themselves over the stones, stumbling in the debris of the ruined houses, taking the shortest route to the city. The cordon of Light troops, still in place, watched in astonishment as the two huge men, one in a stained and damp shirt and wielding a huge blade, the other carrying a seven-barrelled gun, charged at them. A man levelled a musket and gave an uncertain challenge.

'Out the bloody way!' Sharpe's bellow convinced the picquets that the two were British.

Sharpe led the way into the alleyway from which the abortive attack, four days before, had been launched. Civilians were crammed in the streets, hoping for a glimpse of the excitement in the wasteland, but they parted hurriedly before the armed men. Thank God, Sharpe thought, it was downhill to the Irish College where the wounded were taken.

Yet the man who must, surely, have piled the guts of another man onto his stomach, who had smeared himself in blood and soot, who had sought his disguise in a wound so terrible that no one would think he could survive or think he was worth troubling over, had such a lead on them. Thirty minutes, forty even, and Sharpe felt a blind rage at his own stupidity. Trust nothing, and trust no one! Search everyone, and yet the sight of the disembowelled artillery officer had made him turn away in horror and pity. It had been the first officer he had seen inside the first fort and now he was convinced it had to be Leroux. Who could now be free inside the city.

They turned left, their breath coming in humid gasps, and Sharpe saw that they still had a chance. It was not much, but it drove him on. The crowds were holding up the wagons carrying the wounded, jeering at the enemy, and British troops were holding the people back with muskets. Sharpe pushed and forced his way to the nearest cart and shouted up at the driver. 'Is this the first batch?'

'No, mate. Half a dozen have gone already. Gawd knows 'ow they'll get through.'

The driver had mistaken Sharpe for a private. He had seen the rifle slung on the shoulder and, without his jacket or sash, Sharpe had no badge of rank except the sword. He looked for Harper. 'Come on!'

He bellowed at the crowd, pushed at them, and they broke free of the crush around the wounded and ran on, down the hill, and ahead of them Sharpe could see the other carts standing empty at the steps of the College. Sentries barred the door, ignoring the pleas of civilians who seemed to want to get in to finish off what the British bombardment had begun. Apart from the civilians, young men mostly with long, slim knives, there was no excitement at the college. No shouts, no chase, no sign that a wounded man had suddenly sprung to full life and hacked his way to a dubious freedom among the vengeful Salamantine streets.

Sharpe took the steps two at a time and pushed into the crowd that filled the small terrace in front of the great gate. A sentry challenged him, saw the sword and rifle, and made a space for the two men to push through. They hammered on the gate.

Harper looked blown. He shook his head, pounded the studded wood again, and looked at Sharpe. 'I hope you're bloody right, sir.' The Company had been left at the San Vincente, ignorant of where their Captain and senior Sergeant had gone.

Sharpe hammered with the steel guard of his sword. 'Open up!'

A wicket door opened in the gate and a face peered out. 'Who is it?'

Sharpe did not answer. He pushed through, stooping through the small entrance, and a courtyard opened up before him. It would have been a beautiful place, a haven of peace in a peaceful city, a well surrounded by a lawn which, in turn, was surrounded by two storeys of carved cloisters. Today, though, it was the collecting place for the dying, the courtyard filled with the first French wounded who had come to join the men they had wounded four nights before. The courtyard was choked with bleeding men, with order-lies, and Sharpe paused at the archway and looked desperately for the artillery officer who had seemed so terribly wounded.

'What do you want?' A truculent Sergeant came from the gate lodge. 'Who are you?'

'French officer, wounded. Where is he?' Sharpe's tone told the Sergeant he was speaking to an officer.

The Sergeant shrugged. 'Surgeons are straight ahead, sir, across the yard. Officers' wards upstairs. What does he look like?'

'Had his lights hanging out. On a stretcher.'

'Try the surgeons, sir.'

Sharpe glanced at the top cloister. It was in deep shadow, but he could see two or three bored British guards, muskets slung, and doubtless there were wounded officer prisoners in the shadows. He looked at Harper with his huge gun. 'Try upstairs, Patrick. And be careful. Get one of those guards to help you.'

Harper grinned and hefted the huge gun. 'I don't think your man will try anything stupid.' He crossed to one of the curved staircases that led to the officers' wards. Sharpe threaded his way through the wounded towards the sound of screams that indicated where the surgeons worked.

Awnings had been rigged over patches of the lawn to keep the sun from roasting the wounded. A constant trickle of men drew water from the well, ladling from the bucket that was suspended by an intricate iron cage. Sharpe zig-zagged, looking at the men on stretchers, searching the faces of men in the deeper shadow of the cloisters, and going to the unshaded patch of lawn where the first dead, failures from the scalpel or men who died before they could reach the blood-stained table, had been laid out. His instinct told him that Leroux was in this place, yet he could not be sure, and he half expected to find the wounded artillery officer lying in the courtyard. Sharpe could not find him and turned, instead, to the surgeons' rooms.

Colonel Leroux waited on the upper cloister. He needed now only two things, a horse and a long plain cloak to hide the charnel house appearance of his uniform, and both were due to be waiting for him at three o'clock in the alley behind the Irish College. He wished he had asked for them earlier, but he had never suspected that the surrender negotiations would be cut short by the British, and now he peered through the stone pillars of the balustrade and recognised the tall figure of the dark-haired Rifle Officer. Sharpe had no jacket, yet still he was easily identified because of the long sword and the slung rifle. Leroux had heard a clock in the town strike the half hour, he guessed it was now ten minutes short of the hour, and he would have to risk that the horse and cloak had been brought early. So far, at least, things had worked well. It had been a nuisance to be trapped in the forts instead of being with one of his agents in the city, but the escape had been planned with meticulous care, and it had worked thus far. He had been one of the first to enter the hospital and the surgeon waiting in the courtyard had hardly glanced at him. The man had gestured upstairs because it was obvious that no surgeon could save the desperately wounded artillery officer. He could be left to die in the shade of the upper cloister where the officers' wards waited. Leroux watched Sharpe go into the surgeons' rooms and smiled to himself; he had a few moments.

He was uncomfortable. He had piled a dead man's intestines on his stomach and had tucked the entrails into the waistband of the borrowed uniform so that the gleaming, wet, jellied mass would stay in place. He had splashed himself with gore, soaked his blond hair in blood until it was matted and stiff, and then put an unrecognisable lump of flesh over his left eye. He had burned patches of the uniform. The Kligenthal was beneath him, unsheathed, and he prayed that Sharpe would be delayed in the surgeons' rooms. Every minute now was precious. Then he heard the friendly challenge from the sentry at the curved stair's head. 'Sarge, can I help you?'

Leroux heard the newcomer silence the sentry and his instinct told him that this was danger so he moaned, rolled onto his side, and let the guts slide off him. The flies protested. He dug with his hand and twitched the cold entrails free, then reached up and wiped his left eye. It seemed glued shut and he had to spit on his hand, rub again, and then he could see properly. It was time to move.

It all happened terribly quickly. One moment a man seemed to be dying, moaning feebly, and the next he was rising to his feet and in his hand was a long grey blade. He was like something from the pit, something that had rolled and nuzzled and lapped in blood, and he freed the stiffness from his arm with a scythe of the sword and loosed his voice with a great war cry. In the Name of the Emperor!

Harper was looking the other way. He heard the shout, he turned, and the sentry was between him and the demonic figure. Harper shouted at the man to move, tried to force him aside with the squat barrels of the big gun, but the sentry lunged feebly with his bayonet at the ghastly figure and the Kligenthal drove it aside and came back to carve a line diagonally up the sentry's face. The man screamed, fell backwards, and he fell on the seven barrelled gun and the impact made Harper's finger pull on the trigger and the huge gun fired. The bullets hammered uselessly on the flagstones, ricocheted into the balustrade, and the recoil of the huge gun, a recoil that could throw a man clear from the fighting top of a battleship, slewed Harper round and backwards.

The Sergeant fought for balance. There was only the staircase behind him and he stood at the very top at the inside of the curve where the steps were steepest. He was falling and his right hand flailed for support and the sentry, screaming because he could not see, fell at Harper's feet and scrambled for safety and his arm went to the back of the huge Sergeant's ankles and Harper was falling.

Harper's hand caught the balustrade, he heaved on it with all his huge strength, and then he saw the French officer coming for him and the sword was reaching for Harper's chest and the blade seemed to speed up as the Frenchman's strength went into the lunge.

The blade caught him. The point slammed between the tiny carved thighs on Harper's crucifix. He let go of the balustrade, shouting in alarm and warning, and his legs were trapped by the sentry, and he lashed uselessly with his arm for balance and then he fell away from the blade. He toppled.

His head hit the eighth stair down. The sound of it could be heard throughout the courtyard and it was a dull crack. The head seemed to bounce up, light brown hair flapping, the blood already dripping, and then the head slumped down again and Harper's body slipped until it was caught on the stair's bend and he lay, spreadeagled and bloody, head downwards, on the scrubbed stone stairway.

Leroux turned away and shouted at the French wounded to stay out of his way. He ran to his left, the shortest route to the rear of the college, and two sentries, startled, came together and levelled their muskets. One knelt, pulling back his flint, and Leroux checked. They were too far away for him to charge. The one man fired and the ball went harmlessly past the Frenchman, but the other held his fire, waited, and Leroux turned away. He would go the long way round, hoping no sentries waited, and the sword felt marvellous in his hand, like a live thing, and he laughed at the pleasure of it.

Sharpe was inside the surgeons' rooms when he heard the bellowing echo of the seven-barrelled gun and he turned and was running, leaping the bodies laid out on the grass, and he saw Harper fall, saw the huge body bounce on the steps, and Sharpe was shouting with an inchoate anger that cleared the hospital orderlies from his path. He took the curved stairway three steps at a time and he jumped Harper's body from which blood trickled to puddle on the next step down. The Sergeant was silent and still.

Sharpe reached the head of the stairs as Leroux came back past the place where he had lunged at Harper. Sharpe felt an immense anger. He did not know if Harper was alive or dead, but he knew he was hurt, and Harper was a man who would have given his life for Sharpe, a friend, and Sharpe now faced the man who had wounded Harper. The Rifle Captain came up the last curved steps, his face terrifying in its rage, and his long sword sounded in the air as he swept it backhanded at the Frenchman and Leroux parried. Leroux's left hand was grasping his right wrist and all his own strength was in the Kligenthal, and the blades clashed.

Sharpe felt the blow of steel on steel like a sledgehammer strike numbing his right arm. He was rigid with the effort of the blow and the recoil of the blades checked his rush, threatened to topple him backwards, but Leroux too had been stopped, jarred by the two swords meeting, and the French Colonel was astonished at the force of the attack, by the strength that had come at him and still threatened him.

The Kligenthal lunged while the echo of the first clangorous strike still came back from the far side of the courtyard. Sharpe parried the lunge, point downwards, and then turned his own heavy blade with such speed that Leroux jumped back and the tip of Sharpe's blade missed the Frenchman's face by less than a half inch. Again, and again, and Sharpe felt the surge of joy because he had the speed of this man, and the strength, and Leroux was parrying desperately, going backwards, and the Kligenthal could only block the attacks of the old cavalry sword. Then Leroux's back heel touched stone, he was against the wall, and there was no escape from Sharpe. The Frenchman glanced to his right, saw the way he had to go, and then he saw Sharpe's face screwed up with the effort of one last hacking swing that would cut him in half. He brought up the Kligenthal, swinging too, a cut that owed nothing to the science of fencing, just a killing swing in his last defence, and the blades sang in the air, the Kligenthal went past Sharpe and the Rifleman's swing was parried.

The blades met, edge to edge, and again the shock jarred into their arms, shook their bodies, and the sound of it was not a clang, no harsh music, and Sharpe was falling because the sound was dull and his blade, that had been on every battlefield for four years, broke on the impact of the beautiful, silken, grey steel of the Kligenthal. Sharpe felt it go, felt the jarring shock turn into a lurching fall, and he saw the top half of his blade break and tumble as if the steel was no more than baked sugar. It broke, grey and splintered, and the tip fell, harsh onto the flagstones, and Sharpe was left with a handle and a jagged vicious stump. He hit the stones, rolled towards Leroux and stabbed upwards with the stump at the Frenchman's groin, but Leroux laughed in his relief, stepped away, and brought up his sword, point downwards, for the stabbing, killing blow.

The sentry who had not fired his gun pounded around the corner of the cloister, elbowed aside two wounded French officers, and shouted at the blood-stained man whose sword was poised. The sentry jerked up his musket, Leroux saw it, and the Frenchman abandoned Sharpe and ran. The Rifleman hurled the useless sword fragment, missed, and rolled to his feet with his rifle coming off his shoulder.

'Hey!' The sentry's protest was lost as his musket fired. He jerked the barrel up as the flint sparked and he just managed to avoid Sharpe who had erupted into his line of fire. The ball thumped past Sharpe, the pressure of it on his cheek, past Leroux, and flattened itself against the far wall. Leroux was running, no enemies before him, and the Kligenthal was long in his hand.

Sharpe's arm was slow, numbed by the blade-shock, and he fumbled with the rifle flint. Leroux had reached a door at the far end and he tugged at the handle, then beat at the door with his fist. It stayed shut. He was trapped again.

Sharpe stood up. The flint came back and the feeling of the heavy spring compressing was satisfying. It clicked into place, the rifle was ready, and he walked towards Leroux who still hammered at the door just twenty paces from Sharpe. Sharpe jerked with the barrel. 'Still!'

The Frenchman reached down to his boot and as he did the door opened. Sharpe saw the hand come up and in it was a pistol, the barrel octagonal, and he knew Leroux had a duelling pistol. He shouted, began running, and then the Irish priest, Curtis, was standing in the doorway and Leroux pushed the old man aside, went through, and Sharpe shouted at the old man to get out of the way and the door was closing and Sharpe had no time to aim, but just pulled the trigger and the Rifle bullet drove a long splinter from the door's edge. He had missed.

Leroux pulled the door open again and his right hand came up slowly, the pistol barrel foreshortened, and then he smiled, lowered the hand so that the pistol was aimed low at Sharpe and the Rifleman saw the flame in the pan, threw himself sideways, saw the smoke blossom in front of Leroux, and he felt a great blow shudder on his body. Then it seemed as if everything was happening at only half the speed of ordained time. The door closed on his enemy. Sharpe was still running, the rifle falling, clattering, bouncing, and the pain was filling all the world, yet still he tried to run. There was a scream of pure agony, a scream that slashed round the courtyard, and Sharpe did not know it was his own scream, but he was still trying to run and then a knee struck the flagstones, and still he tried, and his hands clutched at warm fresh blood, bright red, and he was screaming, falling, and he slid on the stones, scrabbling still, and the blood spurted behind him, was fanned and smeared by his flailing legs, and the scream still went on.

He slid to a stop at the foot of the door, curled up, clenched against a world of pain that he could never have imagined, and he pumped the scream futilely, and the blood welled between his fingers that clutched into his stomach as if they could reach inside him and pluck the horror that tore at him. Then, blessedly, he stopped screaming and was still.

The Cathedral clock struck three.

CHAPTER 13

Private Batten was annoyed, and let the rest of the Company know it. 'Doesn't give a bugger, does he? Know what I mean?' No one answered. They waited on the glacis of the San Vincente fort and Lieutenant Price looked at his watch and kept glancing at the empty San Cayetano fort. Batten waited for a response. He scratched his armpit. 'Used to be a bleedin' private, he did, and that's what he bloody should be now. Keeping us waiting.' Still no one answered and Batten was encouraged by their silence. 'Always buggering off, have you noticed? Our company's not good enough for him, no, not Mr. Bloody Sharpe. Know what I mean?' He looked round for support.

Sergeant Huckfield had gone to look for Sharpe. The men could see his red coat climbing up the ravine's side towards the San Cayetano. One or two of the men slept. Price sat down on a huge masonry block and folded Sharpe's coat beside him. He was worried.

Private Batten picked his nose and licked the result off his fingernail. 'We could sit here all bleedin' night for all he bleedin' cares.'

Daniel Hagman opened one eye. 'He kept you from swinging by your bloody neck two years ago. He shouldn't have bothered.'

Batten laughed. 'They couldn't have hung me. I was innocent. He don't care, Sharpe. He's forgotten us, till he bleedin' needs us again. He's probably sitting with Harps getting drunk. T'ain't fair.'

Sergeant McGovern, slow and Scottish, stood up and stretched his arms. He marched formally to Private Batten and kicked his ankles. 'On your feet.'

'What for?' Batten dropped into the aggrieved tone of surprise that was his main defence against an aggravating world.

'Because I'm going to smash your bloody face in.'

Batten edged away from the Scotsman and looked at Lieutenant Price's back. 'Hey! Lieutenant, sir!'

Price did not look round. 'Carry on, Sergeant.'

The men laughed. Batten looked up at McGovern. 'Sarge?'

'Shut your bloody face.'

'But, Sarge?'

'Shut it, or get up.'

Batten subsided into what he considered injured but righteous dignity. He busied himself with his right nostril, keeping his remarks just out of the Company's hearing. Sergeant McGovern crossed to the Lieutenant and stood formally at attention. Price looked up. 'Sergeant?'

'It's a bit strange, sir.'

'Yes.' They both watched Huckfield cross the ditch of the central fort. Price suddenly realised that McGovern, formal always, was still at attention. 'Stand easy, Sergeant. Stand easy.'

'Sir!' McGovern let his shoulders drop an eighth of an inch. 'Thank you, sir.'

Price looked at his watch. A quarter to four. He did not know what to do and felt helpless without Sharpe or Harper to guide him. He knew that the Scottish Sergeant was hinting that a decision ought to be made and he knew McGovern was right. He stared at the San Cayetano, saw Huckfield's red jacket appear on a parapet, then disappear, and after a long wait Huckfield came to the top of the crude breach and spread his hands emptily. Price sighed. 'We wait till five, Sergeant.'

'Yes, sir.'

Major Hogan had waited for Sharpe, first at the ravine's head, then at Headquarters, but the fate of Colonel Leroux was not the Irishman's only concern. Wellington, now that the forts were taken, was eager to be out of the city. He wanted reports from the north, from the east, and Hogan worked late through the afternoon.

It was not till half past six that Lieutenant Price, awed by approaching Headquarters on his own responsibility, entered Hogan's room. The Major looked up, smelt trouble, and frowned. 'Lieutenant?'

'It's Sharpe, sir.'

'Captain Sharpe?'

Price nodded miserably. 'We've lost him, sir.'

'No Leroux?' Hogan had almost forgotten Leroux. He had assumed that it was now Sharpe's problem while he could concentrate on discovering what fresh levies of troops were joining Marmont. Price shook his head.

'No Leroux, sir.' Price sketched in the afternoon's events.

'What have you done since?'

It did not add up to much. Lieutenant Price had searched the San Cayetano again, then La Merced, and afterwards taken the Company back to their billets in the hope that Sharpe might have turned up. There was no Sharpe, no Harper, just a lost Lieutenant Price. Hogan looked at his watch. 'Good God! You've lost him for four hours?' Price nodded. Hogan shouted. 'Corporal!'

A head came round the door. 'Sir?'

'Daily reports, are they in?'

'Yes, sir.'

'Anything odd, apart from the forts. Quick, man!'

It did not take long. A shooting and a fight at the hospital, one Frenchman had escaped and the town guard had been alerted, but there was no sign of the fugitive.

'Come on, man!' Hogan pulled on his jacket, snatched his hat, and led Lieutenant Price down to the Irish College.

Sergeant Huckfield, who had gone with Price as far as Headquarter's front door, joined them and it was he who pounded on the gate that was still shut against the revenge of the townspeople. It did not take long to hear the story from the guards in the gate-lodge. There had been a chase. One man was wounded, probably in the wards, as to the other? The guards shrugged. 'Dunno, sir.'

Hogan pointed at Price. 'Officers' wards. Search them. Sergeant?'

Huckfield stiffened. 'Sir?'

'Other ranks' wards. Find Sergeant Harper. Go!'

Leroux at liberty. The thought haunted Hogan. He could not believe that Sharpe had failed, he needed to find the Rifleman because, he thought, surely Sharpe could throw light on the episode. It was impossible that Leroux was free!

The surgeons were still at work, dealing now with the less wounded men, taking out scraps of stone that the bombardment had splintered and driven into French defenders. Hogan went from room to room and none could remember a Rifle Captain. One remembered Sergeant Harper. 'Out of his senses, sir.'

'You mean mad?'

'No. In a faint. God knows when he'll recover.'

'And his officer?'

'I didn't see an officer, sir.'

Was Sharpe still on Leroux's trail? It was a hope, at least, and Hogan clung to it. Sergeant Huckfield had found Harper, had shaken the huge Irishman's shoulder, but Harper was still dead to the world, still snoring, still unable to say a thing.

Lieutenant Price came down the curving stairs. He was blinking, almost unable to speak. Hogan was impatient. 'What is it?'

'He's not there, sir.'

'You're sure?'

Price nodded, took a deep breath. 'But he was shot, sir. Really bad, sir.'

Hogan felt a chill spread through him. There was a silence for a few seconds. 'Shot?'

'Bad, sir. And he's not in the wards.'

'Oh, God.' Huckfield shook his head, unwilling to believe it.

Hogan had held to a live Sharpe, a Sharpe chasing Leroux, a Sharpe who could help him, and he could not adjust to the new information. If Sharpe had been shot, and was not in the officers' wards, then he was . . . 'Who saw it?'

'A dozen French wounded, sir. They told the British officers. And the priest.'

'Priest?'

'Upstairs, sir.'

Hogan ran, the same path that Sharpe had run, and he took the stairs two at a time, his sword rapping the stone, and he ran to Curtis' rooms. It seemed to Price and Huckfield, left outside, that he was in the rooms a long time.

Curtis told his story, what there was of it, of how he had opened the door and found a French officer. 'Terribly wounded, he looked. Blood from top to toe. He pushed me in, turned and fired, and then he closed the door. He went out the window.' He gestured to the tall window that opened onto the back street. 'There was a man there, with a spare horse, and a cloak.'

'So he's gone.'

'Clean away.'

'And Sharpe?'

Curtis clasped his hands, then extended the fingers as if in prayer. 'He screamed, screamed terribly. Then he stopped. I opened the door again.' He shrugged.

Hogan dared hardly use the word. 'Dead?'

Curtis shrugged. 'I don't know.' There was not much hope in the old man's voice.

Hogan insisted on going back over the story, harrying it, as if some detail might emerge that would somehow change the ending, but it was with a harsh expression that he left Curtis' door and walked, slowly, down the curved staircase. He offered no explanations to Price, but just went back to the surgeons. He bullied them, ordered them, used all the weight of Headquarters, but still no news emerged. One of them had treated an officer with a bullet wound and the man had survived, a Lieutenant in the Portuguese Army, but they were quite sure they had seen no bullet-wounded British officers. 'We had a few privates.'

'Ye Gods! A Rifle Officer! Captain Sharpe!'

'Him?' The last surgeon shrugged. 'We'd have been told about him. What happened?'

'He was shot.' Hogan kept his patience.

The surgeon shook his head. His breath smelt of the wine he had been drinking through the long afternoon. 'If he was shot here, sir, we'd have seen him. The only explanation is that he never got this far.' The man shrugged. 'I'm sorry, sir.'

'You mean dead?'

The surgeon shrugged again. 'You've looked in the wards? He's not here?' Hogan shook his head. The surgeon gestured over the courtyard with his bloody knife. 'Try the body-men.'

At the side of the college was a small yard where the servants had lived in the better times when the Irish College had been full of students training for the English-banned Irish priesthood. In the yard Hogan found the body-men. They were working, nailing up crude coffins, sewing rough shrouds for the French dead, and they did not remember Sharpe. The smell in the small courtyard was overpowering. Bodies lay where they had been dumped, the body-men seemed to live on a diet of rum and Hogan found the soberest man he could discover. 'Tell me what you do here.'

'Sir?' The man had only one eye, part of a cheek missing,

but he was understandable. He seemed proud that an officer should be interested. 'We burys 'em, sir.'

'I know. I want to know what happens.' If Hogan could at least find Sharpe's body then the worst question would be answered.

The man sniffed. He had a needle and coarse thread in his hand. 'We shrouds the frogs, sir, 'less they're officers, of course, an' they get a coffin. Nice coffin, sir.'

'And the British?'

'Oh, a coffin, sir, of course, sir, if we got enough, if not they get sewn up like this. Unless we ain't got shrouds, sir, then we just stick 'em and bury 'em.'

'Stick them?'

The man winked with his good eye, he was warming to his explanation. By his knees was a French soldier, the face already waxen in death, and the shroud was half closed with big, crude stitches. The man took the needle and plunged it through the Frenchman's nose. 'See, sir? Don't bleed. Means 'is not alive, if you follow me, sir, and if he were then 'e'd like as not give a twitch. We 'ad one four days ago.' He looked at one of his ghoulish mates. 'Four days ago, Charlie? That Shropshire sat up an' bloody puked?' He looked back at Hogan. 'Not nice to be buried alive, sir.' He gestured at the needle. 'Sort of comfort, really, to know we're 'ere, sir, looking after you and makin' sure you're really gone.'

Hogan's gratitude seemed less than heartfelt. He pointed at a stack of rough-cut coffins. 'Do you bury them?'

'Lord love you, no, sir. The Frenchies, now, we might sling 'em in the pit, or at least the burial detail does, sir. I mean there's no point in making a folderol about them, sir, not seein' as 'ow they've been trying to do us, sir, if you follow me. Their officers, now, they're different. They might get the . . .'

Hogan cut him off. 'The British, you fool! What happens to them?'

The perfectionist in the body-man was offended. He

shrugged. 'Their mates get 'em, don't they? I mean the Battalion, sir, does 'em a proper service, with a priest. That's 'em over there. Waitin' for their interdment, sir.' He pointed to the stack.

'And if you don't know who they are?'

'Sling 'em, sir.'

'What happened to the bodies you got today?'

'Depends, sir. Some 'ave gone, some are waiting, and some, like this 'ere gent', are bein' attended to.' He invested the phrase with dignity.

Sharpe was in none of the coffins. Sergeant Huckfield levered the lids open, but the faces were all of strangers. Hogan sighed, looked up at the swallows, then down to Price. 'He's probably buried already. I don't understand it. He's not here, not in the wards.' Hogan did not believe his own words.

'Sir?' Huckfield was raking through the pile of uniforms that had been slit open, searched, and then tossed into a corner of the small courtyard. He held up Sharpe's overalls, the distinctive green overalls that Sharpe had taken off a dead French officer of the Imperial Guard. Hogan, like Huckfield, recognised them instantly.

He turned back to the one-eyed man whose stitches, now that an officer was present, were smaller and neater. 'Where are those clothes from?'

'The dead, sir.'

'You remember the man who wore those?'

The man squinted with his one eye. 'We get 'em naked, as often as not, an' the clothes come after.' He sniffed. 'Buggers have already searched 'em. We just burn 'em.' He peered at the overalls. 'Must 'ave been a Frenchie.'

'Do you know which bodies are French?'

'Course we do, sir. Buggers tell us when they bring 'em.'

Hogan turned to Huckfield and pointed at the pile of shrouded French dead. 'Open them, Sergeant.' He noticed, almost for the first time, the huge bloodstain on the overalls.

It was vast. No man could have lived through that.

The body-men protested as Huckfield began slitting at the grey shrouds, but Hogan snapped at them to be quiet, and he and Price watched as face after face was revealed. None were Sharpe. Hogan turned back to the body-man. 'Have any been buried yet?'

'Lord, yes. Two cart loads this afternoon, sir.'

So Sharpe was buried in a common grave with his enemies. Hogan felt the beginnings of a sob and he swallowed, stamped his feet as if it were cold, and looked at Price. 'It's your Company now, Lieutenant.'

'No, sir.'

Hogan's voice was gentle. 'Yes. You'd better march in the morning. You'll find the Battalion at San Christobal. You'll have to tell Major Forrest.'

Price shook his head obstinately. 'Shouldn't we find him, sir? I mean the least we can do is dig a decent grave.'

'You mean, dig up the French dead?'

'Yes, sir.'

Hogan shook his head. 'Fire a volley over the grave tomorrow morning. That'll do.'

It was all, Hogan thought as he walked slowly back to the Headquarters, that Sharpe might have wanted. No, that was not right. He did not know what Sharpe wanted, except success, and to prove that a man who came from the gutter could compete with anyone, be as good as the most privileged, and perhaps it was better that he should find peace now rather than strive after that remote dream, and then Hogan dismissed that thought as well. It was not better. Sharpe had been turbulent, ambitious, but one day, Hogan supposed, that restlessness would have found satisfaction. Then, curiously, Hogan found himself resenting Sharpe, resenting him because he had been killed and was thus denying his friendship to those who still lived. Hogan could not imagine being without Sharpe. Just when life seemed to reach an even keel the Rifleman could be relied on to upset things, stir them up, make excitement from dullness, and now it was all gone. A friend was dead.

Hogan wearily climbed the steps of the Headquarters and the officers were coming from the Dining Room as he went into the hallway. Wellington saw Hogan's face and stopped. 'Major?'

'Richard Sharpe's dead, sir.'

'No.'

Hogan nodded. 'I'm sorry, my lord.' He told what he knew.

Wellington listened in silence. He remembered Sharpe as a Sergeant. They had covered many miles together and much time. He saw the distress on Hogan's face, understood it, but did not know what words to say. He shook his head. 'I'm sorry, Hogan. I'm sorry.'

'Yes, sir.' It suddenly struck Hogan that life hereafter would seem anti-climactic, inadequate, and dull. Richard Sharpe was dead.

CHAPTER 14

The surgeons had not lied to Major Hogan. They remembered Patrick Harper, stunned cold by the fall, and they had probed and palpated and found nothing broken and so he had been put into a ward where he could snore until he recovered consciousness.

There was another man involved in the fight on the upper cloister. When he reached the surgeon he was still breathing, but shallowly, and unconsciousness had blessedly released him from his pain. An orderly had stripped off the empty scabbard and sword belt, slit the shirt from the man's back, and seen the old flogging scars. The body was lifted onto the stained table.

The surgeon, spattered with fresh blood that gleamed over the clotted, coagulated stains from the week's operations, caught at Sharpe's overalls, split them down with huge shears, and saw the wound low and right in Sharpe's abdomen. He shook his head and swore. The blood welled up in the small bullet hole, spilt and pulsed onto the wounded man's thigh and waist, and the surgeon did not even bother to pick up a knife. He leaned close to the muscled chest and noted that the breathing was shallow, so shallow as to be almost inaudible, and then he picked up the wrist. For a moment he could not find the pulse, was about to give up, and then he felt it; a thready, weak throb of a tiny heartbeat. He nodded at the orderly, then at the wound. 'Close it.'

There was not much he could do, except stop the man bleeding to death and sometimes he thought that would be a mercy with this kind of wound. One orderly grasped Sharpe's feet, held them tight, the second pinched the skin over the wound, pushing the flesh, blood and driven uniform threads together, and keeping his fingers clear of the welling hole. The surgeon crossed to the brazier, took out the poker, and cauterized the puncture. The wounded man jerked, gasped and moaned, but unconsciousness held him, and the bleeding stopped. Smoke hung over the bloody abdomen, the stink of burned flesh was in the surgeon's nostrils. 'Put a bandage on. Take him away.'

The orderly who had closed the wound nodded. 'No hope, sir?'

'No.' The bullet was inside. The surgeon could take a leg off in ninety seconds, he could probe for a bullet and pluck it from next to a thighbone in sixty, he could set broken limbs, he could even take a bullet from a man's chest if it had not pierced a lung, but no one on earth, not even Napoleon's famous Surgeon-General Larrey, could take out a bullet that had lodged in the lower right abdomen. This was a dead man. Already the breathing was shallow, the skin palloring, and the pulse going. The sooner he died, the better, for the rest of his life would be pain. It would be a short life. The wound would abscess, the rot would set in, and he would be buried within the week. The surgeon, irritated with himself for his thoroughness, heaved up Sharpe's side and saw that there was no exit wound. Instead he saw the flogging scars. A troublemaker come to a bad end. 'Take him downstairs. Next!'

They bandaged him, stripped him naked, and his clothes, such as they were, were tossed into a corner where they could be searched at leisure. Many men hid coins in the seams of their clothes and the orderlies reaped a tidy reward for their work. One of them looked at the pale face. 'Who is he?'

'Dunno. French, I suppose.' Sharpe's overalls were French.

'Don't be stupid. French don't flog their buggers.'

'They do!'

'They bloody don't!'

'Doesn't bloody matter. He's dying. Give 'im to Connelley. That's what the doctor said.'

Sergeant Harper could have told them that Sharpe was a British officer, but Sergeant Harper was unconscious in a ward, and Sharpe had borne no marks of rank, just the scars of a flogging that had been given him by Obadiah Hakeswill in an Indian village years before. He looked like a private, he was treated as a private, and he was carried down the damp steps to the cellar where the doctors left their hopeless cases to die. The death room.

Sergeant Michael Connelley, dying himself of alcoholic poisoning, heard the steps and turned his huge, fatty bulk round. 'What you got?'

'Dunno, Sarge. Could be a frog, could be one of ours, but he ain't saying.'

Connelley looked at the face, at the bandage, and tapped a quick sign of the cross on his chest. 'Poor sod. At least he's quiet. All right, boys, down the far end. We've some wee space left.' Connelley sat down on his bench, tipped the rum bottle to his face, and watched as the new man was carried into the darkness of the dank, bricked cellar. 'Any money on him?'

'No, sarge. Poor as a bloody Irishman.'

'You watch yourself!' Connelley growled. He spat on the floor. 'They should have put me with the officers upstairs. There's some rare money up there.' He drank again.

They pushed Sharpe into the wall, laying him on a thin, lumpy straw palliasse, and his head was in the low space where the brick arch met the floor. There was a pile of dirty blankets under the single window, a small grating at the very top of the arch, and the orderly spread one on the naked body that had curled its legs into the foetal position. 'There you are, Sarge, all yours.'

'And in good hands he is, too.' Connelley was not an

183

unkind man. Few would want his job, yet he did not mind. He tried to make the last hours of his dying charges as gentle as he could, yet even in death he expected men to have standards. Especially if there were Frenchmen dying in his room. Then he would lecture the wounded British, admonish them to die like men, not to disgrace themselves in front of the enemy. 'You'll be getting a proper funeral, will you not?' he would say, 'with the whole regiment and reversed arms, the proper honours, and you're making a noise like a wee girl. Shame on you, man, and will you not die well?'

He gestured to the other end of the room and spoke to the orderlies. 'There is a dead one up there.'

It was cold in the death room. Connelley drank steadily. Some men breathed noisily, some moaned, and some talked. The big Sergeant prowled the central aisle from time to time, carrying a water bucket and ladle, and he would feel the feet of the patients to see if they had died. He came to Sharpe and crouched beside him. The breathing was shallow, moaning slightly in his throat, and Connelley put a hand on the naked shoulder and it was cold. 'Ah, you poor man. You'll catch your death!' He lumbered to the window, found another blanket, shook it as if he could free it of the lice that infested its seams, and spread it on top of the other blanket. A man at the far end cried out, caught in sudden pain, and Connelley screwed himself round. 'Whoa there, lad! Whoa! Gentle now! Die well, die well.'

A Frenchman cried and Connelley squatted beside him, took the man's hand, and talked of Ireland. He told the uncomprehending Frenchman of Connaught's beauty, of its women, of fields so fat that a lamb was full grown in a week, of rivers so thick that the fish begged to be caught, and the Frenchman quieted and Connelley patted his hair and told him he was brave, and he was proud of him, and beyond the small grating the sky darkened into dusk and the orderlies came down again and dragged the Frenchman, who had died, head-bumping up the steps.

The pain was like a dream in Sharpe, and sometimes he floated up through the layers of pain and he cried out and at other times he was deep in its suffocating folds and the dream writhed inside him, separate from him, but part of him, pinned to him like the lance held in the Indian soldier's hands that had pinned him to the tree outside Seringapatam, except this was dark, dark, and he cried out, sobbing because of the pain.

'Whoa there, lad!' Connelley paused with his bottle half way to his lips. 'You're a brave one now, sure you are. Be brave, lad.'

Sharpe was lying on his side. He was a child again, being beaten, tied to the bench in the foundling home and the arm was crashing down and crashing down and the birch was splintering inside him and the face of the supervisor changed to Wellington's face and the face was laughing at him.

He dreamed. Teresa was there, but he did not remember that dream, and he did not know that he dreamed of La Marquesa, and the dusk turned to darkness, night in Salamanca, and it should have been his last night in the wide black-curtained bed and he moaned on the palliasse and Connelley, half drunk, called in his sing-song voice for him to die well.

He slept. He dreamed that the rats were chewing the flour and water paste that was caked onto a soldier's hair. Recruits were forced to grow their hair long and when it was long enough it was pulled back and twisted round a leather queue, pulled so hard that some recruits screamed as the hair was yanked and twisted. The skeined hair was formed into the queue, five inches long, a solid pigtail, and it was caked with flour and water paste so that it was stiff and white and sometimes, in the night, the rats chewed at the queue. Then, surfacing into the pain, he remembered that he had not had his hair powdered and pasted for a dozen years, that the army had dropped the fashion, and that the rats were real, scuffling along the cellar's edge, and he coughed at them, spat weakly, and the pain shrivelled him and he cried out.

'Die well, lad, die well.' Connelley had woken up. He should have been relieved hours ago, but he rarely was. They left him to drink peaceably with the dying men. The Irish Sergeant stood up, groaned as the pain hit him, and called again to Sharpe. 'It's only the rats, lad, they won't touch you if you're living.'

Sharpe knew then that the pain was real, that this was not a dream, and he wished he were dreaming again, but could not. He opened his eyes into the dank darkness and the pain was pulsing in him, making him sob, and he forced his knees up and tensed himself, but the pain was terrible and encompassing.

The rush light on the stairs flickered on the cellar wall. The bricks gleamed damply, darkly, curving down to Sharpe's head and he knew he was in this place to die. He remembered Leroux, La Marquesa, and he knew he had been so confident and now it was all over. He had come so far, from the foundling home to being a Captain in Britain's army, yet now he was as helpless as that small child strapped to the bench while the birch thrashed at it. He was going to die, and he was helpless, childlike, and he sobbed to himself and the pain was like flesh-hooks ripping him apart, and he dreamed again.

The Irish priest was mocking him, was stabbing him in the side with a long spear, and Sharpe knew he was being sent to hell. He dreamed he was in a vast building, so high that the roof was misty, and he was pinned by the long spear to the very centre of the floor, and he was tiny, and the great space echoed with laughter, insane laughter that boomed and banged its way in the huge building, and he knew that in a second the floor would open and he would fall endlessly, fall, down to the pits of hell, and he struggled out of that dream back to the pain. He would not go to hell, he would not, and he would not die, but the pain made him want to sleep or to scream.

The bricks glistened above his face. Cold water dripped slowly onto the palliasse. He knew it was the night's middle, death's kingdom, and the rats scuttled against the wall. He tried to talk, forcing words from the pain's grip, and his voice was like wind stirring thistles. 'Where am I?'

Connelley was drunk, asleep, and there was no answer.

There was no Harper. Sharpe remembered the body on the stairs, his friend, and the blood that puddled on the step, and Sharpe cried because he was alone, and was dying, and no one was there. There was no one. No Harper, no Teresa, no mother, no family, just a damp cellar of rats, cold in death's kingdom, and all the glory of Colours carried into battle-smoke, of a soldier's pride, of the bayonets rippling in sun and the boots going forward across the sparks towards victory ended here. In a death room. No Harper. No slow grin, no shared thoughts without words, no more laughter.

He sobbed, and in his sobs he swore he would not die.

The pain was all over so he forced his right hand down and found his naked legs, and then he moved his left hand and found the bandage and he felt round the bandage, round to his lower stomach, and the pain screamed up inside him in a vast red swell of breaking agony that drove him into unconsciousness again.

He dreamed his sword was broken, splintered grey shards, useless. He dreamed.

A man screamed in the room, a high-pitched quavering scream that startled the rats and woke Connelley. 'Whoa there, lad! It's all right, so it is, and sure I'm here. Hey lad, lad! Gentle now. Die well!'

'Where am I?' Sharpe's voice was unheard in the noise. He knew, though. He had seen death rooms before.

The man who had screamed was crying now, small yelps that peaked in pathetic gulps, and Sergeant Connelley swiftly swallowed some rum, thrust the bottle in a gaping pocket, and lumbered down the room with his bucket of water. Other men were stirring, crying for water, for their mothers, for light, for help, and Connelley called out to them all. 'I'm here, lads, I'm here, and you're brave boys, are you not? Now be brave! We have the French, so we do, and would you want them to think that we're weak?'

Sharpe breathed in short, shallow gasps, and he swore he would not die. He tried to blank the pain out, but he could not, and he tried to remember men who had come out of the death room alive. He could not. He could only think of his enemy, Sergeant Hakeswill, who had lived through a hanging, and Sharpe swore he would not die.

Connelley shushed the men with his rough tenderness. He walked down the room, pausing by some, finding some dead, comforting others. Sharpe drifted in the pain; it was like a live thing, trapping him, and he struggled with it. Connelley knelt by him, talked to him, and Sharpe heard the Irish voice.

'Patrick?'

'Are you called Patrick now? And us thinking you was a Frenchie.' Connelley stroked the dark hair.

'Patrick?'

'And a good name it is, lad. Connelley's my name, and Kilkieran Bay's my country, and you and I will walk on the cliffs there.'

'Dying.' Sharpe had meant it as a question, but the word came as a statement.

'And sure you're not! You'll be chasing the women yet, Paddy, so you will.' Connelley took his rum bottle, lifted Sharpe's head gently, and poured the smallest amount between the lips. 'You sleep now, Paddy, you hear me?'

'I'm not going to die.' Each word was soft, each almost edged with a sob.

'Sure you're not!' Connelley lowered the head. 'They can't kill us Irish.' He backed into the aisle and stood up. The room was quieter now, but Connelley knew that the noise could break out again. They were like puppies the dying. Once one was excited, the whole litter began yelping, and a

188

man deserved some quiet to drink and die in. He sang to them, walking up and down the aisle, and he sang the Corporal's Song that told of the soldier's life and he repeated the refrain over and over again as if he wanted to sing them softly into a soldier's death. 'It's a very merry, hey down derry, sort of life enough. A very merry, hey down derry, sort of life enough.'

CHAPTER 15

The next morning Lieutenant Price marched the Company to the field, west of the city, where a common grave had been dug for the French. The Company were shocked, unbelieving. They stopped by the pit. Price stared into the hole. It looked as if dogs had been clawing at the part where the shrouded bodies had been already covered with earth. A sentry shrugged. 'We caught some bloody madman here this morning, sir. He was trying to dig up the bodies.'

They were in two ranks. Price nodded at McGovern. 'Carry on, Sergeant.'

It seemed terribly inadequate. The commands were given, the muskets and rifles went into the shoulders, the volley echoed back from the houses. It all seemed so flat, so wrong, so inadequate.

As the volley and its echo died away there came a sudden burst of bells from the city, pealing bells, victorious and joyful, and the Company marched away from them, going north, leaving a small cloud of smoke that hung over the grave.

Hogan heard the volley, very distantly, and then came the bells clamouring and he straightened his uniform, took off his bicorne hat, and went into the Cathedral. It was Sunday. A *Te Deum* was to be sung for the liberation of Salamanca, for the destruction of the forts, yet it was a half-hearted celebration. The Cathedral was full, packed with gaudy uniforms, sombre citizens, and robed priests, and the organ thundered in the great space, yet Hogan knew nothing but an immense sadness. The congregation sang and responded, went through the motions, yet they knew that Salamanca was only temporarily freed, that the army of Marmont still had to be destroyed, and some of them, the better informed, knew that four other French armies were in Spain and that no city would be free till all had been defeated. And the price would be high. Already a great part of Salamanca had been destroyed to clear a space around the fortresses. The city had lost cloisters, courts, colleges, and houses; all ground to rubble.

After the service, Wellington stood beneath the fantastic carvings of the great western doors, opposite the Bishop's palace, and acknowledged the applause of the crowd. He pushed through them, nodding and smiling, sometimes waving with his plain hat, but his eyes flicked over the faces looking for someone. He saw Hogan, and the hat gestured at the Irishman.

'My lord?'

'Is it done?'

'Yes, my lord.'

Wellington nodded. 'We march tonight.'

Hogan was left behind by the General's progress. What had been done was to put a discreet guard on El Mirador. It had not been an easy decision. To guard El Mirador meant telling the chosen guard who their ward was and why he was important, yet with Leroux at liberty it was the only course left. Lord Spears, his arm mending, but not yet fully fit for normal duties, had been given the task. At first he had been reluctant, but when told that El Mirador was not to be close-guarded at home, only out in public places, he relented. He would still have time, it seemed, for his relentless gambling. Then he was told El Mirador's identity and he shook his head, disbelieving. 'Bless my soul, sir! One would never have guessed!' No one at Headquarters, apart from Wellington himself and Hogan, knew what Lord Spears' new duties were. Hogan was mindful that Leroux had a source within the British Headquarters.

All had been done, then, that could be done, and it had been done heavily, reluctantly, because Hogan still had not fully understood that Sharpe was dead. Twice that morning he had seen Rifle Officers walking in the streets and both times his heart had leapt because he thought he saw Sharpe, and then he remembered. Richard Sharpe was dead, and the army would march on without him, and Hogan let the crowds disperse and walked slowly, disconsolately through the streets.

'Sir! Sir!' The voice shouted at him from down the hill. 'Major Hogan!'

Hogan looked down the steep street he had been passing. A group of chained prisoners were being led by Provosts, one of whom clubbed with reversed musket at a shackled man. Hogan had recognised the voice. He ran. 'Stop it! Stop it!'

The Provosts turned round. They were the police force of the army, universally disliked, and they watched Hogan's approach with silent truculence. Sergeant Harper, who had shouted, was still on the ground. He looked up at Hogan. 'Would you be telling this scum to let me go, sir?'

Hogan felt an immense relief when he saw Patrick Harper. There was something intensely reassuring about his fellow Irishman, and Harper was so inseparable from Sharpe that Hogan felt a sudden, crazy hope that if Harper lived, then Sharpe must, too. He crouched beside the Sergeant who was rubbing his shoulder where the Provost had clubbed him. 'I thought you were in the hospital.'

'So I was. I got the hell out.' Harper was angry. He spat on the ground. 'I woke up this morning, sir, early, with a head like the very devil. I went to look for the Captain.'

Hogan wondered if Harper did not know yet. He wondered how the big Sergeant came to be arrested. The Provosts stirred sullenly and one suggested to the other that he go and find their own Captain. The man left. Hogan sighed. 'I think he's dead, Patrick.'

Harper shook his head stubbornly. 'He's not, sir.' The

chains clinked as he held up a hand to silence Hogan. 'The guard on the gate told me he was, he said that he'd been buried with the French.'

'That's right.' Hogan had told the gate Sergeant at the Irish College. 'I'm sorry, Patrick.'

Harper shook his head again. 'He's not there, sir.'

'What do you mean?'

'I looked. He's not there.'

'You looked?' Hogan noticed for the first time that Harper's trousers were stained with earth.

Harper stood up, towering over the other prisoners. 'I slit up more than twenty shrouds, sir, right down to the ones that stank. He wasn't there.' He shrugged. 'I thought at the very least the man should have a proper burial.'

'You mean?' Hogan stopped. The hope fluttered in him, and he pushed it down. He turned to the Provost. 'Set him free.'

'Can't do that, sir. Regulations.'

Hogan was a small man, usually mild, but he could be roused to a wrath that was awesome. He released it on the Provost, threatened him with the same shackles, threatened him with punishment Battalions in the Fever Isles, and the Provost, wilting under the onslaught, knocked the bolts out of the manacles. Harper rubbed his wrists as the other Provost, with his Captain, came back. The Captain took one look at the freed prisoner, saluted Hogan, and launched into an explanation. 'The prisoner was found this morning, sir, desecrating the dead . . .'

'Quiet.' Hogan's voice cracked with anger. He looked at Harper. 'Where are your weapons?'

Harper jerked his head at the Provosts. 'These bastards have them, sir.'

Hogan looked at the Captain. 'Sergeant Harper's weapons are to be delivered to me, Major Hogan, at Army Headquarters, within one hour. They are to be cleaned, polished, and oiled. Understand?'

'Yes, sir.'

Harper stepped on the foot of the man who had hit him with a musket. Hogan saw the man's face flinch in agony, Harper leaned harder, then the Sergeant stepped away with a surprised look on his face. 'Sorry.' He looked at Hogan. 'Should we go and look for him, sir?'

Hogan had seen the lump and the blood on Harper's head. He gestured at it. 'How is it?'

'Bloody terrible, sir. Feels as if some bastard scraped my brains out. I'll live.' Harper set off up the street.

Hogan caught up with him. 'Don't be too hopeful, Patrick.' He did not like saying it, but it had to be said. 'He was shot, and the surgeons didn't see him.' Hogan had to hurry to keep up with the huge Sergeant. 'He's probably buried with the British, Patrick.'

Harper shook his head. 'He's not buried at all, sir. He's probably sitting up in bed screaming for his breakfast. He always did have a terrible tongue in his head in the morning.'

Hogan shook his head. 'You didn't hear me. They didn't treat a British officer with a bullet wound.' He hated puncturing Harper's hopes, yet still the Irish Sergeant seemed unmoved.

'You searched, sir?'

'Yes. Officers' wards, surgery, the dead in the courtyard.'

'Other ranks' wards?'

Hogan shrugged. 'Sergeant Huckfield looked for you, he didn't see Sharpe. Why should Sharpe be there?'

Harper screwed his face up with the pain of his head. 'They didn't treat an officer?'

Hogan felt sorry for Harper. At last the truth had sunk in. 'I'm sorry, Patrick. They didn't.'

'Like as not. The bugger wasn't wearing his jacket, and doubtless they saw the scars on his back.'

'He what?' Hogan dodged round a water-seller who was waving his leather spout hoping the Major would buy.

Harper shrugged. 'He left his jacket with the Lieutenant, didn't he? It was so damned hot out there. Then the surgeons must have seen his back. Like mine.' Both Sharpe and Harper had been flogged and the scars never went.

Hogan swore at the absent Lieutenant Price who had never thought to mention Sharpe's jacket. He began to run, the hope suddenly giddy inside him, and they took the steps of the college in two leaps. The hope stayed with him as they went into the mens' wards. Hogan imagined Sharpe's face when he saw them, the relief, the joking that he had been mistaken for a Private, even a Frenchman, but there was no Sharpe there. They searched each room, twice, and the faces on the floor stayed the same. Harper shrugged. 'Perhaps he woke up, told them who he was?'

The orderlies said no. They had seen no officers, no patient complaining about being in the ward. There was no Sharpe. The hope went. Even Harper seemed to be resigned. 'I can dig up the British, sir.'

'No, Patrick.'

One of the orderlies had become involved in their search. He still wandered, hopeful, among the crammed wounded. He looked at Hogan and seemed reluctant to speak. 'Was he shot bad, sir?'

Hogan nodded. 'Yes.'

'Connelley's kingdom, sir?'

'What?' The orderly pointed out of the window to a small door at the far side of the courtyard. 'The death room, sir. The cellar.'

They crossed the grass, beneath the awnings that were still rigged round the wellhead, and Harper pulled open the door. A stench came up into the sunlight, a stench of pus, blood, vomit, foulness and death. There was a light at the bottom of the steps, a feeble, flickering rushlight, and a great bulk of a man peered up in its illumination.

'Who's that?'

'Friends. Who are you?'

'Connelley, your honour. Sergeant. Would you be relieving me, of your kindness?'

'We would not.' Harper went down the steps, treading carefully because they were slippery, and the stink of disease and death grew worse. The room was filled with moaning, with small cries, but the bodies lay utterly still as if, in the darkness, they were rehearsing for the grave. 'We're looking for a man with a scarred face, and scarred back. He was shot yesterday.'

Connelley swayed slightly, the drink rank on his breath. 'Would you be Irish?'

'I would. Now do you know the man?'

'A scar, you say? They all have scars. They're soldiers, not milkmaids.' Connelley groaned and sat heavily on his bench. He waved a hand towards the small barred window. 'We had an Irish lad in yesterday, shot he was. Patrick he calls himself. He was alive an hour ago, but he won't last. They never do.' Hogan had come down the stairs and the fat, drunken Sergeant peered at the officer's uniform. 'Oh, my God, and it's an officer, to be sure.' He lumbered to his feet and his hand wavered to a salute. The salute turned into an expansive wave round the room. 'Ah, and they're all good lads. They know how to die like men, so they do, and there's no call for you to be officering them, sir, they're doing their duty.'

Harper pushed Connelley gently back onto his bench. He took the torch from its bracket and set off to search the room. Hogan watched him and felt the hope inside him shrivel to nothingness. The bodies were so still, so hopeless. The room was like a grave.

Harper crouched under the brick ceiling and held the torch over the bodies. He went left first, into the darkest part of the cellar, and the faces he saw were pale. Some slept, some were dead, and some watched the light go past and there was a terrible hope in their eyes that the torch presaged some help, some miracle. Many shivered beneath their blankets. Fever would kill them if their wounds did not.

Harper could not imagine a man being in this room and living, but this was the death room and they were here to die. The big Sergeant, Connelley, seemed decent enough. Some death-room attendants simply stifled their charges, or slipped a dagger between their ribs, because they could not endure the endless crying, the moans, the helpless, childlike ways of the dying. Harper turned at the end wall and carried the torch down the far side. He stopped a few times and pulled damp blankets away from hidden faces, and he saw the fever and smelt their deaths. He went past the stairs where Hogan stood by Connelley's bench. 'Anything, Sergeant?' Hogan's whisper was an expression of worry. Harper did not reply.

He stopped beside another man whose face was hidden, whose legs were drawn up, and Harper pulled back the blanket that lay right up to the dark hair. There was a second blanket beneath and the man was clutching it, hiding his face, and Harper had to prise the fingers open so he could pull it down.

The eyes were red. Already the cheeks seemed sunken. The face was pale, the hair soaking with sweat and water. Harper could not detect any breath, yet the fingers had not been cold, and the huge Irishman put a single finger onto the long scar. The eyes did not move. They were staring into blankness, into the space where the rats had been in the night. Harper's voice was very soft. 'You silly bugger. What are you doing here?'

Sharpe's eyes moved, slowly, up to the face that flickered in the light of the torch. 'Patrick?' There was no strength in the voice.

'Yes.' Harper looked round at Hogan. 'He's here, sir.'

'Alive?' Hogan's voice was just above a whisper.

'Yes, sir.' But only just, Harper thought, by the thickness of the merest thread, but alive.

CHAPTER 16

Marmont had marched north, away from the River Tormes, forty miles to the valley of the River Douro. The dust of the French retreat spiralled high from the wheels, boots and hooves of the army; dust that plumed in the sun over the wheatfields. It was like the thin smoke trail of an unimaginably large grass fire. It faded, carried eastwards by a breeze from the far Atlantic, and the plains of Leon were left empty except for the hovering hawks, the lizards, and the poppies and cornflowers that smeared colour on a bleached land.

On Monday, June 29th, the feast of St. Peter and St. Paul, the British army was swallowed up in the haze of the immense plain. They went north, following Marmont, and all that came back were rumours. One day the people of Salamanca said that there had been a great battle, that the sky had lit up with the flashes of the great guns, but it was just a summer storm sheeting the dark horizon with silver and the next day there was another rumour. It was said Wellington was beaten, his head cut off, and then it was the French who had lost, who had soaked the Douro red with their blood, dammed it with their corpses. They were just rumours.

The Visitation of the Blessed Virgin Mary came and went, then St. Martin's Day, and a peasant girl in Barbadillo said an angel had appeared to her in a dream. The angel had been armoured in gold and carried a scarlet sword with two blades. The angel had said that the last battle would be fought in Salamanca, that the armies of the north would harrow the city, pour blood in its streets, desecrate the Cathedrals, trample the host, until, in desperation, the earth would open up and swallow the evil and righteous alike. Her village priest, a lazy and sensible man, had her locked away. There was trouble enough in the world without hysterical women, but the rumour spread, and the peasants looked at their young olives and wondered if they would live to see an autumn harvest.

In the north, beyond the Douro, beyond Galicia, across the Pyrenees and France itself, and still further north, a small man led a vast army into Russia. It was an army the like of which the world had not seen since the hooves of the Barbarians came out of the dawn. The war had become unimaginable, so vast that the dreams of a Barbadillo peasant girl were not so far removed from the fears of sober statesmen. Across the Atlantic, beyond the shredded wave crests, the Americans prepared their forces to invade British Canada. It was a world war now, fought from the Great Lakes to the Indian Ocean, from the Russian steppes to the plains of Leon.

Sharpe was alive. A message went north to the South Essex, and another went further north to La Aguja, 'the needle', and it told of her husband's injury and urged her to come south. Hogan was not hopeful that his messenger could reach Teresa; the journey was long and the Partisans used secret paths and hiding places.

Sharpe was moved upstairs. He had his own room, small and bare, and Harper and Isabella curtained off one half and lived with him. The doctors said Sharpe would die. The pain, they said, would stay with him, even increase, and the wound would abscess into constant blood and pus. Most of what they said came true. Hogan had ordered Harper to stay, an unnecessary order, but the big Irish Sergeant sometimes found it hard to endure the pain, the smell, the helplessness of his Captain. He and Isabella washed Sharpe, cleaned away the pus, dressed the wound, and listened to the rumours that came back to the small British force left in the city.

A letter came from the Battalion, written by Major Forrest and signed with scores of names. The Light Company wrote their own, penned by Lieutenant Price, decorated by the crosses and signatures of the men, and sometimes Sharpe was lucid and he was pleased with the letters.

Somehow he hung on. Each morning Harper expected to find his Captain dead, but he lived, and even the doctors shrugged and conceded that sometimes, very rarely, a man recovered from that wound. Then Sharpe took the fever. The wound was still abscessed, its dressing changed twice a day, but now Harper and Isabella had to wipe the sweat that poured from Sharpe and listen to the ravings that he muttered day and night.

Isabella found some Rifleman's trousers, taken from a dead man who was as tall as Sharpe, and she hung them on the wall beneath the jacket and above Sharpe's boots that Harper had found discarded in the small courtyard. The uniform waited for him, but the doctors had again given up hope. The fever would kill him. Harper wanted to know how they would treat a fever and the doctors tried to fob him off, but the Irishman had heard of some miracle cure, a new cure, something to do with the bark of a South American tree. The doctors had very little of the substance, but Harper frightened them and they yielded it up, grudgingly, and Harper gave it to Sharpe. It seemed to help, yet the doctors had very little of the precious substance. It had only reached them the previous year, it was expensive, and they made it go further by mixing the powdered quinine with black pepper. When the quinine ran out they gave Sharpe quassia bark instead, but still the fever raged, and even the Navy's remedy, suggested by Lord Spears, which consisted of gunpowder mixed with brandy, did not work.

There was an army remedy and Harper decided on that.

He carried Sharpe downstairs one morning, stripped him naked, and laid him on the grass of the courtyard just beside the cloister. The Sergeant had already drawn bucket after bucket of well water and carried them to the top cloister where he had filled two rain barrels. He would have preferred to be higher, three floors at least, but the upper cloister was the best he could do. He looked down on the shivering naked body and poured the first barrel in a glittering cold shock that exploded on Sharpe. He cried out, jack-knifed, and the second barrel followed in a cascade that flattened Sharpe, choked him, and then Harper ran downstairs, wrapped Sharpe in a dry blanket, and carried the emaciated body back to the cot. The doctors said that Harper had certainly killed Sharpe with that treatment, yet that night the fever went down and Harper came back from the Cathedral to find Sharpe lucid again.

'How are you feeling, sir?'

'Bloody.' He looked it, too. His eyes were sunk in a pale face.

Harper grinned at him. 'You'll be up soon.'

Harper and Isabella took it in turns to pray. She used the chapel of the Irish College, close and beautiful, but Harper thought God might be nearer to the big Cathedral and he climbed the hill twice a day and he prayed with a childlike intensity. His broad, strong face would screw up in concentration as though the very force of his thoughts could drive the prayer up, past the statues, past the glorious ceiling, and up to a heaven where so many other prayers were clamouring for answers. He lit candles to St. Jude, the patron saint of hopeless causes, and he prayed to him, pleaded with him, and once again the doctors began to cautiously suggest that there was a chance; that sometimes men recovered from the wound, and Harper prayed on. Yet he knew something was missing. They gave Sharpe medicines when they could, prayers that they did not tell him about, and Harper knew there was something else; something that might persuade

Sharpe to live. Something was missing.

Sharpe's weapons were missing. The Rifle had been stolen in the hospital, the sword broken by Leroux. It took Harper three days, a bribe, but in the end a storekeeper with the Town Major opened up a small warehouse and rummaged through the racks. 'Swords,' he muttered to himself, 'swords. You can have this one.' He offered Harper a sabre.

'That's bloody rubbish. It's got bloody woodworm. I want a Heavy sword, not that bent rubbish.'

The Corporal storekeeper sniffed. He found another sword, this one straight. 'Twenty pounds?'

'You want me to try it on you? I've paid already.'

The Corporal shrugged. 'I have to account for this lot.'

'You poor wee man. And how do you account for the stuff you steal?' Harper went to the racks himself, raked through the weapons, and found a plain, sturdy, Heavy Cavalry blade. 'I'll take this one. Where are your rifles?'

'Rifles? You didn't say nothing about any rifles.'

'Well I am now.' The huge Sergeant pushed past the storekeeper. 'Well?'

The Corporal glanced at the open door. 'More than my bloody job's worth.'

'Your job's worth cowdung. Now where are the rifles?'

The Corporal reluctantly opened a box. 'That's all we've got. Don't get many.'

Harper picked one up. It was new, beautiful, the lock greased, but it would not do. 'Are they all like this?'

'Yes.' The Corporal was nervous.

'You can keep it.' Harper put it back. He would have liked one for himself, let alone Sharpe, but these were the new rifles with the carbine bore, smaller than the old rifles, and he knew that they would never be able to get a reliable source of ammunition. The rifle would have to wait. He grinned at the storekeeper. 'Now a scabbard.'

The man shook his head. 'Scabbards is difficult.'

Harper pointed the blade at the storekeeper's throat.

'You've got two dollars of mine. That says scabbards are easy. Now give.'

He gave. The sword was not like Sharpe's old sword. This one had not been looked after, it was dull, but it was a Heavy Cavalry sword and Harper set to work on it. The first day he remade the sword's guard. The guard was slim at the pommel and then it broadened so that it would cover a man's fist and it ended in a broad circle that guarded against an enemy's blade sliding down the sword and slicing into a cavalryman's hand. It was a comfortable guard if a man spent his life in the saddle, but the heavy, steel circle cut into a man's ribs if he wore the sword as Sharpe would wear it. It was too long a blade to hang comfortably at the waist. The slings of the scabbard would have to be shortened so that the handle and guard of the sword would lie at the bottom of Sharpe's left rib cage. Harper borrowed a hacksaw, some files, and he worked on the guard. He cut the right hand side of the circle back, past the small holes that could be tasselled for display, right down to within an inch of the blade. He made an edge that was crude, mis-shapen, and ugly, but he filed it obsessively until the shape of the new guard was smooth and easy on the eye. Then he polished the steel until it looked as if it was fresh from the Birmingham factory of Woolley & Deakin.

The handle of the sword was tight on the blade's tang, but the wooden grip was rough to the palm. Harper took off the backpiece and filed the grip, and then he varnished it with oil and beeswax until the handle was dark brown and shining.

On the second day he remade the blade. The back edge of the sword was straight and the point was made by curving the fore edge back to meet it. That was not the point Sharpe liked. The rifleman liked a blade with two edges, both sharp, and a point that was symmetrical. Harper raked through the workshops of the College and found the wheel the gardeners used to sharpen their scythes. He oiled the wheel, treadled it, and then put the blade onto the stone so that it rang, it shrieked, and the sparks flowed like live-fire from the steel. He worked the back edge, curving the sword's last two inches until the fore and back edges were the same. He had made a balanced point. Then he polished the sword, holding the blade up to the light to make sure the stone marks were even. The steel gleamed.

Finally, as the afternoon wore on, he sharpened the blade. He gave Sharpe an edge that the Captain had never had, and he worked at it, and worked, and the perfectionist in him would not give up until the fore edge, and the top seven inches of the back, were razor sharp. He let the wheel slow to a stop.

He took a rag and poured olive oil onto the sword. He polished it again, oiled it, and the sword was unrecognisable from the blade he had taken from the storekeeper. It was no Kligenthal, but it was no ordinary sword. He had remade Sharpe's sword, done it with care and friendship, and he had put into his work all the Celtic magic that he could muster. It was as if in working on the sword he was working on Sharpe himself, and he held the finished blade up to the westering sun and it blazed white light in a dazzling burst. It was made.

He took the sword upstairs, looked forward to Sharpe's face, and Isabella met him. She was running down the cloister and at first Harper was alarmed, and then he saw the look on her face and she threw herself at him, talked so fast that he had to slow her down, and she gabbled her news. A woman had come, and such a woman! Hair like gold and a coach with four horses! She had visited the hospital and she had given gifts to the wounded men and then – Isabella's eyes still sparkled at the memory – the woman had come to Sharpe's room and she had visited the Captain and she had been angry.

Harper slowed her down. 'Angry?'

The Captain was a hero, wasn't he? La Marquesa had shouted at the doctors, had told them it was disgusting that a

204

hero should live in such a place and tomorrow La Marquesa was sending a carriage that was to take Sharpe to a house outside the town, a house by the river, and the best of it was, and here Isabella jumped up and down beside her huge Irishman, clutching at his jacket in her excitement, that the aristocrat had talked to her, Isabella! She and Harper were to go with the Captain. They would have servants, cooks, and Isabella twirled in the cloister and said that La Marquesa had been kind to her, grateful to her, and by the way the Captain was feeling better.

Harper grinned because of her infectious delight. 'Say that all again.'

She said it again, and this time she wanted to know where he had been. He had missed La Marquesa, the most gracious person Isabella had ever met, a Queen! Well, almost a Queen, and Harper missed her, and tomorrow they were all moving to a house by the river and they were to have servants! And by the way the Captain is much better.

'What do you mean, better?'

'I changed the bandage, *si*? She was here! I thought she might visit us. She visit everyone. So I change the bandage and no muck? Patrick! No muck!'

'No pus?'

'No nothing. No muck, no blood.'

'Where is he now?'

She opened her eyes wide because her tale was dramatic. 'He sit up in bed, *si*? Up! He very happy that La Marquesa see him.' She punched Harper. 'And you do not see her! Four horses! And your friend was here.'

'My friend?'

'The English Lord. Lord Spears.' She sighed. 'He has a blue and silver uniform, all shining, and no arm any more! The bandage is off!'

'You mean his arm is out of the sling?'

'That's what I say.' She smiled at him. 'You would look good in blue and silver.'

205

'Aye. It would make a change from black and blue.' He grinned at her. 'Would you stay here, woman? I want to talk to him.'

He pushed open the door of Sharpe's room and, as Isabella had said, Sharpe was sitting up. There was an expression of wonderment on Sharpe's face as if he expected the clenching pain to come back at any moment. He looked up at Harper and smiled. 'It's better than it was. I don't understand it.'

'The doctors said it might happen.'

'The doctors said I would die.' He saw the sword in Harper's hand. 'What's that?'

'Just an old sword, sir.' Harper tried to keep his voice matter of fact, but he could not hide his grin. He shrugged. 'I thought you might be wanting it.'

'Show me.' Sharpe held out a hand and Harper saw how desperately thin his Captain's wrist was. Harper reversed the sword, held it out, and Sharpe grasped the handle. Harper pulled the scabbard away, the sword was in Sharpe's hand, and the weight pulled it down, almost to the floor, and Sharpe had to use all his feeble strength to bring the long, clumsy blade up again. It shone in the small light from the window. Sharpe's eyes stayed on the blade and his face was all that Harper could want. The blade turned over, slowly, the arm horribly weak as it rehearsed the twist that the sword needed as it lunged into an enemy. Sharpe looked up at Harper. 'You did it?'

'Aye, well, you know, sir. Not much to do, sir. Passed the time, so it did.'

Sharpe twisted the blade back and the light ran down the steel. 'It's beautiful.'

'Just the old '96 pattern, sir. Standard issue. Nothing special. I took the odd nick out the edge, sir. Would it be true, sir, that we're moving tomorrow? To higher circles, I hear?'

Sharpe nodded, but he was not listening to Harper's words properly. He was looking at the blade, letting his gaze go up and down the steel, from the new point on the sword to the place where the steel buried itself into the reshaped guard. The weight was too much for him and it sank, slowly, until the tip rested on the rush matting. He looked up at Harper. 'Thank you.'

'For nothing, sir. Thought you might need it.'

'I'll kill the bastard with it.' Sharpe grimaced with the effort, but the blade came up again. 'I'll slaughter the bastard.'

Patrick Harper grinned. Richard Sharpe was going to live.

PART THREE

Tuesday, July 21st
to
Thursday, July 23rd
1812

CHAPTER 17

Sometimes the river was silver, a sheen of pitted silver, and sometimes it was dark green like velvet. At dusk it could look like molten gold, heavy and slow, pouring itself richly towards the Roman bridge and then on towards its junction with the River Douro and then, the far off sea. Sometimes it was mirror smooth, so the far bank was perfectly seen upside down on its surface, and at other times it was grey and broken, but Sharpe never tired of sitting in the pillared shelter that a previous Marques had built right on the water's edge. It was a private place, entered only through one door, and when the door was shut and bolted, the sounds of the house and garden faded.

He exercised for hours in the shelter, strengthening his sword arm, and he walked further each day so that by the time they had been in the house six nights he could walk the mile to the city and back and the only pain was a dull, tugging ache. He ate prodigiously, wolfing down the beef that, as a true Englishman, he knew to be the only source of strength. Captain Lossow, of the King's German Legion, contrived to send Sharpe a wooden crate that proved to be full of stone-bottled beer. A letter was nailed to the crate. It was very short. 'The French could not kill you, so drink yourself to death. Your Friend. Lossow.' Sharpe could not imagine how Lossow had contrived to find a whole crate of beer in Spain, but he knew how generous was the gift and he was touched by it.

On the fifth day he fired Harper's rifle, letting the butt kick into his shoulder, forcing his tired arms to hold the barrel steady, and on his tenth shot he smashed one of the empty stone bottles into shards and felt content. He was strengthening. He had written to Hogan on the first day without cruel pain and the Town Major's office forwarded the reply and Hogan was delighted at Sharpe's news. The rest of the letter was grim. It told of fruitless marching and counter-marching across the plains, of the army's discontent because the French seemed to be outmanoeuvring the British, beating them without a battle being fought, and Hogan hinted that soon the army might be retreating on Salamanca.

Hogan apologised in his letter because he had still not reached Teresa. The message, he knew, had travelled as far as Casatejada, but Sharpe's wife was not there. She was further north harrying the troops of the French General Caffarelli and Hogan did not know how long it would be before she heard the news. He hoped it would be soon. Sharpe felt guilty, because he did not share Hogan's hope. Once Teresa was in Salamanca then he would be forced to give up the company of La Marquesa. She visited most evenings, coming to the shelter beside the river, and Sharpe found himself looking forward to the visits, needing her company, and Harper kept his wonder to himself.

Major Hogan had spoken of Leroux in his letter. 'You are not to concern yourself, Richard, nor to feel responsible for what happened.' That, thought Sharpe, was kind of Hogan because Sharpe was responsible. The failure nagged at him, depressed him, and he tortured himself by imagining what the Frenchman would do to La Marquesa to make her talk. She thought that Leroux was probably in the city, and Hogan agreed. 'He will lie low, we think, until Salamanca is again in the hands of the French, (for that, I fear, is a possibility if we cannot bring Marmont to battle) and we must hope that his plans are frustrated. If we do fight Marmont, and win, then Leroux will have to leave Salamanca. Perhaps he has already, we do not know, but in the meantime we have put a guard on El Mirador and you are not to concern yourself with anything except a full recovery.'

The mention of a guard puzzled Sharpe. La Marquesa came alone, except for her coachman, postilion, and chaperone. The coachman and postilion would wait in the servants' quarters, the chaperone be sent to read a book in the long, gloomy library of the house, while La Marquesa went alone with Sharpe to the pillared shelter beside the river. He showed her the letter and she laughed. 'It would be a little obvious, Richard, wouldn't it? If I rode out here with an armed man riding beside me? Stop worrying.'

The next evening Lord Spears came with her and they could not hide in the small shelter. They walked in the garden, chatting, and Sharpe had to pretend, though he guessed Spears knew otherwise, that he hardly knew La Marquesa, that she had plucked him from the hospital as an object of charity, and he said 'Ma'am' and 'Milady' and felt tongue-tied and clumsy, just as he had at their first meeting. At one moment in the evening, when the sun was a glorious crimson in the west, La Marquesa went to the low wall beside the river and threw bread scraps to the ducks. Sharpe was alone with Spears. The Rifleman remembered how the cavalryman had so desperately wanted to know the identity of El Mirador; how he had quizzed Sharpe in the Plaza Mayor on the morning after the first assault on the three fortresses. Sharpe grinned at Spears. 'So you found out?'

'About you and Helena? You were hardly discreet, my dear Richard, coming here to her lair.'

Sharpe shook his head. 'No. I meant about El Mirador.'

An extraordinary look of alarm crossed Spears' face. It was followed by anger and a question that was almost hissed at Sharpe. 'You know?'

Sharpe nodded. 'Yes.'

'What the hell do you know?'

Sharpe tried to talk calmly, to quieten Spears' anger. 'I

know that we've put a guard on El Mirador, and I presumed that you were doing that.'

'How did you know?'

'Hogan wrote to me.' It was not the whole truth. Hogan had written that El Mirador was guarded, but he had not named names. The rest had been Sharpe's deduction and he had not expected this near violent reaction. He tried to calm Spears again. 'I'm sorry. I didn't mean to offend.'

'No, no offence.' Spears pushed his hair back. 'Christ! We're told this is the biggest bloody secret since turning water into wine and then Hogan has to write to you! How many more people know?' Spears glanced towards La Marquesa, then back at Sharpe. 'Yes I am, but for God's sake don't tell anyone.'

'I'm hardly likely to.'

'No, no I suppose not.'

Sharpe wished he had not mentioned it. He had traduced Hogan by suggesting that the Irish Major had written everything in his letter, but Spears' anger had made Sharpe decide not to launch himself on a convoluted explanation.

La Marquesa came back and looked at Spears. 'You're looking positively flustered, Jack.'

Spears smiled at her. 'A wasp, Helena, threatening my virtue.'

'Such a tiny thing to threaten.' She looked at Sharpe. 'You're happy here, Captain?'

'Yes, Ma'am.'

She made polite conversation for Spears' benefit. 'The house is rather pretty. My husband's great-uncle built it. He was a leper, so he was forced to live outside the city. The house was built here and he could rot away happily on his own. They say he looked perfectly dreadful which is why there are such high walls.'

Spears grinned. 'I hope you scrubbed the place before you put Sharpe here.'

She looked at him, smiled, then touched his cheek with her

fan. 'Such a charming man you are, Jack. Tell my coachman to get ready, will you?'

Spears half bowed. 'You'll be safe with Sharpe?'

'I'll risk it, Jack. Now begone.'

She watched Spears walk towards the house and then drew Sharpe into the shade of some bushes. A stone bench was set in a small clearing and she sat on it. 'I'm sorry, I shouldn't have brought him.'

'I think you should.'

She seemed unmoved by that. 'Why?'

'He is your guard. It's his job.'

She watched Sharpe for a few seconds. 'How do you deduce that, Richard?'

He felt confused. First Spears had reacted almost violently, and now La Marquesa was quizzing him as if he was rendering the accounts for her estates. Then he thought that she must be frightened. If Spears had told Sharpe, then Spears was not to be trusted. He smiled at her. 'First, he's here with you. Second, I asked him. He didn't offer the information, in fact he was quite angry that I knew.'

She nodded. 'Good. What did he say?'

'That he was the guard for El Mirador.' He smiled. 'La Miradora.'

She smiled at that. 'There's no such word, I've told you. Miradors are masculine in Spanish, they cannot be feminine. He can be trusted?'

'He got quite angry.'

She sighed, then twitched her fan at a fly. 'He's a fool, Richard. He's no money, he's gambled it all away, but he is amusing sometimes. Are you jealous?'

'No.'

'Liar.' She smiled at him. 'I won't let him come again. He insisted tonight.' She laughed at him. 'You remind me tonight of the first time we met. You bristled with dignity. You were so ready to take offence.'

'And you to give it.'

'And something else, Richard.'

'Yes.' He sat beside her. She could see the new colour in his face.

She sat silent for a moment, her head cocked as if listening for a faraway sound, then she relaxed. 'No guns today.'

'No.' No battle, which meant that the French had out-marched Wellington again, that the armies were getting nearer to the city, and that perhaps the time when Sharpe would have to leave Salamanca was getting closer. He looked at her. 'Come with us.'

'Perhaps you won't go.'

'Perhaps.' But his instinct told him otherwise.

She leaned against him, her eyes closed, and then Spears' voice shouted from the house that her carriage waited. She looked up at Sharpe. 'I'll come early tomorrow.'

'Please.'

She kissed him. 'You exercised today?'

'Yes, Ma'am.' He grinned.

She gave him a mock salute. 'Don't give up, Captain.'

'Never.'

He followed her to the house and watched as the carriage went through the high gates, Spears' horse beside it, and then he turned back into the building. It was his last evening with Harper, till God knew when, for on the next day the Sergeant was going north, taking Isabella, going back to the South Essex. Harper was marching with a group of men recovered from their wounds and to mark their final evening the big Irishman and Isabella ate with Sharpe in the formal dining room instead of in the kitchen.

Sharpe spent the next days alone, exercising and walking, and the news from the north went from bad to worse. An officer, posting back to Ciudad Rodrigo, stopped at the house for water and he sat in the garden with Sharpe and spoke of the troops' anger because they were not allowed to fight. Wellington seemed to be giving ground, to be always retreating from the French, and each new day brought reinforcements to Marmont's army. The officer claimed that Wellington was being too cautious, that he was losing the campaign, and Sharpe did not understand it. The army had marched from Portugal with such high hopes and now those hopes were frittered away. The campaign was being lost without a battle and each day's manoeuvring brought the armies nearer to the city, promised that soon Leroux would have the freedom to hunt again, and Sharpe wondered where the Frenchman was, what he was doing, and practised with the big sword in the slim hope that he might see Leroux again.

A month after Sharpe's wounding the bad news was all confirmed. The day had brought clouds of dust to the east and by the evening Sharpe knew that the armies had reached the Tormes, east of the city, and he knew that Salamanca must change hands again. Another letter came from Hogan, hand delivered by an irritated cavalryman who had gone first to the Irish College, then to the Town Major, and finally had found Sharpe. The letter was brief, its message grim. 'Tonight we cross the river and tomorrow we will march westwards. The French outmarch us each day so we must hurry. I fear it will be a race to the Portuguese frontier and I am not certain we can win. You must leave. Pack now! If you have no horse then try to find Headquarters. I will lend you my remount. Say your farewells and go, no later than dawn tomorrow.' The 'no later' was underlined. 'Next year, perhaps, we can twist Marmont's tail, but not, alas, this. In haste, Michael Hogan.'

Sharpe had little to pack. He stood in the garden and stared over the river and saw the goats that lived on the far hills filing down to the low ground. It was a sure sign that heavy rain was coming, yet the sun still shone, but he looked overhead and sure enough there were clouds rolling in from the north. The river was silver, shot through with green.

He put his few things into his pack. Two spare shirts, two spare stockings, a mess tin, the telescope, his razor and he filled the oxhide pack to the top with food that he took from the kitchen. He wrapped two loaves, a cheese, and a big ham. The cook gave him wine bottles that he thrust into the pack and poured a third into his spare canteen. He had no rifle to carry, just the big sword on its short slings.

He went back into the garden again and the sky was darker, almost black, and he knew he would wait for the morning before leaving. He told himself that he had become lazy, that he was going soft because he wanted to spare himself a night in the open, but he knew that he waited for morning in the hope that La Marquesa would come this night. Perhaps their last night. He thought of walking to the city, of going to the Palacio Casares, but then he heard the sound of hooves, the opening of the gate, and he knew she was coming. He waited.

There was something curiously beautiful about the landscape. The sun still shone, slanting steeply beneath the clouds, and it gave the land a luminance that the sky had lost. Above was darkness, grey and black, beneath was a glowing scene of green hills, brilliant white buildings, and the river like oiled silk. The air was heavy. The clouds pressed down as if the weight of water was sinking them. He expected the rain to begin at any second, yet it held off; it was conserving its force. The goats, as ever, had been right. There would be a vast rainstorm this night. He walked to the pillared shelter, built, La Marquesa had told him, in imitation of a small Greek shrine, and he stood on the topmost step that led to the door, pulled himself up on the lintel and he could see over the high wall to the city. Perhaps it would be his last glimpse of Salamanca in the evening. The sun silhouetted the fine stone, edged the great Cathedral with red gold, and then he pushed the door open and waited for La Marquesa. The river was almost black, swirling, waiting for the hammering of the rain.

In the morning he would go. He would walk away from this city and the dust of the roads would have been driven and churned into mud. He had failed this summer. He had promised to take a man, and the man had almost killed him, yet Sharpe did not see that as his greatest regret. He had betrayed his wife, and that saddened him, but that was not his regret. He would miss La Marquesa. He would miss the golden hair, the mouth, the eyes, the laughter and the beauty, the magic world of a woman whom he had glimpsed, wanted, and never thought he could possess. Tonight was the last night. She would stay, in danger, and he would go back to the army. He could recover his full strength in Ciudad Rodrigo and all the time he would wonder about her, remember her, and fear that his enemy had destroyed her.

The first heavy, plangent drop of rain smashed onto the marble ledge that faced the river. It left a mark the size of a penny. He had dreamed once before of a final night in Salamanca, and that hope had ended in the death room. Now fate had given him the night again, though tinged with defeat. He knew he had become obsessed with her, and he had to abandon her, and that was too often the way of women and soldiers. Yet there was this one night.

He heard the footsteps on the grass and he did not turn round. He was suddenly superstitious. To turn round was to tempt fate, but he smiled as he heard the feet on the steps and then he heard the heavy click of a flint being pulled back on a mainspring.

'Good evening, Captain.' The voice was a man's voice, and the man held a rifle, and the rifle was pointing straight at Sharpe's stomach as the Rifleman wrenched himself about to face the door.

The first thunder racketed over the sky.

CHAPTER 18

The Reverend Doctor Patrick Curtis, known as Don Patricio Cortes, Rector of the Irish College and Professor of Astronomy and Natural History at the University of Salamanca, held the rifle as though it were a poisonous snake that might, at any second, turn and bite him. Sharpe remembered how Leroux had run to this man's room, how Spears had described Curtis volunteering to fight against the English, and now the tall priest faced Sharpe. The frizzen that covered the pan of the rifle was up and the elderly Irishman clicked it down into place. He smiled. 'You see? It still works. It's your rifle, Captain.'

The thunder echoed in the sky. It sounded like heavy siege shot being rolled on giant floor boards. The rain was hissing steadily on the river's surface. Sharpe was five paces from the man. He thought of jumping at him, hoping that the priest would hesitate before pulling the trigger, but he knew that the wound would slow him down. He looked at Curtis' right hand and raised his voice over the sound of the rain. 'You have to have a finger on the trigger to make it work.'

The bushy eyebrows went up in surprise. 'It's not loaded, Captain. I'm merely returning it to you. Here.' He held it out. Sharpe did not move and the Irish priest just shrugged and propped the rifle against the wall.

Sharpe jerked his head towards the weapon. 'It's bad for them to stay cocked. It weakens the spring.'

'You learn something every day.' Curtis picked up the rifle, pulled the trigger, and flinched as the spark cracked on the empty pan. He put the weapon down again. 'You don't seem overjoyed to see me.'

'Should I be?'

'You could be grateful to me. I went out of my way to return your gun. I had to get your address from the Town Major and then smuggle it out under my cassock. It would be bad for my reputation if I were seen going fully armed about the streets.' Curtis gave a deprecating smile.

'You could have returned it earlier.' Sharpe kept his voice cold. He wanted this interfering priest gone. He wanted La Marquesa.

'I wish I could have returned it earlier. It was stolen by one of the College's stonemasons. His wife told me and I retrieved it for you.' He pointed at the weapon. 'And here it is, safely restored.' He waited for Sharpe to speak, but the Rifleman was morose. Curtis sighed, walked to the edge of the shelter and looked at the rain. 'Dear oh dear. What weather!' The surface of the river was corruscated by the rain. The sun, perversely, still showed in the west beneath the great cloud bank. Curtis pulled up his cassock and sat down. He gave Sharpe a friendly smile. 'Do you mind if I sit it out? There was a time when I rode in all weathers, but I'm seventy-two this year, Mr. Sharpe, and the good Lord may not look kindly on me getting a chill.'

Sharpe was not feeling polite. He wanted to be alone until La Marquesa came, he wanted to think of her, to wallow in the misery of the anticipation of their parting. This last night was precious to him, something to hold against the bad times, and now this damned priest was settling down for a cosy chat. Sharpe kept his voice harsh. 'I'm expecting company.'

Curtis ignored him. He waved an expansive hand round the small, pretty shelter. 'I know this place well. I used to be the Marques's confessor and he was always kind to me. He let me use this for some of my observations.' He shifted himself so he was looking at Sharpe. 'I watched last year's comet from in here. Remarkable. Did you see it?'

'No.'

'You missed something, you really did. The Marques was of the opinion that the comet affected the grape harvest, that it was responsible for the good vintage. I don't understand that, but undoubtedly last year's wine was excellent. Excellent.'

A great explosion of thunder saved Sharpe the necessity of replying. It echoed across the sky, grew and faded, and the rain seemed to seethe down with more force. Curtis tut-tutted. 'I presume you're waiting for La Marquesa.'

'You can presume what you like.'

'True.' Curtis nodded. 'It concerns me, Mr. Sharpe. Her husband is a man I would call a friend. I'm a priest. You are, I know, a married man. I think I'm speaking to your conscience, Mr. Sharpe.'

Sharpe laughed. 'You came out here, in this weather, to give me a bloody sermon?' He sat down on the curved bench that ran round the inner wall of the shelter. He was trapped here, while the rain lasted, but he was damned if he was going to let a priest start meddling with his soul. 'Forget it, Father. It's none of your business.'

'It's God's, my son.' Curtis spoke mildly. 'La Marquesa doesn't confess to me. She uses the Jesuits. They have such a complicated view of sin. I'm sure it must be very confusing. I have a very simple view of sin and I know that adultery is wrong.'

Sharpe spoke quietly, his head tilted back against the wall. 'I don't want to be offensive, Father, but you're annoying me.'

'So?'

Sharpe brought his head forward. 'So I remember Leroux going to your room, I remember hearing that you fought against the English, and I know that the French have spies in this town, and it would take me about two minutes to tip you into that river and I wonder how many days it would be before they found you.'

Curtis stared at him. 'You mean that, don't you?'

'Yes.'

'The simple solution, yes? The soldier's way.' Curtis was mocking him now, his voice hard. 'Whenever human beings don't know what to do they call in the soldiers. Force ends everything, yes? That's what they did with Christ, Mr. Sharpe, they called in the soldiers. They didn't know what to do with him so they called on men like you and I don't suppose they thought twice about what they were doing, they just banged in the nails. You'd have done that, wouldn't you?'

Sharpe said nothing. He yawned. He looked at the quick ripples where the rain struck the river. The sky was black, the western horizon dark gold, and he wondered if La Marquesa would wait for the storm to end before her coach made its way to the house by the river.

Curtis looked behind him at the rugs and the cushions that La Marquesa had put into the river shelter. 'What are you frightened of, Sharpe?'

'Moths.'

'I'm serious.'

'So am I. I hate moths.'

'Hell?'

Sharpe sighed. 'Father, I do not wish to be offensive, I don't really want to push you into the bloody river, but I do not want to sit here and be lectured about my soul. Understand?'

A thunderclap smashed the sky overhead, so sudden that Curtis jumped, and its lightning seared over the river, the smell of ozone sharp in the air, and the sound of the thunder seemed to roll westwards towards the city, bounce back, and then there was just the rain crashing on the water. Curtis looked at the river. 'There'll be a battle tomorrow.' Sharpe said nothing. Curtis spoke louder. 'There'll be a battle tomorrow, and you will win.'

'Tomorrow we're running away from the French.' Sharpe's voice was bored.

Curtis stood up. His cassock was black against the gloom outside. He stood as close to the river as he could without letting the rain fall on him. He still spoke towards the water, his back turned on Sharpe. 'You English have an ancient belief that your great victories come on the day after a night of thunder.' The priest's hair was white against the black clouds. 'Tomorrow you will have your battle, your soldier's solution, and you will win.' Thunder growled half-heartedly and the priest, to Sharpe, looked like some ancient magician who had conjured this storm from the deep. When the thunder sound had died Curtis looked at Sharpe. 'The dead will be legion.'

Sharpe wondered if he heard the jangling of traces beyond the house. He cocked his head, listened, but he could hear only the rain in the garden, the wind in the trees. He looked at Curtis who had sat down again. 'And when does the world end?'

'That's God's business. Men make battles. Wouldn't you like a battle tomorrow?' Sharpe said nothing. He leaned against the wall. Curtis spread his hands in resignation. 'You didn't want to talk about your soul, so instead I talk about a battle, and still you won't talk! So. I'll talk to you.' The elderly priest looked down as if collecting his thoughts, and then the bushy eyebrows came back up to Sharpe. 'Let's suppose that the thunder tells the truth. Let's suppose there's a battle tomorrow and the English win. What happens?' He held up a hand to stop Sharpe speaking. 'This is what happens. The French will have to retreat, this part of Spain will be free, and Colonel Leroux will be stuck here.' Now he had Sharpe's attention. The Rifleman had sat up. 'Colonel Leroux,' Curtis went on, 'is almost certainly inside the city. He's waiting for the British to leave. Once they do leave, Mr. Sharpe, then he will reappear and no doubt the killing and the torturing will go on. Am I right?'

'Yes.' Curtis had said nothing that anyone else could not have worked out. 'So?'

'So if Leroux has to be stopped, if the killings have to be stopped, then you must fight and win a battle tomorrow.'

Sharpe leaned back again. Curtis was merely a living-room strategist. 'Wellington has been waiting for a battle for a month. It's hardly likely that he'll get one tomorrow.'

'Why has he waited?'

Sharpe paused while thunder sounded. He looked out at the river and saw that the rain was still heavy. It was almost dark. He wished the rain would stop, he wished Curtis would go. He forced himself to make conversation. 'He's waited because he wants Marmont to make a mistake. He wants to catch the French wrong-footed.'

'Exactly!' Curtis nodded vigorously as though Sharpe was a pupil who had grasped a subtle point. 'Now, bear with me, Mr. Sharpe. Tomorrow, am I right, Wellington will be south of the river and then he will turn west, to Portugal? Yes?' Sharpe nodded. Curtis was leaning forward, talking urgently. 'Suppose he didn't turn west. Suppose that he decided to hide his army at the turning place and then suppose the French did not know that. What would happen?'

It was very simple. Tomorrow both armies would cross the river and turn to their right. It was like the bend of a horse-racing course and the British were on the inside. If they wanted to get ahead of Marmont, to win the race to the Portuguese frontier, then they had to come off the bend fast and keep marching. Yet if Curtis was right, and if Wellington hid on the bend, then the French would march past him, their army strung out in a line of march, and it would be easy to trip him up. It would no longer be a race. It would be like a shepherd stringing his flock out in front of a pack of hungry wolves. But it was just conjecture. Sharpe shrugged. 'The French get beaten. There's just one thing wrong.'

'What's that?'

Sharpe thought of Hogan's letter. 'Tomorrow we're marching west, as fast as we can.'

'No you're not, Mr. Sharpe.' Curtis' voice was certain. 'Your General is hiding his army at a village called Arapiles. He doesn't want Marmont to know that. He wants the French to think that he's simply leaving a rearguard at Arapiles and that the rest of the army is marching as fast as it can.'

Sharpe smiled. 'With the greatest respect, Father, I doubt if the French will be fooled. After all, if you've heard of this deception, then so must a lot of others.'

'No.' Curtis smiled. The rain still crashed down outside, hidden now by the darkness. 'I spent the afternoon at Arapiles. There is one problem only.'

Sharpe was sitting forward again, the rain forgotten. 'Which is?'

'How do we tell Marmont's spies that Wellington is really marching tomorrow?'

Sharpe shook his head. 'You're serious, aren't you?'

'Yes.'

The Rifleman stood up, walked to the door and peered into the garden. There was nothing to be seen except the trees lashing in the storm. He turned round, puzzled by the conversation. 'What do you mean "we"?'

'I mean our side, Captain.'

Sharpe walked back to his seat, picking up his rifle as he went, and he felt as if the ground beneath his feet was crumbling away. At first Curtis had provoked him, then mocked him, now he was making Sharpe feel very stupid. He let his fingers run over the lock of the rifle, liking its solidity, and looked at the priest. 'Say what you have to say.'

Curtis thrust his hand into the breast of his cassock and brought out a piece of paper. It was folded into a narrow strip. 'This came to me today which is why I went to see Wellington. It came to me, Captain, sewn into the spine of a volume of sermons. It came from Paris.'

Sharpe ran his finger against the rough edge of the rifle flint. He was unaware of the pain in his wound, he just listened to the elderly priest who had suddenly assumed great authority. 'Leroux is a dangerous man, Captain, very dangerous, and we wanted to know more about him. I asked one of my correspondents, a friend, a man who works in a Ministry in Paris. This is the answer.' He unfolded the paper. 'I won't read it all, because you've heard much of it from Major Hogan. I'll just read the last line. "Leroux has a sister, as skilled in languages as himself, and I cannot discover her whereabouts. She was christened Hélène".'

Sharpe shut his eyes, then shook his head. 'No.'

'Yes.'

'No, no, no.' Thunder drowned his protest. He opened his eyes and the priest was dark in the night. 'You're El Mirador.'

'Yes.'

Sharpe hated to believe it. 'No. No.'

Curtis was inexorable. 'You may not like it, Captain, but the answer is still "yes".'

Sharpe still refused to believe. 'Then where's your guardian?'

'Lord Spears? He thinks I'm hearing confessions in the Cathedral, I often do on Tuesday night. He's saying his farewells to La Marquesa, Sharpe, which is what is holding her up. Half the cavalry officers in town are paying her court at this moment.'

'No! Her parents were killed by the French! She lived in Zaragoza!'

'Sharpe!' Curtis shouted him down. 'She met her husband in Paris just five years ago. He was part of a Spanish government embassy to Napoleon. She says her father was executed in the Terror, but who knows? So many died! Thousands! And no records were kept, Sharpe, no careful ledgers! It's not difficult for Napoleon's men to produce a pretty young girl and claim she's the daughter of Don Antonio Huesca and his English wife. We'd never have known if we hadn't asked about Leroux.'

'You still don't know. There are a thousand thousand Hélènes and Helenas.'

'Captain Sharpe, please think.'

She had claimed she was El Mirador, she was not. He thought of the telescope on the mirador, the telescope that pointed to the San Cayetano fortress where there had been the second telescope. It would have been so easy for her to signal to Leroux, to talk to him using a system like the army's telegraph system. Sharpe still hated to believe it. He swept an arm round the shelter. 'But all this! She's been looking after me!'

'Yes.' Curtis stood up and moved about the floor. The rain had slackened, the thunder was further south. 'I think, Sharpe, that she is more than a little in love with you. Lord Spears says so and, God knows, he would have sinned with her if she had let him. I think she is in love with you. She's lonely, she's far from home. As a priest I disapprove, as a man I'm envious, and as El Mirador I want to use that love.'

'How?'

'You must lie to her, Captain, tonight. You must tell her that Wellington is leaving a rearguard at Arapiles and that he will try to convince Marmont that the rearguard is his whole army. You will tell her that Wellington wants to trick Marmont into staying still, into facing the rearguard while the bulk of the British army escapes. You will tell her that, Captain, and she will believe you because you have never deceived her. And she will tell Marmont, and then tomorrow you can watch the fruit of your labours.'

Sharpe tried to laugh it off. 'She tells Marmont? Just like that?'

'No one in Spain stops a messenger who carries the seal of the house of Casares el Grande y Melida Sadaba.'

Sharpe shook his head. 'No.' He wanted to see her, to hold her, to listen to her voice, laugh with her.

Curtis sat again, near Sharpe, and he talked as the rain

228

pelted on the river, as the storm moved southwards, and he talked of the letters that came to him, hidden letters, coded letters. He talked of the men who sent them and the ruses they employed to get the messages through. Now, it seemed to Sharpe, Curtis was a magician. He conjured the picture of his correspondents who feared for their lives, who worked only for liberty, who had stretched a web across Napoleon's empire that led to this elderly priest. 'I don't remember exactly when it started, perhaps four years ago, but I found the letters coming, and I wrote back, and then I began to hide the letters, to put them inside the bindings of books. Then, when the English army came, it seemed sensible to pass the material onwards, so I did, and now I find that I am the most important spy you have.' Curtis shrugged. 'I did not mean to be. I've trained priests, Sharpe, for years. Many of them write to me, often in Latin, sometimes in Greek, and I have lost only one man. I fear Leroux.' Sharpe remembered La Marquesa telling him how she feared Leroux. She was his sister.

Sharpe looked at Curtis. 'You think Leroux is in the city?'

'I think so. I don't know, but it seems logical that he would hide there until the French came back. Or stay there so he could go on looking for me.' Curtis laughed to himself. 'They arrested me once. They took all my books, all my papers, but they found nothing. I persuaded them that as an Irish priest I had little love for the English. I don't have much. But I do love this country, Sharpe, and I fear France.'

The rain had almost stopped. The thunder was sounding to the south. Sharpe felt utterly alone.

Curtis looked at the Rifleman. 'I'm sorry.'

'For what?'

'Because I think you're fond of her?' Sharpe nodded, and Curtis sighed. 'Michael Hogan said you would be. He didn't know if you were her lover, so I probed you to see how you reacted. Lord Spears said you were, but that young man spreads scandal. I think perhaps I envy you.'

229

'Why?' Sharpe was low; feeling that his life had been dissected. He had been used.

'I'm a professional gelding, Sharpe, but that doesn't mean I never notice the mares.'

'She's very noticeable.'

Curtis smiled in the darkness. 'Jellification.'

Sharpe put the rifle onto the bench beside him. 'What happens if there is a battle tomorrow?'

'We'll look for Leroux in the evening. I suppose we'll have to search the Palacio Casares.'

'And her?'

Curtis smiled at him. 'Nothing. She's a member of the Spanish aristocracy, beyond reproach, beyond punishment.' The wind was chilled by the passing rain. Curtis looked into the night. 'I must go. If she found me here, then I had the excuse of the rifle, but it's better that she doesn't find me.' He stood up. 'Convince her tonight, Sharpe, and I absolve you for this night, for this deed.'

Sharpe did not want absolution, he wanted Helena, or Hélène if that was her name, and yet he feared to see her in case she noticed a difference in him. She had used him, and perhaps he should never have believed that an aristocrat could have a genuine purpose in friendship with a man such as he, yet he could not believe that it had all been a pretence. She had needed him at first because he was the man hunting her brother and he had told her everything, so she had told Leroux, but she had come back for him, had rescued him from the hospital, and tonight he wanted her, whatever the darkness might hatch.

Curtis went through the door into a garden that was heavy with rain. The trees dripped after the storm. 'Good luck, Sharpe.'

'And you, sir.'

Curtis went. Sharpe felt foolish and alone. He wanted her, to lie to her and with her, and he was alone. He waited. To the south, over the village of Arapiles, the thunder bellowed.

CHAPTER 19

The ridge ran north and south. It had been close cropped by sheep, goats, and by the rabbits whose droppings lay like miniature spent musket balls in the thin, springy grass. The ridge smelt of wild thyme.

The day had dawned with a pale, rinsed sky. The only remnants of the great thunder storm were a few high, ragged clouds and a burden of water on the soil that promised to be burned away by noon. The ridge top was already drying when Sharpe arrived.

She had begged him to stay. She had begged him to protect her against Leroux, and he had joined in the lie by begging her to retreat with the army, to go to Ciudad Rodrigo, but she would not.

She had gone back to the city in the early morning, when it was still dark, and she had promised to send Sharpe a horse, a gift, and he had protested, but the horse came. A servant gave it to him and watched, silent, as the Rifleman rode towards the fords east of the city. She had given him a horse, a saddle, a bridle, and he could not guess how much the gift was worth. Soon she would discover that he had betrayed her, as she had him, and he would return the gift. Now he rode the horse down the great ridge towards the place where the hills ended and the plain began; the turning place. This was the bend where the armies went west and the ridge was like the marker on the inside of the curve. He had explained it all to her, in the darkness, and he had said that the French could march faster than the British and so Wellington planned to steal a march. He would leave a Division at Arapiles and send the rest of the army on a fast march, fifteen miles westward and, by staying with the rearguard himself, Wellington would persuade Marmont that the whole army was still in front of Salamanca. She had listened to him, asked questions, and Sharpe had warmed to the lie.

They had lain together in the shelter and when the time came for them to part she had touched the scar on his face. 'I don't want to go.'

'Then stay.'

'I must go.' She smiled sadly. 'I wonder if I'll ever see you again.'

'You'll be surrounded by cavalry officers and I'll be jealous.'

She kissed his cheek. 'You'll bristle with dignity, like the first time you came to the mirador.'

He kissed her back. 'We'll meet again.' The words echoed in his head as his horse, her horse, trotted on the ridge's spine.

To the east of the ridge was a wide sweeping valley where the ripening wheat had been flattened by the rain and where a few dark trees showed the course of a stream. At the far side of the valley was an escarpment, its steep side facing Sharpe, and he knew that beyond the sheer red-rock bluffs at its crest the French army would be marching. The ridge and the escarpment ended in a great rolling plain and it was on that plain that Marmont would swing westward into the home straight; the race to block the Portuguese road.

At the southern end of the ridge the ground fell steeply away and, a short walk from the ridge's end to the west, was a village. It was like a thousand other Spanish villages. The cottages were low, made of rough-dressed stone, and a man could not stand upright in most of the small houses. The houses grew into each other and formed a maze of tiny alleyways that surrounded the simple church, no bigger than a storehouse. The church had a small stone arch built on one end of its roof that acted as the belfry for the one counter-weighted bell. A stork's nest clung to the top of the arch.

The richer peasants, and there were few of them, had painted their cottages white. Roses grew against the walls. Farmyards lay next to some cottages, empty now for the villagers feared the army that the night had brought behind the ridge. The villagers had driven their cattle away, to another village, and the hovels and alleyways had been left to God and the soldiers. The village, which had never been famous, was called Arapiles.

If a man stood at the very bottom of the slope, near to the village, and looked southwards he would have seen an apparently empty, almost level plain. It was covered with wheat and grass. The horizon was dark with trees and jumbled because, beyond the plain, the country was rough and hard. If the man turned to his right he could see the village of Arapiles and, just beyond the village and so close to it that it seemed as if its rocks grew out of the small cottages, was a hill; the Teso San Miguel. Between the southern end of the ridge and the Teso San Miguel was a small valley, just two hundred yards wide at its narrowest point, and if a man were to walk up the valley's centre, keeping the ridge to his right and the Teso San Miguel to his left, then he could see straight ahead of him, four miles to the north, the big tower of Salamanca's New Cathedral. If the small valley were wreathed in cannon smoke, silted with musket smoke, then a man might be grateful for that landmark.

In the east was the escarpment, then the wide valley, then the high ridge which smelt of thyme and lavender and was pretty with cabbage white butterflies, and then the small valley, and then the Teso San Miguel with Arapiles at its foot, and beyond the village and the small hill the plain stretched to the west. Yet none of those things were strange in this landscape. Sharpe stood his horse at the southern end of the ridge, and his soldier's mind took in the escarpment, the valleys, and the village, but his wonder was at the plain that stretched away to the treeline to the south. The plain, which was pale with ripening wheat, was like a great sea that lapped against the escarpment, ridge and Teso San Miguel, and in the sea were two strange islands. Two hills, and to a soldier the two hills were the key to the plain.

The first hill was small, but high. And, being small and high, it was steep, too steep for the growing of crops and so it had been left for the sheep, the rabbits, the scorpions that lived in the rocks that littered the slopes, and the hawks that nested on its flat summit. The small hill lay just to the south of the ridge, so close that the valley between them was like a saddle. From the air the ridge and the small hill would look like an exclamation mark.

If a stork flew directly south from its nest on Salamanca's New Cathedral, over the river, and on into the farmland, it would cross the small hill. And if it still flew south, into the great plain, it would cross the second hill just three quarters of a mile from the first. This hill was truly isolated in the wheat. It was bigger than the first, but lower, and it was like a flat-topped slab that lay, like a dash, beneath the exclamation mark. It was as steep as the first hill, just as flat-topped, and the hawks and ravens lived there undisturbed for no man had a good reason to climb the steep sides, no reason unless he had a gun. Then he would have every reason for no infantry could hope to dislodge a force that was on the flat hill-top that stood like a great gun platform in the sea of wheat. The two hills were called by the villagers 'los Hermanitos', which means 'the little brothers'. Their proper name was taken from the village itself. They were the Arapiles; the Lesser Arapile and, out in the plain, the Greater Arapile.

When God made the world he made the big plain just for the cavalry. It was firm, or would be when the sun had dried off the night's rain, and it was mostly level. The sabres could fall like scythes in the corn. The Arapiles, Greater and Lesser, God made for the gunners. From their summits, conveniently made flat so that the artillery could have a stable platform, the guns could dominate the plain. God had made nothing for the infantry, except a soil easily dug into graves, but the infantry were used to that.

All that Sharpe saw in a few seconds, because it was his trade to see ground and understand its use for killing men, and he knew, too, that if he had deceived La Marquesa then this would be the killing ground. Some men had already died here. In the wide valley between the British ridge and the French escarpment, Riflemen were fighting a desultory battle with French skirmishers. The Rifles had pushed the enemy back to the very crest of the escarpment, killing a handful, but no one was taking that battle very seriously. The second outbreak of fighting was serious. Portuguese troops had been sent to take the Greater Arapile, out in the plain, and the French infantry raced them to its summit, then poured musket fire down the precipitous slope and so the Portuguese had failed. The French had taken one of the two gun platforms that dominated the killing ground and already Sharpe could see French cannon on its summit. Two British guns sat silent on the Lesser Arapile. Their crews let their uniforms dry off from the night's rain and they wondered what the day would bring. Probably, they thought, another desperate, scrambling march to get away from the French. They wanted to fight, but too many days of this campaign had ended in despondent retreat.

He rode close to the small farmhouse that was built at the southern end of the ridge crest. It was busy with staff officers and Sharpe stopped the horse and slid uncomfortably to the ground. A voice made him turn round. 'Richard! Richard!'

Hogan walked towards him with his arms outstretched, almost as if he wanted to embrace Sharpe. The Major stopped, shook his head. 'I never thought to see you again.' He took Sharpe's hand and pumped it up and down. 'Back from the dead! You look better. How is the wound?'

'The doctors say a month, sir.'

Hogan beamed in delight. 'I thought you were dead! And

when we took you from that cellar.' He shook his head. 'How do you feel?'

'Half strong.' Sharpe was embarrased by Hogan's pleasure. 'And you, sir?'

'I'm well. It is good to see you, it is.' He looked at the horse and his eyes widened in surprise. 'You've come into money?'

'It's a gift, sir.'

Hogan, who loved horses, peeled back the stallion's lips to look at its teeth. He felt its legs, its stomach, and his voice was filled with admiration. 'He's a beauty. A gift?'

'From La Marquesa de Casares el Grande y Melida Sadaba.'

'Oh.' Hogan reddened. 'Ah.' He patted the stallion's neck, glanced at Sharpe. 'I'm sorry about that, Richard.'

'Why? I suppose I made a fool of myself.'

'I wish I could with her.' Hogan grinned. 'Did you tell her?'

'Yes.'

'And she believed you?'

'Yes.'

Hogan smiled. 'Good, good.' He could not resist his pleasure. He danced a few ludicrous jig steps on the grass and beamed at Sharpe. 'Oh good! We must tell the Peer. Have you had breakfast?'

'Yes, sir.'

'Then have more! I'll have my servant stable your horse.' He stopped and looked at Sharpe. 'Was it hard?'

'Yes.'

Hogan shrugged. 'I'm sorry. But if it works, Richard . . .'

'I know.'

If it worked there would be a battle. The great drying plain south of the village, around the hills, would become a killing ground, spawned in a dark night of thunder, betrayal, and love. Sharpe went for more breakfast.

CHAPTER 20

The sun rose higher, its heat stronger, and it dried the killing ground and baked the rocks till they could not be touched. It hazed the horizon and made the air shimmer above the flat rock summits of the two Arapile hills. The gunners spat on the barrels of their cannon and watched the spittle hiss and boil away, and that was before the guns fired. Insects were busy in the grass and wheat, butterflies flickered above the poppies and cornflowers, and the last ragged clouds of the rainstorm died and disappeared. The land crouched beneath the heat and it was seemingly empty. From the ridge or the escarpment, from any of the hills, a man could not see more than one hundredth of the hundred thousand men who had gathered at the Arapiles that day. Wednesday, July 22nd, 1812.

Auguste Marmont was thirty-six years old. He was Duke of Ragusa, which meant little to him compared with being the youngest Marshal of France, and he was impatient. The Englishman, Wellington, had beaten every French General who had opposed him, but he had not beaten Marmont, nor would he. Auguste Marmont, son of an ironmaster, had outmanoeuvred the Englishman, outmarched him, and all that had to be done now was to outrun him to Portugal. Yet now, as the morning came towards its end, he was uncertain.

He rode his horse to the rear of the Greater Arapile, dismounted, and climbed the steep slope on foot. He used the wheel of a cannon for his telescope rest and he stared long and hard at the Lesser Arapile, at the village, and at the farm buildings at the southern end of the ridge. Other officers were using their glasses and one of them, a staff officer, pointed at the farm on the ridge. 'There, sir.'

Marmont squinted as the sun flashed off the brass of his telescope, trained it, and there, clear in the lens' circle, was a man in a long blue coat, grey trousers, and a plain dark hat. Marmont grunted. Wellington was on the ridge. 'So what's he doing?'

'Lunch, sir?' The staff officers laughed.

Marmont frowned at the hint. 'Going or staying?'

No one answered. Marmont panned the telescope to his left and saw two British guns on the Lesser Arapile and then more guns, perhaps four, on the hill behind the village. That was not many guns and he did not fear them. He straightened up from his glass and stared westward. 'How's the ground?'

'Dry, sir.'

The plain stretched invitingly to the west. It was empty; a great golden road that might take him ahead of Wellington. Marmont itched to be moving, to be outmarching the British so he could block the road and win the victory that would tell France, Europe, the world, that Auguste Marmont had destroyed Britain's army. He could taste that victory already. He would choose the battlefield, he would force the red-jacketed infantry to attack up some impossible slope that he would have lined with his beloved artillery, and he could already see the roundshot and canister flailing at the hopeless British lines. Yet now, on the Greater Arapile, he could feel doubt in his mind. He could see redcoats in the village, guns on the hills, but were they just a rearguard, or something more? 'Is he going or staying?'

No one answered. A Marshal of France was a fine fellow, second only to the Emperor, and he wore the dark blue uniform edged with golden leaves, and his collar and shoulders were heavy with gilt decorations. A Marshal of France was given privileges, riches, and honour, but they had to be earned by answering the difficult questions. Was he going or staying?

Marmont stumped about the top of the Greater Arapile. He was thinking. His boots were tight and that annoyed him, any man who took one hundred and fifty pairs of boots to war was entitled to find a pair that fitted. He pulled his mind back to the British. Surely they were marching? Wellington had not offered battle in a month, so why should he on this day? And why should Wellington wait? Marmont went back to the gun and peered again through the telescope. He could see the unadorned figure of his enemy talking to a tall man in the green jacket of a Rifleman. The Rifles. Britain's light troops. Fast marchers, even faster than the French. Suppose Wellington had left his Light Division at this village? Suppose that the rest of the army was already on the road, marching west, escaping the vengeance of the French Gribeauval guns? Marmont put himself in his enemy's place. He would want to steal this day's march. He would want the French to stay here, thinking that the British army threatened them, and how would he do that? He would leave his finest troops at the village, stay himself, because if the General is present, then the enemy assumes the army is present, and still Marmont knew he had to make a decision. Damn these boots!

To do something was better than doing nothing. He turned to his staff officers and ordered an attack on the village itself. It was, he knew, a holding move. It would discourage the British rearguard from venturing onto the plain and it would form a screen behind which he could march west; yet he knew he still had to make the decision, the big choice, and he was frightened of it. His servant was spreading a linen tablecloth on the grass, setting it with the silver cutlery that travelled everywhere with the Marshal and his one hundred and fifty pairs of boots, and Marmont decided the war would have to wait till after an early lunch. He rubbed his hands together. 'Cold duck! Excellent, excellent!'

A horseman rode down the southern slope of the escarpment, past the troops that waited for the orders that would send them west or keep them waiting for a day. His horse splashed through a shallow ford, past an ancient footbridge that spanned the stream with flat stone slabs, and then he spurred towards the strange Arapile hill where he had been told Marmont waited. He carried a letter in his sabretache. He put the horse at the slope, urged it as high as it could climb, and then he dismounted, threw the reins to an infantryman, and scrambled up the last few steep feet. He ran to the Marshal, saluted, and handed over the folded, sealed paper.

Marmont smiled when he saw the wax seal. He knew that seal, knew it could be trusted, and he tore the paper open and called for Major Berthon. 'Decode it. Quick!'

He looked again at the enemy held hills. If only he could see what was on the far side! And maybe the letter would tell him, or maybe, his thoughts became pessimistic, it was merely some piece of political news, or a report on Wellington's health, and he fretted while Berthon worked at the numbers written on the paper. Marmont pretended to be calm. He offered the cavalryman who had brought the message on the last lap of its journey some wine. He complimented him on his uniform, and then, at last, Berthon brought him the paper. 'The British march west today. A single Division remains to persuade you that they plan to fight for Salamanca. They are in a great hurry and fear to be overtaken.'

He had known it! The message merely confirmed his instinct, but he had known it! And then, as if in confirmation of his sudden certainty, he saw the tell-tale plume of dust that was rising in the western sky. They were marching! And he would overtake them! He tore La Marquesa's note into shreds of paper, finer and finer, and he scattered them on the hilltop and he grinned at his officers. 'We've got him, gentlemen! At last, we've got him!'

Five miles away the British Third Division, which had been left to screen Salamanca on the north bank of the Tormes, marched through the city and across the Roman bridge. It was an uncomfortable march. The citizens of Salamanca jeered them, accused them of running away, and the officers and sergeants kept a tight rein on their men. They marched beneath the small fortress on the bridge and turned right onto the Ciudad Rodrigo road. Out of sight of the city they turned off the road, to their left, and went further south till they had reached a village called Aldea Tejada. They were close now to the great wheat plain that could yet become a killing ground.

It took the Third Division more than two hours to march past a single point on the road. The men were tired, dispirited at a further retreat, and ashamed that they were deserting the city. Some of them, in their tiredness, dragged their feet. The dust began to move. The road had dried and the dust rose, was stirred, and the air over the Ciudad Rodrigo road was misted with fine, white powder. The army's baggage, sent ahead in case the British did have to retreat, added to the mist that smeared the western horizon.

Marmont had the message, had seen the dust, and now his tight boots were forgotten. He would have his victory!

There was no such elation on the British ridge. The waiting had made Wellington's officers irritable. Sharpe had slept for a while, for he had had little rest the previous night, and now he stared at the great plain and it was empty beneath the hawks that slid against the steel-blue sky. There was no sign that Marmont had extended his left, that he had fallen into the trap, and Sharpe knew it must be past midday. He had been woken by the cannons firing on the French attack on the village. He had watched for a while as the British roundshot ploughed through the ranks of the enemy Battalions, as the skirmishers met for their private war in the wheat stalks, but the French attack was stopped at the village's outskirts. Marmont did have one success. His guns on the Greater Arapile drove the British guns off the summit of the Lesser Arapile. Sharpe watched the gunners, helped by infantry, manhandle the great weapons down the steep slope. Round one to France.

The French attack was not heavy. About five thousand men had come from behind the Greater Arapile and advanced on the village. Sharpe could hear the sharper sound of the Baker Rifles from the plain and he knew that the French skirmishers would be cursing the British Riflemen, that Voltigeurs would be dying in the wheat, and it all seemed so far away, like a child's battle with toy soldiers seen from an upstairs window. The blue uniforms came forward, stopped, and the white smoke rills showed where the musket volleys were fired, puffs showed where shrapnel burst over the enemy, and the sound would come seconds after the smoke appeared.

The attack stopped just outside the village. This was not a true battle, not yet. If the French had been serious, if they had really wanted to capture the miserable cottages, they could have marched in their great columns, the Eagles bright above, and the massed drums would have driven them on and the artillery would have blasted a path ahead of them, and the noise would have swelled to a great crescendo in the afternoon heat while the French wave swept over the village, up the small valley, and then there would be a battle. Sharpe dozed off again.

Hogan woke him with an offer of lunch; two legs of cold chicken and diluted wine. Sharpe ate in the shadow of the farmhouse wall and he listened to the small sounds of the skirmishers bickering by the village. Still the great plain was empty to the west, the French were not taking the bait, and Hogan had gloomily admitted that in a couple of hours the Peer would probably order a full scale retreat. Another day gone.

Wellington was pacing up and down in front of the farm. He had been down to the village once, seen that the defenders were in no trouble, and now he fretted as he ate cold chicken and waited for Marmont to show his hand. He had noticed Sharpe, welcomed him back 'to the living', but the Peer was in no mood for small talk. He paced, he watched, and he worried.

'Sir! Sir!' A horseman was spurring up the ridge, coming from the west, and his horse was lathered with sweat. He jumped from the saddle, saluted, and offered a scrap of paper to the General. He was an aide-de-camp to General Leith and he did not wait for Wellington to read the paper. 'Sir! They're extending their left!'

'The devil they are! Give me a glass! Quickly!'

There was dead ground on the rolling plain, hollows in the wheat that hid themselves from the ridge, and the French were in the hollows. General Leith, off to the west, had seen the movement first, but now the French could be seen, climbing a track from the dead ground, and Sharpe, his own telescope extended, saw that the enemy was marching. The sheep were on the wolf-ground. Wellington rammed his glass shut, threw the chicken leg he had been eating over his shoulder, and his face was jubilant. 'By God! That will do!'

His horse was ready, he mounted, and he spurred off to the west, outrunning his staff officers, and the dust spurted from behind his horse. Sharpe kept staring to the south-west, at the great plain that stretched so invitingly in front of the French, and he saw the troops come out of the dead ground and into plain view. It was a beautiful sight. Battalion after enemy Battalion had turned themselves into the order of march and they were going westward in the blistering heat. The attack on the village was supposed to do no more than pin down the British rearguard while the French left, safe in the knowledge that their foes had already marched, were now eagerly trying to outmarch them. The heat simmered the air above the plain, yet the French were full of heart, full of ambition, and they swung along the dirt tracks between the thistles and the wheat, and their weapons were slung and their hopes high. They marched further and further west, stringing the French army finer and finer, and none of them could know that their enemy was waiting, ready for battle, hidden to their north.

Hogan was replete with happiness. 'We've got him! At last, Richard we've got him!'

CHAPTER 21

Battles rarely start quickly. They grow like grass fires. A piece of musket wadding, red hot, is spat onto grass, it smoulders, is fanned, and a hundred other such tiny sparks flicker on the dry ground. Some fade, others catch into flame and may be stamped out by an irritable skirmisher, but suddenly two will join and the wind catches the fire, blows it, swirls the smoke and then, quite suddenly, the little wadding sparks have become a raging flame that roasts the wounded and eats the dead. There was no battle yet at the Arapiles. There were sparks that could yet turn into an inferno, but the afternoon wore on and the officers watching from the farm at the southern end of the great ridge felt their elation turn to boredom. The French batteries still fired at the village over the heads of their troops who had settled in the grass and wheat, but the cannonade was slower, almost half-hearted, and the British used the lull to manhandle two guns back up the Lesser Arapile.

The afternoon smouldered. Three o'clock passed, then four, and to the men on the ridge, to the Battalions behind the ridge, the sound of battle was like a distant storm that had no effect on them. The French left wing, a quarter of the army, was marching westwards and it heard the guns behind and thought it was merely the bickering of the rearguard.

The British gunners of the Royal Horse Artillery who had dragged and forced two guns to the crest of the Lesser Arapile served their bucking monsters in the muck sweat of the heat. The guns crashed back on their trails, splintered rocks on the other Arapile hill, and after each shot the gunners had to lever the trails back into position, the monster had to be fed, and the smoke stung their eyes and fouled their breath. A gunner pushed a spherical case-shot into the barrel. It was Britain's secret weapon, invented twenty-eight years before by Lieutenant Shrapnell, and still no other country had succeeded in copying the shell. This was a small case-shot because the gun, a six pounder, was the biggest that could be worked up the steep hill-slope. The hollow iron ball of Shrapnell's invention had sixty musket balls packed round its central powder charge. The fuse had been cut so that the ball would explode over the Greater Arapile and the rammer thrust it down the gun's throat, stood back, and the Sergeant who ruled this gun checked his crew, touched fire to fuse, and the gun wheels jarred off the rock, the trail slewed, the smoke slammed forward and the case shot thundered over the plain.

The battle was smouldering. It could ignite at any moment and Fate, who is the soldiers' Goddess, was taking an interest in the sparks that flickered and threatened about the Arapiles. An artillery officer on the Lesser Arapile saw the case-shot leave the smoke, he saw it as the faintest trace of a grey pencil-like line in the air and then it exploded, just over the far edge of the Greater Arapile, and it was a black-grey air burst shot through with deep red and the ground beneath and ahead of the explosion was spattered by the lead balls and the shattered casing. Most went harmlessly to ground, some ricocheted off the hot stone, but two balls, with Fate's malevolence, took Auguste Marmont in the side and France's youngest Marshal was down. He was not killed, but he would not lead his army again this day, an army he had already pointed to destruction.

Wellington was far away. He had ridden to the Third Division and he had pointed them in a new direction, eastwards, and they had begun their march. The French marched west, thinking they were in a race to head off the

British, but the British were coming towards them, and waiting behind them, and they could not know it. And the British, soured by the weeks of march and counter-march, of retreat, wanted to fight.

Between the Third Division and the Arapiles, hidden in a deep fold of ground, there were more British. Horsemen. The Heavy Cavalry, newly come from Britain and eager to try out their mounts and their long thirty-five inch straight blades, blades they said were too heavy for a swift parry, but wonderful for killing infantrymen.

The sun had bleached the plain pale. The killing ground was beginning to fill, as a stage might fill, but still it waited for the spark that would fan into a battle. It came in the west as the Third Division hit the head of the French column and to the men, up on the ridge by the farmhouse, it came as the distant muffled sound of muskets that were like a far-off thornbush fire. Smoke came from the west, and sound, and the dust that added to the smoke, and then the telescopes could make out a little of what was happening. The French column was being crumpled, thrown back, and the battle, that had started in the west was coming east, back to the Arapiles.

The French battalions recoiled. They were outnumbered, outgunned and outgeneralled. They had thought they were the vanguard of a march, and found they were the front line of a battle, and their defeat was about to become disaster.

Sharpe watched it. He hated the cavalry as all infantry-men hated cavalry and he was used to seeing the British cavalry ill-led and ineffective, but Fate was capricious to the French on that hot Spanish afternoon. The British Heavy Dragoons, some from the King's own bodyguard, came on the French from the north. They wanted to fight. They came up from their dead ground in two ranks, trotting to keep their order, and the black horsetail plumes on their shining crested helmets rippled as they moved. Sharpe, watching through the glass, saw a shiver of light, a glitter, and the swords were up and the horsemen were booted knee to booted knee.

He did not hear the trumpet that put them into the canter, but he saw the line go faster, and still they kept their discipline, and he knew what they must be feeling. All men fear the moment of going into battle, but these men were on their big horses and the smell of the powder was in their nostrils and the trumpet was setting their blood on fire and the swords in their hands were hungry. The French were not ready. Infantry can form square and the textbooks say that no cavalry in the world can break a well-formed square, but the French had not known the danger and they were not in square. They were falling back from a massive infantry attack and they were firing and loading, cursing their General, when the earth shook.

A thousand horses, the best horses in the world, and a thousand swords came from the dust and the trumpets spurred the horsemen into the final charge, the moment when the horse is released to run like the devil and the line will stagger and bend, but it does not matter because the enemy is so close. And the horsemen, who had been given a target that every cavalryman dreamt of, opened their mouths in a triumphant scream and the great, heavy, edged blades came into the French with all the weight of man and horse. The fear had turned to anger, to craziness, and the British killed and killed, split the Battalions, rode down the French and the huge blades fell and the horses bit and reared, and the French, who could do no other, broke and ran.

The horses ran with them. The swords came from behind. The Heavy Dragoons drove paths of blood and dust through the fugitives and there was no difficulty in killing. The French had their backs to the horses so the swords could take them in the neck or over the skull and the horsemen revelled in it, snarled at their enemies, and the swords had so many targets. The musket sound had gone. It was replaced by the thunder of hooves, by screams, and by the cleaving sound of a butcher's block.

Some French ran for help to the British infantry. The red ranks opened up, helped them in, because all infantry feared that moment when they were not in square and when the cavalry hit them at the full charge. The British soldiers shouted at the French, told them to run to the British lines, and the red-coated men watched in awe what the Heavy Dragoons were doing and knew that Fate could have decreed it otherwise and so they helped their enemy to escape the common enemy of all infantry. The spark had turned into a running flame.

Sharpe watched from the hill, privileged as a spectator, and he saw the French left wing chewed into fragments between the horses and the Third Division. He watched the Heavy Dragoons, superbly led, reform again and again, charge again and again, and they fought till the troopers were too weary to hold the heavy swords.

Eight French Battalions had been broken. An Eagle had been lost, five guns captured, and hundreds of prisoners, their faces blackened by the powder and their heads and arms sliced by the swords, had been taken. The French left had been split, shattered, and massacred. Now the horsemen were spent. Fate was not all on the British side. She had decreed the death of the Heavy Dragoons' General who would never again be able to show British cavalry how to fight, but their job this day had been done. Their blades were thick with blood, they had ridden to glory, and they would remember the moments for ever when all a man had to do was lean right, cut down, and spur on.

Wellington was launching his attacks, one by one, from the west to the east. The Third Division had marched, then the cavalry, and now more men were launched onto the great plain. They came from both sides of the Teso San Miguel and they drove southwards, aiming at the hinge of the French line, its centre, dominated by the Greater Arapile. Sharpe watched. He saw infantry spread out from the small valley between the ridge and the Teso San Miguel and march past the village. Their colours had been stripped of the leather casings and they flew over the Battalions and Sharpe felt the pang of extraordinary pride that the sight of the colours gave every soldier.

The guns on the Greater Arapile shifted their aim, fired, and the first gaps were blown in the British lines, the Sergeants shouted at men to close up, close up, and they marched on, attacking in line, and Sharpe saw the yellow colour of the South Essex.

It was the first time ever that he had not fought with them and he felt a deep guilt as he watched his men, the skirmishers, run ahead into the wheat. He watched them fearful for them, and he knew that the wound still hurt, that the doctors had said that it could re-open and bleed, and that the next time it might fester and he would die.

Portuguese troops were marching for the Greater Arapile. The Fourth Division, survivors of the main breach at Badajoz like Sharpe's own South Essex, were marching to the right of the French hill. The shots kept coming. The French had arrayed guns on the plain beside the hill and the batteries bellowed at the British and Portuguese lines and the gaps appeared, were filled, and small knots of red or blue coated men were left behind on the trampled wheat. The French troops who had been attacking the village fell back in the face of the Fourth Division. It marched on, its colours high, and they threatened the French guns in the plain, the troops who retreated in front of them, and the troops who were coming back from the carnage in the west. Sharpe rested his telescope on Hogan's shoulder and found his own men, paired in the wheat, and he saw Harper and kept him in the glass. The Sergeant was gesticulating to the Company, keeping them spread out, keeping them moving, and Sharpe felt a terrible guilt that he was not there. They would have to fight without him, and he could not bear the thought that some would die and that he might have saved them. He knew that there was little he could have done that Lieutenant Price and the Sergeants were not already doing, but that was small comfort.

So far, he knew, the battle was falling to the British. The French left had gone, and now the centre was being assailed and Sharpe could not see how the centre could hold out against the attacks. Surely the Fourth Division would take the ground to the right of the Greater Arapile, the French guns would limber up and go, and it seemed to Sharpe, watching from the thyme-scented hilltop, that the French had somehow lost the will to fight back. The wheat and grass were skeined with smoke, the air thundered with the round-shot, canister and shrapnel, and the thousands and thousands of men marched into the plain and the red jackets, everywhere, beat back the French. It seemed that, this day, Wellington's men were remorseless, unbeatable, and that only nightfall would save a few Frenchmen. The sun was already sinking towards evening, still bright, but the night was coming.

Marmont did not know what was happening. He had been taken away, treated by the surgeons, and his second in command was wounded, and a third man, General Clausel, took over the army. He could see what was happening and he had not lost the will to fight. He was still a young man and he had been a soldier for half his life and he did not intend to lose this battle. His left was gone, surprised and broken, and the centre was threatened, but he was playing his own game. He had been taught to fight by a master, Napoleon himself, and Clausel was content to let the centre fight while he collected his reserves, massed them, and drew them up behind the shelter of the Greater Arapile. He commanded a massive force, thousands of bayonets, and he held them back, waiting for the moment when he would release them like a huge counterpunch that would be aimed at the very centre of Wellington's army. The battle was not yet lost, either side could win it.

The Portuguese climbed the steep slope of the Greater Arapile and Clausel watched them and timed his counter-attack so that they would be the first to suffer. The signal went. The crest of the hill was lined with infantry, the muskets could not miss at a few paces, and the Portuguese, helpless in the face of the last precipitous feet, were tumbled backwards. No bravery could compensate for those last sheer feet. The Portuguese were blasted away by the French muskets, and even their defeat would not have mattered if the Fourth Division had been able to attack past the hill and surround it, for then the French on the Greater Arapile would have fled.

The Fourth Division did not get past the hill. From behind it, coming out to Sharpe's right, the counter-attack rose from the small patch of dead ground next to the hill's western end. The French columns came forward. Twelve thousand men, their Eagles aloft, their blades as thick as the wheat they trampled flat, and Sharpe heard, through the guns, the drums of the French beating the *pas-de-charge*. This was war as France had taught the world war. This was the mass attack, the irresistible force, driven by blurred drumsticks, the collection of men turned into a great human battering ram that would be marched against the enemy to smash through the enemy's centre and make a hole through which the cavalry would pour and tear at the flanks.

The British line, two deep, could usually stop the column. Sharpe had seen it happen a dozen times and there was a cold mathematical logic to the process. A column was a great filled rectangle of men and only the men on its outer edges could use their muskets. Each man in the British line could fire and, even though the column had more men than the line, the line would always win the firefight. The frightening thing about the column was its size, and that scared un-steady troops, overawed them, but it was vulnerable to good troops. The column took the punishment, as Sharpe had seen other columns take punishment, and again he was amazed by the French soldiers who stayed so steady under horrific bombardment. Cannon balls struck the columns and successive ranks soaked up the balls' passages, and shrapnel cracked over their heads, yet still the column moved. The drums never stopped.

This was the might of France, the pride of France, the tactic of the world's first conscript army, and this column, Clausel's counter-attack, ignored cold mathematical logic. It was not defeated by the line.

It pushed the Fourth Division back. The British had fired their clockwork volleys, the muskets flashing rhythmically through the smoke cloud, and Sharpe had seen the Light Companies go back to their Battalions, form line, and join in the musket fight. The Fourth Division was awed by the column. Perhaps the British had seen too much blood at Badajoz, had thought that any man who lived through that ditch had no right to die on a summer's field, and they took a step back before reloading, and the step became two, and the columns still came on and the officers shouted, the Sergeants tried to dress the ranks, but the lines went backwards.

The drummers paused to let the thousands of voices chant their war cry. 'Vive l'Empereur!' And the drums started again, the old rhythm that Sharpe knew so well. Boom-boom, boom-boom, boomaboom, boomaboom, boom-boom. That rhythm had sounded from Egypt to Russia, had driven the columns to rule Europe, and between each phrase the drummers paused, the shout went up, and the column came on as the drummer boys, tight in the column's centre, let the sticks fall again. With each shout the bayonets went up in the air and splintered the slanting sunlight into twelve thousand shards and to the left of the column, in the space between the two strange hills, the French cavalry hacked into the remnants of the Portuguese.

'No.' Sharpe spoke to himself. Hogan saw his right hand gripping and re-gripping the sword handle.

The Fourth Division were beaten. Some men climbed the

lower slopes of the Lesser Arapile, some the slopes of the Teso San Miguel, while some took refuge in the village. The column carved through the defeated Battalions, ignoring them, marching steadily on towards the small valley that led to the very heart of the British line. Some of the Fourth Division, like the South Essex, still went backwards in front of the column, but they were beaten, and the column came to the small valley and the guns, on either side of the French, poured death into their ranks. The British roundshot lanced at the column, the shrapnel exploded above it, but still the Frenchmen closed up, marched on, stepped over their dead, and they left a trail of mangled, shot-torn bodies in their wake like a blood-slime beneath the smoke.

The noise was the noise of French victory. The drums, the cheers, the guns that could not stop them, and the noise filled the valley as the French Battalions went towards the distant landmark of the new Cathedral's largest tower. The Eagles were bright above their heads.

Wellington's messengers galloped at break-neck speed down the slope. They went to the Sixth Division, the new Division, the Division that had taken so long to take the fortresses, and it was the only Division between Clausel and victory. The Fourth Division had been beaten and now the Sixth had to win or else Clausel would have plucked victory from disaster.

Battles rarely start quickly. Sometimes it was difficult to know when a skirmish had become a battle, yet the height of a battle was easily determined. When the Eagles were flying and the drums were sounding, when the guns of both sides were in frenzy, then the battle was fully joined. It had yet to be won and Sharpe, who had watched the South Essex go backwards through the smoke-torn valley, could not bear that it might be won or lost without him. He shook off Hogan's restraining arm, called for his horse, and went down into the smoke.

CHAPTER 22

From the ridge crest there had been a pattern to the battle, often disguised, always shrouded by smoke, but a recognisable pattern. The French left had been broken, the centre had yielded and then delivered a splintering counter-attack, while the French right, like the British left, was still in reserve. Wellington was hooking his attacks from the west, one by one, but Clausel had forced a new pattern and was even now daring to hope for victory. Once in the valley there was no pattern. It was familiar, for Sharpe had been on many battlefields, but for the men who loaded and fired, who looked desperately into the smoke banks for a sign of danger, the valley was a place without pattern or reason. These men could not know that the French left was broken, would not know that the blood was drying to a crust on the flanks of the Heavy Dragoon horses, they only knew that this valley was their fighting place; the ground where they must kill or be killed.

It was a confused place, but it had a simplicity that Sharpe needed. He had been fooled by La Marquesa and his foolishness had led to the escape of his enemy. He had been outwitted by the clever people of the secret war, but in this valley there was a simple job to do. He knew that La Marquesa would be hearing the guns like an echo of last night's thunder. He knew she must know that he had turned the tables on her, lied through his love as she had lied through hers, and he wondered if she thought of him.

255

Politics, strategy, cleverness and guile had brought on this battle. Now it was up to the soldiers.

He could see to his right where the Sixth Division marched in small columns towards the great French column. It would be, perhaps, two minutes before the new Division formed its two deep line and the muskets could try again to stop the massive French attack, and he knew there was a job for the South Essex in that short time. The Battalion were at the valley's end, the Grenadier Company hard against the Teso San Miguel and acting as a hinge. The other nine companies were swinging back in the face of the French and the Light Company, on the left of the line, were swinging fastest and loading slowest. Sharpe could see Major Leroy, commanding the left five Companies, swearing at them and gesturing. Sharpe understood why. If the small Battalion line swung fully back to the hillside then the column could pour out into the open ground of the British rear. Leroy wanted to hold the South Essex, force the column to edge to its right and thus straight onto the muskets of the Sixth Division. The South Essex was like a desperately frail breakwater that had to force a tidal wave away from empty ground and into a channel prepared for it.

The space behind the Battalion was littered with wounded, and the bandsmen were tugging them backwards, away from the heels of the retreating companies, and Sharpe rode there and beckoned to a drummer boy. The lad gaped up at him as he slid from the horse. 'Sir?'

'Hold the horse! Understand? Find me when this is over. And don't bloody lose it!'

He could hear the drums, the cheers of the French, and the crackle of muskets seemed drowned by the great noise. The attack was in the valley, coming forward, and the South Essex thought they were the last obstacle between the French and Salamanca. They fought, but they stepped back after each shot, and Major Leroy galloped his horse behind the thin line and his voice pierced at Sharpe's ears. 'Still, you bastards! Stand still!' The Major was nearing the Light Company, who stepped back the fastest, and he swore at them, cursed them, but while he checked the Light Company the others bent backwards and Leroy was seething in his anger. He saw Sharpe and there was no time for a greeting, for surprise. The American Major pointed at the Company. 'Hold them, Sharpe!' He galloped right, to the other Companies, and Sharpe drew his sword.

Harper's gift. It was the first time he had carried it in battle and the blade was bright in the valley's gloom. Now he would find if it was lucky.

He stepped past the flank of the Company and the men were red-eyed, their faces smeared black with powder, and at first no one noticed him. They knew Leroy had gone and they were stepping backwards, their ramrods awkward in their hands, and suddenly a voice they knew, a voice they feared never to hear again, was shouting at them. 'Still!' They checked in their surprise, began to grin, and then they saw the anger on Sharpe's face. 'Front rank! Kneel!' That would stop the bastards. 'Sergeant Harper!'

'Sir!'

'Shoot the next bastard who takes a step back.'

'Yes, sir.'

They stared at him as if he was a ghost. They froze, bullets half rammed down barrels, and he bellowed at them to load, to hurry, and it was the first time he had shouted in a month and the strain tugged at the huge, tender bruise low on his stomach and Harper saw the twinge on his Captain's face. The front rank was kneeling now, more frightened of Sharpe's anger than the French, and the Riflemen were tap loading their guns, not bothering with the greased leather patch that gripped the grooves of the barrel. Sharpe knew it was a waste of a good weapon. 'Rifles!' He pointed to the open end of the line, nearest the French. 'Move! Load properly!'

The sound of the French was close, overwhelming, and he

wanted to cringe from it, to turn and watch it, but he dared not. His men were loading again, their training overcoming their fear, and he watched as the ramrods came up and out of the barrels and were propped against mens' bodies. The muskets were levelled towards the French. He glanced to his left and saw that number Five Company had already fired and he had to trust that no man in the Company disliked him enough to aim deliberately at him. 'Fire!'

The balls hammered past him. 'Load!' He watched them, daring them to move. The Riflemen were now in a small group at the open end of the line and he looked at them. 'Kill their officers. Fire in your own time.' He looked back at the men. 'We stay here. Aim at the corner of the column.' He suddenly grinned at them. 'Nice to be back.' He turned round, his back to the Company, and now all he could do was stand, to be still, to deny this tiny patch of grassland to the French. He stood with his legs apart, the sword resting on the ground, and the great column was shouting and drumming its way towards them.

The small volleys of the South Essex battered the column's nearest corner, threw men down so that the ranks behind edged right to avoid the bodies, and still the Company volleys came from the South Essex and the Frenchmen, who had been raked with shrapnel and canister, lanced with roundshot, angled their march so they would go past the single Battalion. The breakwater was holding. The French fired at them as they marched, but it was hard to load a musket and keep walking, harder still to aim in the rhythm of the march, and the column did not win by firepower. It was designed to win by sheer weight, by fear, by glory. The drums hypnotised the valley and drove the Frenchmen on and they passed just fifty yards in front of Sharpe. He watched the packed ranks, saw their mouths open rhythmically when the drums paused and the great shout went up, 'vive l'Empereur!' Another volley pitted the corner, more men fell, and then an officer tried to drag a group of men out of the column to fire at the Light Company and Daniel Hagman put a bullet through the Frenchman's throat. Sharpe watched the enemy infantry strip the dead officer as they marched past, successive ranks bending down to go through the officer's pockets and pouches, and still the drums bore them on and the shout filled the valley, and Sharpe wondered where the Sixth Division were and what was happening on the rest of the field.

He watched the enemy soldiers, so close, and except that they liked moustaches, they looked little different to his own men. Sometimes a Frenchman would catch Sharpe's eye and there was a curious moment of recognition as though the enemy face was that of an old half-remembered comrade. He saw the mouths open again. 'Vive l'Empereur!' One man caught Sharpe's eye as he chanted the words, shrugged and Sharpe could not help grinning back. It was ridiculous.

'Fire!' Lieutenant Price's voice shouted. The Company pulled their triggers and the column jerked spasmodically away from the balls. Sharpe was glad to see the man who had shrugged at him was still alive. He turned round. 'Stop firing!'

There was no point in firing now. They might kill a few men on the column's flanks, but their job had been to push the ponderous column a few yards to its right, and they had done it. They could save their loaded muskets for the column's retreat, if it did retreat, and Sharpe nodded to Price. 'The Company can retire, Lieutenant, as far as the hill.'

The rear of the column was marching past now and Sharpe saw the wounded limping behind, trying to catch up with their comrades, and some of them fell to add to the droppings of the great attack. He looked south, into the smoke, and he could see no cavalry yet, no guns, but they could come. He turned and walked towards his Company and the men grinned at him, called out to him, and he was ashamed because he had feared that one might aim for him. He nodded to them. 'How are you?'

They pounded his back, shouted at him, and they all seemed to have inane grins on their faces as though they had won a great victory. He pushed through them, noticing how foul was their breath after his month away from troops, but it was good to be back. Lieutenant Price saluted. 'Welcome back, sir.'

'It's nice to be back. How is it?'

Price glanced at the closest men, then grinned at Sharpe. 'Still the best Company in the Battalion, sir.'

'Without me?'

'They had me, sir.' They both laughed to cover a mutual pleasure. Price glanced at Sharpe's stomach. 'And you, sir?'

'The doctors say another month.'

'Harps said it was a miracle.'

Sharpe smiled. 'He performed it, then.' He turned to watch the column go on. It was like some mindless machine that was grinding its way northwards, aiming at the city, and he knew that soon the valley would fill with French guns and cavalry unless the column could be stopped. One of his men shouted over the swell of drums and French cheers.

'Harps says you was living in a palace with Duchess!'

'Harps is a bloody liar!' Sharpe pushed through the knot of men and grinned at the big Sergeant. 'How are you?'

'I'm doing all right. Yourself, sir?'

'It's fine.' Sharpe looked north to where the valley was littered with bodies. 'Casualties?'

Harper shook his head. He sounded disgusted. 'Two wounded. We went back too bloody fast.' He nodded at Sharpe's shoulder. 'You got the rifle back?'

'Yes. But I need ammunition.'

'I'll fix that for you, sir.' Harper turned as a new sound filled the valley. It was like a hundred children dragging sticks along park railings, the sound of the volleys that the Sixth Division were slamming into the column's head. The Sixth swore that this day they would restore the reputation that had been sullied by the time they took to capture the three fortresses. They had approached the great column in small columns and then, in the enemy's face, they swung into line and waited for the French to come into musket range.

The two-deep line curled round the head of the column. The men fought like automatons, biting the cartridges, loading, ramming, firing on command so that the volleys' flames ran down the face of the line, again and again, and the bullets twitched at the fog of powder smoke and hammered the French. The British volleys made the column's head into a pile of dead and wounded men. Frenchmen who had thought themselves safe in the fourth or fifth rank suddenly had to cock their muskets and fire desperately into the smoke bank. The column checked. The drums still sounded, but they no longer paused for the great shout. The drummer boys worked their sticks as if they could force the men over the barricade of the dead and onto the Sixth Division, but the men at the column's front were flinching from the murderous fire. The men behind pressed forward, the column crushed and bulged, and the drummer boys faltered. Some officers, brave beyond duty, tried to take men forward, but it was hopeless. The bravest died, the others shrank back from the British fire, and the column heaved and jerked like some giant snared animal.

There was a pause in the British volleys. It was filled with a new sound, a scraping and clicking as the hundreds of long bayonets were taken from belt-scabbards and fixed on the muskets. Then a cheer, a British cheer, and the long line came forward with their blades level and the great column, that had so nearly turned the battle, turned instead into a panicked crowd. They ran.

The French had tried to send galloper guns through the small valley to blast the Sixth Division away, but the guns had been broken by the British artillery. The French gunners who still lived put their wounded horses out of their agony with their short carbines. The valley floor was thick with the remains of battle. Bodies, guns, canteens, pouches, haversacks, spent cannon balls, dead horses, the wounded. Everywhere the wounded. The French column was a running mass of fugitives, fleeing the steady line of the Sixth Division that came forward into the small valley which was covered by a tenuous awning of smoke. The sun touched the smoke layer with red. The Fourth Division reformed itself, drew bayonets, and went on with the Sixth. The British went forward, the French back, and Clausel's centre was gone. It had extracted a price for its defeat, a high price, but it was over. The Eagles went back, they left the Greater Arapile, the French were running from the field. The French left had been destroyed, utterly destroyed, in just forty minutes. The centre had tried and failed, and now all that could be done was for the French right to form a barrier on the edge of the plain to stop the British pursuit.

The sun was sinking into a cushion of gold and scarlet, it touched the killing ground with crimson and it promised to give enough light for a little time more. Time enough for more blood to be spilt on an earth that already reeked with the stench of it.

CHAPTER 23

To the spectators on the great ridge the battle had appeared as something like a surging spring tide seething into a place that was usually above the high water mark. The tide had surged from the west, running swiftly over the plain, and then it had struck the obstacles of the Arapiles. The fighting had churned. For a moment it had looked as if the French centre would flow irresistibly towards the city, through the small valley, but it had been held, the two Divisions in column broken, and the fighting had surged back, past the Arapiles, and now the fighting drained off to the south and east; away from the city.

The fighting was not done, yet already the scavengers were on the field. The wives and children of the British were stripping enemy corpses. When it was darker they would start on men of their own side, slitting the throats of the wounded who resisted them, but for the moment they plundered the French while the Bandsmen cared for the British wounded. The South Essex followed the Sixth Division for a small way, but then orders came for them to rest and the men dropped where they were.

The drummer boy, with the worried intensity of a child given a great responsibility, had clung to Sharpe's horse and the Rifleman was grateful for the saddle. The wound throbbed, he was tired, and he forced himself to respond to the greetings of Leroy and Forrest, of the other officers, and they teased him for having a horse. He was tired, but still restless.

Musketry came from the south. The fighting still went on.

Sharpe sat on his horse, her horse, and he watched, without really seeing, as a small child tugged at the ring on a finger of a naked corpse. The child's mother was stripping another Frenchman nearby, slicing open the seams, and she snapped at the child to hurry because there were so many corpses and so many looters. The child, dressed only in a cut-down skirt of her mother's, picked up a discarded French bayonet and began hacking at the ring finger. Prisoners were being herded, disarmed, and led to the rear.

The French had been beaten. Not just beaten, they had been utterly defeated. Half their army had been broken and the survivors were running for the road that led eastwards through the southern woods. Only a rearguard stopped the vengeful British and German cavalry from hacking into the fugitives, but the cavalry pursuit could wait. The French were stumbling, discipline lost, back through the cork woods and oak trees to the town of Alba de Tormes. The battle had been fought in a huge bend of the river and Alba was the only town with a bridge that could take the French east to safety. Many men would use the fords, but most, with all the baggage, the guns, the pay chest, and the wounded, would make for the mediaeval bridge at Alba de Tormes. And there stop. The Spanish had a garrison in the town, a garrison that commanded the bridge, and the French were trapped in the great river bend. The cavalry could ride in the morning and round up the fugitives. It was a great victory.

Sharpe stared at the smoke that lay above the battlefield in long pink ribbons. He should be feeling the elation of this day. They had waited all summer for a battle, wanted it, and no one had dared hope it would be this decisive. This year they had taken Ciudad Rodrigo, Badajoz, and now they had defeated the so-called Army of Portugal. Yet Sharpe was haunted by failure. He had protected La Marquesa, who was his enemy, and he had failed to capture Leroux. He had been beaten by the Frenchman. Leroux had put Sharpe in the death room, he had broken Sharpe's sword, and Sharpe wanted revenge. There was a man alive who could boast of beating Sharpe, and that hurt; it throbbed like the wound, and Sharpe wanted the pain to go. He was restless. He wanted one more chance to face the Kligenthal, to possess it, and he touched the hilt of his new sword as if it were a talisman. It had yet to be blooded.

The South Essex were piling their arms, going to the village to steal doors and furniture that could be broken into fires, and Sharpe did not want to rest. There was unfinished business, and it frustrated him because he did not see how to finish it, and he wondered if the Palacio Casares was even now being searched for Leroux. He could go back to Sala-manca now, but he could not face La Marquesa.

Major Forrest walked over to Sharpe's horse and looked up. 'You look like a statue, Sharpe.' He held up a captured bottle of brandy. 'Join us?'

Sharpe looked to the southern edge of the battlefield where smoke was still rising from the fight. 'Do you mind if I see the end of it, sir?'

'Help yourself.' Forrest grinned at him. 'Take care, I don't want to lose you again.'

'I'll take care, sir.' He let the horse find its own way between the grass fires and the wounded. The sun was almost gone, already a pale moon was high in the evening sky, and he could see where the French rearguard sparkled the dusk with their muskets. A dog whimpered beside the dead body of its master, barked as Sharpe's horse came too close, and then ran back to its vigil.

Sharpe was depressed. He had always known that he could not possess La Marquesa, yet he missed her, and he was saddened because they had both deceived, there was so much left unsaid. It too was unfinished business. He rode slowly towards the gunfire.

The last French Division had arrayed itself on a small, steep ridge that blocked the tracks into the wood. The ridge allowed six and sometimes seven ranks of men to fire at the

British, each rank firing over the heads of the ranks in front, and the twilight was stabbed by the French flames.

The Sixth Division, that had already defeated Clausel's brave hopes, advanced against the obstacle. They had already won a great victory and now they thought that this rearguard, this impudent line, would melt before their musket fire in the dusk. The musket duel began. Line against line, and the cartridges were bitten open, the powder tipped, and the flints snapped forward, and the French line held. It fought gloriously, hopelessly, in the knowledge that if they collapsed and ran for the road that led eastwards through the woods, the cavalry would come after them. Darkness was their hope, their salvation, and the last French Division stood on their small steep ridge and they galled the Sixth Division, flayed it, and the Battalions shrunk man by man.

British artillery jangled its way over the plain, turned, and unlimbered on the Sixth Division's flanks. The horses were led away, the guns' trails unhooked from the limbers, and the red-bagged ammunition was piled beside the weapons. Canister. The gun-layers eyed the French line dispassionately; at this range they could not miss.

Nearly every ball from the splitting tin containers would count on the French ridge. The guns jumped backwards, smoke belching, and Sharpe saw the French fall sideways like wheat hit by buckshot. Still they fought. Fires had started in the grass, adding to the smoke, and their flames were lurid on the underside of the battle smoke that hung in skeins over the spitting muskets. The French held their place, the dead fell on the slope, the wounded struggled to keep firing. They must have been terrified, Sharpe thought as he watched them, because they knew that the battle was lost, that instead of marching to the gates of Portugal they would have a long harried retreat into Spain's centre, yet still they fought and their discipline under the onslaught of musket and canister was awesome. They were buying time with their lives, time for their shattered companions to make

266

their way eastwards towards the bridge at Alba de Tormes. And there, the British knew, a Spanish garrison waited to complete the destruction.

The fight could not last, whatever the bravery of the French, and the end was signalled as the Fifth Division, which had attacked the French left beside the cavalry earlier in the day, were marched onto the French rearguard's flank. Two British Divisions fought a single French Division. More guns came in a slew of dust and chains and their canister split apart in the heart of the guns' great flames. More fires caught in the grass, their flames throwing wavering black shadows as the twilight turned to night, and the end had to come. There was a pause in the musket fire of the Sixth, an order was repeated from Company to Company, and there was the great noise of the scraping bayonets coming from scabbards. The line flickered with reflections from the seventeen inch blades.

'Forward!' The last light was draining in the west over Portugal, there was a cheer from the British, the line surged forward towards the battered French, but the battle had one surprise left.

Sharpe heard the hooves behind him, and took no notice, and then the urgency of the sound, the speed of the single horse, made him turn. A lone cavalry officer, resplendent in blue and silver, his sabre drawn, was galloping at the French line. He was shouting like a maniac. 'Wait! Wait!'

The Company nearest Sharpe heard the sound, checked, and a Sergeant forced a gap in the files. Officers shouted at the cavalryman, but he took no notice, just urged on his horse that was labouring with the effort, raked by spurs, and the turf flew in clods behind the hooves. 'Wait! Wait!' The officer went for the gap and the French, on the ridge, were just shadows as they turned and ran for the safety of the dark woods.

The cavalryman went through the gap in the British infantry and he still screamed defiance at the French as they disappeared. He set his horse at the bank of the ridge, scrambled up, and his sabre flailed like a whip as he forced his horse after the enemy. Sharpe urged his own horse forward. The cavalryman was Lord Spears.

Spears had disappeared into the dark trees and Sharpe, pulling his clumsy sword free of the scabbard, went round the flank of the British line, in front of the silent, smoking guns, and the slope of the small ridge was horrid with French dead. Officers of the Sixth Division shouted at him, cursed him, because he was in their line of fire, but then his horse tipped over the crest and he was riding for the deep shadows. He could hear shouts ahead, then musket fire, and Sharpe ducked his head as La Marquesa's horse went into the trees.

Spears was in a small clearing among the trees, fighting a crazy lone battle with French fugitives, and Sharpe came too late. The cavalryman had ridden the length of the clearing, chopping down with his sabre, and as Sharpe arrived he was turning the horse, hacking down, and a French Sergeant was on his other side, musket raised, and Sharpe saw the flash, saw Spears go rigid, and then the French fled into the trees. Spears' mouth opened, silently, he seemed to shake, and then he slumped in the saddle. The sabre hung beside him, his arm limp, and he was gasping for breath.

Sharpe rode to his side. Spears' right hand was clasped to the silver and blue of his uniform and, between the fingers, dark blood stained the cloth. He looked at Sharpe. 'I was almost too late.'

'You're a fool.'

'I know.' Spears looked past Sharpe to the three bodies he had made in the clearing. 'It was good swordwork, Richard. You know that, don't you.'

'Yes, my lord.'

'Call me Jack.' Spears was fighting to control his breath. He looked disbelievingly at the blood that stained his hand and jacket. He shook his head. 'Oh, God.'

Sharpe could hear the infantry of the Sixth Division

coming into the trees. 'Come on, my lord. A doctor.'

'No.' Spears' eyes glistened. He blinked rapidly and seemed ashamed. 'Must be the musket smoke, Richard.'

'Yes.'

'Get me out of here.'

Sharpe sheathed his sword for the second time that day, and both times it had been unbloodied, and he took the reins of Spears' horse and led it out of the trees. He skirted the advancing infantry, not wanting to be fired on by a nervous man, and they came out onto the small ridge a hundred yards from where the last fighting of the day had happened.

'Stop here, Richard.' They were at the top of the bank. The fires and the darkness of the battlefield were spread out in front of them.

Sharpe still held the reins of Spears' horse. 'You need a doctor, my lord.'

'No.' Spears shook his head. 'No, no, no. Help me down.'

Sharpe tethered both horses to a misshapen, stunted tree. Then he lifted Spears from the saddle, and laid him on the bank. He made a pillow from his own greatcoat. He could hear the Sixth Division hacking at branches with bill-hooks and bayonets, making their fires, and the battle, at last, was truly over. Sharpe opened Spears' jacket, his shirt, and he had to tug the linen away from the wound. The bullet had driven some threads of the shirt into the chest and they stuck out, matted and obscene, like thick hairs. The hole seemed very small. Blood welled in it, glistened black in the moonlight, then spilt dark on Spears' pale skin. Spears grimaced. 'It hurts.'

'Why the hell did you do it?'

'I didn't want to miss the battle.' Spears put his fingers on the blood, lifted them away and looked at his fingertips in horror.

'It was a crazy thing to do. The battle was over.' Sharpe cut with his pocket knife at Spears' shirt, tearing away the clean linen to make a pad for the wound.

Spears gave a lopsided grin. 'All heroes are crazy.' He tried to laugh and the laugh turned into a cough. He put his head back on the pillow. 'I'm dying.' He said it very calmly.

Sharpe put the pad on the wound, pressed gently and Spears flinched because the bullet had broken a rib. Sharpe took his hand away. 'You won't die.'

Spears twisted his head and watched Sharpe's face. His voice had some of his old, impish charm. 'Actually, Richard, at the risk of sounding frightfully heroic and dramatic, I rather want to die.' The tears that were in his eyes belied his words. He sniffed and turned his head back so he stared upwards. 'That's awfully embarrassing, I know. Apologies.' Sharpe said nothing. He stared at the fires that threaded the battlefield, grass fires, and at the mysterious lumps that were broken bodies. A wind came off the field and brought the smell of victory; smoke, powder, blood, and burning flesh. Sharpe had known other men want to die, but never someone who was a lord, who was handsome, charming, and who now apologised again. 'I did embarrass you. Forget I spoke.'

Sharpe sat beside him. 'I'm not embarrassed. I don't believe you.'

For a moment neither man spoke. Musket shots came flat over the battlefield; either looters being discouraged or men putting other men out of their misery. Spears turned his head again. 'I never slept with La Marquesa.'

Sharpe was startled by the sudden, strange confession. He shrugged. 'Does it matter?'

Spears nodded slowly. 'Say thank you.'

Sharpe, not understanding, humoured him. 'Thank you.'

Spears looked up again. 'I tried, Richard. God, I tried. That wasn't very decent of me.' His voice was low, directed at the stars.

It seemed a strange guilt and Sharpe still did not understand why Spears had raised the subject. 'I don't think she took offence.'

'No she didn't.' Spears paused. 'Crazy Jack.'

Sharpe drew his feet in, as if to get up. 'Let me fetch a doctor.'

'No. No doctor.' Spears put a hand on Sharpe's arm. 'No doctor, Richard. Can you keep a secret?'

Sharpe nodded. 'Yes.'

Spears took his hand away. His breath was heavy in his throat. He seemed to be making up his mind whether to speak or not, but finally he said it. His voice was very bitter. 'I've got the Black Lion. Dear God! The Black Lion.'

CHAPTER 24

'Oh, God.' Sharpe did not know what to say.

The two men were on the edge of the battlefield, the edge of an immense expanse of misery. Shadows crossed in front of the intermittent flames, dogs howled at the half moon that silvered the humped shapes of the wounded and dead. The guns that had shattered the French rearguard were left where they had fired, and their barrels cooled in the night wind. From far across the dark field came the sound of singing. A group of men round a fire were celebrating their survival. Sharpe looked at Spears. 'How long have you known?'

Spears shrugged. 'Two years.'

'Oh, God.' Sharpe felt the hopelessness of it. All men feared it, of course, it lurked in the shadows like the dark beast that the army nicknamed it. The Black Lion, the worst kind of pox, the pox that killed a man through senility, blindness, and gibbering madness. Sharpe had once paid his pennies to walk through Bedlam, the mad-house in London's Moorfields, and he had seen the syphilitic patients in their small, foul cages. The patients could earn a small pittance, thrown farthings, by capering and displaying themselves. The Insane of Bedlam were one of the sights of London, more popular even than the public executions. Spears faced a long, filthy, agonising death. Sharpe looked at him. 'Is that why you did this?'

The handsome face nodded. 'Yes. You won't tell?'

'No.'

Spears' sabretache was lying on the bank and he reached

for it, failed, and flapped a hand at it. 'There are cigars in there. Would you?'

Sharpe opened the flap. A pistol lay on the top, which he put to one side, and beneath it were wrapped cigars and a tinder box. He blew the charred linen into a small flame, lit two cigars, and handed one to Spears. Sharpe rarely smoked, but tonight, in this sadness, he wanted a cigar. The smell reminded him of La Marquesa. The smoke drifted away on the breeze from the dead.

Spears made a small sound that could have been a laugh. 'I didn't even have to be here.'

'At the battle?'

'No.' He drew on the cigar, making the tip bright. 'In the army.' He sighed, shifted himself. 'My elder brother got the inheritance. He was such a tedious man, Richard, so utterly tedious. We had a mutual, brotherly hatred. Then two weeks before he was to get married, God answered my prayers. He fell off his bloody nag and broke his fat neck. And I got everything. Money, estate, houses, the lot.' His voice was low, almost hoarse. He seemed to want to talk. 'I was already over here and I didn't want to go back.' He turned towards Sharpe and grinned. 'There's too much joy in this war. Does that make sense?'

'Yes.' Sharpe knew the joy of war. No other thing gave such excitement, or asked such a price. He stared at the grass fires which scorched the flesh of the wounded and dead. War had brought Sharpe promotion, a wife, La Marquesa, and it could yet kill him as it was killing Spears. Capricious Fate.

Spears coughed and this time he wiped blood from his lips. 'I gambled the whole lot away. Jesus God! Every bloody penny.'

'All?'

'Twice over. You don't gamble, do you?'

'No.'

Spears grinned. 'You're very tedious for a hero.' He coughed and turned his head to spit blood on the grass. Most

273

of it went onto Sharpe's greatcoat. 'It's like standing on a clifftop and knowing you can fly. There's nothing like it, nothing. Except war and women.'

The wind was cooler now, chilling the skin of Sharpe's face. He pulled Spears' jacket over the wound. He wished he had known this man better; Spears had offered friendship and Sharpe had been wary of it. Now he felt very close to Spears as the blood seeped into the lungs.

Spears pulled on the cigar, coughed again, and the blood flecked his cheeks. He turned his face towards Sharpe. 'Will you do something for me?'

'Of course.'

'Write to my sister. Hogan's got her address. Tell her I died well. Tell her I died a hero.' He smiled in self-deprecation. 'Do you promise?'

'I promise.' Sharpe looked upwards. The stars were the camp fires of a limitless heavenly army. Beneath them, the fires of the victorious British were dull. The muskets sounded far away as men dispatched the wounded.

Spears blew out a spume of smoke. 'Her name's Dorothy. Ugly name. I do like her. I want her to know I died well. It's the least I can do now.'

'I'll tell her.'

Spears seemed to ignore Sharpe's words. 'I've ruined her life, Richard. No money, no inheritance, no dowry. She'll have to marry some bloody tradesman to get his money and in return he'll get her body and some noble blood.' His voice was very bitter. 'Poor Dorothy.' He took a deep breath that rasped in his throat. 'I'm broke, I'm poxed, and I've disgraced the family. But if I die a hero, then at least she has that. A lot of people won't cash my notes of hand. Bad behaviour when a fellow has just died for King and Country.' Spears laughed, and the blood was dark on his skin. 'You can live as bad as you like, Richard, as long as you can, but if you die for your country you'll be forgiven everything. Everything.' Spears turned away from Sharpe so he could stare into the immensity of the battlefield's sadness. 'I used to get dragged to bloody church every Sunday. We went into the private pew and all the peasants tugged their forelocks. Then the bloody preacher got up on his back trotters and warned us about gambling, drunkenness, and fornication. He gave me all my ambitions in life.' He coughed again, worse this time, and there was a pause as he forced air into his lungs. 'I just want Dorothy to know I was a hero. They can put a marble plaque in the church. The last of the Spears, dead at Salamanca.'

'I'll write.' Sharpe took off his shako and pushed a hand through his hair. 'I'm sure the Peer will write.'

Spears turned his head to look at Sharpe again. 'And tell Helena she broke my heart.'

Sharpe smiled. He did not know if he would ever see La Marquesa again, but he nodded. 'I'll tell her.'

Spears sighed, smiled ruefully, and stared at the battle-field. 'I could have done my bit for England. Given her the pox.'

Sharpe grinned dutifully. He supposed that it must be near eleven o'clock. So many people in England would be going to bed and they would be quite ignorant that at tea-time the Third Division had smashed the French left, and that by the time the bone china was cleared away the French had lost a quarter of their army. In a few days, though, the bells would ring out in all the villages and parsons would give thanks to God as though the deity were some kind of superior General of Division. The squires would pay for hogsheads of beer and make speeches about the Tyrant Broken by Honest Englishmen. There would be a fresh crop of plaques in the churches, for those who could afford it, but on the whole England would not show much gratitude for the men who had done their bit this day. Then he remembered what Spears had said. 'Given her the pox', 'done my bit for England' and Sharpe was suddenly cold inside. Spears knew she was French and he had betrayed it because he could not resist the joke. Sharpe kept his voice calm. 'How long have you known about her?'

Spears twisted to look at him. 'You know?'

'Yes.'

'Jesus. The things people say in bed.' He wiped blood off his cheek.

Sharpe stared into the darkness. 'How long have you known.'

Spears tossed his cigar down the slope. 'A month.'

'Did you tell Hogan?'

There was a pause. Sharpe looked at Spears. The cavalryman was watching him, conscious suddenly that he had said too much. Slowly, Spears nodded. 'Of course I did.' He smiled suddenly. 'How many do you think died today?'

Sharpe did not reply. He knew Spears was lying. Hogan had only discovered that La Marquesa was once Hélène Leroux yesterday. Curtis had received the letter in the morning, seen Hogan in the afternoon, and then come to Sharpe. Spears had never told Hogan, nor did Spears know that Curtis had seen Sharpe. 'How did you find out?'

'It doesn't matter, Richard.'

'It does.'

There was a flash of anger in Spears. 'I'm a bloody Exploring Officer, remember? It's my job to find things out.'

'And to tell Hogan. You didn't.'

Spears breathed heavily. He watched Sharpe, then shook his head. His voice was weary. 'Christ! It doesn't matter now.'

Sharpe stood up, tall against the night sky, and he hated what he had to do, but it did matter now, whatever Spears thought. The sword hissed out of the scabbard, came free, and the steel was pale in the half-moon.

Spears frowned. 'What the hell are you doing?'

Sharpe put the blade beneath Spears, pushed away a protesting arm, and then levered with the steel so that the cavalryman was half rolled over, facing away from Sharpe, and then the Rifleman put one foot on Spears' waist and the sword blade against Spears' back. There was anger in

Sharpe's voice, a cold, frightening anger. 'Heroes don't have scarred backs. You talk to me, my lord, or I'll carve your back into bloody ribbons. I'll tell your sister you died as a poxed coward, with your wounds behind.'

'I know nothing!'

Sharpe leaned on the blade, enough for its razor point to go through cloth. His voice was loud, strong. 'You know, you bastard. You knew she was French, no one else did. You knew she was Leroux's sister, didn't you?' There was silence. He pushed the sword.

'Yes.' Spears choked, spat blood. 'Stop it, for God's sake, stop it.'

'Then talk.' There was silence again, except for the wind rustling the leaves of the trees behind them, the crackle of flames from the fires of the Sixth Division, and the desultory, far-away musket shots. Sharpe lowered his voice. 'Your sister will be disgraced. She'll have nothing. No money, no prospects, not even a dead hero as a brother. She'll have to marry some ironmonger with dirty hands and a great belly and she'll whore herself for his money. You want me to save your bloody honour, my lord? You talk.'

Spears talked. His words were punctuated by the coughing, the spitting of blood. He whined at times, tried to wriggle, but the sword was always close and, bit by horrid bit, Sharpe took the story from him. It depressed Sharpe, it saddened him. Spears pleaded for understanding, forgiveness even, but it was a tale of honour sold. Spears had told Sharpe, weeks before, that he had been nearly captured by Leroux. He had told of escaping through a window, tearing his arm to shreds, but the story was not true.

Lord Spears had never escaped from Leroux. He had been captured and had signed his parole. Leroux, he said, had talked to him through a long night, had drunk with him, and found the weakness. They had made a bargain. Information for money. Spears sold Colquhoun Grant, the army's finest Exploring Officer, and Leroux gave him five hundred Nap-

277

oleons and all had been gambled away. 'I thought I might get the town house back, at least.'

'Go on.'

He had sold the list stolen from Hogan's papers; the list of men paid by Britain for information. He had made ten gold coins a head, then lost it at the tables, and then, he said, Sharpe spoiled everything. He had chased Leroux into the fortresses and Spears thought his paymaster was gone, trapped, and then Helena had asked for him, talked with him, and the money had started coming again. And all the while Leroux had Spears' parole, the piece of paper that proved Spears was a liar, that he had been a prisoner once, and the paper was held against Spears. If he double-crossed them, he said, then Leroux threatened to send the paper to Wellington. Leroux had made a slave of Spears, a well-paid slave, and who would ever suspect an English lord? The clerks, the grooms, the servants, the cooks, the lesser people of the Headquarters had all been under suspicion, but not Lord Spears, Crazy Jack, the man who livened parties and used his wit and charm to entrance the world, and all the time he was a spy.

There was more. Sharpe knew there would be more. He had taken his sword away, was sitting beside Spears, and the cavalryman confessed all, almost glad to spill it out, yet there was a reticence at the end of his story. The grass fires were dying. The moaning and the musket shots were lower and fewer from the battlefield, the wind had reached its night chill. Sharpe looked at the grey blade that stretched in front of him. 'El Mirador?'

'He's safe.'

'Where?'

Spears shrugged. 'He's in a monastery today. Bowing and scraping.'

'You didn't sell him?'

Spears laughed, and the sound was harsh and bubbling because of the blood in his throat. He swallowed and grimaced. 'I didn't need to. Leroux had already found out.'

As Hogan had suspected. 'Sweet God.' Sharpe stared at the field after battle. He had once feared for La Marquesa's body beneath Leroux's torture, now he flinched from the thought of the elderly priest racked on a blood soaked table. 'But you said he's safe?'

Curtis was safe, but he was an old man. Old men worry, Spears said, about dying before their work is done, and so Curtis had written the names and addresses of all his correspondents in a small, leather book. It was disguised as one of his notebooks of astronomical observations, filled with star charts and Latin names, but the codes could be broken.

Leroux had bided his time. He had planned to take Curtis when the British had gone, but then came news of a great British victory, and he had demanded that Spears fetch the priest. Spears' voice was small now. 'I couldn't do that. So I fetched him the book instead.'

Leroux no longer needed El Mirador. With the book in his hands he could find all the correspondents who wrote faithfully from throughout Europe and he could take them one by one, kill them, and Britain would be blind. Sharpe shook his head in disbelief. 'Why didn't you just lie? Why did you have to give them the book? They didn't know about it!'

'I thought they'd reward me.' Lord Spears was pathetic.

'Reward you! More blood money?'

'No.' Blood was dark on his cheek. 'I wanted her body just once. Just once.' He made a choking sound that could have been a laugh or a sob. 'I didn't get it. Leroux gave me back my parole instead. He returned me my honour.' The bitterness was rank in his voice.

The dark bulk of the Greater Arapile was topped by two small fires. It blocked Sharpe's view of the lights of Salamanca. 'Where's Leroux now?'

'He's riding for Paris.'

'Which way?'

'He's going to Alba de Tormes.'

Sharpe looked at Spears, dying on the ground. 'You didn't

tell him the Spanish were there?'

'He didn't seem to care.'

Sharpe swore softly. He must go. He swore again, louder, because he liked Spears and he hated this sudden weakness, this collapse of a man, this sale of honour. 'You sold all our agents for one parole?'

No. There had been money, too, Spears said, but the money was to be paid when Leroux reached Paris and it would go to Dorothy in England. A dowry, Spears' last treacherous gift, and he pleaded with Sharpe, told Sharpe he could not understand; family was all, and Sharpe stood up. 'I'm going.'

Spears lay on the ground, defeated, broken. 'One last promise?'

'What?'

'If you find him she won't get the money.'

'No.'

'Then keep my honour for her.' The voice was husky, close to breaking. 'Tell her I was a hero.'

Sharpe lifted the sword, put the point in the scabbard, and drove it home. 'I'll tell her you died a hero. Your wounds in front.'

Spears rolled onto his side because it was easier to void the blood. 'And one thing more.'

'I'm in a hurry.' Sharpe had to find Hogan. He would rouse Harper first, because the Sergeant would want to join this final hunt, this last chance against their enemy. Leroux had killed Windham, killed McDonald, he had come close to killing Sharpe, he had tortured Spanish priests, and he had taken the honour of Lord Spears. Sharpe had been given one more chance in the wreckage after the battle.

'I'm in a hurry, too.' Spears waved a feeble hand towards the battlefield. 'I don't want those bloody looters to kill me, Richard. Do that much for me.' He blinked. 'It hurts, Richard, it hurts.'

Sharpe remembered Connelley. Die well, lad, die well. 'You want me to kill you?'

'The last office of a friend?' It was a plea.

Sharpe picked up Spears' pistol, cocked it, and crouched beside the supine cavalryman. 'Are you sure?'

'It hurts. Tell her I died well.'

Sharpe had liked this man. He remembered the chicken being tossed like a howitzer shell at the ball, he remembered the great shout in the big Plaza on the morning after the first night on the mirador. This man had made Sharpe laugh, had shared wine with him, and now he was a miserable, broken man who had given his honour first to Leroux, and now to Sharpe. 'I'll tell her you died well. I'll tell her you were a hero. I'll make you into Sir Lancelot.' Spears smiled. His eyes were on Sharpe. The Rifleman brought the pistol close to Spears' neck. 'I'll tell her to build a new church big enough for the bloody plaque.' Spears smiled wider and the bullet went beneath his chin, up through the skull, and erupted at the top of his head. It was the kind of wound that a hero, on horseback, might fetch. He died instantly, smiling, and Sharpe's greatcoat was spattered by the wound. He pulled it out, then threw it down, hating it. He turned and hurled the pistol into the trees, heard it crash through branches and twigs, and then there was silence. He looked down on Spears and cursed himself that he had ever become involved. Spears had talked of the joy that war could bring, the irresponsibility of unshackled youth, but there was little joy in this secret war.

He bent down and picked up his greatcoat, shook it out, and walked to the horses. He mounted his own, led Spears' by the reins, and went down the bank. He paused at its foot, looked back, and the body was a dark shadow against the grass. He told himself that the tears in the corners of his eyes were just irritation from the smoke of battle; something any man could expect.

Revenge was at Alba de Tormes, his heels scraped the horse's flanks, and the Cathedral clock, above the Palacio Casares, struck twelve.

CHAPTER 25

Alba de Tormes was a town on a hill to the east of the River Tormes. The hill was crowned with an ancient castle and covered with jumbled roofs that led down to the magnificent convent where the body of St. Teresa of Avila was revered by pilgrims. Beside the convent was the bridge.

The French needed the bridge to take their shattered army to the relative safety of the eastern bank and away from the pursuit that they knew would come with sabres in the dawn, but Wellington had denied them the bridge. Weeks before, when his army first came to Salamanca, he had put a Spanish garrison into the Castle and into the defence works at the bridge's eastern end. The Spanish guns could rake the length of the bridge, rattle its stones with canister, and so the French were trapped in the great river bend.

From Alba de Tormes the river flowed nine miles north and then, in a great curve, it turned westwards and flowed for ten miles before its waters passed beneath the arches of Salamanca's Roman bridge. Within that great bend the French fled eastward through the night. Hundreds crossed by the ford, but most went towards the town that had the only bridge they could use. The French guns, baggage, pay-chest, wounded, all went to Alba de Tormes and to the bridge that was guarded by the guns of the Spanish.

Except the Spanish were not there. They had fled three days before; fled without sight of an enemy. They knew the French were coming south, feared a British defeat, and so the Spanish garrison packed its baggage and marched south.

They deserted their post. The bridge was left open to the French and, all night, Marmont's men went eastward. A great victory had been devalued. The stragglers of the defeated army were collected on the eastern bank, formed into ranks, and marched away. A rearguard, that had not fought the previous day, barred the eastward road a little beyond the town and its empty bridge.

The news reached Wellington's Headquarters at the same time that Sharpe was persuading Hogan that Britain's spy-ring had been betrayed. One notebook, just that, and a hundred doors would be beaten down from Madrid to Stettin, El Mirador's correspondents would be dragged away and the French firing squads would be busy. Hogan shook his head. 'But how do you know?'

'Lord Spears found it missing, sir.' Sharpe had already described a hero's death for Jack Spears.

Hogan stared suspiciously. 'Just that? Nothing else?'

'Isn't it enough, sir? He died before he could say anything else.'

Hogan nodded slowly. 'We must tell the Peer.'

Then there was the explosion of anger, of cursing, because Wellington in the next room was hearing from a cavalry patrol that the French were crossing the bridge at Alba de Tormes. The defeated army were escaping, not trapped as he had thought, because the Spanish had fled. The door between the two rooms was flung open.

Sharpe had seen Wellington's anger before. It was a cold anger, hidden by stillness, expressed in bitter politeness. Not this night. The Peer hit the table with his fist. 'God damn them! God damn their bloody souls! Their bloody, rotten, filthy souls!' He looked at Hogan. 'They deserted Alba de Tormes. Why didn't we know?'

Hogan shrugged. 'Because they didn't see fit to tell us, sir.'

'Alava!' Wellington bellowed the name of the Spanish General who was the liaison officer with the British. The staff officers were very still in the face of the General's anger. He hit the table again. 'They think we fight for their bloody country because we love it? They deserve to bloody lose it!' He stalked from the room, slammed the door, and Hogan let out a long, slow breath.

'I don't think the Peer's in any mood for your news, Richard.'

'So what do we do, sir?'

Hogan turned to a staff officer. 'What's the nearest cavalry?'

'KGL Light, sir.'

Hogan turned for his hat. 'Get them.' He looked at Sharpe. 'Not you, Richard. You're not well.'

Sharpe rode, despite Hogan, and Harper rode beside him on Spears' horse. Captain Lossow, with his troop, were their escort, and the German officer greeted Sharpe with undisguised pleasure. The pleasure was dissipated by the long, chafing ride. Hogan was at home on a horse, he rode straight backed and long stirruped, while Harper had been bred in a valley of the Donegal Moors, had ridden the ponies bareback as a child, and he sat easily on Spears' horse. Sharpe was in a nightmare: He ached in every bone, the wound throbbed, and three times he nearly fell as sleep tried to claim him. Now, at dawn, he sat in agony above the Tormes and stared at a grey landscape through which the river twisted, sinewy and silver, past the silent town with its castle, convent, and empty bridge. The French had gone.

And Leroux? Sharpe did not know. Perhaps the French Colonel had lied to Lord Spears. Perhaps Leroux planned to stay in Salamanca until the British moved on again, this time eastwards, but somehow Sharpe doubted it. Leroux wanted to take his treasure back to Paris, decode it, and then loose the cruel men against the names inside. Leroux had ridden, Sharpe was sure, but where? Alba de Tormes? Or had he gone directly east from Salamanca towards Madrid? Hogan doubted it. Leroux, Hogan was certain, would try to find the security of the French army, surround himself with muskets

284

and sabres, and the great doubt in Hogan's mind was simply whether Leroux had been given too great a start. They spurred down the hill towards the river that slid chill beneath the mockingly empty bridge.

Sharpe had been given his last chance. He had ridden for it through the night and in this dawn his hopes were at their lowest. He wanted to take his sword, his unblooded sword, against the Kligenthal. He wanted Leroux because Leroux had beaten him, and if a man thought that was a bad reason, then a man had no pride. Yet how could they discover a lone rider in this immense countryside, skeined with early mist? Sharpe wanted revenge for the deaths of the crucified Spaniards, for the deaths of Windham and McDonald, for the pistol shot on the upper cloister, and for Spears whom Sharpe had liked, whom Sharpe had killed, and whose honour he protected.

Hogan twisted in his saddle. He looked tired and irritable. 'Do you think we've overtaken him?'

'I don't know, sir.' In the dawn there was no certainty.

They clattered over the bridge, the sabres of Lossow's Germans drawn in case the French had left a rearguard in the town, and then the iron of the horses' hooves filled the narrow streets with echoing din. As they breasted the hill at the town's head they saw the horizon, that till now had been grey touched with spreading pink, suddenly blaze with the top edge of the rising sun. It was scarlet gold, dazzling, and the western wall of the castle keep was coloured rose. The new day.

'Sir!' Harper was pointing, exultant. 'Sir!'

In the sunrise, in the glory of the new day, the doubts were put to rest. A rider, alone, going eastwards, and in the telescope, through the flare of the light, Sharpe saw green and black overalls, boots, a red jacket, and an unmistakeable black fur hat. A Chasseur of Napoleon's Imperial Guard, alone, trotting eastwards. It had to be Leroux! The lone figure turned dark and blurred against the dawn, then dropped into a dip of the road. He had not looked back.

They followed, urging the horses into a fast trot for their strength had to be conserved even though the riders all wanted to sound the pursuit, go into a gallop, and bring their sabres against the fugitive. Twice more they saw the Chasseur, each time closer, and on the second glimpse Leroux turned round, saw his pursuers, and the chase was on. Lossow's trumpeter let go with the challenge, the spurs went back, and Sharpe tried to tug the huge sword from its clumsy scabbard.

He was easily outstripped by the Germans, good riders all, and he cursed as his scabbard flapped and banged against his thigh. He lurched, unbalanced by the sudden gallop, then the blade came free, was shining in the dawn, and he saw Leroux once more. The Frenchman was less than half a mile ahead, his horse jaded, and Sharpe forgot his aching thighs, his sore seat, and clapped his heels to persuade more speed from his horse.

The Germans were still ahead of Sharpe. They rode through a small village where Leroux, mysteriously, had turned left. They followed his northward course, the horses plunging a shallow bank into a stream, scattering the water silver bright in the dawn, then onto fields of the far bank. There were hills ahead, shallow hills, and Sharpe wondered if Leroux was hoping for a hiding place. It seemed a forlorn hope.

Then Lossow was shouting, holding a hand up and signalling a stop, the troop pulled left, slowed, and Sharpe caught them up and his protest at abandoning the pursuit died in his throat. Their horses slowed to a walk, stopped. Leroux was safe.

Leroux would reach Paris, the notebook would be decoded, and the Frenchman would win. If they had been given another two miles they might have caught him, but not now.

Leroux was trotting his horse along the face of a shallow

286

hill that sloped up from the wide valley. Lined on the slope was the French rearguard, a thousand cavalrymen, and Lossow spat in disgust. 'We can't do anything.' He sounded apologetic as if he thought Sharpe might truly expect him to charge a thousand enemy with just a hundred and fifty men. He shrugged at Sharpe. 'I'm sorry, my friend.'

Sharpe was watching Leroux. 'What's he doing?'

The Frenchman was not joining his cavalry. He trotted along the face of the ranks and Sharpe could see that he raised his sword in salute to the French squadron commanders. Leroux was still going north, past the cavalry, and Sharpe urged his horse into a trot so he could follow the Frenchman. Sharpe led Lossow's troop north, a half mile to the west of the French line and watched as Leroux went on riding, past his cavalry, and dropped into a valley at the end of the hill. Leroux was now in dead ground, invisible to them, and Sharpe pushed his tired horse into a canter.

There was a hill ahead of them that would overlook the dead ground, and they rode up its slope, the dew sparkling where the hooves hammered the turf, and then it was Sharpe's turn to hold up his hand, to slow, and to curse. He had half hoped that Leroux was planning to ride on, to go eastwards again with his own cavalry behind him, but Leroux had reached true safety. In the small valley were French infantry. Three Battalions in square and, some way behind them, another two Battalions who guarded the rear of the hill where the French cavalry barred the road east.

Leroux was walking his horse towards the Battalions in square. Sharpe swore again, pushed his sword into its scabbard, and slumped in his saddle.

Hogan leaned on his pommel. 'That's that.'

One of the French squares opened its ranks, Leroux walked his horse inside, and for all Sharpe could have done Leroux might as well be in Paris already.

Patrick Harper flexed his borrowed sabre and shook his

head. 'I was just beginning to look forward to a cavalry charge.'

'Not today.' Hogan stretched his arms, yawned.

Further eastwards, perhaps three miles away, the road was filled with retreating troops. Going east to safety. Leroux had reached the rearguard, was safe, and would soon be escorted by this infantry to the rest of the French army. Lossow had just a hundred and fifty men. The French rearguard was at least two and a half thousand men, infantry and cavalry, and Sharpe's last hope vanished like the mist that faded from the landscape.

It promised to be another beautiful day. The meadows of the gentle hills were lush with pasture, lavish with wild flowers, and the first warmth of the climbing sun was on Sharpe's face. He hated to give up this pursuit, yet what else was there to do? They could ride back to Alba de Tormes, sit by the river's edge, and drink harsh red wine till all the disappointment was drowned in the vintage of last year's comet. There would be other days to fight, other enemies, and Curtis' men were not the only brave people who sent messages to England. There was hope, and if the hope was not bright then there was always wine in Alba de Tormes.

It was pointless, of course, to deal in what might have been, yet Sharpe cursed because they had not left the battlefield an hour earlier. He imagined what he could do if he had just a single battery of nine-pounder guns. He could open those squares with shot after shot, and if he had just two good British Battalions he could finish them off! Hogan must have thought the same for he looked gloomily at the three French squares. 'We'll have no guns or infantry till this afternoon. At the earliest!'

'They'll be long gone by then, sir.'

'Aye.'

This rearguard would stay just long enough to hold up the cavalry pursuit while the rest of Marmont's army stole a march on the British. Without guns or infantry the squares could not be broken. Leroux was safe.

Lossow's men rested their horses. They were north of the enemy now, on a hillside that gave them a wide view of the countryside. The enemy cavalry were on another hill a half mile to the south, the infantry closer, in the small hidden valley, while to Sharpe's right stretched the wide valley where the two roads met from the river. The furthest road was the one Leroux had led them on, from Alba de Tormes, and where it passed through the small village it was met by the closest road that came from the fords across the river. The enemy dominated both roads, blocking the pursuit. Leroux was safe.

There was movement on the Alba de Tormes road. British Light Dragoons, three hundred sabres, trotted towards the French, saw them, and stopped. The horses bent their necks and cropped at the grass. They formed a single line, facing the French cavalry, and Sharpe imagined their officers squinting through the rising sun at the outnumbering enemy.

Then, from the north west, from the fords, came more cavalry. Four hundred and fifty men walked their horses into the valley behind the British, and the newcomers looked strange. They wore red jackets, like infantry jackets, and on their heads they wore old fashioned black bicorne hats held on by brass-plated straps. It was like seeing a regiment of infantry Colonels. Each man was armed with the long, straight sword like that at Sharpe's side. They were Heavy Cavalry, the Heavy Dragoons of the King's German Legion. They stopped behind the British Light Dragoons, slightly to their left, and Hogan looked from them to the enemy and shook his head. 'They can't do a thing.'

He was right. Cavalry cannot break a well-formed infantry square. It was a rule of war, proved time and again, that as long as the infantry were solidly ranked, their muskets tipped with bayonets, horses will not charge home. Sharpe had stood in squares and watched the cavalry charge, seen the sabres raised and the mouths open, and then the muskets had fired, the horses fell, and the surviving cavalry sheered away down the sides of the square, were blasted by the muskets. The squares could not be broken. Sharpe had seen them broken, but never when they were well formed. He had seen a Battalion attacked as they formed square, seen the enemy penetrate the unclosed gap and slaughter the ranks from the inside, but it would never have happened if the gap had been closed. He had seen a square break itself, when the men panicked and ran, but that was the fault of the infantry themselves. The South Essex had broken once, three years before at Valdelacasa, and then it had been because the survivors of another square had run to them, clawed at the tight ranks, and the French cavalry had ridden in with the fugitives. Yet these French squares, below him, would not break. Each was of four ranks, the front rank kneeling, and each was solid, calm, and ringed with bayonets. Leroux was safe.

Leroux was safe because he had taken shelter with the infantry. The enemy cavalry, facing west on the hillside, were vulnerable to a British pursuit. Their safety lay in their greater numbers, yet Wellington's men had the greater morale. Sharpe heard the far-away sound of a trumpet, he looked right , and he saw the British Light Dragoons begin their charge. Three hundred men against a thousand, an uphill charge, and Captain Lossow whooped at them with glee.

The cavalry were charging.

CHAPTER 26

A cavalry charge begins slowly. The horses walk. The troopers have time to see the advertisement engraved on their sabres, 'Warranted Never to Fail', and feel the fear that the same guarantee does not apply to men.

Dust showed behind the walking horses. It drifted across the lush valley. The shadow of the Light Dragoons was long behind them, the sabres were upright, curved, slashing light from the rising sun. The valley was quiet, the enemy still.

A second trumpet. The horses went into the trot and still the men were knee to knee. The triangular banners, guidons, were high above the line of blue and silver uniforms. The faint drumming of hooves came to the hilltop where Sharpe watched. The French cavalry did not move.

Lossow wanted to take his men into the valley to join the charge, but Major Hogan shook his head. 'We must watch Leroux. He might make a run for it.' He knew it was unlikely. Leroux was in the safest place; in a square's centre.

Harsh voices came thin from the valley; orders. Sharpe looked right and saw four hundred and fifty heavy, clumsy swords drawn into the light. The German Heavy Dragoons were in six squadrons, three ahead, three behind, and each squadron was in two ranks. The ranks were forty yards apart so that, should they charge, the second line would have plenty of space to swerve or jump over the dead of the first. The Germans were behind and to the left of the British Light Dragoons who trotted towards the enemy cavalry on the hill.

A trumpet sounded, much closer, and Lossow's horses

moved impatiently. The German squadrons were advancing at the walk and Sharpe frowned. He looked to his left. 'They can't see them!'

'What?' Hogan looked at Sharpe.

'The infantry!' Sharpe pointed. 'They can't bloody see them!' It was true. The French squares were shadowed in the small valley, hidden by a spur of hillside, and the German Heavy Cavalry were unaware of their presence. The Germans were riding towards ambush. Their line of charge against the French cavalry would take them past the small valley, inside musket range, and the first they would know of the presence of French infantry would be the flaming muskets.

Hogan swore. They were too far from the KGL squadrons to give them warning, they could only watch as the cavalrymen walked towards disaster.

The British Light Dragoons were ahead, trotting towards the hill, and their advance was well beyond the infantry's range. Sharpe drew his sword. 'We can't just sit here!'

Hogan knew they could not warn the Heavy Cavalry, but to do nothing was worse than making a hopeless attempt. He shrugged. 'Go.'

Lossow's trumpeter blew the full charge, no time now for a decorous walk that would gradually speed up into the full gallop, and Lossow's men threw themselves into a reckless downhill gallop. If their Heavy comrades just saw them, if they just wondered why they came so fast and waved so frantically, then they might avert disaster. But the six squadrons of the Heavy German Cavalry went on stolidly, the trumpet sounded and they went into the trot, and Sharpe knew they were too late.

Another trumpet sounded, far ahead, and the British Light Dragoons went into the canter. They would stay at the canter until the final few yards when they would be released into the full gallop. A cavalry charge works best when all the horses arrive at once; a solid, moving wall of men, horses and steel. The British reached the bottom of the hill, began to climb it, and still the French did not move.

The German Heavy Cavalry still trotted, still ignorant of the ambush that waited fifty yards ahead. Some of the faces beneath their strange black bicornes looked curiously at Lossow's men. Sharpe was lurching in his saddle, praying that he would not fall, and the sword was in his right hand and he wished that there were no squares, that he could face Leroux in open battle, but Leroux was safe.

The British trumpet released the Light Dragoons. It threw them forward, shouting, in the final gallop that put the weight of a charging horse behind the sabre. They were outnumbered, they charged uphill, yet they urged their horses on. The French, at last, moved.

They ran. They ran without a fight. Perhaps no man wanted to die after the previous day's carnage. There was little glory in defeating this cavalry pursuit, no man would win his Legion of Honour medal today, and so the French turned, spurred eastwards, and the British Dragoons chased them, swore at them to fight, but there was no fight in the French cavalry. They would run to fight another day.

The German Heavy Dragoons saw the French run, saw their chance of a fight fading, and so the trumpet put them into the canter. The notes of the call sounded close to Sharpe and then they were drowned by the sound he had been dreading, the sound of an infantry volley. The nearest faces of the squares disappeared in smoke, the leading German squadrons tumbled in dust, falling horses, and cartwheeling swords. Men died beneath their horses, crushed, men screamed. The ambush had worked.

There was no need to warn them now. The French squares had turned one squadron into a shambles, hurt two more, and the other Germans must know they were beaten. Suddenly they had found infantry, well formed infantry, and cavalry cannot break well-formed squares.

The black bicorne hats turned left, the cavalry saw the

squares with horror, and the trumpets pealed above the defeated charge. Sharpe knew the squadrons were being called away, called off, that they would ride away from the squares. He looked at Harper and grinned ruefully. 'No cavalry charge today, Patrick.'

The Irishman did not reply. He slammed his heels back, whooped with mad joy, and Sharpe jerked his head back to the Germans. They were pulling at their reins, but not to ride away. They were turning towards the squares, were charging them, and the trumpets were pushing them on. It was madness.

Sharpe pulled at his reins, kicked back, and let the horse ride with the others. The sword felt good in his hand. He saw the French infantry reloading, calm and professional, and he knew this charge was doomed.

The German squadrons were still at the canter. They wheeled left, they aligned their ranks, and the madness came on them. The trumpets threw them on.

Lossow, his men, Sharpe and Harper, came up behind the Heavy Squadrons as they began the final charge. Sharpe knew this was madness, knew this was doomed, but it was irresistible. The sword was long in his hand, his blood sang with the trumpet's challenge, and they went on; galloping into the impossible charge.

CHAPTER 27

The German Heavy Dragoons were jealous. The day before the British Heavy Cavalry had charged to glory, had bloodied their swords to the hilts against French infantry that had not had time to form square. The Germans did not like the British having all the glory.

The Germans were also disciplined, the most disciplined of all Wellington's cavalry. Not for them the British habit of charging once and then going berserk in a mad chase that left the horses blown and their riders vulnerable to the enemy's reserves. The Germans were coolly efficient about war. But not now. Now they were suddenly enraged, enough to attempt the impossible. Four hundred and fifty men, less those who had already died, were charging fifteen hundred well formed infantry. The trumpet hurled them into the gallop.

They had no chance, Sharpe knew, but the madness was driving sense out of his head. Artillery could break a square, infantry could break a square, but cavalry could not. There was a mathematical logic that proved it. A man on horseback needed some four feet of width in which to charge. Facing him, in four ranks, were eight men. An infantryman only needed two feet, slightly less, and so the horseman was charging down a narrow corridor at the end of which waited eight bullets and eight bayonets. And even if the infantry were unloaded, if they only had their bayonets, then the charge would still fail. A horse would not charge home that solid wall of men and steel. It would go so far, then swerve, and Sharpe had stood in squares often enough to know how safe they were. This was an impossible charge.

There was terror and madness in the air. The Germans had turned into this charge in a sudden explosion of anger. Their long heavy swords were raised for the first stroke, the hooves slung up great clods of turf, and the French square nearest to the charge fired again. Eighty yards to go.

Screams came from ahead of Sharpe. He had a glimpse of a horse sliding on its belly, head up and yellow teeth bared to the sky. A man rolled over and over, blood whipping from his neck, his sword stuck straight up and quivering in the ground. The trumpet again, incoherent challenges, and everywhere the hammering of hooves that filled the valley.

A horse drummed the earth with its legs, dying on its side, blood frothing as it lashed its neck and screamed in pain. The second rank gathered itself, jumped, and the French had saved one rank's muskets for the moment. Smoke pumped from the square, bullets lashed at the charge, and a man was hit at full jump. He came backwards from his horse, a halo of blood about his face, and the horse went on alone. A standard bearer was down, his horse dead, and he ran with the standard, holding it aloft, and another German leaned left from the saddle, took the staff at the full gallop, and again the banner was high and taking them on in the impossible charge.

The earth quivered with the heavy horses, with the hammer of their hooves. The ranks had loosened in this madness so the valley seemed filled with big men on big horses, the sunlight catching their swords, the brass-plated straps of the bicornes, and the gleaming hooves that drove them on. The hooves threw up earth that stung Sharpe's face. The horses seemed to strain towards the enemy, their eyes wild, their teeth bared, and Sharpe let the madness flow up in him to conquer the terror. He rode past a dead horse, its rider crouching for safety behind the corpse, and Sharpe had never done this. He had never ridden with the cavalry in a charge and there was a splendour to it that he could not have dreamt. This was the moment when a man became a god, when the air was noise, when speed lent its strength to the sword, a glorious feeling in those minutes before a bullet turned the god into dead meat.

A cavalryman, wounded, was being dragged by his stirrup. He screamed.

At fifty yards another rank of the square brought up their muskets, looked into the storm of anger, and fired. A horse and rider tumbled, hooves high in the sunlight, falling, and the blood streaked impossibly far on the grass, then the next rank was past, manes flying, and still the French had one more loaded rank.

The square blossomed smoke. A bullet hammered past Sharpe, but he did not hear it. He could only hear the hooves. An officer ahead of Sharpe was hit. He saw the man shaking with the pain, imagined the scream that he could not hear in this valley of noise, and saw the long sword dangle useless by its wrist strap. The man's horse was hit too, jerking its head in sudden pain, yet it charged on. A dying man on a dying horse leading the charge.

The trumpet hurled them at the enemy. One trumpeter was down, his legs broken, yet he played on, played the charge again and again, the notes that could drive a man into wild glory. These screams in the valley, horses and men, screams of pain drowned by the trumpets. The guidons were lowered like lances, it was the final moment, and crossfire took them from another square and one guidon went down, point first into the earth and the man who had held it seemed to fall so slowly, then suddenly he was rolling and screaming, streaking the grass with his blood, and still the charge was led by a dying man on a dying horse. The man died first. He fell forward onto the neck of his horse, yet the horse still obeyed its last command. It charged. It used up its blood, its great heart pumping to the dying limbs, and the horse fell to its knees. Still it tried to charge as it slid on the grass, slick with blood that pumped from its chest, and it slid with its dead burden and died itself. And as it died, and could not turn, it slid like a great missile of dead meat into the front face of the square. Man and horse, in death, smashing the ranks back, opening the gap, and the next rank of Germans saw it.

They saw daylight. They twitched the reins, they screamed, and the French tried desperately to remake the line. Too late. A horse was there, the first sword came sobbing down, and then the horse was hit by a musket ball, it fell, made more space, and two more horses were in the gap, the swords hissed, and the horses leaped the pile of dead and were within the square. The French were dead men.

Some ran, some surrendered, others fought. The Germans came at them with their long swords and the horses fought as they were trained to fight. The horses killed with their hooves, hammering at skulls, they bit so that a man could lose his face in one horrid second of bowel-loosening fear, and the dust rose with the screams as the last German squadrons tugged right and went for another square.

Survivors of the first clawed at the second square, they tore into its ranks and the horsemen came too. Harper was there, the sabre fast in his hand, and Spears' horse was trained for this. It moved constantly so no infantryman could hamstring it, it lined up the targets for the sabre, and the Irishman was chanting his Gaelic war cries, the slaughter-madness on him, and the valley was filled with the horsemen, the swords, and the hopeless infantry.

The second square collapsed, broke apart, and the Germans grunted as they brought the heavy blades down in the killing blows. The trumpeter, his legs broken, still lashed them into a fury, though now the notes were of pure triumph. Sharpe's horse, not trained for war, swerved from the chaos and he swore at it, tugged at the reins, and then a mounted French infantry officer came for him, sword held like a lance, and Sharpe lashed with his great sword, missed, and he cursed this horse that would not take him to the target. Leroux?

Where in God's name was Leroux?

He could see Harper. The Irishman was in among the fugitives from the second square. One man came at the Sergeant with a bayonet and Harper kicked up with his foot, caught the bayonet, and then sliced down with the sabre. The man fell, and his shako was ludicrously stuck on Harper's sabre. It stayed there through two more strokes, then shook itself off as the huge Sergeant killed a French officer.

Sharpe could see Hogan. The Major, his sword not even drawn, was circling among the infantry shouting at them to surrender. The muskets were being thrown down, the hands going up, but still Sharpe could not see Leroux.

The third square was retreating up the hillslope. Back there somewhere, Sharpe knew, were two more French Battalions. A new trumpet call rang out, reforming two squadrons, and then Sharpe saw Leroux. He was in the third square. He had been on foot, but now swung himself into his saddle, and Sharpe kicked with his heels and rode towards the unbroken square. Its men were nervous, panicked by the smell of blood and fear, and as Sharpe rode so did the trumpet throw the reformed squadrons against the square.

The first two squares were ended. Most had surrendered, many were dead, and the Germans, who had done a fine thing, wanted to do more. Individual riders spurred towards the unbroken square.

The square fired, not at the cavalry, but at survivors of the first squares who wanted to break into its ranks. The infantry were frantic with fear, stumbling as the square inched backwards, and the first Germans came, were blasted from the saddles, while one man rode down the face of the square, his face a mask of blood, and his long sword beat uselessly at the bayonets, rattled against muskets, and then a shot threw him onto the ground.

More Germans charged home, the swords fell, and there was no reason for the square to break, yet its men were terrified of the fate of their comrades. Some threw down their muskets, raised their hands, and Sharpe could see the mounted officers in the square's interior tearing at their standard. This Battalion did not carry the Regiment's Eagle, they carried a flag which they tore into strips to hide in their uniforms. The square was dying and Sharpe saw the surrender and still he charged, wanting to break through the ranks to get his enemy, Leroux.

Leroux had not yet given up. He had not expected this – what man could? He had ridden all night, looping far to the south to avoid British cavalry patrols, and at Alba de Tormes, in the dawn, he had pulled off the heavy cassock that had been his disguise. He had thought himself safe in the square. He had never seen a square broken, never, not even when he had charged with the Emperor himself. And now this!

Leroux could see the German horsemen all around the surrendering square, yet there were not many. Most had ridden on to the two French Battalions in the rear. It would still be possible for the Frenchman to break out, to ride north for a mile before turning east, and he rode to the north side of the square, shouted at the ranks to split, and then he saw Sharpe coming directly at him. That damned Rifleman! He had thought Sharpe dead, wished him dead, had treasured his memory of the screams on the upper cloister, and then his idiot sister had taken a fancy to the man, protected him, and the bastard was back. This time he would kill him. He drew the pistol, the deadly, rifled pistol, from its chest holster and levelled it over the ranks of the square. He could not miss. He pulled the trigger.

Sharpe hauled on the rein, leaned back, and La Marquesa's horse reared up, hooves flailing, and the bullet took the horse in the throat. Sharpe kicked the stirrups free, pushed desperately away from the saddle, and then he was rolling on the grass as the horse fell at the French ranks. The men shrank back, pushed back, and Sharpe snarled at them, picked up his sword, and plunged into their ranks.

They could have killed him, any one of them, yet they wanted only to surrender. They let Sharpe through, their faces dull, and he snatched a musket from a man in the rear rank. The French soldiers watched the tall Rifleman, feared him, and not one lifted a finger against him.

Leroux was shouting at another face of the square, beating with the flat of his Kligenthal, and Sharpe propped his own sword against his leg, checked the unfamiliar pan of the musket, and levelled it. His rifle was on his back, still without ammunition, and this heavy, strange musket would have to suffice. He pulled the trigger.

Powder stung his face, the kick slammed his shoulder, the smoke blinded him. He tossed the musket down, picked up his sword, and Leroux was hit! He was clutching his left leg, blood showing, and the ball must have passed through the flesh of his thigh, through the saddle, and stung the horse. It reared up in sudden pain and Leroux had to snatch at its mane, he tried to control it, but it reared again and he was falling.

The square had surrendered. Some Germans already pushed their way into its centre and one of them took a strip of the tasselled gold cloth that had been the French standard and waved it high, shouting at his comrades. The French soldiers sat down, muskets beside them, resigned to their fate.

Leroux struck the ground, was winded, and the pain in his left leg made him wince. He had dropped the Kligenthal and he could not see because his big, round, fur hat had slipped over his eyes. He knelt up, pushed the hat back, and the Kligenthal was on the ground. A boot was across the blade. Leroux slowly looked up, past the black trousers, past the tattered green jacket, and he saw his own death in the eyes of the Rifleman.

Sharpe saw the fear in the pale eyes. He stepped back a pace, releasing the Kligenthal, and smiled at Leroux. 'Get up, you bastard.'

CHAPTER 28

The two French Battalions at the rear were not shaken by the breaking of the squares. They fired coolly, their discipline tight, and the German horsemen were cut down by the volleys.

In the small valley the squares had been broken. Prisoners were being herded, many with the dreadful cuts on their heads and shoulders where the great blades had fallen. The horses heaved to get their breath. Cavalrymen stood still, disbelieving what they had done, and their swords were held low and blood dripped from the tips. They had done the impossible. Some men laughed in relief, an almost wild laughter, and the French prisoners, now passion was spent, offered the victors wine from their canteens.

Patrick Harper threaded his way into the third square and looked down on Sharpe and Leroux. The Frenchman still knelt, the Kligenthal was still on the ground. Harper looked at Sharpe. 'What's his trouble?'

'Won't fight.' Sharpe's sword was still clean.

Leroux stood up, wincing as the wound in his left leg hurt. 'I surrender.'

Sharpe swore at him, then gestured at the sword. 'Pick it up.'

'I surrender.' Leroux's pale eyes looked right for help, but Harper blocked the view.

Sharpe tried to see a likeness between this man and La Marquesa, but he could not. What in her was beauty had become hard in her brother. 'Pick up the sword.'

Leroux brushed grass from the fur trim of his red jacket. 'I have surrendered.'

Sharpe swung the flat of his sword so it hit the fur hat, knocking it off. 'Fight, you bastard.' Leroux shook his head. Sharpe would not take the surrender. 'You surrendered before, remember? Not this time, Captain Delmas.'

Leroux smiled, gestured at the Kligenthal. 'You have my sword.'

Sharpe crouched, his eyes still on Leroux, and picked up the Kligenthal in his left hand. It was beautiful, balanced to perfection, a weapon made by a master. He tossed it towards Leroux. 'Fight.'

Leroux let the blade fall. 'I am your prisoner.'

'Kill the bastard, sir.' Harper growled.

'I'm going to.' Sharpe levelled his sword, put it to Leroux's breast, and pushed. The Frenchman went backwards. Sharpe stooped and picked the Kligenthal up once more. He held it out, handle towards the Frenchman, and went forward again and again. Leroux went backwards. The French soldiers watched.

Then Leroux could go no further. He was backed into a corner of the square and Sharpe brought his sword up so that the tip was at Leroux's throat. The Rifleman smiled. 'I'm going to kill you. I don't give a damn whether you fight or not.' He pressed with the sword, Leroux's head went back, and suddenly the pale eyes showed alarm. He really was to die and his arm came up, snatched at the Kligenthal, and Sharpe stepped backwards. 'Now fight, you bastard.'

Leroux fought. He fought because he thought that if he won this fight, then he could surrender. He knew Sharpe would kill him, he had recognised that, so he must kill Sharpe. And if he succeeded in killing the Rifleman then there was always hope. He might escape again, make his way back to France, and it would always be possible to arrange for Curtis' capture. He fought.

The Kligenthal felt good. He gave two short, hard strokes

that loosened his wrist, and he felt the shock of the blades' meeting, and then he settled into a rhythm, probing the Rifleman's weakness, letting the Kligenthal tease the older blade to one side in preparation for the lunge. The point always beats the edge.

Sharpe went backwards, letting Leroux get out of the corner, and Harper rode alongside just as if he were the referee at a prize fight. Some of the French shouted for Leroux, but not many, and some of the Germans came to watch.

Sharpe watched Leroux's pale eyes. The man was strong, and faster than Sharpe remembered. The blades rang like anvils. Sharpe was content to let his long, straight sword do the work for him, he let its weight soak up the attacks, and he planned this man's death. La Marquesa, Leroux's sister, had asked him once if he enjoyed killing, had even accused him of enjoying it, but that was not true. Some deaths a man can enjoy, the death of an enemy, and Sharpe was paid to have enemies. Yet he did not wish death on the French. There was more satisfaction in seeing a surrendered enemy, a defeated enemy, than in seeing a slaughtered enemy. A field after battle was a more horrid place than anything the people in England, who would soon celebrate Salamanca, could imagine. Death stopped war from being a game, it gave it glory and horror, and soldiers could not be squeamish about death. They might regret the moment when rage conquers fear, when it banishes all humanity and makes a man into a killer, but that rage could keep a man from being dead and so the regret was mixed with relief and a knowledge that, to be a good soldier, the rage would one day be back.

Sharpe parried a lunge, twisted his sword over the Kligenthal so the blades scraped, and lunged himself, checked, lunged again, and he saw the pain in the pale eyes as Leroux was forced onto his back foot. Sharpe would kill this man, and he would enjoy it. He would enjoy the retribution as a man could enjoy the death of a child murderer at Tyburn, or the shooting of a deserter after battle. Death was sometimes public because people needed death, they needed retribution, and Tyburn's gallows gave more pleasure than pain. That might be bad, but that is the way of people, and Sharpe's sword tip hit the guard of the Kligenthal, forced it wide, came free when Leroux's arm was off balance and Sharpe brought the blade scything back so it cut across Leroux's chest, then back again so the sword cut Leroux's forearm, and Sharpe knew this man would die.

He would die for McDonald, for Windham, for the un-named Spaniards, for Spears, for El Mirador, for Sharpe himself, and Leroux knew it, for he became desperate. His right arm was wounded so he held his wrist with his left hand and scythed the Kligenthal in a glittering, air singing blow and Sharpe stepped back, let the blade pass, and then shouted his exultation as he lunged forward, picking his spot, and he did not hear Hogan shouting at him, nor Harper's cry of acclamation, for the blade was going into Leroux's body at the exact place where Leroux had wounded Sharpe, and Leroux let the Kligenthal go, his mouth opened, and his hands clutched at the blade that still pierced him, a flesh-hook that tortured him, that went through skin and muscle and tore the scream from him.

He fell. He was not dead yet. The pale eyes were wide. He drew up his legs as Sharpe had drawn up his legs, he gasped air into his lungs so that the scream could fight the pain that he had made Sharpe fight for two weeks, and then Sharpe twisted the sword free, held the point above Leroux's throat, and finished him off.

He left his sword swaying above the lifeless Frenchman and stepped back. Leroux was dead.

Hogan had watched Sharpe's anger. He rarely saw the Rifleman fight. He had been awed by Sharpe's skill, troubled by the turbulence of his friend, and he saw the distaste that crossed Sharpe's face when it was all done. Leroux was no longer the enemy, no longer Napoleon's man, he was a pathetic, cringeing corpse. Hogan's voice was mild. 'Wouldn't he surrender?'

'No, sir.' Sharpe shook his head. 'He was a stubborn bastard.'

Sharpe picked up the Kligenthal, the sword he had wanted so much, and it could have been made for him. It settled in his right hand like a part of himself. It was a beautiful and deadly weapon.

He unclipped Leroux's snake-clasp belt, tugged the sword slings free from the body, and strapped the scabbard over his own scabbard. He pushed the Kligenthal home. His Kligenthal.

Leroux's black sabretache was spotted with blood. Sharpe lifted the flap and there, on top, was a small leather note-book. He opened it, saw a star chart surrounded by a strange language, and tossed it to Hogan. 'That's what we wanted, sir.'

Hogan looked at the dead in the valley, at the prisoners, and he looked at the survivors of the King's German Legion Heavy Dragoons who walked their horses back from the unsuccessful attack on the remaining two French Battalions. The Germans had won a great victory, at great price, and the valley was stinking of blood. Hogan looked at the book, then at Sharpe. 'Thank you, Richard.'

'My pleasure, sir.'

Sharpe was taking Leroux's overalls. He had worn overalls exactly like these until the fight in the Irish College. Now he had killed another Chasseur Colonel. Leroux's overalls still had the silver buttons down their legs and Sharpe grinned as he held them up. He wiped his sword clean on them.

Leroux's sister had once asked Sharpe if he enjoyed killing and he had given her no answer. He could have replied that sometimes it was terrible, that often it was sad, that usually it happened without any emotion, but that sometimes, rarely, like this day, there were no regrets. He picked up his own sword, the crude sword that had won the fight, and smiled at Harper. 'Breakfast?'

EPILOGUE

Salamanca was honeyed gold in the sunlight. A city built like Rome on hills above a river.

The morning sunlight slanted the shadows long in the Great Plaza. The wounded, two days after the great battle at the Arapiles, still died in the hospital.

Sharpe stood on the Roman Bridge and stared down at the sinuous green weeds. He knew it was foolish to be here, maybe a waste of time, but he waited.

A company of Spanish soldiers was marched across the bridge. The officer grinned at him, waved a cigar. The men looked curiously at the two swords that hung by the grim Rifleman's side.

A farmer drove cattle past him. Two priests went the other way, arguing violently, and Sharpe paced slowly behind them, stopped at the small fortress arched over the roadway, and walked slowly back.

The clock on the hill struck ten.

A cavalry Sergeant drove a dozen remounts into the river. They drank while he rubbed them down. The edge of the river was very shallow. Children played there, running easily to a small island, and their voices carried up to the bridge.

She might not even come this way, he thought, but she did.

Two liveried servants first, mounted on horseback, then the dark blue coach with its four white horses, and after that another coach that he presumed was for luggage or servants.

He pushed against the stone of the parapet, watched the

servants ride past, then the four white horses, and then the barouche, its cover up, was opposite him.

She saw him.

He had to walk a few paces to where the barouche had stopped. He looked up. 'I tried to see you.'

'I know.' She was fanning her face.

He felt awkward. The sun was hot on the back of his neck. He could feel sweat trickling below his armpit. 'Are you well, Ma'am?'

She smiled. 'Yes. I find myself temporarily unpopular in Salamanca.' She shrugged. 'Madrid may be more welcoming.'

'You may find our army in Madrid.'

'Then I may go north.'

'A long way?'

She smiled. 'A long way.' Her eyes dropped to the two swords, then back to Sharpe's face. 'Did you kill him?'

'In a fair fight.' He was embarrassed again, as he had been at their first meeting. She seemed no different. She was still beautiful, unbearably so, and it seemed impossible that she was an enemy. He shrugged. 'Your horse died.'

'Did you kill it?'

'Your brother did.'

She half smiled. 'He killed very easily.' Her eyes went back to the sword again, then back to Sharpe. 'We were not very fond of each other.' He supposed she meant she and her brother, but he could not be sure she was not talking of himself. She shook her head. 'Did you wait for me?'

He nodded. 'Yes.'

'Why?'

He shrugged. To tell her he missed her? To tell her that it did not matter that she was French, a spy, released only because she was a Spanish aristocrat and Wellington could not afford the scandal? To tell her that amid all the lies there had been some truth? 'To wish you well.'

'And I wish you well.' She mocked him gently. To Sharpe

308

she seemed untouchable, unreachable. 'Goodbye, Captain Sharpe.'

'Goodbye, Ma'am.'

She spoke to the coachman, looked back at Sharpe. 'Who knows, Richard? Maybe another day.' The coach lurched forward, the last he saw was her golden hair going back into its shadows. He thought to himself that he had nothing of hers to remember her by, only memory which was the worst souvenir.

He felt in his new ammunition pouch and fingered the message that had been delivered that morning from Wellington himself. It thanked him. He supposed that Napoleon would have written similar messages to Leroux and La Marquesa if Sharpe had not taken the notebook from the shattered squares at Garcia Hernandez. After the battle they had found that was the name of the village near to the hill and the valley.

Major Hogan was expansive at lunch. Sharpe was to stay in Hogan's old lodgings, to be fed well by the landlady, and Hogan drank well before he left. 'You're to stay and recuperate, Richard! General's orders! We want you fully strong again.'

'Yes, sir.'

'Forrest will wait for you, don't worry. Your Company's safe.'

'Any news of a new Colonel?'

Hogan shook his head, belched, and patted his stomach. 'Not yet. I think Lawford would like it again, but I don't know.' He shrugged. 'Forrest might get it. I don't know, Richard.' He pushed a forefinger into Sharpe's side. 'You should be thinking about it.'

'Me! I'm a captain.' Sharpe grinned and bit into cold beef.

Hogan poured more wine. 'Think about it! A majority next. Then Lieutenant Colonel. It could happen, Richard. It's going to be a long bloody war. We just heard the Americans are in now, they may be in Quebec for all we know.' He sipped his wine. 'Can you afford a Majority?'

'Me!' Sharpe laughed. 'They're two thousand six hundred pounds. Where do you think I can get that kind of money?'

Hogan smiled. 'Don't you usually get what you want, Richard?'

Sharpe shrugged. 'I get the rainbows, sir. Never the pots of gold.'

Hogan twisted his glass in his hands. 'There was one other thing, Richard, a smallish thing. I've been talking to Father Curtis and he did say something odd. He says that notebook was well hidden, truly well hidden, and he can't imagine how Leroux could have found it.'

'Leroux was a clever man, sir.'

'Aye, maybe. But Curtis was sure it was too well hidden. Only Lord Spears, he says, knew where it was.' His shrewd eyes were on Sharpe.

'Really, sir?' Sharpe poured more wine.

'Does that strike you as odd?'

'Spears is dead, sir. He died well.'

Hogan nodded. 'I hear his body was some way from all the others. Some way from the fighting, in fact. Odd?'

Sharpe shook his head. 'He could have crawled away, sir.'

'Yes. With a hole in his head. I'm sure you're right, Richard.' Hogan swirled the wine in his glass. His voice was still neutral. 'The only reason I ask is that I do have a responsibility for finding whoever was the spy in our head-quarters. I can make myself unpleasant, I suppose, turn over a lot of stones, but you do understand me, I'm sure.'

'I don't think you need to be unpleasant, sir.'

'Good, good.' Hogan grinned at Sharpe, raised his glass. 'Well done, Richard.'

'What for, sir?'

'Nothing, nothing.' Hogan toasted him all the same.

Hogan rode away that afternoon, going eastwards to the army that now marched towards Madrid. Harper left with him, mounted on one of Hogan's spare horses, and for the second time that day Sharpe found himself on the Roman Bridge. He looked up at Harper. 'Good luck.'

'We'll see you soon, sir?'

'Very soon.' Sharpe touched his stomach. 'It hardly hurts.'

'You've got to be careful, sir. I mean it killed that Frenchman.'

Sharpe laughed. 'He wasn't careful.'

Hogan bent down and shook Sharpe's hand. 'Take your time, Richard! There won't be another battle.'

'No, sir.'

Hogan smiled at him. 'And how long are you going to wear two swords, eh? You look ridiculous!'

Sharpe grinned and unclasped the Kligenthal. He offered it to Hogan. 'You want it?'

'Good Lord, no! It's yours, Richard. You won it.'

But a man only needs one sword. Harper watched Sharpe, he knew how Sharpe had craved after the Kligenthal, he had seen Sharpe hold the sword last night. The Kligenthal had been forged by a genius, shaped by a master, a weapon of contained beauty. To look at it was to fear it, to see it in the hands of a man who could use it, like Sharpe, was to understand the mind that had made this sword. It seemed to weigh nothing in Sharpe's hand, so perfectly balanced was the steel, and the Rifleman drew it out now, slowly, so the steel shone like oiled silk in the sun.

The sword at his side, the sword that Harper had given him, was crude and ill-balanced. It was too long for an infantryman, it was clumsy, and it was stamped out with hundreds more in an ill-lit Birmingham factory. Beside the Kligenthal it was raw, cheap, and crude.

Yet Harper had worked the cheap sword as a talisman against Sharpe's death. Something more than friendship had gone into the blade. It did not matter that it was cheap. The cheap sword had beaten the Kligenthal, the expensive sword, and there was luck in the blade. Dozens of similar swords had simply been left at Garcia Hernandez after the charge, not worth the bother of picking up, and the peasants would fashion them into long knives. Yet Sharpe's sword was lucky. There was a soldiers' goddess and her name was Fate and she had liked the sword Harper made for Sharpe. The Kligenthal was stained with the blood of friends, with the torture of flayed priests, and the beautiful sword contained not luck, but evil.

Harper watched as Sharpe drew his arm back, checked for a second, and then threw. The Kligenthal wheeled up into the sunlight, circling, dazzling with quick flashes as the steel caught the light. It seemed to hang for a second at the top of its arc, speared light at the three men, and then fell. It fell towards the Tormes' deepest part, still turning, and then the sun left it so the steel was grey and then it struck the sheen of the water, broke it, and was gone.

Harper cleared his throat. 'You'll frighten the fishes.'

'That's more than you ever did.'

Harper laughed. 'I caught some.'

The goodbyes were said again, the hooves sounded on the bridge's stones, and Sharpe walked slowly back to the town. He did not want this leave to be long. He wanted to be back with the South Essex, in the skirmish line where he belonged, but he would wait a week and eat his food and rest as he had been ordered.

He pushed open the door of the small courtyard of the house that was his new address, registered with the Town Major, and he stopped. She looked up. 'I thought you were dead.'

'I thought you were lost.' He had been right. Memory was the worst souvenir. Memory told him she had long dark hair, a face like a hawk, a body that was slim and muscled from the days of riding the high border hills. Memory forgot the movement of a face, the life of a person.

Teresa put the cat on the ground, smiled at her husband,

and came towards him. 'I'm sorry. I was far north. What happened?'

'I'll tell you later.' He kissed her, held her, kissed her again. There was guilt inside him.

She looked up at him, puzzled. 'Are you all right?'

'Yes.' He smiled. 'Where's Antonia?'

'Inside.' She jerked her head towards the kitchen where Hogan's 'motherly old soul' was singing. Teresa shrugged. 'She's found someone else who wants to look after her. I suppose I shouldn't have brought her, but I thought she ought to be near her father's grave.'

'Not yet.' They both laughed because they were embarrassed.

The sword scraped on the ground and he took it off, laid it on the table, then hugged her again. 'I'm sorry.'

'What for?'

'Worrying you.'

'Did you think this marriage would be calm?' She smiled.

'No.' He kissed her again, and this time he let his relief pour out of him, and she held him tight so that the wound hurt, but it did not matter. Love mattered, but that was so hard to learn, and he kissed her again and again till she drew away.

She smiled up at him, happiness in her eyes. 'Hello, Richard.'

'Hello, wife.'

'I'm glad you're not dead.'

'So'm I.'

She laughed, then looked at the sword. 'New?'

'Yes.'

'What happened to the old one?'

'It wore out.' Not that it mattered. From now on this old sword, with its dull scabbard, would be his sword and Fate's weapon; Sharpe's sword.

HISTORICAL NOTE

It may seem wilful, even perverse of me to introduce yet more Irish characters into Sharpe's adventures, yet Patrick Curtis and Michael Connelley existed and, in *Sharpe's Sword*, play the roles they played in 1812. The Reverend Doctor Patrick Curtis, known as Don Patricio Cortes to the Spanish, was Rector of the Irish College and Professor of Natural History and Astronomy at the University of Salamanca. He was also, at the age of 72, the spy chief of his own network that extended throughout French-held Spain and well north of the Pyrenees. The French did suspect his existence, did want to destroy him, but they discovered his identity only after the Battle of Salamanca. As modern spy novels would say, Curtis' cover was 'blown', and when the French did make a brief reappearance in the city he was forced to flee for British protection. In 1819, when the wars were over, he received a British Government pension. He finally left Spain to become the Archbishop of Armagh and Primate of All Ireland, and he died in Drogheda at the good age of 92.

Archbishop Curtis died of the cholera, Sergeant Michael Connelley of the soldiers' hospital in Salamanca died of alcoholic poisoning not long after the battle. I have no evidence that Connelley was in the hospital (which was situated in the Irish College) before the battle, in fact I would rather doubt it, but he was certainly there after the events of July 22nd, 1812. I have traduced his memory by putting him in charge of the death room when in fact he was appointed to be Sergeant of the whole hospital. Rifleman Costello, who

315

was wounded at Salamanca, wrote about Connelley in his memoirs and I have shamelessly stolen my description from his book. He was, indeed, attentive to the sick. He did, as Costello says, 'drink like a whale', but his chief distinction was his anxiety that the British would die well in the face of the French wounded. Costello quotes him. 'Merciful God! What more do you want? You'll be buried in a shroud and coffin won't you? For God's sake, die like a man before these 'ere Frenchers.'* Sergeant Connelley was immensely popular. The funeral of the Duke himself, Costello says, would not have attracted more mourners than did Connelley. One of the pallbearers, a cockney ventriloquist, rapped on the coffin and imitated Connelley's voice. 'Let me out, won't you? oh, merciful Jesus, I'm smothered.' The cortege stopped, bayonets were produced, and the lid prised off to reveal the still dead Sergeant. The incident was thought to be extremely funny, a joke in good taste, and it does not seem to be out of character with Wellington's men.

Colquhoun Grant, the Exploring Officer, also was a real character who was captured shortly before the Battle of Salamanca. He escaped from his captors in France and spent some astonishing weeks at liberty in the streets and salons of Paris. He continued to wear full British uniform and if he was challenged he claimed that it was the uniform of the American army. His story, more incredible than fiction, can be found in Jock Haswell's 'The First Respectable Spy' (Hamish Hamilton, 1969).

The French did use codes and Captain Scovell, mentioned in Chapter 4, was the man who broke the enemy codes. Any reader who would like to see how the codes worked can find all the details in Appendix XV of Volume V of Oman's 'A History of the Peninsular War'. For the details of the espionage background to *Sharpe's Sword* I owe a debt to Jock

*'The Peninsular and Waterloo Campaigns' by Edward Costello. 1967 edition, edited by Antony Brett-James, Archon Books, London. p 109.

Haswell's book and, for that and much more besides, to Oman's vast and brilliant history.

Salamanca is still one of the most beautiful cities of the world. The Plaza is virtually unchanged since the Sixth Division paraded there on June 17th, 1812 (although the bullfights have been moved to a modern arena). The Plaza is, simply, magnificent. The area where the French created a wasteland around their three fortresses has been rebuilt, alas uglily, but enough of the old city remains and it well repays a visit. The Roman Bridge is now reserved for pedestrians only. The crenellations and the small fortress were removed in the middle of the nineteenth century, restoring the bridge to its original appearance, though the stone bull is still there above the eleventh arch. It marks the place where the bridge was broken in the floods of 1626. Only the fifteen arches nearest the city are Roman, the other eleven are reconstructions from the seventeenth century. The Irish College is unchanged from the days when it was the army's hospital in 1812.

The battlefield is a particularly pleasing site to visit, for the ground has scarcely changed since July 22nd, 1812. Some trees have gone in the years since and a railway line now runs between the Greater and Lesser Arapile and on into the small valley where the Sixth Division halted Clausel's counter-attack. There are a handful of modern houses south of Arapiles, but not enough to spoil the ground. To find the battlefield take the road south from the city, the N630 to Caceres, and the village of Arapiles is signposted to the left. The side-road to the village roughly marks the left hand limit of the Third Division's advance and the Heavy Cavalry must have charged just about where the village is signposted on the main road. It is well worth taking a good account of the battle, with good maps. I have simplified the story of the battle a little, concentrating on the events around the Arapiles, and anyone interested enough to visit the site would be well rewarded by reading one of the many splendid

317

accounts that are available as non-fiction. Once at the Arapiles the ground becomes obvious, thanks to the hills, and there is a memorial obelisk, now sadly weathered, on the crest of the Greater Arapile. Climbing to the memorial makes one wonder at the Portuguese troops who had to make the same climb, in full kit, against a defended skyline. They truly had a hopeless task.

I spent more than a week walking the battlefield and, as ever, received much help from the local people.

Salamanca was a great victory. Wellington suffered close to five thousand casualties (of whom about one thousand were killed outright on the field and no one knows how many dying later of their wounds). Marmont, fearful of Napoleon's wrath, tried to hide his casualties. He told the Emperor he had lost about six thousand men. In fact he lost fourteen thousand, one Eagle standard, six other standards, and twenty guns. It was a shattering defeat that told the world that a French army could be utterly beaten. It cleared the French from western Spain, and the defeat would have been even more crushing had the Spanish garrison at Alba de Tormes obeyed orders and stayed at their guns. Their defection from the war allowed Marmont's remaining 34,000 soldiers to escape and it led, also, to the strange and 'impossible' victory at Garcia Hernandez. The Germans lost 127 men in the charge. The French, including a whole Battalion taken prisoner, lost about 1,100 from 2,400. The first square broke in much the same way as the description in the novel.

To find Garcia Hernandez, follow the road to Alba de Tormes from Salamanca. It is well signposted because Alba de Tormes (thanks to St. Teresa of Avila) is still a busy place of pilgrimage. Go through the town and follow the signs to Penaranda, and the village is some seven kilometres beyond Alba de Tormes. Today it calls itself 'Garcihernandez' and the road by-passes it, but turn left into the village, cross the only bridge that leads over a small stream, and the track (suitable for cars) leads into the lee of the hill where the

King's German Legion made their magnificent, extraordinary charge.

I owe a great debt to Thomas Logio, physician and friend, who supplied me with a 'suitable' wound for Richard Sharpe. He saved me from my own medical ignorance, though I fear I may have embellished the information to his embarrassment. For that, I beg his forgiveness. Whatever is accurate about Sharpe's injury, treatment and recovery belongs to Dr. Logio.

The rest is all fiction. No Leroux, no Lord Spears, no codename 'El Mirador', not even, alas, a Marquesa de Casares el Grande y Melida Sadaba. Sharpe and Harper are just shades of the real men who marched and marched and finally fought on that burning July day in the valley by the Arapiles. It was a great victory and they must have been relieved, the survivors, and perhaps a little apprehensive for they knew, surely, that the war that in 1812 was spreading around the world would need many more such 'great' victories if it was ever to end. Sharpe and Harper will march again.